MW01232071

To Judy!
Best wishes
much love!
Marilyn [illegible]

# LILY

# LILY

## A STORY OF LOVE

BY

MARILYN STUART

This is a work of fiction. Names, characters, places, and incidents are products of the author's imagination, and any resemblances to actual events, locales, or persons, living or dead, is entirely coincidental.

© 2003 by Marilyn Stuart. All rights reserved.

No part of this book may be reproduced, stored in a retrieval system, or transmitted by any means, electronic, mechanical, photocopying, recording, or otherwise, without written permission from the author.

ISBN: 1-4033-9268-4 (e-book)
ISBN: 1-4033-9269-2 (Paperback)
ISBN: 1-4033-9270-6 (Dust Jacket)

Library of Congress Control Number: 2002095627

This book is printed on acid free paper.

Printed in the United States of America
Bloomington, IN

COVER CONCEPT by JAMES NUDERA

COVER DESIGN by IRA

1stBooks Library: www.1stBooks.com

1stBooks - rev. 01/13/03

It is with a thankful heart that I dedicate this book to the two men in my life, who have been instrumental in helping me achieve my goal. To Jon, my late husband, who convinced me I had the talent, discipline, and imagination to write. To Charlie, my present spouse, who, because he believed in me, supported my dream, and allowed me the freedom to pursue it. I love you both.

To my four daughters, who I have enjoyed as grown, sensitive loving women. Through the years, we have developed close emotional bonds, which provided me with the poignant viewpoint for my story. Without which I could only have imagined what a mother must feel like when faced with the ultimate decision. I love you.

# CHAPTER 1

She gasped for breath as the struggle intensified. Somewhere in that space between wakefulness and sleep, Lily finally freed herself from the illusive world of dreams and sat up with a start. The knot in her stomach tightened and her heart started to pound like an African drum. While beads of perspiration trickled down the valley of her breasts her eyes darted about the room searching for validation that she was no longer trapped in the nightmare. To ease the panic that had seized the moment, she pulled both knees to her chest and pressed her throbbing forehead against her naked thighs.

Moments later she eased out of bed into the chilly room and began to shiver. She quickly wrapped a silk dressing gown around her frigid body, crossed the room to the window, and opened the white brocaded drapes. The ominous clouds swirled in the ashen morning sky adding to her feelings of dismay.

Safely enclosed in her marble shower with the hot pelting water streaming down her nude body, the tensions began to ease from her taut muscles.

Refreshed, she threw on some clothes, raked a brush through her damp, shoulder length hair, and rushed downstairs, anxious yet hesitant, to convey her foreboding feelings to her husband.

When Lily entered the breakfast room, Henry glanced up from his morning paper. Her brows were raised and her lips were turned down as if a scowl had taken root.

"Morning," he mumbled and scanned her expression as if trying to determine the source of the troubled look. Postured at the carved mahogany breakfast table in a three-piece charcoal suit, he continued to read the morning paper. His vest buttons strained to contain a conservative maroon tie and a midsection paunch. Highly starched French cuffs displayed a set of tasteful platinum cufflinks, with a raised diamond encrusted 'H', that peeked out from his jacket sleeves.

She was keenly aware that his stone blue eyes were staring and it felt like a cold ocean wave had suddenly washed over her.

"Didn't sleep well? You look tense, just like I feel when I'm about to begin a summation."

Lily ignored the question and sat down.

He shrugged off her silence and resumed reading the paper.

She glanced across the table and tried to find the right words to explain her anxieties. He looks younger than fifty, she thought. Round face, horseshoe fringe of brown hair, and an aquiline nose perched high above a prominent chin provided a visual of a Roman Emperor sans toga.

He looked up again and smiled, his steely eyes peered over his gold-rimmed glasses, then jumped back to the editorial column.

She stared at the printed words on the newspaper across from her, then cleared her throat. As her lips parted, Emma, their rotund housekeeper, lumbered into the room carrying a silver pot filled with hot Brazilian coffee. Her shuffle was silent, though labored, and a white crisp apron protected her massive uniformed girth which strained at the seams in it's attempt to cover her mid-section.

"Morning, Miss Lily." Azure eyes, surrounded by a plump face, twinkled as she filled her employers cup. Emma's gray hair was pulled back and wrapped in a bun exposing her aging, leather-like skin. "I do hope you had a pleasant rest, Mum."

"Yes, thank you."

Emma stood silent and waited to hear what Lily would choose for breakfast.

"Um, just whole wheat toast. Dry." Lily cleared her throat again. "Henry."

He lowered his paper and arched his bushy brows. "Hmm?"

Her voice faltered. "I, I have this strong feeling," she grabbed her stomach, "something's wrong." She paused. "Something's about to happen."

He laid down his paper and shook his head as if annoyed.

"Honestly Lily the—"

"I'm serious," she pleaded, "I woke up with this sense of eminent danger," she started to chew on her lip, "and try as I may I, I can't seem to shake it."

Emma waddled back into the room. Plagued with flat feet and bad circulation, she often talked about going back to Ireland to live out the rest of her days. Lily knew she would never be able to replace her, after all she was like family.

Emma leaned over and put the rack of toasted bread in front of Lily. "You have to listen to those feelings Mum," Emma's eyes flashed, "heed the message," she whispered, then glanced back at Henry, shook her head, and shuffled back into the kitchen.

Henry's thin lips moved in a straight line as he contemplated his response. "Don't get weird on me Lily. All that feeling stuff is crap. You women have the tendency to dramatize everything, especially at certain times of the mo—" he stopped in the middle of the sentence, as if his lips were frozen. He swallowed hard when he caught the hateful glare in his wife's eyes. His cheek muscles twitched as he straightened his shoulders in readiness to defend his statement.

Irked by his condescending, chauvinistic attitude, she braced herself and pushed against the back of the chair in anticipation of his boring verbal gymnastics that were sure to come. His argument was predictable.

"There's a logical explanation for everything, including your pre-cognitive feelings."

"Aha, so you admit I have premonitions?"

"I admit nothing," he said and began to explain the scientific facts concerning pre-cognitive visions.

Lily winced at his black-and-white logic and slammed her cup on the table as she interrupted, "you're right counselor, its a woman's thing." She swept her hair off her neck. "Mark my words," she snarled and wiggled her index finger at him, "something's going to happen.

Something big. I can feel it. And I look forward to saying 'I told you so'."

His smile remained as cold as the air-conditioned room as he attempted to change the subject, but she had already tuned him out and only caught bits and pieces of his treatise on logic. Years of marriage taught her how and when to shut out his dull monotonous tone. It was either that or scream. This morning she chose not to challenge him and could only hope to enjoy her coffee. He's got some nerve, she thought, making fun of my feelings. Oh, the hell with it, I just won't say anything about my premonitions ever again.

She started to nibble at her toast, all the while scrutinizing his every move, like a mongoose leering at its prey. One drop of cream, then one, two, three spoons of sugar, stirred exactly three times, and the finishing touch to the ritual was the sound of his spoon clanking against the rim of the cup, and god forbid if the orange marmalade wasn't on the table. You'll see, my premonitions are always right—

"Well I'll be damned," he chuckled as he smacked the paper with the back of his hand. "After all these years, look who's moving back to town?" Lips drawn, he glanced up at Lily, then back to the paper. "Loyola! How the hell did he manage that?" He took another sip of coffee. "Hmm. I wonder why he didn't keep in touch? I'll call him when he gets in. Should make for an interesting reunion, don't you think?" His stare was as cold as the coffee in her cup.

"Who are you talking about?"

He carefully folded the paper and laid it in front of her. Then he leaned over, kissed her cheek and turned to leave. "I'll be late tonight, got a few briefs to finish."

Despite his absence from the breakfast room, her lips moved in silent protest against his elitist attitude. When she heard the front door close she sighed, relieved that he was finally gone. She picked up the newspaper and skimmed the first line of the article. Her pulse started to race.

"It can't be," she exclaimed.

RENOWNED WAR JOURNALIST AND PULITZER PRIZE WINNER EDMUND *VILANTE* TO TEACH AT LOYOLA.

Her hands started to tremble as she opened the folded newspaper. She scanned the entire article. He'd been living in California: freelancing for Newsweek, Time, and National Geographic. The column mentioned a novel he had penned and quoted him as saying 'that he was looking forward to moving back to Chicago and renewing old friendships'.

A chill shot through her. The panic that had lived beneath her skin for years finally burned through to the surface, paralyzing her where she sat. She began to shiver. Why, why now? She reread the article. July 15th. Six weeks. She reached out to touch the black and white photo, then hesitated as if it were a hot coal. She smoothed the folds of the paper, hesitated, than began to trace a fine line along the curvature of his lips.

"Damn you." She slammed the newspaper on the table and rushed into the kitchen. She pulled open one drawer, then another. She couldn't find any. She needed one. There has to be an old pack of cigarettes around here somewhere, she thought. Frustrated, she gripped the edge of the counter-top and ran her nails across the granite as she thought about possible hiding places. Her search had yielded nothing. Although it had been years since she had a cigarette, she needed one now. Aggravated by her inability to satisfy her craving, she kicked the bottom drawer shut and hurried back into the breakfast room.

Drawn to his picture, like metal to a magnet, she ran her fingers across the entire image, this time studying every detail of the handsome face. His hair was still wavy, his broad smile, still warm and charming. More handsome now, she thought. I wonder how many women those lips–? She chided herself for such thoughts and hastened to the forefront of her thoughts, long forgotten memories of their childhood. She moved back in the rigid chair and observed pictures from her past as they floated to the surface of her mind, like leaves stirred by a summer wind. Good memories. Happy memories. She lingered in the warm recollections and remembered...

The scar below his left brow...she threw the stone just at the exact moment he turned back into its path. The blood oozed from his brow, over his eye, and down his face. Despite his many reassurances that he was all right, she wasn't convinced that the stone had not taken out his eye. What if she had blinded him? The gash below his brow didn't require stitches, but the scar was still visible, even now, forty years later, making him look even more like the rogue he was.

"More coffee ma'am?"

Lily lurched forward and hit the empty coffee cup with her hand. "Emma!" she yelled, "you're gonna give me a heart attack." Lily took a deep breath. "Cough or make some kind of noise, but don't ever sneak up on me again." Her fingertips braced her temples.

"I'm sorry, I keep forgettin, Mum." The big woman maneuvered behind Lily's chair and filled her coffee cup. "I come into a room without anybody realizin I'm there. I'm not that little either." She chuckled and waddled back into the kitchen.

"Oh my God!" Lily's hand covered her mouth as memories of her waking experience surfaced. "That's it! That's what the ominous feelings were about. He's coming back." Her skin tingled as if tiny ants were crawling over her entire body. She tried to scream, but no sound came from her throat. Then a merging fear seeped into the core of her being and forced her to gasp for breath. She tightened her robe, sat straight up, and crumbled the newspaper, as if doing so would make him disappear.

"Don't you dare come back!" Tears made a jagged descent down her cheek as she continued to twist the paper as if wringing out a wet towel. A calendar leered at her in big letters. JUNE. July was only weeks away.

The air-conditioned Mercedes offered little relief from Chicago's heat and humidity. Her sleeveless linen sheath wrinkled the moment she buckled her seat belt. "Damn this heat," she muttered and dabbed the beads of sweat from her forehead with a tissue.

When she arrived at the rectory she checked her makeup in the visor mirror. She carefully removed a fleck of coral lipstick from the corner of her mouth and blew a wisp of copper hair from her brow. The hell with how I look, she thought, and started across the parking lot to the rectory. How did Jim manage to get himself appointed to a parish so close to home? Odd, that after all these years, he was never transferred to a different parish, as were so many priests before him.

She climbed the chipped concrete steps of St. Joseph's rectory, a monument of Christian faith that had been maintained by generations of Chicago Catholics, but had now fallen on hard times. The surrounding parish buildings reminded her of an old woman without makeup, shamelessly exposing their aging process.

Just as she reached the top step the door swung open. Jim welcomed her into his lean arms and gave her a hug. "How are you, Sis?" He kissed her on the cheek, took a step back, and held her at arms length. "You look great."

"I can always count on you for a hug," she leaned her head against his chest and squeezed his minimal waist. His humor normally matched hers, but today there was no bantering. His cinnamon eyes appeared serious, more so than she remembered.

"C'mon," he took her by the arm and led her into the living room. She felt a quiver in his grip, evidence that he was tense.

"It's been over three weeks since I've seen you." She pulled away and playfully smacked his arm.

"Yep," his answer was flat. "What's the occasion? I mean for the visit. Everything all right at home?"

He moved a strand of hair from her eyes and tucked it around her ear. "There, that's better." He took out two glasses and filled them with wine. "Salud," he clicked her glass with his and took a big swallow.

She was surprised that he was serving wine so early in the day, but said nothing.

"How's the volunteer work going?" As he spoke his head tilted to the right, a self-conscious habit to hide his mangled ear. One night in Nam, his story went, Napalm hit the rice paddies, engulfing everything around him in scalding flames. His collar had caught the destructive jelly and burned his neck, hair, and ear. No pain at first, only the stench of burning flesh. Then he heard a piercing scream. It was his. An army buddy heard his cries for help, wrestled him to the ground, than smothered the flames with his own body. He dragged Jim to the perimeter of the fire and onto safety, but a piece of Jim's blackened ear was ripped off as he was being pulled across the rocky terrain. And to this day he has refused restorative surgery.

Lily wrinkled her nose at the musty odor in the old parish house. Despite numerous coats of paint on the old plaster walls, a dank smell continued to hang in the air. An old air conditioner rattled in the living-room window, throwing off a feeble flow of cool air.

Jim wore khaki's and a sport shirt, too hot to wear a collar. Though she'd seen him ordained; stood at his side when he baptized Jody; attended many a mass with him as the celebrant, Lily never got use to the idea that her brother was a Jesuit. Her mother often accused her of being disrespectful. Lily's standard reply, 'That's no priest, that's my brother,' made Lenore bristle. Jim often encouraged her disrespect, as if trying to irritate his mother.

As his frail hand brushed through his thin, brown hair, Lily studied the streaks of silver that ran through his tresses. He's only fifty-three, she thought. His face, gaunt and heavily lined, magnified the light brown eyes that starred out from beneath a furrowed brow.

"Why don't you petition the diocese to bring in another priest? You're spending far too many hours on pastoral work."

"There's a shortage of committed men that are willing to dedicate their life to God. Young people today don't understand the Church's refusal to update its policies; its lack of action to embrace the modern world."

"You're probably right, but I didn't come here to discuss the Catholic Church. Have you seen this mornings paper?"

His eyes lit up, "No, I haven't. Why? Have you made the front page? Arrested for speeding?"

"Very funny." Her forced smile turned to a frown. "All joking aside, I need to talk to you." She put her glass down, unfolded the newspaper, and handed it to him. "This morning's Trib, it's about Edmund." She moved closer and pointed to the picture. "A professorship at Loyola."

"Impressive. I wonder what subject he'll be teaching?"

"Who gives a crap what subject. Not one word in twenty five years and he shows up on our doorstep," she gulped the last of her wine. "Why now?"

"When did any of his actions ever make sense? Think back when we were kids. While we were playing ball, he was home carving wood." Jim snapped his fingers as something came to mind. He jumped up and moved to the desk where he grabbed a wooden statue of an owl perched on a tree branch. "I still have this." He handed the carved bird to his sister.

She thrust the statue back into his hands and stepped to the window. "Do you remember when he ran off to Mexico, supposedly to rescue his brother? Well, we never saw him again." The sadness in her voice hung in the air like an unfinished melody. She turned to the window, hoping to hide her disappointment from her brother's probing eyes. "Years later you wrote, from Vietnam, that you'd been assigned to Edmund's company."

Jim gripped her by the shoulders and spun her around. "So, why so upset?"

Her silence spoke loudly of the thoughts she didn't dare share. She moved her stare to the worn carpeting.

He cupped his sister's face and tilted her head till their eyes met. "Out with it, why the major concern?"

"He was a good friend. Then nothing. Never wrote, never called. Not a damn word for twenty-five years."

"I don't know why he chose silence, but he's still my friend and I thought he was yours too. What's with the anger?" His eyes were like beacons in search of the truth as they scanned her face. "It's more than anger, isn't it Sis?"

As if dispelling a chill, she began to rub her arms.

"You're afraid to see him, aren't you?"

She started to break away but Jim grabbed her by the hand, led her back to the couch, and forced her to sit down. "What's really upsetting you?"

"You're right. It's stupid. I'm upset over nothing. Edmund chose to end our friendship. There was nothing I could have done."

Jim retrieved a silver framed picture from the desk and moved his fingers over the glass. "These are some of the men I served with in Nam." He handed Lily the photo. "There's Edmund, a true brother during those horrible days. Our weapons of choice were similar, his, a pad and pencil, mine a missal. We fought side by side till I was wounded," his head tilted, "we handled our descent into hell the best way we knew how."

Those eyes had seen much and she could only watch as her brother struggled to keep his apparent anguish hidden. "That's my point," she exclaimed, "if you were so close, why the long silence?"

He leaned his forearms on his knees, clasped his hands and looked at her. "You know there's an old Italian expression Edmund's mom always used, 'Only the spoon knows what's in the pot.' He leaned back and gripped the frayed arm of the couch. "I'm sure he had his reasons and I wouldn't think of questioning him. My friendship is unconditional. All I know is that he was there for me when I needed him. He was always high on life and I need to feel that positive energy again."

"Well I sure as hell would question him."

Jim shook his head. "You wanted the good life. A big house; membership in a country club; influential friends; a big car, a healthy bank account, and your marriage to Henry secured all that." He took her hands in his. "And I also must commend you for your patience with Mom. I know that you two never see eye to eye on anything. In fact, I don't know how you stand it. She's totally unmanageable and always making unreasonable demands. Can't you be half as generous with Edmund?"

She straightened her dress. "You do what you have to, but I'm not going to see him. I've no reason to rekindle that relationship." She hugged him and started for the door.

"Is it because Edmund dropped you?"

Lily spun around and winced. She felt as though she'd been punched in the stomach. "What the hell are you talking about?" She turned and walked back to the couch. "We never even dated. Remember, it was you, me, Henry and Edmund, hanging together. I was dating Henry."

"From where I stood, you and Edmund were good buddies, you should have been dating him. The two of you always had your heads together, joking about things you two thought were funny. When he called the house you'd be on the phone for hours. If I didn't know better," he said coyly, "I'd say—"

"You don't have your collar on and this isn't the confessional," she snapped. "We were friends, that's all. Things are different now. I don't need to look back. Anything else you want to know?"

In mocked surrender he raised his hands high above his head. "I'm not the enemy, Sis." He took her by the shoulders, "Henry will probably invite Edmund to the house. What then?"

"I don't know." Her heart raced at the thought.

"According to the paper he won't be here for a few weeks, so that should give you enough time to deal with it."

Jim opened the door and kissed his sister on the cheek. "Now get out of here."

She stood on her toes, kissed his cheek and ran to the car. A quick turn of the key, and the pedal to the floor, caused the Mercedes to lurch forward and the tires to screech as they punished the road. With a steel-like grip on the wheel, Lily raced toward the intersection of Touhy and Clark and hit the brakes when the light jumped to red. Easy girl, she told herself, you'll figure it out, you always do.

## CHAPTER 2

The cramped office was battleship gray and matched the sooty hue of the tiled floors and metal desks. Two scratched and dented filing cabinets filled the corner, leaving little room for additional seating. A single window, on the far wall, peeked out onto the back lot of the hospital where delivery and maintenance vehicles were parked.

Lily had chalked up thousands of volunteer hours in ten years and was considered, by her supervisor, to be a natural at handling distressed callers. During those years she had a few close calls, like the time she kept shouting into the phone to keep a girl awake who'd just swallowed a bottle of sleeping pills. Her hoarse voice cajoled and pleaded with the drugged girl to keep talking. Thank god the EMT's got to her in time.

That was over four years ago, and now she was even more committed to helping those in trouble. Like the young girl, Lily had learned the hard way about emotional entanglements, convinced that if she didn't control her emotions, she'd get hurt...much too high of a price to pay for loving someone. The day Edmund walked out of her life, the door to her heart slammed shut.

Seated at her desk, Lily kicked off her shoes, relieved that her tired feet could relax for a few hours. Her supervisor, Dorina Brown, known as Dory, was on the phone, and acknowledged Lily with a nod.

Lily met Dory the day she applied for the volunteer position. Dory's, gentle, coffee-colored eyes, immediately set Lily at ease. Proud of her climb out of the ghetto, despite growing up without a father in the Cabrini projects, Dory was subjected, by her mother, to numerous fleeting male personalities. At fourteen she escaped to the streets and found herself pregnant and on drugs. Several times she'd tried to kill herself, and like everything else, she'd botched that too.

Dory claimed she owed her life to Rev. Moody, a minister who stepped into her life and took her under his wing. He stood by her side, and helped her put her life back together. When she surfaced from the pit of despair, and free from addiction, she knew what her life's work would be.

Working days in the busy hospital kitchen she finished high school at night. The kindly minister helped her get a scholarship to college where she earned a degree in Psychology. When the Crisis-line was established, Dory applied for the position of Director, and was hired. Time proved her heart as big as her girth, with patience and understanding her trademarks.

The big black woman hung up the phone. "How are you girl," she chuckled and leaned back in her chair. "You look good and cool in that yellow dress. I'd sell my soul to have your figure. How in this world do you stay so small? Lordy, I was born big and it seems that I keep on getting bigger." She ran her hands over her ample body.

"You just missed it. I've been on the phone with an old man who swallowed a load of pills. Crippled with arthritis, he could barely get around. With no family or friends to watch out for him, his neighbors called HRS. The state made arrangements at one of them nursing homes, but he preferred death. Can't say I blame him."

"That's so sad."

"I know. But he was a smart old geezer. Waited almost an hour before he called us, makin sure the pills had time to work, knowin there'd be no intervention. All he wanted was for someone to know there'd be a body. We talked, then he hung up just as Emergency Services broke down the door."

"I presume, by the report you're filling out, they were too late."

Dory nodded. "DOA. Phone still clutched in his hand." She looked away, her big brown eyes saddened by the event. "My voice was the last thing that poor creature heard. You know Honey, I sure do get discouraged about the lack of dollars for this place, but it's days like this that makes it all worth while."

The afternoon passed quickly. Lily stretched her arms above her head and glanced at the large clock on the wall. Her shift was over. She slipped on her shoes, waved good-bye to Dory, and hurried out of the hospital.

As she drove home she dialed her good friend Pat on the cell phone. Four rings. No answer. Then she remembered Henry would be late and pulled into the parking lot adjoining Andy's Steak House. She walked past the bar toward the hostess desk.

"Lily! Over here." A fashionably dressed petite figure floated from the cocktail lounge towards her. A sleeveless, white linen, sheath was draped tight around the 5'3" frame and accented her pert breasts and shapely hips.

"Where've you been?" Lily asked, "I've been calling all day?" The two women embraced with cheeks brushing and kissing the air.

Straight blond hair, short and swept to one side, framed Pat's face. She grabbed Lily's hand. "Come on, I want you to meet someone."

Lily pulled back. "I really don't feel like socializing. If you don't mind I'll meet them some other time. Go ahead, I'll just grab a bite to eat and head home."

As always, at the first sign of trouble with her dear friend, Pat issued an order. "No you won't," then proceeded to study her friend. "Listen, I'll excuse myself and join you. Then we can talk."

A few minutes later she was seated across from Lily, ordering a martini with two anchovy olives. She sucked one olive off the miniature plastic spear and bent her head below Lily's downcast eyes. "Okay, give. What's bothering you?"

Lily hesitated and continued to nibble on the celery in her Bloody Mary.

Pat leaned forward. "I've told you a lot of shit through the years and if you don't tell me what's bugging you I'll be awake all night wondering. And I do need my beauty sleep."

Lily glanced around the dining room. She scanned the shiny brass tubes that served as dividers between tables. Her voice was a lifeless monotone as she started talking about Henry; explaining about Edmund's picture in the paper; and her anger about her husbands attitude. She sipped her spiked tomato juice and continued to nibble on the celery stalk that stood high in the tall glass.

"Well that makes sense. Now give me the punch line."

"What do you mean?" Lily's brows lifted high and almost touched her hairline. "I'm telling you exactly what happened."

Pat leaned on the table. "Calm down, I just want you to be realistic. You know Henry's going to see him, and so is Jim." She paused and stared at Lily, her blue eyes intent on discovery. "I know there's more. What's really bugging you about this man?"

Lily averted her friend's eyes.

"I agree with your brother. You're probably pissed off because he dropped you."

Lily dabbed at her lips with a napkin. She really wanted to get up and run, but knew Pat would follow. A hollow laugh covered her annoyance. "You and Jim don't know what you're talking about. In fact you're so far off base, it's ridiculous."

"Yeah! Sure." Pat sucked in her cheeks and rolled her eyes. "It's so ridiculous that you're about to explode." Pat stirred her martini with her finger.

Maybe I can tell her, Lily thought, and ordered another drink. She scooted forward and swore her friend to secrecy. "I grew up with Edmund and had a crush on him ever since I can remember. All through high school and college we hung out, my brother Jim, Henry, Edmund, and me. He was all I ever dreamed about. Then one day we made love."

"So?" Pat sipped the last of her vodka martini.

"The next thing I know, he's gone."

"Damn!" Pat exclaimed as she fell back in her chair. "I've known you over twenty years and you never said anything about this man." She slapped her hand on the table. "When are you going to learn you're not alone. You have me to confide in."

Lily fiddled with her plastic straw. "I was worried about your reaction, I didn't want to shock you."

Pat laughed. "Me? Shocked?" She put her hand to her throat in mock surprise. "I'm the last to be surprised at anything. I'm upset because you never told me about Edmund."

"I couldn't. When I married Henry I made up my mind to be a good wife. If I hadn't put Edmund out of my mind I couldn't have carried it off."

Pat shot straight up in her chair, as if being called to attention. "What do you mean, 'carried it off'?"

"I couldn't let the past effect the present. But now he's coming back. That's what's got me ups—I mean curious."

"Bullshit. You were right the first time." Pat smiled and wiggled her finger at Lily. "You're upset! Quit kidding yourself, the man you loved is coming back to town and you don't trust yourself." She pursed her shiny red lips. "Have you thought about what you're going to do when he shows up at your front door?"

"Don't be silly," Lily gulped, "why would he do that?"

"Why not? Until you face your real feelings, you won't be free of him. Listen to your heart, that's your only priority."

"Why do you have to be so, so honest? You face everything head on."

"Hell, it's a waste of time and energy to do otherwise." She thrust her palm up. "Enough about me. Why do you think you never heard from him? Do you really believe he took advantage of you? There are some guys who won't commit to anything or anybody." She moved her chair closer to Lily's.

"If your appraisal of him as a 'User' is true, he'd have stuck around and gotten all he could and as often as he could. Admittedly you were a willing partner."

Lily leaned her elbows on the table. "It wasn't a one night stand. It was much more. We cared about one another. How could he know his brother would get in trouble. Edmund had to go, there was no one else."

"Bullshit! Quit trying to justify his actions. He could've written; he could've called; if he cared as much as you did, he could've sent you a damn telegram, even used carrier pigeons if he had to. Face it my friend, he used you. What you thought was the love of your life was just a roll in the hay. What makes you think it was anything more than a good fuck? After all you weren't a teen-ager, you were in college and it wasn't like it was your first tim—" Pat's voice broke off, her lashes flew up and her mouth dropped when she saw the coy look on Lily's face.

"I'll be damned! It was your first time? You really believed that Catholic bullshit about no sex before marriage?" Pat threw her napkin on the table. "I can still remember the nuns preaching that garbage in school, telling us men only marry virgins. If that were true, there'd have been no weddings because there were no virgins." She paused. "You know what I used to do when they started preaching that shit about going to hell and everything? I'd picture Sister Aloysius, my home room nun, having sex with one of the priests."

Lily's eyes opened wide like saucers and the two women looked at one another, then started giggling. Soon their laughter turned to hysteria.

"Can you picture it? Imagine trying to get that long black robe over her head."

"I don't remember ever seeing any buttons on it." Lily added, "now that you mention it, I wonder how the heck they took it off to sleep?"

"Talk about putting a bag over her head..." Lily's stomach muscles ached as Pat kept adding sordid details to her images.

"Can you imagine Sister Ludmilla, the nun with the hairs growing on her chin, having sex? She'd probably ball the poor priest to death." Pat gulped her martini and continued laughing. "I wonder if she's the reason old Father Mulchey died. He probably had a heart attack trying to get it in that tight assed bitch."

"You're going to hell for sure."

"Yeah," Pat giggled, "but all those nuns will be there to greet me."

Teary eyed from laughing, Lily threw back her head. "Stop, my sides hurt." She wrapped her arms around herself and continued to giggle. "Please, if you don't stop I'll pee in my pants." Their laughter finally subsided and Lily wiped the tears from her eyes.

"Seriously Lily, I never realized you waited till you were in college. My first time was in high school," Pat nodded and continued, "in the back seat of a Ford. And I don't mind telling you it wasn't anything like it was cracked up to be. Hormones, that's all it was Lily. Hormones."

Pat took a deep breath, excused herself and walked to the ladies room. The men at the table across the aisle stopped talking and turned to look as she walked by. Lily pushed her plate away and thought about what Pat had said. Pat's ideas about hormones was all wrong. Her first time with Edmund was special. It was more than sex. It was love. She knew it by the way he looked at her. The way his hand trembled when he touched her body.

Lily glanced around the busy dining room, fearful that others would hear her most secret thoughts. The restaurant was a buzz with quiet conversations, business people entertaining clients, couples visiting, and women enjoying friends, along with the best steaks in town.

On her way back to the table Lily watched Pat weave across the highly polished oak floors. Once again the men stopped talking to ogle the petite blond as she passed their table. One of the men stepped in her way and introduced himself. She smiled, then politely brushed past him, and headed back to the table. Lily knew Pat liked the way men looked at her, and she thrived on the attention. She used her looks to her advantage and knew how to handle herself in every situation. Maybe being married three times gave her the experience, Lily thought.

"You know they're looking at you, don't you?"

"Of course. And I love it." She cocked her head and smiled at the men across the way. "That's the fun of it. It's all a game, Lily. A big fucking game. You can't take it serious, it'll drive you bonkers."

"What I don't understand is, how you know when a man is serious, or, well, you know what I mean." She twisted her wedding band.

"You just know. They're all made out of the same mold," she started to laugh, "they even talk about the same things, business, sports, women, and expensive toys. After a few times in bed you just know when it's over. The only question is who's going to break it off first. Sometimes it's a very nice thank you and good-bye, other times you never hear from them again. Sound familiar?"

Lily squirmed in her chair. The waiter approached with a round of after-dinner drinks, compliments of the gentlemen at the far table.

"See how easy it is." Pat turned, faced the gentlemen, raised her glass, tilted her head, and smiled. "Now, back to you. Twenty-five years ago there were four of you. Right?"

Lily nodded.

"You dated Henry, but you liked Edmund. And you felt that Edmund liked you. Is that correct?"

Lily nodded again.

"But Mamma Nora didn't like Edmund because he was Italian, an automatic thumbs down. And even though you cared for Edmund, you kept dating Henry because your mother felt he was more reliable, and had a better future. There'd be more money, prestige, and a bigger house if you married Henry. Am I on target?"

"You make it sound like I did whatever my mother told me."

"Well, didn't you? I'm sorry to say, but you still do."

Lily opened her mouth to defend herself but Pat stopped her with a raised hand.

"Let me finish. So Henry goes to Harvard, enrolls and finds a summer course that will enable him to graduate six months ahead of his class."

Lily sipped her Drambuie while twirling and bending the straw out of shape. "Even before Henry left for Harvard he always cracked the books, that's why we didn't see much of one another that summer. It wasn't enough for him to pass the courses, he had to be at the top of his class."

She paused, studied her straw, and continued. "Edmund and I were together every day. Sometimes Jim would join us at the drugstore and we'd talk for hours. But I didn't want Jim around, I wanted to be alone with Edmund. He was exciting, interesting, and always challenging me to widen my views about the world and the people in it. Then one day, after spending the afternoon together, it happened. We were alone at his house and...you know, one thing led to another."

Lily stared at a copy of Van Gogh's 'Sunflowers' that hung on the far wall. As she thought about her and Edmund, she could feel his arms around her. The warmth of his mouth on hers, his bare chest pressed against her breasts, his hot hands caressing her as his lips brushed butterfly kisses on her neck. Her heart started to beat faster and she felt the heat from the blood rushing up her neck and face, causing a flush. She patted her cheeks in an effort to quell the river of heat flowing through her.

"You're flushed my friend," Pat's eyes twinkled. Her sly grin widened as she leaned across the table and stared into Lily's eyes.

"What are you smiling about?"

"Look at you. Just talking about Edmund and you get a hot flash. And don't tell me its' menopause. Face it girl, you still got the 'hots' for this man. You've been carrying that torch all these years, that's why this situation has you upset. You don't know what the hell you'll do when you see him again." Pat slammed the table with her palm. "You're still in love with Edmund."

Flustered, Lily reached for a glass of water. It slipped through her fingers and tumbled onto the table, splashing water and ice cubes across the white cloth.

Pat snickered. "Go on, deny it. I dare you. Look at you, you're like a young school girl, all nervous just talking about him."

Eyes blurred with tears, Lily fumbled in her purse for a tissue. Loneliness gripped her heart as echoes of the truth moved through her like a slow moving train. She prided herself on being able to handle anything, but Edmund was proving to be her Achilles heel.

She stood up and threw her napkin on the table. "I don't want to think about it anymore."

Before Pat could say more, Lily motioned the waiter for the check and started toward the door where Pat finally caught up with her.

"Where are you going? I'm sorry if I said anything to upset you. You know me, I've got a big mouth and I say what I think. So I overstepped my bounds this time."

"It's not you. It's what you said that struck a chord, and I don't like what I'm feeling." Lily reached for Pat's hand. "You've helped me more than you'll know." She kissed Pat on the cheek and hurried out of the restaurant.

On the drive home Lily kept one eye on the speedometer. Wilmette had a posted speed limit of 35 mph and enforced it. Henry often lectured her to drive carefully and not get a ticket for speeding. God forbid that the wife of a prominent attorney shouldn't be perfect.

She thought about what Pat had said. Was she right? Did she still love Edmund? Henry wasn't that bad. He didn't drink, didn't cheat, and provided more than a comfortable lifestyle. As a child she watched her parents scrape by, never knowing what the next week would bring, and she swore it wouldn't be that way for her.

Wilmette was comfortable, and where she belonged. She knew everyone, and they accepted her. So what if Henry was a little boring? After all, he wasn't home much, giving her more time to spend with Jody.

Not much had changed in twenty years on Chestnut Street. Large stately homes lined the street, resembling majestic sentinels that had weathered the onslaught of time. The Douglas's, her golfing friends, sat on their screened porch enjoying the cool breezes off Lake Michigan. Sam and Dotty Winchester were walking their white poodle Samantha and waved as Lily drove by.

She pulled into the driveway, drove to the rear of the house, and parked behind Henry's blue Mercedes. She hurried up the back steps then stopped in her tracks. Shit, I forgot to lock the car. 'Always lock the car', he told her. If it's ever stolen we wouldn't be able to collect on the insurance. She ran back, locked the car, and then ran into the house.

"Henry? I'm home. Where are you?"

A light from the den found him with his glasses down from the crown of his nose, buried in a law book. He was wrapped in a silk burgundy smoking jacket, and except for the tone of flesh from his face, his gown was an exact match to the hue of his leather chair, giving the illusion that only his head was present. Lily smiled at the imagined vision.

"Have a nice time?" he asked, and never looked up from his book. Then he mumbled something about dinner and kept on reading.

Disappointed at his inattention, Lily left the room. He had more of a rapport with Emma than he did with her. I'm glad he has his own room, she thought. I could have been a serial killer, or standing nude and begging to be ravaged, he wouldn't take that nose of his out of a law book for anything.

Lily stared into the mirror as she brushed through her copper hair. She remembered the first time she laid naked in Edmund's arms. Despite the fact that twenty-five years had passed, memories of their time together were closer to the surface than she realized...she recalled a need to shower after their love making, but couldn't break away from him. Instead she melted into the deep curves of his arms and wedged herself against his broad chest. She became aware of their rhythmic breathing and moved her hands up and down his back, dragging her fingernails over his naked body. His sighs excited her. How different things will be now, she remembered thinking. Now she belonged to him. They'd tell Henry, then they'd be together forever.

Starting over wasn't easy. He knew he had to bury his ghosts before he could move into a new life.

After spending hours packing boxes filled with computers, scanners, and office equipment, he stood up, arched his back, and applied pressure to his lower spine with his thumbs. He scanned the bare living room, empty but for a faded armchair. The tan sculptured carpet revealed deep lines where furniture once stood. Nail holes dotted the bare walls, and the red brick fireplace still contained traces of charred logs.

He pushed aside piles of crumpled newspapers and plopped into the old green chair. His large hands moved lovingly over the faded, arms. He smiled and remembered the day it was delivered. Mai Lyn refused to sit in it for almost a year, 'the material was too pretty to sit on,' she said. Now time had its way, the brocade was discolored and worn. Hopefully the Salvation Army would find some use for it.

The house had sold quickly, asking three hundred thousand, when it was worth nearly four, helped. The Realtor had pleaded with him to consider its market value and raise the price. 'I want out now and don't give a damn about the loss,' he'd reply.

With his Meerschaum in his mouth, he sucked the smoke into his lungs before blowing out the match. A terrifying realization washed over him, he tried hard to ignore the truth, but it persisted. Twenty years of his life in a handful of cardboard boxes. Damn!

His lids were heavy from lack of sleep and his heart numbed by the events of the past three months. He inhaled deep and rested his head against the chair. Smoke rings filled the room with a Cavendish aroma. He rested his pipe in the ashtray and ran his large hands through his thick, wavy hair.

The Pulitzer, along with numerous writing awards, meant nothing now. They couldn't ease the numb, dead feeling inside. Accepting the professorship at Loyola University was a logical move and offered him a retreat into the womb of childhood. His pulse slowed, his muscles relaxed, allowing the tension to ease from his body.

He was comfortable with the hastily made decision to get the hell out of California. A faculty member found him a house near Winnetka, not far from the Chicago campus, and from the pictures he'd seen, it appeared more than sufficient for his needs.

Mai Lyn's flair for interior decorating dotted their old Marin County home. He urged her to take courses at the University to develop her talent. Unable to speak English and fearful of new places and people, she never considered the idea. Content to stay at home, she catered to their daughter Christine and him. Her obsession to please often made him edgy and uncomfortable.

He loved her, but the excitement of uncovering a covert operation, involving foreign governments, or trekking through the jungles of third-world countries, was the thing that set his adrenaline flowing. Like a seductive siren, the call to adventure enticed him to new horizons. Writing first-hand of unfolding events provided the life force that pumped through his veins.

Time had sent him into the Soviet Union to cover the CIA's search for two missing spies. Instead, he got wind of the upheaval in Russia, and his instinct for trouble, along with astute timing, had him present at Yeltsin's, now famous stand outside the Kremlin. A much bigger story then two spies, and as the fates would have it, earned him the Pulitzer Prize.

Despite the highs of his journalistic challenges, guilt remained his constant companion. For three months, when Mai Lyn was ill with malaria, he was forced to care for his wife and daughter, it was the longest period of time he had ever spent at home.

After Christine was born in Nam, he often stood by her straw mattress and stared at the cherub like creature, touching the tiny fingers that clung to his. Amazed at the miracle of birth, he was awed that his coupling with Mai Lyn could create such a beautiful baby. She grew to be a gentle, serenely wise, and beautiful young lady.

He swallowed repeatedly at the convergence of memories. The vision of his twenty-year old daughter, sporting long dark silken hair draped halfway down her back, brought tears to his eyes. Her dark brown eyes were flecked and ringed with gold and resonated with a faraway gaze. With her high cheekbones and delicate nose, professional photographers often pursued her in hopes of capturing her beauty on film. But she always refused.

Unaware of her exotic beauty, she focused intently on her studies. After working part-time at the television studio, she'd spend hours with her mother trying to keep her informed of world events. For Christine, her mother always came first. Her friends had apartments in the Bay area but she opted to live at home.

He'd have given his life for his daughter, but God had gypped him of the opportunity. Old memories, new guilt, and a thousand 'if only's' swirled through his mind. His haunting regret: if only he'd been home the morning she and Mai Lyn left the house for the last time.

His reverie concluded, he moved through the empty house and poked his head into the vacant rooms as if listening for sounds from the past. When he reached Christine's room a tear surfaced and rested in the corner of his eye. He placed his large hand on the door jam and studied the empty space. His eyes darted back and forth as if expecting to catch a fleeting glimpse of her. Unable to establish visual contact, he arched his body, drew the back of his hand across his moist eyes, and pushed his hands deep into his back pockets.

While fighting the pain from grief, he had barely managed to complete the rewrites on his novel. The publisher had been on his case. Coaxing, then finally demanding he finish: the publication date was looming.

He walked back into the living room, picked up the boxes and stacked them in the Explorer. He placed two identical black boxes on the floor and threw his suitcases into the back seat.

As he drove off, tears slid down his tanned cheeks. God, please get rid of this pain, he prayed. Let the heartache be behind me. He gripped the wheel while his knuckles strained to break through his skin, as he fought the urge to look back. Then, like an invisible cloak, a cold chill descended upon him as he reached the end of the block. He slammed on the brakes, made a screeching U-turn, and drove back down the street. As he neared the house he took his foot off the gas and coasted past the vacant dwelling. He stared at the old house and nodded, then stepped on the gas. He had one more stop before he could start the long journey home.

Edmund eased the Explorer onto the deserted rock strewn road, careful to steer around the loose boulders as he climbed the hills high above San Francisco Bay. The motor labored on the steep grade and forced him to downshift. Sunlight splashed through the windshield as he drove the serpentine road. He finally arrived at the summit, parked, and got out.

Below him sprawled the famous orange bridge. The famous span swayed in the untamed coastal winds as the vast Pacific churned below. Cars crawled across the Golden Gate Bridge and appeared like soldier ants marching to their mound. He set the two black boxes on the ground near the cliff's edge. The gusting winds blew through his streaked hair and whistled around the hillside like a boiling teapot.

He picked up the wooden box bearing a gold imprinted M. The wind instantly claimed its contents, swirling his wives ashes out over the ravine in a thin gray cloud.

"Mai Lyn, I return your body to the earth. May your spirit soar and roam the heavens free of prejudice." His words mixed with the ashes as he upended the box. "Thank you for the beauty and gentleness you brought into my life. Most of all, thank you for our daughter." He stepped to the crumbled edge and hurled the empty container into space.

The knot in his stomach tightened. His brown eyes, normally so full of life, now reflected intense pain and sorrow at the thought of his next task. He picked up the second box and clutched it to his heart.

"God damn Mexican!" he shouted as he fought the bitterness welling up inside. He struggled with his anger, wanting this last moment with his daughter to be filled with love. His shoulders heaved and the dam of sorrow finally burst, blinding him with tears as he caressed the box that held his little girl. He took a deep breath and opened the lid to let the wind catch the muted gray ashes.

"Christine, my beloved daughter, I set you free." His voice cracked. "In death, as in life, you chose to be with your mother. God sealed my fate when he took you from me. Now I'll never have the chance to prove that I can be a good father. I love you Christine. Your arms are wrapped around my heart forever."

He gazed upward and closed his eyes in silent prayer. Then he swung the box as hard as he could. It tumbled down the hillside, and bounced off the jagged rocks into a deep gorge, landing close to the first box. He straightened his shoulders and stared at the far off horizon, as if doing so would close the door to a lifetime of memories.

# CHAPTER 3

Michael, the owner of Sabin's greeted Lily with a smile. "Good afternoon Mrs. Halston, you're right on time. Your mother and brother are at your usual table." He spun around and led her into the dining room.

The first Saturday of each month found mother, brother, and sister having lunch at the renowned Goldcoast eatery that served gourmet food, in a posh setting, at exorbitant prices.

When Lily reached the table, Jim stood and hugged her. She squeezed his hand before leaning over to kiss her mother. Michael stood behind the chair and waited to seat her.

"Isn't that dress a little tight dear? Gaining weight?"

The sound of Nora's caustic voice caused Lily to grit her teeth. Lily spread the white napkin across her lap. "Do you ever offer a compliment, Mother?"

Nora pointed her nose into the air and waited for Lily to be seated. "I'm only telling you what I see."

Jim's eyes shot a message across the table to his sister and cautioned her not to start an argument.

"As a matter of fact, I've lost a couple of pounds." She sat back and took a sip of water and tried to ignore her mother's shrill voice that sounded like chalk scratching the surface of a blackboard. She pretended to listen and nodded at the appropriate times.

Ever since Lily could remember her mother always wore a hat in public, and today was no different. Her variety of chapeaus was the one thing that made their luncheons interesting. Today Nora was sporting a white picture hat with a wide brim that bobbed up and down every time she exhaled. Lily bit her cheek in an effort to suppress a smile.

Nora's A-line dresses hid her thick waistline, while her face, accented by prominent cheekbones, appeared to rest on her shoulders; there was no hint of a neck. Nora sipped at her wine and then brushed a napkin across her mouth. Her blunt chin was set and determined, and every time she spoke it thrust forward in a challenging manner. At seventy-four her head was covered with a wealth of dark hair, every strand neatly tucked in place.

Nora leaned back into the chair with her hands folded in her lap, and waited for an opportunity to inject her brand of sarcasm. Her brows were bunched together in an agonizing expression. "Thank goodness for your stepfather Al and his stocks, Lord knows where I'd be today if it weren't for him." She took a deep breath and explained about seeing an attorney to transfer her holdings into a Living Trust. At her death the stocks would pass to them with no major tax consequences.

Nora was taunting them and her crafty smile caused the left side of her thin lip to turn up, but they weren't buying any of it. "You should be grateful that I think of you first."

Lily rolled her eyes. "Yes Mother, you've told us many times, but we don't need or want your money. Spend it on yourself." Lily shook her head, sat back, then started to admire the European chandelier counting the myriad of sparkling crystal tear-drops that hung over the table.

Nora's reply was sharp. "I read that Edmund Vilante is coming back to Chicago. Did you see the article?"

Lily knew the old woman was fishing for information and she wasn't about to give her the satisfaction of a straight answer. She glanced at her brother who had just finished his second martini and was raising his empty glass to catch the waiter's eye.

"Yes, I saw the article." She held the stemmed glass to her lips and took a sip of iced water. "Henry plans to invite him to dinner."

"What!" Nora strained forward. "Why would he do that? Why does Henry want to see that, that, Italian drifter? He's never showed any sense of responsibility, never had a real job." Nora took a sip of wine. "I doubt he'll keep his teaching position. He'll get bored and take off for parts unknown again." She pointed her finger on the tabletop. "Just like before. Remember?" She looked at Lily and took a deep breath. "And I didn't mind saying good riddance."

Lily leaned toward her mother. "He's a Pulitzer Prize winner and highly respected in his field. It's the most coveted and prestigious award in Journalism." Lily leaned back and started to pick imaginary lint from her skirt while attempting to contain her annoyance. "When you make statements like that it shows how little you know about journalism."

Lily looked to Jim. "Why don't you jump into this conversation? He's your friend too."

Jim pushed his glasses up on his nose. "The literary world claims his stories about post war Vietnam, and the struggle of the people to rebuild their lives, is his best work. Of course, marrying a Vietnamese woman added depth to the effort."

"Really!" Lily erupted. "When did marriage become a prerequisite to study a culture?"

Jim raised his bushy eyebrows. "Did it ever occur to you that he might have loved the woman he married?"

Lily excused herself and retreated to the Ladies room. She slammed her purse on the vanity and sat down in front of the mirrored wall.

"Damn! Get a hold of yourself girl," she muttered to the face staring back at her. The idea that he had married, infuriated her. Face the truth girl, he dumped you for someone else. You're not the first woman it's happened to.

She fussed with a curl that had fallen onto her forehead, then started to check her makeup. She slid coral lipstick across her full lips, then blotted them with a tissue. She stood up, turned sideways, sucked in her stomach and slid her hands over her hips. She leaned in close to the mirror, shook her head and walked out.

As she moved closer to the table she heard Jim talking about the war and how it brought strangers like Edmund and his wife together. "Bullshit," she snarled, and sat down.

Nora straightened her back as if someone had suddenly slipped ice cubes down her dress. She threw a piercing stare at her daughter.

"Edmund couldn't love someone like that." Lily took a sip of wine, then held the glass up to the light. "I doubt if he could love anyone except himself, so don't give me that crap about love." She took an ice cube from her water glass and added it to her wine. Then she picked up a silver spoon and pointed it at her brother.

"The article didn't mention anything about his wife. If he were such a devoted husband he wouldn't have been globetrotting. And besides he could've written, after all you were his buddy."

"Let me tell you something about army buddies." Jim took a swig of his martini and smacked his lips. "Just because a group of men experience hell together," his voice cracked, "it's not a strong enough tie to bind them for a lifetime. Some of us carry raw memories and we don't want reminders."

Lily watched his eyes haze over in remembrance.

Jim's smile echoed sadness. "Seeing old buddies brings back ugly memories. The world is different after you've experienced the ravages of war and the killing that goes with it. It forces you to..."

His cheek quivered. Again his eyes burned with that faraway look, his mouth pulsated, and his voice became hoarse. "I intend to see Edmund." He pushed his eyeglasses up to the bridge of his nose. "In fact," he took another sip of his martini, "I'm looking forward to renewing our friendship." He stared at Lily as if to say it's your turn now.

"Mother, I don't think it's any of your business who Henry and I see. It's our life. We make our own decisions."

Nora screwed up her pudgy face. "He's no good! He's never amounted to anything and never will. I'll bet he doesn't have a penny to his name. Just like his parents."

"What are you talking about?" Lily spat. "Did you hear what I just said about the Pulitzer Prize?"

Nora's chin jutted out as sarcasm dripped from her lips. "How much money did he get?"

"I don't know, and I don't care. Is that all you think about is money? What about Daddy? He worked hard all his life and you got by."

Nora turned to Jim. "That's your third martini! It's a good thing you don't have your collar on." Her small eyes furtively checked the room. "What would people say?"

"There's nothing wrong with a couple of drinks before lun---"

"That's what your father use to say, and he was an alcoholic."

"Daddy wasn't an alcoholic," Lily cried, "he just drank beer."

Nora closed her eyes, shook her head, and started to mutter. "You don't know the half of it, Missy." Her voice grew loud and shrill. "I lived with him and his drinking," her mature eyes blazed, "I can see all the signs in him," she thrust her chin at Jim, "and it scares me."

"I only drink when I'm out to lunch. Why are you making it a federal case?"

"I'm not." Her eyes narrowed and one side of her mouth turned up. "Your sister is the one that's arguing and telling me that your father wasn't an alcoholic." Nora leaned forward and pointed to herself. Suddenly a red flush spread up her neck.

"I know different," she slumped in the chair, "I was married to the man. I know about the crying jags; stumbling into bed at night; hidden bottles of whiskey; pee on the bathroom floor. And the women–" she raised her eyes to the ceiling, clasped her hands to her breast and made the sign of the cross. "God only knows about the women. I lived through it all. I know."

Lily was stunned, her facial features remained motionless as if paralyzed. "If that was the case, why did you stay? Why didn't you leave him?"

Nora blew her nose and dabbed her eyes with a handkerchief. "Simple, I was married in the church. The vows I took were for better or worse. People didn't get a divorce because a man drank. They lived with it. Keeping the family together was more important. I had the two of you to think about."

Lily's laugh was sarcastic. "Who do you think you're kidding, you stayed because of his weekly pay-check. You never loved him."

Nora's lips twitched. "I'm still your mother, don't you dare talk to me that way. I demand respect."

Lily leaped from her chair. "Then don't talk about Daddy like that," she threw her napkin on the table. "He was my father and I loved him," she hesitated, "you're right about one thing, he was a fool. He had to be to put up with you."

"Hey c'mon, sit down," Jim took his sister by the arm, guided her back to her chair and started to rub her back. He looked at his mother, "she didn't mean it."

"You don't care who you hurt, do you?"

Nora's mouth dropped and her eyes peered over her fat cheeks. "I know you loved your father but it's against all of God's laws to take your own life. His cowardice left the two of you without a father and me to raise you all by myself. It was a struggle, and don't you think that I've forgiven him, because I haven't."

"Well if you don't mind, keep your opinions about my father to yourself."

Jim suggested they order lunch and signaled the waiter.

Defiant at her mother for attempting to manipulate them, Lily tossed her head and as she did, her hair swished around her shoulders, like an impatient stallion. Still upset, and her stomach in knots, she glanced at the menu. Nothing appealed to her and she wanted out of this situation. Now.

Nora started again about Edmund. She insisted on knowing exactly when he'd be back in town and was unusually curious about where he was going to live.

"Tell me Mother, why so curious about Edmund? You're asking questions that neither Jim or I can answer."

"I was just wondering." Nora busied herself with the menu even though she had already ordered.

"There's always a method to your madness, Mother. What's your agenda this time?" Lily's eyes narrowed with suspicion as she scanned her mother's stoic face in search of a clue.

Suddenly Nora's hands started to shake.

Lily eyes darted across the table to Jim's. He mirrored her concern. "What's wrong with your hands?"

"Nothing," Nora assured them. She quickly clasped her hands and held them in her lap.

Jim blinked and quickly pushed his glasses up on his nose. He pulled his chair next to his mother's and wrapped his hands around hers. "You never said anything about this, how long have you had these?"

"On occasion...for the past year or so. It's nothing to worry about. It only happens when I get upset. The doctor said I should avoid stress." She glared at Lily.

"I'm sorry we upset you, Mother," Lily whispered.

A strained silence blanketed the table while their waiter served lunch. Lily picked at her chicken pecan salad and watched Jim drain his third martini. He looks pale and washed out. Come to think, she thought, he hasn't looked good the last couple of times I've seen him. Was Mom right? Was Jim drinking too much? If so, why?

Her mother's high-pitched voice interrupted her thoughts. "Lily, did Edmund ever say why he was stuck in Mexico for so long?"

"What made you think of that?" Lily hesitated. "What do you mean stuck, he went there to find his brother."

"Remember," Nora said, after swallowing a bite of quiche, "you told me he had to go to Mexico because his brother was in trouble with the police."

"Yes, but what makes you think he was detained? I never said that."

"I, I just assumed," she stammered and tried to avoid Lily's stare. "When he didn't come back in time for your wedding, I assumed he was in jail like his younger brother."

"If Edmund was detained in Mexico he would have written, called, or done something to get in touch with me."

"You're right," Nora bore a sheepish grin, "silly of me. I just thought he'd have been at your wedding. By the way, I never hear from Jody. Doesn't she realize she has a grandmother?"

Before Lily could answer, Nora signaled the waiter to clear the table and ordered coffee for all. "When you talk to her, tell her to call me. I wish she'd settle down and get married." She peered down her nose. "I've been calling her for the past week but she's never home. I keep getting that darn answering machine. It makes me nervous."

"Mother, she's twenty-four years old and has a life of her own. I can't tell her how to live it. Besides, what makes you think she'd listen to me? She's stubborn and does as she pleases."

"You and Henry should stop supporting her then she'd have to get married. She'd have to find a husband to support her."

"We don't support her," Lily's nostrils contracted, "Henry gives her a monthly allowance towards the rent. He would've done the same if she went to college, and it would have cost a lot more." Her insides tightened at the idea of having to explain her actions to her mother. "In fact Jody fought us about that. But when she couldn't find a job, she finally accepted our offer with one stipulation, no obligations. And Henry and I agreed. Now she works part-time at the Tribune."

Nora sneered, "in my day kids weren't subsidized by their parents. They lived at home until they got married. There wasn't enough money for anything like that. They had to go to work. Don't you remember Lily, I didn't have money for your college. You worked hard and saved every cent for your tuition." Nora looked at Jim, "I'll always be grateful to the Diocese for your scholarship."

"Is that the reason for your generous contributions to the church? Do you feel beholden because they paid for my education?"

"Don't be silly. Me grateful? You're the best thing that's happened to this diocese."

"Don't make comments like that, Mom." His cheeks turned red and he reached for his handkerchief. "God is the only one that can see into our hearts and know the secrets that dwell there. We can't hide from Him." Jim wiped his glasses with his handkerchief and positioned them back on his face.

Nora turned to Lily. "Jody will learn the hard way," she squinted, "she's had it all handed to her on a platter. God will teach her a lesson."

Jim swished a fresh martini in his glass. "Do you know how God works, Mother? Damn it, the harder I try to figure Him out, the more vague the answers."

"Don't swear!" Nora hissed and looked around the restaurant to see if anyone had heard him. "You're not to question His will."

Jim threw his napkin on the table. "It's ideas like yours that are stagnating the Church. God gave us a brain and He expects us to use it. That's the only way the Church can move into the twenty-first century. It must start relying on modern day theologians to give us new direction. It must listen to its members and realize that without the people there is no Church. The people are the Church."

"No! The church will never change. It can't. God's Law is God's Law and no modern-day priest can change that. It's bad enough mass is in English."

Jim turned to Lily and shrugged, then dropped his fork on the desert plate, he was ready to leave. Lily pushed her plate away and stood up. Nora paid the check and insisted they call her next week.

Relieved that the ordeal was finally over, Lily drove to Jody's apartment. She hated the foul-smelling streets of the city where miserable houses were crowded close together, leaving no room for the sunlight to brighten their meager lives. At least the stench of the hot city didn't permeate Jody's apartment. Why her daughter turned down the condominium they'd rented for her, even though it was only five blocks from Wilmette with the rent paid for a year, was beyond her comprehension. But Jody had to do it her way and move into a two-bedroom apartment in this crowded neighborhood.

Despite Jody's stubborn nature, Lily was proud of her petite, blonde beauty. Those wide-eyed, innocent, green eyes and disarming smile, always brought warmth to Lily's heart. She was their only child and she cared less about the law. High spirited and feisty, her very nature questioned authority. She voiced her many opinions and challenged the very legal system that provided her comfortable lifestyle.

Lily secretly cheered her daughter's challenges to the legal system and her father's logic, and often encouraged her freethinking and anti-establishment views. Jody couldn't condone the word 'Justice' as she'd seen it practiced by many attorneys, and used every opportunity to chide the system and what it stood for. Her world was devoid of absolutes: no black and white, only shades of gray. Compromise was her forte', forcing her to seek the arena of the arts which welcomed her views and creative personality. She believed in and supported freedom of speech and found her niche in the world of journalism.

"Hi, Mom," Jody's greeting held a hint of laughter that lingered in the air, "it must be the first of the month. Lunch with Grandma, right?"

Lily wrapped her arms around her daughter and gathered her close.

Jody stepped back. "What's wrong? You seem upset?"

"Nothing. I'm just glad to see you." Lily took her daughter's hands and pulled her onto the couch beside her. "Did I ever tell you how glad I am you're my one and only daughter?"

"Many times. And I never get tired of hearing it. I love you Mom and always will." Jody's eyes took on a serious hue. "Tell me what Grandma said or did this time that's got you so down?"

Barefoot, and seated cross-legged on the old patterned couch, Jody grabbed two green throw pillows and propped them behind her.

How could Jody watch TV on that 19" screen? Christmas would be a good time to buy her a big screen TV. She wouldn't return a Christmas gift, or would she?.

"Are you going to tell me what's wrong?"

"She pushes my buttons and frustrates the hell out of me. Then I feel guilty for feeling that way." Lily cocked an eyebrow. "She says she hasn't heard from you in over a month."

"I talked to her last week. It was only for a few minutes, but I did call her." Jody laughed. "I think she's funny. I can see where you get your traits from, especially your stubborn streak."

"I'm not stubborn."

"No? What about the condominium? Then there was that fellow I was dating in col—"

"I just want what's best for you. He wasn't the right one. And time proved me right."

"You're right, he wasn't. But now I can't be bothered with commitments. There's lots of interesting people to meet and places to go." Her face lit up. "And besides, most guys are either married or engaged. The pickings are slim these days, but thankfully I enjoy doing my own thing."

Lily stood up and brushed the black cat hair off her yellow skirt. She looked around. "Where's 'Nostradamus', he's usually climbing all over you?"

"I haven't seen him this morning. He's probably asleep on a pile of clothes."

"Oh, before I forget," she placed a hand to her cheek, "I'm going to need your help. I'm having a party for your Dad's fiftieth birthday and you've always got great ideas."

Jody jumped off the couch. "C'mon, let's go to the Flea Market. We can browse around and see what's happening. I love shopping there."

"Aren't you going to change or at least put some make up on?"

"See, you're doing it again. What's wrong with jeans and a tee shirt? As long as they're clean." A smile of defiance crossed her face. "Nope, no makeup, I look fine. You're the one that needs to grab a pair of my flats. Those heels will kill you before we get half way through."

"Now who's giving orders?"

Jody looked at her mother and laughed.

While browsing the aisles of the open air market they nibbled on Funnel cakes and spilled powdered sugar every time they took a bite.

"Oh, by the way," Jody snapped her fingers, "I forgot to tell you. The Trib wants me to take some creative writing courses, so I've enrolled at Loyola."

Lily's mouth opened wide and her eyes shot up. "When do you start?"

"I'm not sure. I have to check my schedule. I don't remember the classes or the days. Why?"

A shiver of panic fluttered up Lily's spine, making it feel like a spider scurrying to its nest. Impossible, she thought.

"Mom, you've got a strange look on your face. What's up?"

Lily swallowed hard. "Are you enrolled at the downtown campus?"

"Yes, it's close to the office and to my apartment. Why?"

Lily cleared her throat as relief filled every part of her body. Her mind raced for a plausible explanation.

"Well I thought if you were going to the main campus you could come for lunch, and if you were attending evening classes, you could spend the night. Your old room is always ready."

"You never miss an opportunity to get me back home. I love you for it but I'll be taking classes downtown. Thanks for the offer anyway, I'll keep it in mind."

A smile played at the corners of Lily's mouth.

"My legs are killing me," Jody said and found an empty table, "let's sit, we've been at it for over two hours. Better yet, let's get out of here, I'll treat you to an iced tea."

Lily put her hand on her daughters shoulder. "You, tired? Since when? You usually run circles around me."

"I know, it's probably the heat. Besides, I didn't get much sleep last night." She dropped her eyelids and turned the edges of her mouth. "I was out with some friends—"

"Are you sure you feel okay? You look pale?"

"Stop it Mom, there's nothing wrong. Remember, I don't have make up on." Jody reached for her mother's hand, "but thanks for worrying."

At the Burger King, around the corner from Judy's apartment, Lily slipped into a booth while Jody ordered drinks. She looked so thin, Lily thought. Was she eating regularly? She chuckled at her daughter's radical ideas and recalled a few years back when Jim and Jody got into it at Sunday dinner. Jody's views about the church holding itself up as God and not allowing the people to think for themselves, upset Jim. Jody delighted in disagreeing with him on everything the Church stood for, including his vow of celibacy. Her pet peeve, the unequal treatment of women.

It disturbed Lily that Jody no longer attended mass, but Jim cautioned her to leave it alone. God works in strange ways, He'll get her back on track.

"A penny for your thoughts," Jody slid into the booth.

"I was envying your petite figure. What kind of diet are you on?"

"I'm not on a diet. I'm one of the lucky ones, must be my metabolism. I'm like Dad, tall and thin, only I have hair." They laughed.

"Now tell me," Lily lowered her voice, "what does the Tribune have in mind for you? Why are they sending you back to school?"

Jody's face lit up. "My editor said I have a unique point of view. Remember the feature story I did in the Magazine section last year? Well, they want to give me more assignments like that but he said I need polish." She rolled her eyes and grinned. "I'm real excited about it."

Jody rested her head on the back of the booth and stared at the ceiling. A smile crossed her lips and touched two dimples, making her face look as if loving fingers had squeezed her cheeks. She rolled her head and looked at her mom. "I never realized writing could be so fulfilling. It's what I want to do Mom; maybe the newspaper, a magazine; possibly a book. I'm hoping this class will give me direction."

"I'm glad you found something you really like and feel good about. When I went to college I couldn't find that elusive direction, fulfillment seemed to evade me. That is, until you were born. You were what was missing in my life." She reached over and pushed Jody's hair off her face.

Jody sucked on her straw.

"You made my life worth living. When you moved out I put in a lot of hours at the Crisis line. It filled a void and made me feel needed again."

Jody sat up, reached across the booth, and grabbed her mother's hand. "I'll always need you Mom, but not in the same way I did when I was little. Just knowing you're there, gives me strength. If I need anything, I know I can count on you. No matter what."

"Your dad is there for you too. He loves you just as much as I do."

"I know," a frown moved across her face, "but he's hard to talk to. If I ask him anything it turns into a question-and-answer session. He makes me feel like I'm on the witness stand. Sometimes he can be a pain in the ass."

"Jody, he's your father. Don't talk like that?"

"Why not, it's true. He's unbending and refuses to listen to alternative ideas." Jody stared at the floor. "I love him, but it's difficult to be around him. I suppose its because he wanted a son and blames me for being a girl. He's never said anything, but I feel it when I'm around him."

"I'll admit he wanted a boy, but when you were born he went out and bought you a pink teddy bear that was so big you couldn't even play with it until you were almost three. He was so proud of his baby girl. When guests would arrive, he'd run upstairs, wake you, than carry you downstairs, half asleep, to show you off to our guests. Many nights he'd sit in the nursery and rock you to sleep. One time I even heard him singing to you, if you can imagine that."

Jody smiled.

"As you got older his law practice expanded and he wanted to provide us with all the good things that life had to offer and worked hard for them. Please Jody, don't ever think like that, I assure you, you're wrong."

Jody gulped, "then why is it if I don't hug him, he never comes close? And when I do put my arms around him, he seems uncomfortable? Uncle Jim hugs everybody. Why can't Dad? I've never seen him hug you?"

Lily took her handkerchief, reached across the table, and dabbed the tears that glistened in the corner of her daughter's eyes. "Your father loves you, he just doesn't know how to show it. He was taught not to display emotion, it was a sign of weakness. I don't ever remember seeing his parents hold hands, hug one another, or kiss in public."

Jody's mouth took on an unpleasant twist and brought a frown into her features.

Lily nodded. "It's true."

"I've never seen you and Dad hold hands, either. How can you live with someone without ever being touched?"

Her laugh was choked and desperate. "Each of us lives our own definition of marriage. Mine is, security, respect, and understanding."

"What about love? You didn't mention that. How can you live with someone without loving them?"

"I love your father. I never said I didn't. It's just that we have different ways of showing it and there's nothing wrong with that."

Jody shrugged. "You're probably right but there's one thing I know for sure," she said smugly, "the man I marry won't be able to keep his hands off me. I want to be hugged, touched, and kissed whenever he's around, and we'll probably spend most of our time in the sack, getting it on." She wiggled her penciled brows. "You're blushing Mother, does showing affection embarrass you?"

"No, it just hasn't dawned on me that my daughter is a grown woman and we're discussing things that I never imagined talking about." Jody scooted across the booth.

"Come over for dinner this evening. Your dad will be glad to see you."

"Not tonight, I've got plans. Maybe next week."

They said their good-byes and Lily watched the fragile figure turn and head across the street. She saw her nod to her neighbors as she moved into the lobby of her apartment building. Jody was all grown up, and all that was left of the little girl she once held in her arms, were memories. Her heart skipped a beat and she swallowed hard. She longed for that time when her world was her daughter, and wondered if she had to do it over again would she make the same decision.

# CHAPTER 4

"Professor." He turned his head and hesitated when he heard himself call out his new title. It sounded strange, but he knew it was true. He continued to knot his black tie and slipped it tight around his neck. He thought about the commitment he had made as he tucked his shirt into his trousers. His contract demanded a two-year commitment to Loyola and in return he was awarded a Professorship. Despite the perks the world of academia offered, he was still nervous about the commitment. "Professor Edmund Vilante," he crooned into the mirror as he slipped into his charcoal sports jacket.

"Who'd have thought...talk about destiny."

As he crossed the crowded campus he found the cool September morning invigorating. The towering oak and maples were still cloaked with green. He inhaled the cool crisp air and thought about the coming winter days. Northern California had its mountains and cold weather, but the drastic seasonal landscape changes of his mid-western hometown were unique, and stirred boyhood memories deep inside his belly.

He adjusted his tie and walked toward building C. As he stood before the ominous gray structure, he scanned the façade, grabbed a few quick puffs on his pipe, than smacked the pipe bowl on the sole of his shoe. He put the pipe in his jacket and started up the steps. His fingers moved across the dark suede elbow patches on his jacket and he smiled. Suddenly he felt like he was being strangled, as though someone had their hands around his neck and wouldn't let go. He gasped for air and realized how tense he was. He smiled and put his finger inside his heavily starched collar, hoping it would ease his nervousness. But it persisted in pinching his neck.

With his jaw rigid as stone he walked into the classroom and stared at a sea of faces. Amid the many sighs and whispers, he smiled and nodded a thank you. He knew his finely tuned athletic body, tanned skin, and rugged good looks didn't fit the stereotype of the professors they were use to.

He moved to the podium, introduced himself, and immediately began to outline the semester's work. He paused, then walked back to his desk and threw one leg over the edge. As he sat down he started to loosen his tie. A burst of applause brought a smile to his face and he immediately tore off his tie and tossed it on the desk. No more white shirts and ties for him.

He informed his students that anything beyond one absence would be grounds for an F. If they wanted to learn, they had to make a commitment and stand by it. His heart skipped a beat at the word 'commitment', but he ignored it and proceeded to call the role, attempting to place names with faces. He reached the next name and stopped. He looked out at the rows of students before him.

"Jody Halston!"

A hand in the third row broke above the student's heads. He tried to see the face but couldn't without being obvious. "Miss Halston, after class please, I need to speak with you."

When roll call was finished the students began filing into the halls as Edmund made his way to Jody's desk. He sat down on the opposite desktop. "Do you have a few minutes?" He couldn't take his eyes off the young woman sitting across from him, and suddenly realized he was staring. It's definitely Lily's daughter, he thought. The shape of her face, that wide-eyed innocent look, Lily's manner of tilting her head to one side, just like the young lady sitting before him.

Suddenly thoughts of his daughter Christine surfaced and he had to swallow hard. In an effort to scatter the memories, he shook his head and smiled. "I had a friend by the name of Henry Halston who was studying to be an attorney, any chance you're related?"

Her eyebrows shot up, "he's my father. How do you know him?"

"We practically grew up together."

"Then you must know my mother?"

He cleared his throat. "Yes, I knew your mother as well. We were all friends before you were born. How are your Mom and Dad?" Had he made the right decision to come back? Twenty-five years evaporated as recollections of happier times surfaced.

"Daddy is in partnership with Grandpa. They have two offices, both downtown. Mom and Dad live in Wilmette. She's busy with the Crisis Line."

His eyebrows shot up as if questioning her last remark.

"It's an emergency phone number for people with problems." She smiled. "Do you know Uncle Jim?"

He nodded. "We were part of the same crowd and served in Vietnam together."

She smiled and shook her head. "I wonder why Mom and Dad never spoke of you?"

He shrugged and smiled at her. "Remember I haven't seen them in over twenty-five years. I never bothered to write, and knowing your mother, I'm sure her nose is out of joint, but my assignments made it difficult to correspond with anyone. Besides, I'm lazy. In the field all-day and writing all night, I had no inclination to fill reams of paper with small talk, but I intend to call them now that I'm back. By the way how is your grandmother still bossing your mother around?"

She stifled a giggle. "Boy, you got that right Professor Valenti. She still tries to tell Mom what to do. In fact, Grandma schedules a monthly luncheon with Mom and Uncle Jim just to keep tabs on us. Daddy ignores her but Mom still lets her dictate. I don't understand why she puts up with it."

"Thirty or forty years ago children were taught not to talk back to parents or express an opinion." He studied the young lady's features. "Has anyone every told you how much you look like your mother? If it wasn't for the blond hair you'd be identical, at least the way I remember her," he hesitated, "has she changed much?"

"I've seen pictures of her when she was young. She wears her hair different now and she's put on a few pounds, but I think she looks better. More beautiful! Daddy's got less hair, just a little ring around his head."

He nodded, not trusting himself to speak, and glanced at the wall clock. "Listen, I have to get ready for another class. Would you do me a big favor?"

Her face brightened at the question. "Sure, if I can."

"Don't say anything to your mother or father that we've talked, I'd like to surprise them. Okay?"

Her eyes twinkled. "Do you think they'll really be surprised to see you?" Jody stood and turned as if to leave, then turned back to face him. "By the way, why did the University cancel this class at the downtown campus?"

"There weren't enough students signed up at that location. I hope it's not too much of an inconvenience?"

"No. Except those classes were at night and these are during the day. I'm lucky my boss is giving me time off to attend."

The first of October rolled around and found Edmund busy reviewing his student's short stories. When assignments needed to be critiqued he was always in class early to make sure his assessments were as thorough as possible. No matter how bad a story; ineffectual a plot; or shallow the characters, he always found some good in the writing.

He paused and recalled his promise to Jody. A month had passed and he still hadn't called Jim or Lily. He hadn't had time. He tilted back in his swivel chair and sat staring at the ceiling.

She didn't wait, he thought. He slapped his palms on his muscular thighs, then ran his hands through his hair as if trying to sort out his thoughts. I wasn't in Mexico that long, he huffed, next thing I know she's married to Henry. She never answered any of my letters. It wasn't like her. I even sent a telegram. Maybe I just don't understand women.

As the students began to fill the class he was forced to focus on the assignments in front of him. He shuffled through the stack, only a few left to edit. The stories had been a pleasant surprise, quite a few of his students showed promise and Jody was one of them. His own novel came to mind and he was pleased that he disguised his characters as well as he did. He knew Lily would recognize herself, but he didn't want anyone else to know their story.

As he studied the youthful faces of the promising writers, a curtain of loneliness momentarily blocked life's sunshine, engulfing him in the gloom of loss. Then Jody strolled into the room and his sadness ebbed.

"Congratulations Students!" The undergraduates glanced at one other, surprised by the unexpected accolades. "I never realized there was so much talent in this room. Quite a few of you have the potential to be Pulitzer Prize winners."

His students smiled, chattered among themselves, and applauded as he walked down the aisles and handed out their edited stories. Back at his desk, he watched them read the red-inked critiques. He focused on Jody, her petite chin on her hand, a bemused smile crinkled across her lips at his comments.

Pleased by his remarks, pride sparkled in her eyes as she stopped by Edmund's desk.

"You have talent young lady, don't waste it. As you see from my notes there are a few areas that need improving. Overall, you have a strong unique voice. Your editor at the paper was right, you should write poignant pieces. It would be a great loss to stifle that talent and not share your insights with others. Don't let anyone, and I mean anyone, talk you out of expressing your views."

"Thank you, Professor. Mom hasn't mentioned hearing from you and I'm dying to tell her. Why haven't you called?" Her eyes opened wide as poker chips. "Listen, I've got a great idea."

He smiled and listened. They were startled when a beautiful young woman walked into class.

"May I help you?"

"You don't know me Professor Vilante, but I've heard about you."

Jody rolled her eyes.

"My name is Marianne Adler, I'm in the Masters program."

What a body, he thought.

"I'd like to invite you to a dinner, my advisor is having some of his students over on Saturday. They're bringing their spouses, and since I don't have a partner, I thought I'd ask you."

There was a time, not long ago, that he would've jumped at the opportunity to be with this beauty. But those days were over for him.

"I'm sorry but I already have plans. But I'm flattered you asked."

She thanked him and left the room.

Jody rolled her eyes again.

"What's the matter? Haven't you ever seen a guy get hit on?"

"Yeah, but not one your age."

"Thanks a lot." He moved closer and wrapped her across her arm with his hand, pretending to hit her. "Now let's get back to what we were discussing, you were trying to get me to your house.

"I'll pave the way. Mom is planning a party for Dad's fiftieth birthday, November ninth. Why don't you come to the house and surprise everybody? They'll all be there, everyone you know, including Grandma."

He roared with laughter then squinted one eye and wiggled a finger at her. "You're a trouble maker, young lady. Do you want to give them all a heart attack?"

"How can you say I'm a trouble maker?" She cooed and batted her long lashes. "I want to be there when you surprise the family. I love a drama. Just to see the look on everyone's face when you walk in." Her eyes sparkled.

"I'll see. It's still some time away. I was hoping to see them before then."

"So. You can still come to Dad's birthday party. Wouldn't you like to see your old buddies, including Uncle Jim?"

* * *

Several weeks passed since Jody's impromptu invitation to the Halston bash. Edmund still hadn't made up his mind whether he would attend. Apprehension never played a part in his life until now, and he wasn't comfortable with the feeling. While on assignment in China, without a thought for his own safety, he smuggled out stories describing the grievous disregard for human rights. No fear, no hesitation, just doing the damn job.

When the AP Wire Services picked up his account of happenings behind the Bamboo Curtain, all hell broke loose. Suddenly China was in the unwanted spotlight as the world read his shocking stories. He was quickly smuggled out of the country and none too soon. When he landed in San Francisco, he read about the uprising in Tehnemen Square and mourned the deaths of those who'd helped him.

Here he was, years later, agonizing over how to open lines of communication with his past. He had to make amends. As he made his way toward the exit he heard his name called.

"Edmund! Hey Edmund, hold on there."

He spun around. A tall trim figure hurried toward him. When the figure passed under the overhead light, Edmund's mouth dropped.

"I was hoping I'd run into you. Why haven't you called you son of a gun?"

He was quick to rally and extended his hand. "Henry! You're the last person I'd imagine meeting here. What the hell are–"

"I just finished a lecture on ethics. It broke earlier then I expected so I took this short cut. And I'll be damned if I don't run into you."

"This is weird," Edmund exclaimed as he released Henry's hand. "I was just thinking about you. In fact, I was making plans to see Jim this week-end and then pop in on you and Lily."

"I was wondering when you were going to get in touch," he said and tapped Edmund on the arm. "You know twenty-five years is a hell of a long time."

Edmund slapped his old friend on the back. "You can say that again. Too damn long. I've missed all of you. But practicing law seems to agree with you." He patted Henry's paunch. "You look good," he glanced at the top of his head and frowned, "but what's happening up there?"

Henry passed his palm over his bare scalp and shrugged.

"Are your girls driving you–"

"You could say that again." He squinted and cocked his head to the side. "How did you know I had a daughter?"

"Jody's my student and she's been filling me in."

"That's odd, she never said anything," he dismissed the idea with a wave of his hand, "she seldom discusses things with me. Her mother is her buddy, the one she always talks to."

"I asked her not to say anything."

Henry's eyes flickered.

"I wanted to surprise the family. I hope I haven't created any problems?"

Edmund thought he detected a noticeable edge to Henry's voice and forced a tight smile. "Of course not. I understand. Now that I've spoiled your little surprise, let's get together. What say we meet for dinner? Next week?

"That'll be great." Edmund smiled and extended his hand. "There's so much we have to catch up on. It'll be like old times. Be sure to say hello to everyone for me."

Henry turned, walked back into the shadows and called over his shoulder, "I'll call you about the time and place."

Outside the building Edmund paused, pleased that fate had intervened and made the decision for him. She would finally know he was back. He sat for a moment in the Explorer trying to imagine the surprised look on her face when Henry told her about their meeting. And Jim Was his faith strong enough to carry him through those black moments? Memories of Jim weeping in his arms came to mind. Did his friend ever find the solace he so desperately needed?

Suddenly feelings of guilt and shame rippled through him. He had neglected Jim because of his anger at Lily, or so he had told himself. And the harder he ignored the truth the more it persisted. He'd never told his wife he loved her either, never said the words. Never committed himself to her or to the relationship. Now he didn't like the truth he was facing. All those years, all those lies...

"God damn," he muttered and covered his eyes with his hand. During his marriage to Mai Lyn he'd managed to bury his feelings. The position at Loyola, although timely, was a ploy. Why didn't she wait? Did she ever love him? He started to panic. His pulse quickened and he shuttered as the thought of commitment froze in his brain.

* * *

"Hi," he called out as he strolled into the family room. Startled, Lily jumped into a sitting position and caused her book to spill to the floor. "Oh!"

"I'm sorry, I didn't realize you were dozing."

She rubbed her eyes and tried to waken. Her jade dressing gown fell loosely around her when she propped the overstuffed pillow behind her.

"Do you want some tea?" he asked, "I'm going to make a pot." She reached down to retrieve the fallen book. "No thanks, I don't feel like anything." She followed him into the kitchen and sat down at the table.

"You'll never guess what happened."

"Was the crowd receptive to your ideas?"

He nodded. "A good crowd. Better than I expected, over three hundred people. When I finished I wanted to avoid the crowd and ducked down the back stairs to the parking lot."

The teapot whistled and he moved quickly to remove the boiling water from the burner. He poured himself a cup of herbal tea and joined her at the table.

"So, what happened?" She yawned and rubbed her eyes.

"Behold, a ghost." He smiled and fluttered his eyebrows. "I ran into Edmund as he was walking out of his class. I recognized his swagger. Can you believe it? After twenty-five years I run into him at Loyola. He looks good." A smug smile crossed his face as he sipped the hot tea. "Much better than I remember. Of course he immediately noticed my diminishing hair line," he ran his hand over his head, "we joked about it. His sense of humor hasn't changed."

Awakened by the startling news, Lily shivered and wrapped her gown tightly around her.

"I know, I'm just as shocked as you. So was Edmund. He said he was planning to call or stop by this weekend. It'll be like old times, don't you think?" His eyes were sharp and piercing.

A myriad of thoughts raced through her head. He's coming here? Never. She felt like a trapped animal scrambling to avoid capture. Get away. Don't see him. Did he ask about me? Why would he? Surely Henry didn't invite him here.

"Oops, I almost forgot," Henry grinned and took another sip of tea. "Jody's one of his students. Imagine, our daughter being taught by our old friend. Small world isn't it?"

It felt like someone had kicked her in the stomach. Her pulse was erratic, her mind a crazy mixture of hope and fear. She braced herself when she stood, then walked to the cabinet.

"Is there any tea left, I've changed my mind." Her hands were trembling as she took a deep breath.

"Are you all right?"

"Of course, your news just surprised me." Her throat felt dry and constricted as she carried her cup back to the table, careful not to let him see her nervousness. After several sips she spoke. "I can't believe it. Jody in Edmund's class? She told me she was going to the downtown campus." She tried to sound offhand and casual. "I wonder why she changed her mind? What else did he have to say?"

"He asked her to keep it a secret, said he wanted to surprise us. He wants to see Jim too. He asked about you and how you were doing."

"What did you tell him?" Lily clenched her hand under the table and her fingernails dug into her palm.

"Nothing. He told me that Jody filled him in on the details of the past twenty years." Henry took his cup to the sink and rinsed it. "In fact, I'm meeting him next week for dinner." He turned and stared at her. "Why don't you join us at the club?"

"No!" she answered. "He couldn't be bothered with us all these years, so why should I go out of my way to see him now."

"Well," he shrugged, "it's not like you're going out of your way. I'm inviting you to have dinner with us."

Lily felt his eyes assessing her as she took another sip of tea. She fought to keep her voice calm and contained. "I don't think so. I've got a busy week ahead. One of the girls is going on vacation and they've asked me to work extra hours at the hotline. You go. Reunions are not my cup of tea." She wrinkled her nose and smiled at the pun. "I'll see you in the morning," she said and moved toward the stairs.

"I think I'll invite Edmund to my birthday soirée," he called out. "Do you have any objections?"

She smothered an emerging breath and froze on the first step. Her hand on the banister, she turned to face him. His brows were raised, his face set, his mouth clamped shut. It was as though he were ready to start a cross-examination.

"It's your birthday," she said, and fought to contain any hint of emotion, as she continued up the stairs. "Invite whomever you want."

She walked into her room, closed the door, and nearly collapsed against the bedroom door. Her breathing was hard and fast as her mind raced with unanswered questions. Tonight held little sleep and she hoped the same for him.

*Marilyn Stuart*

## CHAPTER 5

The illuminated hands of the clock announced that she had three hours before the light of day would rescue her from the demons of the night. Despite efforts to clear her head, she couldn't escape the myriad of images that moved through her roused mind. The snail like crawl of the dark night edged on. Finally, the first light of dawn seeped under her draped windows. Thankful for the light of day, she crept out of bed and busied herself till it was time to go downstairs.

Silence surrounded the breakfast table. Henry was reading his paper and Lily found herself still lost in her burdensome thoughts. She sipped at her coffee and gazed out into the back yard, nodding at her husband's occasional comments about world happenings. When he finally left for the office she rushed next door to Pat's.

"Well you're up and about early, in fact, you look like you haven't been to bed. Or have you? What's his name?"

Lily glared at her. "This isn't funny. Henry ran into Edmund last night. Can you believe it," Lily rattled on, "I'm so pissed at Henry. He had the nerve to ask me to have dinner with them next week. Can you imagine?"

"Sure! He doesn't know how you feel. He assumed you wanted to see Edmund as much as he did. It makes perfect sense to me."

"What do you know," Lily scowled, "all your marriages failed and you're telling me that Henry makes sense."

A ringing silence surrounded the two friends. Lily grabbed Pat's hand. "I'm sorry. Please forgive me? I have no right to talk to you that way. You're always ready to lend a sympathetic ear and here I am biting your head off."

"Nothing to forgive, you're venting and I just happen to be within striking distance."

While Pat filled their coffee cups Lily related the encounter between Edmund and Henry, including Edmund's intention to stop by the house.

"Listen, there are two problems here. One, you're angry with Henry because he asked you to join them for dinner. And you're also mad at him because he wants to invite Edmund to his birthday party. Right?"

Lily nodded.

Pat took a sip of coffee. "You're angry at Edmund for," she paused, "for what Lily? I'm still trying to figure that one out."

Barefoot, Lily strolled to the French doors, opened them wide and walked out onto the large Victorian porch. A brisk fall wind had blanketed the Olympic-sized pool with dried leaves, leaving only an occasional glimmer of clear water.

Pats questions made Lily uncomfortable and she tried to stall for time. Time to find some answers. Maybe telling Pat her deep dark secret might feel good. She pulled her white cashmere around her shoulders and sat down on the porch swing. It creaked when she set it in motion.

Pat picked up both mugs of coffee and followed her friend onto the porch. "Mind if I join you? You don't have to talk if you don't want to. I'll just sit and enjoy the beautiful morning."

"What if I told you something so awful...it might effect our friendship? Would you want to know?" Lily stared into her cup.

"Lily, look at me." Pat turned and forced Lily to do the same. "There is nothing you could do that would change the way I feel about you. I'm not a fair-weather friend," she paused, "Lily, are you trying to come out of the closet?"

"Will you be serious for once."

"Even if you murdered someone, and I can't imagine that in my wildest dreams, it wouldn't change the way I feel about you. I wouldn't condone the act, but as your friend I'd stand by your side. Now tell me, in twenty words or less, what's buggin you. Why these questions? Planning to kill off Henry?"

Lily giggled, then drew her lips in. "You have to promise never to reveal what I'm about to tell you. I've carried this secret for twenty-five years and I've never felt safe sharing it with anyone, that is until now." She clasped her hands and looked off in the distance.

"This is happening because I'm being punished for my sins," her voice faltered.

"Spit it out."

"Edmund is..., he's Jo, Jody's father!"

Pat's emerald eyes flew open. Her lips moved but no sound escaped, she could only form soundless words. Finally she snapped her mouth shut and compressed her lips for fear she'd say something before thinking. She failed.

"Holy shit!"

"See I told you, it's a shocker." Slowly, as if trying to convince herself that she wouldn't be struck by lightening, Lily repeated the words. "Edmund Vilante is Jody's father."

Pat let out a long deep breath that ended with a prolonged sigh. "Lily I don't give a damn who Jody's father is. I worry about you carrying this burden, not having confidence that our friendship could handle it."

"That's not true! When I met you, almost twenty years ago, he'd been out of my life over five years. I survived by burying all memories of my past. I almost had myself convinced that Henry was Jody's father." She paused. "And everything was fine till he decided to waltz back into my life. I never expected to see him again. As far as I was concerned he was dead."

Pat threw her arms around Lily. "Thank you for trusting me enough to confide in me."

Lily picked up her empty cup and turned it upside down. "I feel like this cup...empty to the core."

"Gerta," Pat yelled. Within seconds her housekeeper appeared and filled their cups with hot coffee. "Now it all makes sense. He left you pregnant and never bothered to find out if he had a son or daughter. Even worse, that son of a bitch never offered support, not that you or Henry needed it. But it's just the idea that he might have offered it."

"Wait a minute you're way ahead of me, and as always you've jumped to the wrong conclusions. You're right about one thing, Edmund never checked to see if I was all right or how the baby was because," Lily paused and looked away, "he doesn't know."

"What?" Pat slid off the swing and left Lily swaying back and forth. She moved to the end of the porch and leaned her backside against the railing.

"How could you not tell him? It's his daughter. He has the right to know. You know how men feel about daughters, and from what you've told me about him, he would have been head over heels in love with her. But you never gave him that chance, Lily. What were you thinking?"

"Think back thirty, forty, years ago before you judge me. Standards were different then. If I had come home and told my mother I was pregnant she literally would have killed me. Having sex was a mortal sin and good girls didn't do it till after they were married. And I didn't know how to get an abortion, nor did I have the money. But even if I did, I couldn't have killed my baby, besides it's a mortal sin to take a life. God never would have forgiven me. I would've been condemned to hell."

Pat shot back. "I'm not judging you, but shit, you sound like a god damn Baptist preacher. Don't you realize that your guilt has been your hell? Through all these years you've paid the price over and over again. When are you going to let it go? Quit playing the martyr?"

"I'm not playing the martyr! I'm just reminding you what it was like back then."

Admiration filled Pats eyes. "How the hell did you pull it off? I can't imagine Henry ever agreeing to claim Jody as his own. You must have really promised him the world."

"He doesn't know. He thinks Jody's his daughter." Lily paused. "Edmund and I planned to tell Henry about how we felt about one another, but we never got the chance. While waiting for Henry to return from school Edmund was notified that his younger brother was in trouble with the Mexican authorities. He had to go to Mexico and see if he could help. He was supposed to be back in a few days, a week at the most. Back then my periods were every twenty-eight days, like clock work. When I was two weeks late, I knew."

Lily took a deep breath. "When I discovered I was pregnant I knew I didn't have much time, I had to find Edmund. For three weeks I called, I wrote, I called again. I tried everything, but all efforts to reach him failed. I had to do something and fast."

Pat walked over to the swing and sat down again.

"Then I decided to drive to Harvard. It was the July Fourth weekend and the place was teeming with tourists. I hoped there would be vacancies at the local motels, and there were. The hard part was convincing Henry to let me stay with him. He was a prude about such things, but I knew that after a few drinks, and some cozy pillow talk, along with help from a new black negligee, he wouldn't be able to resist. So that night—"

"What! You mean you were engaged and never slept with the guy? My god girl you must think I'm a slut. Compared to me you're the Virgin Mary."

Lily laughed. "The following morning I left for home and continued my efforts to find Edmund. After two more weeks of calling all over Mexico the light finally dawned. He could've gotten in touch with me. He could've called or written. It was a long hard road to reach that conclusion, but there was no other answer."

"I called Henry and told him that I was pregnant. Like me he was worried what his family would say, so we concocted a story about being married three months earlier by a Justice of the Peace, and now we wanted a big wedding. His folks, as well as my mother were delighted, especially when we told them I was pregnant, another lawyer to carry on the Halston tradition."

Lily flew off the swing. "There's one more thing. Last night I found out that Jody is in Edmund's class."

"Holy shit! No wonder you haven't been able to sleep."

Lily's voice was shaky. "I'm upset. I'm angry, worried, and scared. I don't know what I am anymore. I'm having a hell of a time sorting through it all. One thing I know for sure, I'm married, and so is Edmund. So why am I upset?" She paused, than crossed her arms under her breasts as if to protect herself from verbal assaults.

"When I finally realized Edmund didn't want me, I never dealt with the anger." Her eyes widened. "Now those feelings have come back to haunt me."

"Gerta's finished in the kitchen, c'mon lets go back in." Pat slipped her arm through Lily's as they passed through the French doors. The over-sized kitchen was filled with wall-to-wall cabinets, glossy canary yellow walls, and coordinated designer wallpaper, a decorator's delight.

"Pat, I have to be honest. I'm afraid I still love him. But it's been so long, I just don't know for sure. I could be in love with a memory. And besides I've got too much to lose in this marriage. I've got to be careful. I've got everything I've ever wanted and I'm not about to jeopardize my security."

"Yes you have everything," a smile moved across Pat's face, "except a four letter word and I don't mean fuck. I'm talking about love."

"I've lived without love for so long what difference would it make now? After all I have Jody to give me the love I need."

"That's a cop out. It's not the same and you know it. Jody fights for her independence and you continue to smother her. She doesn't like you fussing over her. Loosen the strings or you'll lose her."

They two women starred at one another.

"Lily, there's one more thing," Pat said.

"What's that? We might as well say it all."

Pat starred at Lily and a devilish look flashed across her eyes. "You have to learn to say 'fuck' whenever you get mad or frustrated."

Lily gasped, covered her mouth with her hands, threw her head back, and laughed out loud. "I don't know about you! I can't believe that someone as beautiful as you could have such a dirty mouth. Where did you learn to swear like that?"

"Growing up in Chicago teaches you a lot more than you learn in school. You're forced to live by your wits and your mouth. Once the words are out, I feel better. You should try it some time."

The door chimes interrupted their conversation. "Who the hell could that be this time of morning? I'm not expecting anyone."

Gerta walked into the kitchen. "Mrs. Chernak is here to see Mrs. Halston."

Lily and Pat glanced at one another as Nora marched behind the thin Nordic housekeeper. Lily jumped up. "What are you doing here Mother? How did you know where I was?"

"Emma told me. Why, is it a secret?" Nora glanced at Pat whose body was rigid with defiance. A small gray feather stood up, RobinHood Style, on the side of Nora's smoke gray hat. "What could be so important that you had to come here?"

"Pat and I had a few things to discuss. I really wish you had called first."

Nora's chubby hands were planted firmly on her hips. "This was too important to wait. Can we go to your house, after all this is a private matter. No offense Pat, it's just that I have something personal to talk to Lily about." With that Nora turned and walked out of the room.

"Boy does she have big balls. How do you put up with it? You deserve some kind of a medal."

Lily rolled her eyes. "She's my mother."

"She may be your mother but she has no right to order you around. Why do you allow it?"

"It's easier not to challenge her. Keeps the peace. Listen, I've got to go before she orders you out of your own house."

A hard glint shone in Pats eyes. "Hah, that'll be the day. She may lord it over you but I'll tell her to take a flying fuck before I let her dictate to me."

Lily giggled, shook her head and left the kitchen. Nora stood at the front door, impatiently tapping her foot. Her smile was as phony as her words. "That's a colorful slack outfit you have on dear, is it new?"

"No Mother, I've had it for quite some time. What's so important that you couldn't talk to me on the phone about it?" Lily hurried her mother across the lawn, through the front door, and into the living room.

Nora looked around the parlor. "I've always loved this room," she smiled as she rubbed the toe of her shoe on the carpet. "I know this Persian rug must be expensive. How much did you say you paid for it?"

"Why, do you want to buy it?" Lily compressed her lips into a fine line and stood with her arms folded, impatient to hear her story. "Will you get to the point. What's so important?"

Nora's aggression ebbed. "I'm upset about Jim. Last week at lunch, you saw for yourself how he gobbled down three martinis." Her mothers gray eyes glistened with moisture. Her concern for Jim was evident and a first. Was it warranted or was she over reacting, merely trying to use Lily to manipulate her son?

"Yes I saw, and I'll admit I was surprised. I don't ever remember seeing him drink three martinis. Something terrible is bothering him. Has he said anything to you?"

"No. None of my children confide in me," she pouted, "you know that."

For the first time Lily saw an unselfish side to her mother and a warm feeling surged through her. Then guilt reared it's ugly head as she remembered silently cursing her, wishing she were gone and out of her life. But this was different, Lily had to agree with her about Jim's drinking.

"What makes you think he'll tell me anything?"

Emma brought in a tray of homemade oatmeal cookies and a pot of hot coffee. Nora's demeanor changed again. She looked down her nose and jutted out her chin. "Thank you Emma. Pour me a cup, then you can go."

Emma poured the coffee, smiled, and handed her the cup along with a napkin.

"You were close as children. Don't you remember how you used to sit at the dinner table and whisper to one another. Then the two of you would start giggling. Then your father would get mad and you'd run into the back yard and sit in your tree house for hours, playing, talking, and eating candy. I remember you had a secret code and no one was allowed in your tree house unless they knew it. Every time I'd find out what it was, you'd change it, as if I needed a secret word to get into your clubhouse." Nora thought a moment about her request. "Yes, I'm convinced if there's anything wrong he'll tell you before anyone."

"You may be right, but I don't think we should interfere. He can take care of his problems." Her words had a hollow ring.

"That's just the point," her mother pleaded, "something is eating away at him. A mother knows these things. This didn't just happen. It's been coming on for years and I'm afraid it's getting out of hand. I recognize the signs. Even if you refuse to believe about your father, I see the same signs in your brother Jim. And I don't know how to stop it." Nora's eyes were flat and unreadable as stone as she chewed on Emma's oatmeal cookies.

"If you want me to help you I don't want you to talk about Daddy that way."

Nora pleaded. "But Lily it's true. Why won't you believe me?"

The phone rang.

"I'll get it Emma."

"Listen, Lily," Pat whispered, "your Mother's been there for awhile. I'm giving you a way out if you want it."

"Of course, I haven't forgotten about our meeting."

Pat giggled on the other end of the phone.

"I appreciate your calling. I'll probably be leaving shortly. See you then." Great friend.

"Who was that? I didn't realize you were going out?"

"Yes Mother, I have an appointment in an hour and I can't miss it. I'll think about what you said. Now if you don't mind I have to get dressed." She jumped up and waited for her mother to finish her fourth cookie. Lily picked up her mother's purse, handed it to her, than kissed her on the cheek. She grabbed her by the elbow and ushered the surprised woman to the front door as she continued to brush cookie crumbs off her bosom.

"I'm glad we had this chance to talk. I'll call you if I find out anything." Lily locked the front door, leaned against it, and heaved a sigh of relief. She'd never done that before. Damn it felt good. She smiled as she thought about that word. 'Fuck'. Who knows, maybe one of these days.

Having gathered newly found confidence at the way she handled her mother, Lily decided to visit her brother. Maybe her mother was right about his drinking. She walked into her closet. Beige slacks, beige tops; brown skirts and slacks; white dresses, white slacks, and white tops; her entire wardrobe choreographed by color. Henry's idea, one of the few to which she agreed.

She reached for the phone and dialed. Jody answered on the first ring. "Hi Honey, how are you? You looked pale and tired the last time I saw you, why don't you take some B12?"

"I know what the problem is. I've been doing a lot of reading lately and when I read too long my eyes start to hurt and I end up with a migraine. I probably need glasses."

"Since when have you been having migraines? Why didn't you say something? I'll make an appointment at the Ophthalmologist. What's the best time for you?"

"Mom, I can take care of this, I'm not a child, and besides I'm going to an Optometrist. He'll check my eyes and probably prescribe reading glasses. It's nothing major."

"Why don't you let me come with you? I'll pay for the glasses?"

"Mother you're doting again."

"Really Jody, how many times do your father and I have to tell you that we'll gladly help with any medical expense. What's money for if not to help your children?"

"I know, but I like the feeling I get when I do it myself. Can't you understand?"

* * *

Mrs. Divanski ushered Lily into the rectory. Jim wasn't in, but expected back shortly. Lily decided to wait. She glanced at her gold watch. "Do you know when he'll be back?" The housekeeper shrugged and let out a deflated sigh. It was evident that the woman was holding back.

"Are you sure you don't know where my brother is? I have to talk to him. It's important."

Mrs. Divanski plopped down on the worn brown sofa, next to Lily, and started to ring her hands. Her gray eyes flickered as they moved from Lily's face to the floor.

"What's wrong, Mrs. Divanski? Please tell me, maybe I can help." She touched the woman's arm. "Has anything happened to my brother? Please, you're scaring me."

The old housekeepers' voice was fragile. "I know this is none of my business but I've been taking care of the priests here at St. Joseph's for all these years and I know when there's a problem." The woman's voice broke.

"Mrs. Halston, I don't want to lose my job." Her eyes were brimming with tears. "I love working for the church and it breaks my heart to see the unhappiness," she blurted, "night after night I see him drowning himself in the devil's brew. I worry that the parishioners might see him or, heaven forbid, if he's called to give the Last Rites." The woman made the sign of the cross.

"What I mean is, I don't know how he'd drive. There are times, in the mornings, when I come to work, I find him sleeping on this very couch. I know he hasn't been to bed because the blankets haven't been turned down. I'm really worried Mrs. Halston. He's a good priest."

The housekeeper crumbled her handkerchief as a tear trickled down her cheek. She did her utmost to avoid eye contact.

Lily leaned over and touched the woman's hands. "I'm grateful you told me, I only wish I'd known sooner. I promise you, this is our secret." The housekeeper stood, straightened her shoulders and smiled. She thanked Lily and walked out of the room.

An hour passed. Lily vowed to do something and rehearsed how she'd bring up the subject. The stark sound of the front door bell startled her. The floor creaked, like a door needing oil, under the weight of her brother's steps and caused the old wooden boards to give, enabling her to track his movement toward the living room. It seemed odd that Jim would ring the bell but he probably forgot his keys. She cleared her throat then turned and gasped.

Frozen by the vision of the formidable figure in the doorway, she could only stare at the dark eyes looking out from a sun burnished face. His eyes were open as wide as hers and mirrored her astonishment. She shot up from the couch as ripples of electric shocks ran through her. Barely able to control her reflexes she searched for her voice. Her heart was pounding. She put her hands on her cheeks and felt the warmth from her flush then straightened her shoulders and cleared her throat.

"Edmund, to say I'm surprised would be an understatement. What are you doing here? I thought you were Jim." She prayed her knees would stop shaking.

He was devastatingly handsome and had a rugged look about him that she hadn't seen before. He was dressed in a blue sport shirt that opened enough to show the salt and pepper hair on his chest. His gray fitted slacks brought her to a quick breath. The picture in the paper didn't do him justice. His black hair was in total contrast to the strands of silver at his temples and created a sensual air about him. The smell of Jasmine and musk, his after-shave, wafted across the room. She heard his intake of breath.

"Oh my God!" He smiled and strolled toward where she stood.

She could only stare at the approaching figure, mesmerized by his compelling brown eyes. His strong mouth curled as if on the verge of laughter as he reached for her hand. Like a frightened doe in the woods she was ready to bolt. In a protective motion her hand moved to her neck. The warmth of his large palm sent a shiver coursing through her and she pulled her slender hand back. She forced a smile along with a nod as he began to speak.

"I called Jim last night hoping we could get together for a late lunch. I gather he's not here? That's good," he smiled, "it'll give us a chance to talk."

When Edmund dropped down beside her, Lily quickly moved to the edge of the couch. "You're as beautiful as I remember. Time has been gentle to you and you wear it well. I'm really glad to see you," he paused and continued to stare. "I was planning to have dinner with Henry next week, hoped' you'd join us." The huskiness of his voice lingered.

She swallowed hard, lifted her chin, and met his gaze, all the while trying to force her breathing to slow down. Damn it, she'd sworn not to see him, and here he was. She searched for and finally captured an aloof tone.

"Henry mentioned that he'd seen you at Loyola. He asked me to join the two of you next week, but I have plans. Possibly some other time." She avoided eye contact, afraid that he would know she was lying. Despite her erratic heartbeats she remained calm and watched him out of the corner of her eye. His furrowed brow revealed a somber curiosity and she relished the moment.

"I understand that Jody is one of your students."

"Yes, I recognized the name and asked her if she was your daughter. She's beautiful Lily, and she looks just like you. You must be proud."

"I am. Henry and I have always been proud of Jody." She wanted to ask him about his wife and daughter but, on second thought, didn't want to know anything about them. Suddenly she heard Jim's voice.

"It's about time you showed up," Lily exclaimed.

Edmund let out a whoop as the two men embraced like long lost brothers. A sense of relief filled Jim's eyes. They pounded each other's backs, shook hands, and talked incessantly. Jim winked at Lily and she caught her breath. The physical embrace gave her time to gather her thoughts.

"Hi Sis, what are you doing here? Aren't you supposed to be at the 'Crisis line'?" Before she could answer he looked at Edmund. "Listen, I've got an idea. Why don't the three of us have lunch? It'll be like old times." He looked from one to the other. "C'mon guys, it should be fun."

"It will never be like old times," she responded sharply and started to fuss with her dress, straightening and removing imaginary lint. "Besides, I'm due at the hospital." She walked over to Jim, kissed him on the cheek, turned, and started to walk out of the living room.

Edmund's voice sliced through the air and stopped her in mid-step. "Wait Lily. When am I going to see you? We have twenty-five years to catch up on."

She turned and arched her brows, placed her hands on her hips, then tossed her head, causing her hair to slosh around her face. "It's of no importance to me. The past is the past. There's nothing to talk about."

His lips tightened at the rebuff.

She quickly turned, walked out of the rectory, and slammed the door behind her.

Amused, but unmoved by her retort, Edmund turned to Jim, shrugged his shoulders and smiled.

Jim put his arm around Edmund's shoulder. "You can never figure out women. I'm glad that dealing with the gentler sex is not one of my problems. Despite what people think, the vow of celibacy has its good points. I don't think I'd fare too well with the fairer sex. I have other demons to handle." A shadow crossed Jim's face, much like a cloud eclipsing the sun. The moment passed and a smile returned to his face as he ushered his old army buddy out the rectory to a long awaited reunion.

# CHAPTER 6

Shaken by the sudden appearance of her past, Lily hurried out of the rectory and to her car. The cool crisp air alleviated the flush from her cheeks and gave way to memories of that night, long ago. She brushed her hand across her lips and could still feel the warmth from his touch. She shook her hand and started the car.

In what seemed to be only minutes, she found herself in front of the hospital. She parked the car and left her memories inside the leather interior of the Mercedes. She nodded at Dorey and headed toward her desk, plopped into her chair, kicked off her shoes and pushed them under her desk. She knew she was riding an emotional storm, and was being whipped about by her turbulent feelings, like a cork tossed about by the rip tide. She peeked into her compact mirror and realized her make up needed retouching; her nose was shiny, her lips were pale and showed only a hint of color, while a curl fell loosely across her forehead.

"Lordy, child," exclaimed Dorey. "You look like one of those ad's. You know, headache #49."

"I'm fine," she said, and leaned back in her swivel chair, "been racing around all day." As she freshened her makeup she glanced around the tiny space. A large map of Chicago and the surrounding suburbs hugged the wall, tied into the phone company in a crosspatch system so that when an incoming call activated the board, it showed the approximate location. If the call was an emergency they could forward it to the dispatchers at 911 who had a similar set up.

Lily's neck ached. Her lower back was spasmodic and her stomach was giving her fits. She couldn't keep up this emotional pace without it taking its toll. She needed to be alone with her thoughts and this was not the place to think. The phone rang.

"Crisis Line. May I, he—hello." The caller hung up. She scooted across the cement floor toward the back of the room where a fresh pot of coffee was brewing. She poured a cup and sniffed the nutty aroma. The phone rang again.

"I'll get it," she hollered and scrambled to her desk. Lily wrinkled her nose as she listened. The distraught young girl was eager to talk and even though she was rambling, Lily sensed she was holding back. What was really bothering her?

After a few minutes Dorey looked up from her paperwork. From Lily's conversation Dorey realized the caller was serious about committing suicide.

"How old are you?"

Twenty-three came the answer.

"I have a daughter two years older than you and I wouldn't care what she did. I'd still love her. I'm sure your mother feels the same way."

A tear-choked voice whispered, "I don't have a mother, or a father. They're dead."

Lily listened to the sobbing. "I've been on my own for the past ten years and handled everything that's been thrown my way."

Lily continued to give moral support. She pointed out her choices and tried to convince her that suicide was not the answer.

"Please tell me your name. I'd like to know what to call you."

"Jessica."

"That's a beautiful name. Did you know it means rich in Hebrew? Isn't there any family or maybe a Rabbi that could help?"

Dorey signaled Lily that she was plugging into her line. The final decision whether or not to send the police fell on her shoulders.

Lily wrote on a pad of paper in large printed letters, WAIT I CAN TALK HER OUT OF IT. Dorey shook her head, raising her hand with all five fingers extended.

Five more minutes. Experience taught Dorey that if she sent the police out before they talked the caller out of committing suicide, within twenty-four hours the caller usually finished the job.

Lily's heart was pounding. "Jess I can be there in fifteen minutes, we can talk. Please let me help."

Dorey glared at her. That suggestion was against the rules. Trained individuals are available to make those personal visits, not crisis line volunteers.

"No." Jessies' voice was firm but fragile. "If you make any attempt to come here I'll shoot myself now!"

Lily's heart thrust into her throat. She grabbed the phone with both hands and gasped when she heard the click of a gun hammer being cocked.

"All right Jessie, calm down. I won't come. Please put the gun down! I know you have it in your hand. I beg you, please! I promise I won't make any attempt to see you." Lily switched to a more soothing voice. "Jessie you're not telling me everything. What's really wrong? Don't be afraid. Trust me."

Jessie started talking. "I've been diagnosed with Aids and I'm going to die a horrible death. Just the thought of it..." Lily looked over at Dorey. She was finally getting the callers confidence.

Lily swallowed hard. How could she tell Jessica she was wrong? How could she tell her she wasn't going to die? How could she convince her that the future wasn't what she thought it would be? In her silence Lily uttered a prayer for guidance and forced her stomach to settle down.

"Jessie, I've got an idea. You said I couldn't possibly know how you feel and you're right. But I know a girl about your age who has full-blown Aids and doing well. I'd like to call her and let you talk with her. You'll like her." Lily started flipping through the Rolodex on her desk.

"She works with young people who've been diagnosed with the same disease. Wouldn't you like that?" The long silence ripped through the phone. "You're not alone Jessie. You're never alone. If you like, I can pray with you."

"You've helped, more then you'll ever know." Jessie paused. Another sob was heard through the phone.

"Thanks," Jessie whimpered.

The prolonged silence was deafening. Fear sat like a lump inside Lily's knotted stomach. She started to tremble. Goose bumps dotted her skin. Then an explosion pierced the silence. The sound of a gunshot reverberated in Lily's ear.

"Jessie! No!" she screamed, "Jessie, answer me."

Dorey jumped up and hit a button alerting 911 as Lily continued to shout into the phone. Immobilized, Lily stared at the black instrument in her hand.

"Jessie, answer me...Jessie..."

Lily ran to the board and committed the address to memory. She had a vague idea where the north Clark street address was and mentally formulated her drive as she ran barefoot to her car, shoes and purse in hand.

Dorey ran after her, shouting at the speeding car as it swerved out of the parking lot. Lily drove to Clark Street in record time, only twenty minutes. She scanned the addresses on the buildings, desperate to find Jessie's apartment. Then she saw the flashing lights of a police cruiser, then more police cars and ambulances. Traffic was at a stand still. She whipped around the corner and left the car up on the curb and ran to Clark Street. Her lungs were aching as she headed down the block toward the gray three-story building.

As she pushed through the crowds a policeman grabbed her arm and stopped her on the stone steps. "You can't go up there Lady, there's been an accident." His voice was courteous but firm. "You'll have to step back." He took her arm and escorted her down the steps. "They're bringing the body down now."

"Please officer," Lily's voice broke as she pulled away, "I have to see her. I have to see Jessie."

"You knew the deceased?"

"No, I mean yes. I was talking to her when she shot herself." She looked up the steps and saw the EMT's struggling down the narrow steps with the stretcher behind them. Lily clenched her jaw and her breathing turned ragged. She put a knuckle in her mouth to stop the sobs.

"Please officer", she cried, "I've got to see her. She has to know that somebody cared." Tears blurred her vision.

As the body passed, the officer stopped the EMT's and motioned for Lily over to his side. He nodded to the attendant and he unzipped the black bag.

Desolation swept over Lily at the sight of the beautiful young black girl's face. A bullet hole in her temple, the size of a quarter, oozed with crimson fluid from the jagged flesh. Lily covered her face and screamed in silence. Bile was on her tongue and she swallowed hard.

"What a shame, she was pregnant," he said shaking his head. Lily turned to the EMT. "What?" Guilt started gnawing at her as the attendants zipped up the bag and carried Jessie's body to the ambulance. She stood and watched as they maneuvered the black bag into the vehicle and suddenly it felt like an elephant was sitting on her chest and it caused her to gasp for breath. When the ambulance door finally closed Lily turned and ran.

Safe inside her car she wept out loud. "Why God? You put me at the phones so I could help, then you let this happen. What's the point?" She rested her head against the car window and continued to sob as the traffic cleared. Isn't there anything I can do right? What did I say, or maybe didn't say, that caused Jessie to pull the trigger? Could I have prevented it? I botched my opportunity to save Jessie's life.

The dashboard clock read four, Dorey would still be on duty. She dried her tears and proceeded to on to the hospital, all the while seeing images of the bullet hole in the young girls head. As she drove into the hospital parking lot images of her childhood exploded and flashed unrelentingly across the screen of her mind. She jumped out of the car and ran inside. Dorey sprung out of her chair and sat Lily down, then ran to the ladies room for a cold cloth. Lily closed her eyes.

Ghostly images whirled around her head, causing her face to bear hideous contortions as if she were in terrible pain. She was five years old again. She leaned forward in her chair and grabbed Dorey's hand.

"Breathe slowly girl. I've never seen you like this. What's the matter? I told you not to go. What happened? What possessed you? Was it bad? Talk to me."

Lily looked at Dorey. "It has nothing to do with today," she sobbed. Her head hung down and her hands were clasped between her knees.

The big woman squeezed Lily's hands between hers. "Hush Honeychild it'll be all right, you'll see."

In between sobs Lily started to speak of her childhood. "They let me see Jessie. She was a beautiful young thing, tan skin, shoulder length hair and a gaping hole in the side of her head." Lily gasped as the vision of the dead girl returned.

Dorey ran and brought Lily a glass of water. "Keep talking baby," she hollered from the sink, "that's the best thing you can do." She handed her the glass of water.

"But that's not it," she said, "it was seeing Jessie that way". Terrible pictures...memory of my dad." She covered her face with her hands. "Scenes from when I was little. Mom, Dad, their arguments. I was five when it happened. I remember lying in bed and trembling whenever I heard them fight. I was so scared I use to pull the covers over my head because I didn't want to listen. I wanted to tell them I was sorry for being a bad girl."

She took a deep breath as Dorey handed her a box of tissue. Lily pulled out a handful, wadded them together and wiped her eyes. She took a sip of water and continued her story as Dorey listened with eyes as wide as saucers.

"I remember this particular night lying in bed and listening to them fight. Their voices kept getting louder and louder. Then they stopped. I jumped out of bed and went to my bedroom door to see if I could hear what they were doing. The quiet was as frightening as the screaming. I could hear mom crying, then I started to cry. Next I heard drawers opening and closing. Then it was quiet again."

"Suddenly," Lily's lips moved uncontrollably, "there was an explosion. The sound rattled the windows and I jumped out of my skin and nearly wet my pants. I remember opening the door and looking into the living room. I saw my mother running from the kitchen. Then I heard her scream. I thought she was hurt so I ran after her. Half asleep, my brother peeked out of his bedroom, I can still see him standing there and rubbing his eyes."

"I'll never forget what I saw. My mother was shaking all over. One hand was clutched at her stomach, the other covered her mouth as if trying to retrieve her bloody scream. My dad was sprawled on the floor and my mother was leaning over him. Her screams filled the room. I remember thinking that he'd tripped and fallen, so I ran to his side. I froze when I saw all the blood seeping onto the rug. Pieces of loose flesh hung from the ragged head wound. I'll never forget the funny smell that lingered in the room. Gunpowder. I started yelling, 'I didn't mean it Daddy, I didn't mean it.' The next thing I remember is my brother standing beside me, crying while he wiped my tears with his pajama top. The rest is a blur."

Lily blew her nose and wiped her eyes. "I remember a lot people coming to the house, telling my mother how sorry they were. Nobody said anything to Jim and me, it was like we weren't even there." Lily started to shiver and wrapped her arms around herself. "I miss him. He was the only one that talked to Jim and me."

The kindly black woman stood up and nodded. "Makes sense now. Runnin after Jessie was a second chance to save your father. Since you couldn't do it as a child you made up your mind that you were going to save as many people as you could, Voila', the Crisis line."

"Your wrong Dorey, I love helping people in trouble. It makes me feel good and fills the emptiness inside. Besides, suicide is wrong. Imagine how different my life would've been if my father didn't take the coward's way out. Look at Jessie, she had a full life ahead of her."

"Well I don't know about your father but you can't say that Jessie had a great life to look forward to. She was facing hell, and she knew it, and so was her baby. I don't agree that she had the right to take her life but the Lord only knows how long she might have lived." Dorey gathered Lily in her arms and stroked her hair. "I know how it must hurt Sugar." She rubbed Lily's back, cooing to her until Lily's sobbing had subsided.

"I'd be willing to bet that after today's episode some of those holes in your heart will disappear. It's clear now why you've been so dedicated and puttin in so many hours." She eased Lily away from her. "Definitely not a healthy hobby."

"I really don't believe in suicide. It's against God's commandment. I believe that no one has the right to act as God. Only He can decide when and how we'll die. That was ingrained in me as a Catholic and I still believe it with all my heart. Look at the great work Hospice does. I can't think of any circumstance where suicide is warranted." Her body still quivering, Lily eased into the chair.

"Shh, it's gonna be all right."

It was a few minutes after five and Lily's replacement was at her desk ready to answer the phone. "C'mon Lily let's clock out, I'll buy you a drink, you deserve one after today. I'll just bet your life is gonna be a little sweeter now that some of that shit is gone."

They drove to the cafe around the corner. "I've never been here," Lily said, "what kind of place is this?" A sea of black faces stared at her as they walked in and sat down in a booth.

"Don't worry, you're with me. The food is good and they just got a liquor license." The jolly black woman chuckled as she squeezed into the booth. The sweet smell of Bar-B-Q ribs and greasy fried chicken filled the small cafe. Dorey's mouth watered. "Damn, I've got to do something about this figure of mine," she said, patting her huge hips.

Lily giggled.

"I don't know if you realize it girl but you've been going about this job like someone obsessed. Do you realize how many volunteer hours you've racked up this year?" Dorey ordered two beers, unzipped her attaché case and rifled through her papers.

"Look," Dorey held a chart and pointed, "here, in September, you worked ninety-five hours. This month isn't over and you already have sixty hours logged. Are you trying for volunteer of the year?"

Dorey sprinkled salt on Lily's beer. She took a sip and wrinkled her nose when the foam touched the tip of it. The bitter taste made her shudder.

"Have you ever had a beer?"

Lily shook her head.

"You haven't lived unless you have pretzels and beer." Her white teeth sparkled as she bellowed out for a basket of pretzels. A young black man brought the basket along with a side order of butter.

"Now take a pretzel and swipe it across the top of this butter, bite it and follow with a swig of beer." Dorey grinned. "Do I have to teach you everything, Girl?"

Lily followed a ritual, a sip of beer, a bite of pretzel, than another sip of beer. After the second sip the beer didn't seem as bitter. When Dorey's glass was empty Lily ordered another round. Hungry, she continued eating pretzels dipped in butter. The salt made her thirsty and she ordered still another beer. She chugalugged the drink, then giggled and slammed the glass on the table, proud that she could drink a whole glass of beer without stopping.

Dorey yanked at Lily's hand and shook her head no to the waiter as Lily signaled for another round. "That's enough for you my friend, you have to drive home. I don't want you getting sick on me." Dorey paused. Her dark eyes starred at Lily as she chose her words carefully.

"I'm glad we've had a chance to talk." Taking Lily's clasped hands in her bark-colored hands, she gave a squeeze. "It's no good to devote so much time to the Crisis line. Trust me, it can get you down. Everyone's troubles can be depressing. So...," she said leaning back in the booth, "as of today you are off the schedule for the next sixty days."

"What? Dorey, no! I can't. I have to do this." Lily looked away and thought for a moment. "No, I don't have to do this, I want to. It gives me a sense of accomplishment."

"Listen Girl, what happened to you today is probably going to have far-reaching repercussions. There's bound to be some fallout and you're gonna need time to process it. As of today you are officially off the schedule. End of discussion."

Lily sighed and dropped her brows. "Well Dorey, I do have Henry's birthday party in three weeks and I'm going to need time to get ready for that. You're coming aren't you?"

Dorey's booming laughter filled the small cafe. "Of course, I wouldn't miss seeing how the rich folks live."

*Marilyn Stuart*

# CHAPTER 7

Despite its ripe old age of eighty, the old red brick house was sturdy and boasted of twelve-inch plastered walls and hardwood floors. Unlike his home in San Francisco, that suffered major damage with every quake, this old Wilmette girl had withstood everything Mother Nature sent her way. The only thing that creaked was the heavy front door.

Edmund walked through the empty foyer and into the living room. The rust-colored couch was pushed against the wall, and beside it an end table with two brass lamps, exactly where the movers had left them, two months prior. Coffee spots dotted the glass table in front of the couch, along with an ashtray that overflowed with pipe ashes. The windows were bare and his favorite chair, a brown leather Lazyboy, sat next to the fireplace.

He flicked on the lamp, grabbed the ashtray and plopped in his chair. He pushed back and heard it scrape the wall behind him as the footrest lifted his legs. Boxes were stacked three high in the middle of the room, paintings remained in their crates, and the carved curio cabinet stood empty. Statues that once graced the lighted shelves were still wrapped and boxed. Mai Lyn had treasured each and every one of her collectibles but he had no idea what to do with them. He'd taken a hell of a lot for granted and never realized all the work involved in making a house a home. But now he was living alone. Who'd see it?

He needed someone to come in and clean. He needed more time to...to do what? He no longer had a family; he wasn't traveling; and his nights were long enough. Get with it, he told himself. Things will never be the same. My life's changed, he thought, there's no going back. "All you have is time, buddy. If you don't want to turn into a lonely old man you'll have to change your attitude." He tapped his pipe to get rid of the ash then added fresh tobacco.

"It was okay when you were running around the world, but now you've put down roots. Extend yourself, make that commitment." He lit his pipe, leaned back on the leather headrest, and watched the smoke hang in the air. Good to see Jim. He'd aged beyond his years and looked tired. Maybe the weight loss is what made his face look pale and drawn, or possibly the responsibility of being a pastor, all these years, was getting to him. I'm sure glad I drove to lunch the other afternoon, he thought. With the celebrating we did Jim was in no condition to get behind the wheel.

There, directly before him, an image of her face, smiling through the cloud of smoke. As he relaxed more images began to dance in his head. Despite his resolve not to think about her she intruded with such persistence that his determination to keep her out of his thoughts finally gave way. No harm in thinking.

He remembered the young boy sitting in the kitchen feeling the heat of the open oven door as the pans of 'Brioche' were removed. The aroma spread its tentacles through the kitchen as the sun dried tomatoes melted down the sides and caused his saliva to flow before he even took his first big bite.

A change of memories brought him different visions of his youth, playing hide and seek in the streets of Chicago at dusk, the gang running across the neighbors lawns, behind houses, and through the alleys. He surprised Lily by jumping out of the bushes and kissing her on the cheek. Memories rocketed like a kaleidoscope of time, exploding on the screen of his mind.

The sound of the phone caused his memories to evaporate as quickly as they appeared. He jumped up, limped into the kitchen, and grabbed the phone. "Henry! How are you?" He cradled the phone with his shoulder and proceeded to open cabinet drawers in search of matches to light his pipe. "Next Wednesday would be good for me too. I'm not sure I remember where the club is." He listened to directions and struck one match, then another, and threw the burnt ones into the sink. Finally he was able to suck in enough smoke to still his craving for nicotine. "That'll be great. Looking forward to it. See you then."

He hung up the phone and started to wander about the house. He flipped on the lights as he walked into every room, then stopped to listen for a sound, any sound in the silence of the large house. With an uneven stride he limped to the stereo, turned on his CD player, and plopped back into his recliner. He elevated his legs in hopes of easing the gnawing ache. The damn leg was really bad tonight, he thought. The doctors told him he'd never be free of pain and the only thing he could do was to maintain a lean weight and not run any marathons. Despite the advice, he never pampered himself, setting out instead to prove the doctors wrong by taking on rough assignments.

He remembered the pain shooting through his leg as he trudged up the steep Ruandan mountain path, his guide and cameraman close behind. He couldn't let the mountain slope stop him so he clenched his teeth and kept climbing. He could handle it. He couldn't let anyone know about the severed ligaments...that damn VC.

He recalled the time, in South America, when we was chasing a story in the Amazon jungle, trying to find out who was paying the tribal natives to cut down the Rain Forests. One day, his group of three came upon a rope bridge swinging two thousand feet above the gorge. They had to get to the other side, but never realized how dry and brittle the support ropes were. After years of exposure to the elements, a disaster was looming.

Not sure if the bridge would bear the weight of all three, they decided to cross the narrow bridge one at a time. His camera man first, then his guide, inched their way across the swaying bridge. Now it was his turn. His heart started to pound. The steely taste of fear lay sour in his mouth. He tested each narrow slat before taking a step. He didn't dare look at the jagged rocks below.

Half way across he noticed storm clouds approaching. Suddenly high winds surged into the canyon. The bridge swayed wildly. He clutched the side ropes to steady himself and looked across at his buddies to let them know he was all right, and as he did he stepped on a rotted slat. Suddenly he slipped through the aged wood. "God damn it," he yelled as his good leg dropped like a leaden weight and dangled between the rotten slats. He shouted at his companions to stay back, any added weight on the bridge could cause the ropes to give way.

He pushed up with his bad leg under him until the muscles in his good leg started to spasm. Despite his numerous efforts he couldn't lift his body. He clutched the frizzy hemp rail and struggled to free himself. The rope railing had too much give. No support. He'd always been cool under fire, but this situation was different.

The dark swirling clouds quickly descended and the heavy rains soaked his aching body. Frustrated, helpless, and completely immobilized, he prayed and waited for help. Mike, his camera-man, threw down his equipment and took off his heavy hiking boots. He weighed the least of the three and slowly inched his way out onto the swaying, slippery, bridge. Would the span hold their combined weights? Edmund held his breath and watched the lean man inch his body across the swaying bridge. Finally Mike was at his side. As the torrential downpour washed over them, Mike wrapped his arms around Edmund's chest and started to pull him up, just enough so he could gain leverage and lift himself the rest of the way.

After two or three false starts they finally succeeded, Edmund was extricated from his deadly circumstance. Moments later, when Ike, the cameraman, was off the bridge and on solid ground, Edmund made his move. As his facial muscles twitched across his stern face, he crawled, slat by slat, to the far side of the gorge. As he neared the ledge, a foot from solid ground, a crackling sound suddenly filled the air. Without warning, the rope suddenly became slack and gave way as Edmund lunged for the ledge. His cameraman grabbed for his hand and caught his jacket, just as the bridge slammed against the side of the mountain. They slowly pulled him off the ledge, up the rocky mountain-side to safety.

Once again Lily's face drifted into his mind's eye, more beautiful than he remembered. Her glistening copper hair cascaded around her head like a halo and highlighted her slender white neck. Those sensuous lips begged to be kissed. How could such beauty be forgotten?

Muted tones of 'The Impossible Dream' filled the air from his CD. A lump swelled in his throat accompanied by a hollow ache. Than a tingling current, like a thousand butterfly's walking on his skin, spread through him, ending at the juncture of his thighs. The melody drew him in deeper, like a leaf caught in a whirlpool, sucking him down in a crescendo of remembrance. Erotic images of Lily. His heart pounded. The blood flowed. His hardness throbbed.

Filled with conflicting emotions he shot up and shut off the stereo. What the hell am I doing, he thought. "God damn it, stop it. She's a happily married woman. She has a beautiful daughter and a full life. Don't get yourself into a situation you'll be sorry about. These aren't strangers, they're old friends." He threw up his hands in disgust, walked to the window, pulled the curtain aside, and watched the wind toss the dried leaves around his front lawn.

"I need to talk to her. I have to know." The book would be out in a few months. Get Lily a copy before it hits the bookstores, he thought. When she reads it she'll know how her marriage to Henry affected me. She'll know that I meant every word I ever said to her.

Fatigue eased into his body like a slow-rolling fog and finally settled into his muscles. Achy and exhausted, as though a giant cork had been pulled, he forced his spirit to ebb like warm bath water swirling down a drain. He pressed his hands over his weary eyes. The throbbing finally subsided and he fell fast asleep.

* * *

He pushed up the sleeves of his beige sweater and explained to his students how to convert life's experiences into a creative life of their own. He was trying to bring another dimension to their vision. Writing current news for daily papers was one thing, but his students could take the same material and express themselves on the pages of fiction. As he started illustrating his point he found himself distracted. Jody kept moving her head, back and forth, as if trying to shake something off.

"Professor," a raised hand waved a pen and caught his attention. "How are you able to settle down to a boring life and what will you do for new material?"

"Well, I'm not sure how staying in one place will effect me. I'm hoping to make the transition with as little pain as possible. Keep one thing in mind when you write," he walked around to the front of his desk and sat on the corner with one leg dangling over the edge, "everything you see, hear, taste, touch, and smell, becomes part of you. It's stored in your sub-conscious. Whenever you write, you unconsciously draw from that place. Because of my past I have mountains of data to draw from, so no matter where I live, I'll always have plenty of material. Life thrives on diversity. The secret is to be aware."

Another student wearing a ring in his ear bellowed out, "Yo Professor, you can't leave, we just got you trained. You're cool man and you don't give heavy reading assignments." The class laughed.

"Thank you Mr. Rapulos. Don't worry I have a two-year contract so you'll probably see me next year. I've made a commitment." He smiled at the thought. "In fact I've been asked to teach an additional class, short-story writing. But I guarantee you that class will have plenty of written assignments." His warmth echoed through the class and his students applauded.

"Well, after that gracious act of acceptance, I just might unpack. It's rough at my age to live out of boxes." He picked up William Zinsser's book on 'Writing Well' and made reference to specific pages to study.

As the classroom emptied, Jody slid into a desk in the front row. Her walk had a sunny cheerfulness that matched her constant smile. She propped her arms on her books, watched him gather the loose papers on his desk and sweep them into his briefcase.

"How do you ever find anything? I can imagine what your office looks like."

He smiled. "Thank god for my computer. I do all my work on it. Now all I have to do is unpack my office equipment and I'll be ready to go."

"Were you serious when you told the class that you hadn't unpacked?"

"Yes, why?"

"Well, I was thinking. I'm in jeans and not working the rest of the week, how about I give you a hand?"

Edmund shook his head. "What would your folks say if they knew you were helping me?"

"They'd be glad I was doing something constructive," she said, "besides it'll give us time so you can tell me more about Mom and Dad, you know all the interesting stuff that happened when they were growing up, things they wouldn't tell their daughter."

He hesitated.

"Oh please say yes. I don't have anything to do today and I'd really appreciate the company. It'll be too quiet at the apartment because I've lost my second roommate, she's moved in with her boyfriend."

"All right, but on one condition. Tell me what's going on with you. You seem bored in class. The way you were fidgeting, it looked like you were ready to get up and run out."

"That's not it. I just had a splitting headache," she rubbed her temples, "no matter what I tried it wouldn't go away. I finally popped four aspirins." She smiled. "It seemed to have helped."

He frowned, "have you thought about going to an eye doctor?"

"I was to one a couple of days ago, he said I didn't need glasses, I have twenty-twenty vision. He gave me the name of an Ophthalmologist should the headaches persist."

At that moment a graduate student walked into the classroom. The tall auburn haired beauty ignored Jody and moved next to Edmund. "Professor Vilante, I understand there's a party this evening at Professor Handley's home. Would you like to go?"

Edmund appeared taken back by the unexpected invitation. There was a time he'd have jumped at the opportunity to be seen with such a lovely woman. But he was through with that life. He smiled, "I'm sorry but I have plans."

She smiled and shrugged her shoulders. She touched his hand, turned, and walked out of the room.

"Well? Aren't you the one. Does this happen often?"

"No," he said, still reeling from the invitation.

"Okay, but am I going to help you unpack or not?" She stood, hands on her hips, head tilted, her gaze holding his. Just as Lily used to do, he thought, then chuckled. He was lost to her charm and couldn't say no. The house did need a woman's touch, maybe Jody could unpack the statues Mai Lyn had collected, almost like having Christine back, if even for a moment.

"All right," he smiled and shook his head, "on one condition." He held up a finger and then another, "no make that two. First of all you let me buy dinner when we're finished, and second, if you think this is going to get you an A, you're badly mistaken, young lady."

Her laughter resounded in the empty classroom.

As they left the building, he looked around and raised his brows. He appeared puzzled. His nose wrinkled when he questioned her. "Where are you parked?"

"Right here."

She pointed to the red Harley and climbed onto it.

"You're kidding. I can't believe that someone as tiny as you could handle one of these. I pictured you driving a Mercedes 550 SL convertible."

She slipped her helmet on and scrunched her face. "Oh," she said and tucked her hair into the protective head gear, "you forgot to give me your address. Where do you live?"

"In Wilmette, 224 Lexington Avenue, not to far from here."

"I know where it is." She turned the ignition key and the engine's roar shattered the stillness of the afternoon. She gunned the engine several times then shouted, "its not far from Mom's house. C'mon I'll race you." Her tires squealed across the crowded parking lot.

Jesus, he thought, he and Lily live only blocks from each other. Even though the house was bought sight unseen, he liked the location and the ambiance of the large old homes around him, never even thinking that Lily and Henry would choose such a neighborhood. He ran to his Explorer, jumped in, and roared out of the lot, determined not to let his student beat him. Then he remembered a short cut. He weaved in and out among the rows of parked cars and barely stopped at the street. His tires squealed. He was determined to win.

He chuckled, he felt like a teenager again and took a few sharp corners at speeds he shouldn't have. He couldn't remember having so much fun. His adrenaline was flowing. He whooped out loud as he sped through the yellow light at the intersection, then glanced in the rearview mirror to make sure no cops were around. In another minute he'd be on Lexington, and quickly scanned the street for the red motorcycle.

He made the turn into his driveway, and sitting on his front steps, helmet in hand, shaking her blond hair loose, was Jody. She looked at her watch and shook her head as he screeched to a sudden halt.

"What kept you, Professor?" She faked a yawn, "I could've told you about that short cut, it's been a one-way street for about five years. Too bad."

He threw back his head and laughed. "You're a smart-ass young lady. Didn't your mother ever teach you to respect your elders?"

"Yes," she winked, "but Daddy taught me that there's no better feeling than being a winner. You know he was right, it feels great. I beat ya, Professor." She laughed and wagged a finger in his face as they walked up the front steps into the large gothic-styled home. Jody threw her helmet on the couch and looked around. "Geez, you weren't kidding when you said you were living out of boxes. How the heck do you find anything? Mother would kill me if my apartment looked like this."

"Yes, I know. She always did like things in their proper place. But your father," he grimaced, "he was something else. I can remember all his notebooks had to be facing one way. At the dorm we couldn't sit on the bed because he didn't want it wrinkled. I remember the time a bunch of the guys got together, and when your father was in class, we tore the blankets and sheets off his bed and flung them out the window. I sure wish I could've been a fly on the wall to see the look on his face when he walked into the room. To this day I don't think he knows who did it."

Jody smiled, "he hasn't changed much, only now he drives my mother nuts with his neatness. I think he's compulsive."

After Edmund gave Jody a tour of the house, they started unpacking boxes and Jody began to bark out orders as to where he should put things. They hung three pictures in the living room, another on a large wall in the dining room, two signed and numbered prints in the hall, and a gold-framed mirror on the wall of the foyer.

"This is beautiful," she said, and moved her fingertips across the gold-leafed frame that surrounded the oval mirror.

"My wife found it at an antique auction in San Francisco."

Jody swirled around to face him, her eyes were wide as saucers. She gulped, than blurted out, "where is she? How come she's not here unpacking? Are you divorced?"

Edmund walked into the living room with two cold cans of Pepsi. He handed Jody one and motioned her to sit down. As he lit his pipe and took a few puffs, she ran her hand across the worn rust velour. Suddenly he shot up, darted into the dining room, and started to rummage through an unpacked box. He pulled out an 8x10 silver framed picture and returned to the living room. Jody was sitting barefoot, Yoga style, sipping her cola. He sat down beside her.

"This is a picture of my wife Mai Lyn, and Christine, our daughter. They were killed in an accident earlier this year. A drunken Mexican immigrant ran a stop sign. They still haven't caught him. If they do they'd better not let me know, cause they'll need a roadmap to find the bastard's parts."

Jody gasped at the revelation and covered her mouth with her hand in order to still her muffled intake of breath.

"I'm sorry about the graphics but I get so angry whenever I think about it."

"Don't apologize for the language, I've used worse than that. I'm just sorry about your family. I didn't mean to pry, especially into a sorrowful part of your life."

"It's not your fault. I just assumed," he paused, "that your mother or father would have mentioned that I was married to a Vietnamese woman."

"They didn't even tell me about you. What makes you think they'd mention anything about your family? How old was your daughter?" Jody stared at the picture of the two women standing with their arms around each other. "She's beautiful."

"Christine would have been twenty in September. I miss her terribly," he stared at the photo, "her mother as well." His gut tightened.

Jody leaned over and kissed him on the cheek. "I'm sorry you don't have a daughter anymore. I imagine it must feel terrible, like a deep hole you can't fill."

He gulped hard, "I appreciate your thoughtfulness young lady." Then he turned and put the picture on the coffee table and cleared his throat. "What say we get back to work, remember it was your idea to help me get settled."

He carried a box of figurines to the curio cabinet where Jody carefully began to unwrap the statues. He thumbed through his collection of CD's, hoping he still had some of Christine's favorites. He wanted Jody to feel at home and found artists Christine liked and slid them into the CD. As soon as Tony Bennett began singing

'I Left My Heart In San Francisco' Jody started swaying with the music and continued to unwrap the collectibles and place them on the sparkling glass shelves.

Hours passed, and the final statue, a gold cherub, was placed on the edge of the top shelf. Edmund looked around at his surroundings. To his delight most of the unpacking was finished. A warm sense of belonging filtered through him. Imagine, getting excited about putting things away. Must be getting old, he chuckled as he watched Jody set the crystal lamps on the tables beside the couch.

Jody stood back, hands on her hips, and marveled at her decorator touch. "Now doesn't that look better?"

"I'm glad you talked me into letting you help. As you've surmised, I'm a procrastinator." They smiled at each other. "C'mon kid I'll buy you dinner, you deserve that much." He put his arm around Jody's shoulder, just as he use to with his daughter, then they stepped out the front door.

"Let's go in my car."

"Live it up," she said, "ride with me. You're the great adventurer who's scaled mountains and traveled the back roads of China. My little cycle shouldn't intimidate you. Or does it?"

He wasn't about to let her browbeat him. He bent over, tucked his pant legs into his socks, and climbed onto the back of the bike. He quickly wrapped his arms around her waist. She gunned the motor, leaned back against him, and shouted over the roar of the engine. "This is something I've always wanted to do with my dad but he never had the time, or at least that's what he said. Hang on Professor you're in for the ride of your life."

"That's what I'm afraid of," he shouted as he tightened his grip around her waist. She laughed out-loud, than gunned the engine and peeled rubber as she squealed out of the driveway. His head snapped back, then lunged forward as it recoiled from the sudden start.

She giggled.

For the first time in months the adrenaline was pumping and his heart felt full. He muttered a silent prayer of thanks as they pulled into traffic.

# CHAPTER 8

The bitter taste of beer lingered in her mouth, a constant reminder of earlier in the day. Lily wrinkled her nose at the unaccustomed sour taste. Why did she have to drink three? Her stomach continued to churn while the searing pain, that hid behind her eyeballs, intensified. Her drive home was unsteady, but cautious, as she kept belching and giggling at her bad manners. If Henry could see her now, she thought. In fact she could hear his preachy words, 'One must have the civility to conduct such activities in the privacy of ones home'.

"Bullshit!" She laughed to herself, "I don't care what he thinks. Beer isn't bad, once you get use to the taste." Her stomach lurched and she quickly opened the window, hoping the cool wind would make her feel better. Shouldn't have had that last beer...get stopped now and I could end up in jail...Henry would have a shit fit. She giggled at the vision of her oh-so-tight-assed husband having to bail her out, every vein in his shiny forehead bulging as he fought to maintain his professional demeanor. No matter what she did, she always had to worry what Henry would say.

"Fu...fuck him." Her eyelids popped up and a smile lit up her face. Pat was right. It felt good to say it and she continued to smile at the possibility of being taken to the police station. He'd be more horrified than she.

"Fuck him," she laughed, then turned into her driveway and hiccupped. Still blurry-eyed, she discovered she had mistakenly driven into Pat's driveway. Why not, she thought and blew a wisp of hair out of her eyes as she stumbled out of the car and weaved her way across the lawn to Pat's back porch. She clutched the rail and tried to steady herself, then stumbled up the steps, and plopped down on the wooden swing. The chains made a scraping noise as it started to move. She swung back and forth and let her head fall back, leaving her red hair trailing down the rear of the swing.

Suddenly she felt like Dorothy on her way to the Land of Oz. The porch was spinning and she broke into a cold sweat. Her stomach started to lurch. The beer was in her throat. She covered her mouth as the contents of her stomach forced itself up, leaving a searing sensation running down her throat. She darted to the porch railing and held on for dear life. Her insides started to heave, each spasm worse then before. She sank down to the cool wooden deck, leaving her head to rest against the slats of the railing. She grabbed a handkerchief from her purse and wiped her mouth. The sour taste was horrible. Her stomach retched again and she pulled herself up. Again and again the wrenching continued until there was nothing coming from her stomach. When the heaves finally passed she sank to her knees in prayer and swore never to drink again.

Suddenly the porch light came on. Pat rushed to her side, knelt down beside her, and started to smooth back her disheveled hair.

"Are you all right?" She leaned over and helped her up. "My god you look terrible. What the hell happened?"

"You know you're the second person today that's told me how terrible I look," Lily hiccupped, "talk about low self esteem."

"Lily Halston! You're drunk! Where the hell have you been?" Pat looked around and wrinkled her nose. "You've puked all over my beautiful bushes. How dare you." Pat's laugh was contagious.

Lily tried to steady herself then burst out laughing. She quickly crossed her legs, "if you don't stop making me laugh I'll pee in my pants." She glanced towards her house and put a finger to her lips, then looked at her dress and attempted to smooth the wrinkles. She started to brush the dirt from her knees and that's when she noticed she was barefoot.

"Where are my shoes, have you seen them?" She weaved about the porch searching for her missing footwear. "I don't know what the hell I did with them?"

Pat propped Lily against the railing and disappeared, then returned with a pair of black shoes in hand. "You left them in the car. Now let's go inside, I can't let Henry see you this way. How the hell did you drive home?"

"I'm not drunk, just sick to my stomach. I shouldn't have sat on your damn swing. That's what did it. It's your fault. I was fine when I left the cafe."

"What cafe? Who were you with?"

Lily relayed her story to Pat.

"Three glasses? What kind of a place were you in?"

"It's around the corner from the hospital."

"What? You went out in that neighborhood. Are you nuts? You're lucky you weren't mugged or worse yet, raped. I'm surprised that moron took you to a place like that. White women aren't safe in that neighborhood."

"Pat, Dorey's black. She knew the owners, and I was as safe as I would have been at Andy's Steak House. Relax, I'm safe and sound, aren't I? Could I have some coffee, black if you don't mind, I have to get rid of this terrible taste."

After showering in the guest bath, Lily looked into the mirror and was startled by her image. She finally understood the negative comments. Her mascara was smeared, her cheeks were pale and not even a hint of lipstick on her mouth. She put a hot washcloth over her face and began to breath in the warm moist air. After a few minutes she brushed her teeth and ran a brush through her matted hair. Feeling human again, she made her way down to the kitchen.

"That's much better. Now you look like the woman I know. Despite your age, you've got a beautiful complexion Lily."

"Well if I were sixty-five like you, I'd probably look just as bad." The hot black coffee stung her tongue but slowly began to clear the sponginess from her brain. "I'm famished."

"Well," Pat said, "you're going to have to settle for a cold turkey sandwich and some left over slaw. Do you want a glass of wine with your snack?"

Lily wrinkled her nose. "Please! Any thought of alcohol makes me want to barf."

"All right friend you've used my swing; you've thrown up on my bushes; now your eating my food; this entitles me to the inside scoop." Pat's brows were arched as she stood by the table, her arms folded in anticipation of Lily's wild story. "What the hell is going on?"

Lily maintained her silence. A somber look crept across her face as she continued to sip the hot brew.

Impatient at her friend's prolonged silence, Pat pulled her chair close to the table and started to tap her nails on the table. "Hey, talk to me."

Lily broke her stare and began to relay the details of the earlier events.

Pat listened and shook her head in disbelief. "I didn't know your father killed himself. You never told me."

"I didn't remember the details, but when I saw the bullet hole in Jessie's head it all came back, all the horrible memories, it was like experiencing it for the first time." Tears filled her eyes. "It was Dorey who helped me through a lot of shit."

Lily pushed away her empty plate. "Dorey believes the reason I spend so much time at the Crisis Line is because I've got some crazy mixed up idea that it was my fault that my father killed himself. And you know what Pat, it makes sense." Lily slumped forward and rested her head in both hands. Her fingers formed a visor to shade her eyes. "How the hell I could think that my behavior, at the age of five, could've caused my father's death, blows my mind."

"Does that mean you're hanging it up?"

"The Crisis Line? Hell no!" She smiled, "I'm going to take a few months off then go back. I still believe that suicide is wrong. The difference is that I no longer have that desperate feeling to save everyone."

Pat got up and started to clear the table.

"And I don't want you to blame Dorey for the puke on your bushes, she just took it for granted I liked beer. I couldn't hurt her feelings, besides how was she to know I hadn't eaten all day. I'm glad I had the pretzels or I'd really be in bad shape." Lily sipped the last of her coffee, dabbed her lips with a napkin, and took a deep breath.

"See you did it again. God damn it Lily, you have to learn to say no. You could've told her you didn't like beer and ordered a glass of wine instead. I'm sure those kind of places serve wine, even 'Ripple'. Why do you feel you have to please others? There's nothing wrong with exerting your own wishes."

"I'm not doing it to please others. It's just that I want to be—."

"Go on, keep talking. Maybe you'll be able to figure it out. I've seen you with Henry and no matter what he wants to do you go along with it. Remember the time you and I made plans to have dinner and go to the opera? Henry called and said it was important that you join him and a very influential client for dinner. You never even told him that we had tickets for a show. Why? What were you afraid of?"

Lily avoided Pat's glare. "I'm not afraid of my husband. That's a dumb thing to say. Why would I be frightened of Henry?"

"I don't mean physically afraid, but for some reason you don't want to provoke him, so you give in to all his whims." Pat finished stacking the dishes in the sink and walked into the pantry. She returned to the kitchen table with a corkscrew and a bottle of Leifermichel.

"I'm such a fucking genius, I think I'll celebrate my intelligence with a glass of wine. Are you sure you won't have some?" She goaded Lily with the wine.

Lily pretended to gag and shook her head as Pat wrestled with the opener. "You never say 'no' to Henry because you're grateful." Pat waved her down as she started to protest. "That's right, you're grateful to him for having married you and taken care of Jody, and you think you owe him."

Pat took a sip of wine and smacked her lips. "This explains a lot about you. Don't you see, you feel guilty because you don't love him. Yet you're trying to justify your marriage. You can rationalize all you want but it's not going to change the facts. You're in love with someone else."

Lily's mouth flew open as if to protest, then clamped shut just as quickly.

"You can placate Henry till the cows come home, it's not going to change your feelings about Edmund."

Lily started fidgeting, her thin fingers tensed in her lap.

"You tip toe around him whenever you want something instead of just asking for it. You never question anything he says, you just bite your tongue and agree. Can't you see the high price you're paying?"

"I need a cigarette," Lily said, "I don't have to sit here and take this shit without a smoke. Do you have any in the house?"

"No I don't, and you don't need one either. You quit a couple of years ago. Now's not the time to start. What you really need is a dose of courage."

"Bullshit!"

Pat sipped her wine. "Henry probably does love you, but his love is based on control."

"He's been good to me and Jody, why shouldn't I do what he wants. It's not like he's asking me to rob a bank."

"Don't you understand anything I've said." Pat knelt in front of her. "It's not about Henry, It's about you, and being your own person. You don't know how to say no, even to your mom. You let people use you, and in the process they walk over you."

Lily stood up and started to shout. "Because I...I don't know what I want." Tears stung her eyes. "Are you happy, now? You don't know when to stop, do you? Maybe I should learn to say no to you." She grabbed a napkin, dried her face, and threw it on the table. "Why don't you leave me alone?"

Pat raised a brow.

"How come you have nothing to say? You're the one with all the answers."

"You confided in me as a friend and you've honored me with your trust. You know I'll always tell you the way it is, and you respect that. But I've said enough for now. You've got a lot to think about. You're the one that has to figure out who you really are and what you want, or who you want."

"Henry gave you everything except the love you needed."

Lily stared at Pat.

"He'll never be able to give you the love you need, it's not in him," their eyes locked as Pat nodded, "he never will. It's okay to stay with Henry, but stay with him knowing why you're there. Don't delude yourself any more, it's time to decide what you're going to do with the rest of your life. It doesn't have to be today, or next week, or even next year. But one of these days you're going to have to face your greatest critic."

"And who's that? You?"

Pat shook her head. "You're your own worst critic, your own worst enemy. You have to see that. I love you Lady but I can't get into your heart to give you those kinds of answers. Only you have the key to that doorway. Use it."

Lily walked over to Pat and put her arms around her. "How the hell did you get so smart? You're wasting your time selling real estate, why don't you hang out a shingle, you'd probably make a lot more money."

"You're right, but I wouldn't have as much fun, and I do like to have fun. Do you Lily?"

Lily ran barefoot across Pat's front lawn and rushed up the gray stone steps. She fumbled for her keys and peeked through the side window. She could see a light shining in the den. Henry was still up. She was anxious to tell him about Jessica along with the memories of her father's suicide, as well as her first glass of beer. She dropped her shoes on the front porch and turned the key in the heavy walnut door.

"Lily, is that you? I'm in here."

She stood in the foyer and braced herself. Then took a deep breath and walked into the den. Henry glanced at her bare feet as she dropped into the winged back chair. His eyes were sharp as he assessed her demeanor. A frown crossed his brows as he turned up the right side of his mouth in disgust.

She smiled, looked down, and began to wiggle her toes in the think carpet. "My feet are swollen. When I took my shoes off I couldn't get them back on, so I walked across the lawn barefoot," in a sarcastic tone she added, "don't worry I wiped my feet on the rug at the front door."

Henry gathered his papers and slipped them into his briefcase.

"I'm sorry Henry but I've had a horrendous day."

"You look upset, to say the least. Care to tell me about it?"

She could feel his steely blue eyes attempting to penetrate her reserve. "What could be so bad as to have you in such a funk?" He tapped his finger on the edge of the chair.

Lily repeated the day's events until she got to the part about the bullet hole. Her voice cracked as she gulped. She saw him look away, embarrassed by her display of emotion.

"What's wrong? Why can't you look at me? You act as though I've done something wrong."

"It's not that," he replied in a cold tone. "I just don't like it when you get upset and lose control. I don't know how to comfort you," he shrugged, "I've never known how."

He handed her a handkerchief and started to pace the room as she continued with the details of her father's death. His hands moved across the back of the burgundy leather chair, with his well-manicured nails stopping at each brass nail-head. He finally blinked. "Why didn't you ever tell me this?" He turned away from her and looked down at the floor. "Why did you keep it a secret? I would've understood." His eyes swept slowly to hers, his hands lay flat against his chest. "Why can't you confide in me? I'm your husband." He thrust his hands deep into his pockets. "After all these years you should be able to trust me."

"I've never told anyone," her voice was low and raspy, "I couldn't admit it to myself, until today. It has nothing to do with trust, it has to do with me not remembering. For some reason I couldn't face the fact that my father killed himself." She started to massage her temples, "in some mixed up way I blamed myself for his death."

"That's absurd. You were a child, there's no way you could have prevented it. Where did you get these silly notions?"

"They weren't silly at the time. Don't you understand, he was my father, I loved him." She met his icy gaze and tossed her hair across her shoulders, then stood, "you don't know what it was like to hear the yelling. Try hiding under your bed covers and see how it feels. You don't know what it's like to see your father laying on the floor, his face covered with blood. You don't know..." tears flowed as she wrapped her arms about herself in a protective embrace.

Henry stepped towards her, his arms open and outstretched. He hesitated, than slowly wrapped his arms around her. "Now, now Lily," he patted her back, "it'll be all right. Shhh...you'll have to work through those memories. It's that damn Crisis Line, it's the cause of all this. Why don't you get yourself a different hobby."

She began to feel the fury of his remark in her throat, and it was starting to choke her. "How dare you call the Crisis Line a hobby. You're so far removed from the everyday world you don't know what the hell you're talking about. You have no idea the amount of the people that need help. If they didn't have someone to talk to, who knows what would happen."

She moved back towards him, her face inches from his, then started to snarl. "You're so busy taking care of your well-healed clients you wouldn't recognize a plea for help if it bit you in the ass."

He slowly backed away and moved around the winged chair as if fearful of what her anger would bring. He picked up his book from the seat and sat down. A vein was bulging on his shiny forehead as he glared at her. He took off his glasses and began cleaning them with a handkerchief.

"You know, everything is not black and white," she said, almost to convince herself more than him. "Life is not relegated to law books, as you would like to believe. Everything has to be just so in your book, if not it doesn't compute."

"Let me tell you a few things. The state has a vested interest in preventing suicide and discouraging citizens who are inclined to participate, especially those in the medical profession."

"Then for once we're on the same side."

"Not really. I'd prosecute the doctors or anyone who'd help someone die, while you'd probably coddle them."

Lily started to stand but changed her mind as he continued his sermon in an incensed voice. "While we're having this discussion, let me tell you a few things. Those law books you have such contempt for have provided you with a damn good life. Funny, I've never heard you complain when you spent the money on your big parties or shopping sprees or when you went gallivanting around the world with your girlfriends."

He took a deep breath. "I don't understand you, I never did. I don't know what you want. I thought you wanted this life. I'm influential in the community and well respected for my work in the corporate world. I don't know what's gotten into you? Let me reiterate, the law is what pays the bills for this life style." He swung his arms about, than pointed a trembling finger near her face.

"So before you decide to mouth off again maybe you should see your Gynecologist."

Her green eyes blazed. How dare he call the Crisis Line a hobby. How dare he suggest she see her doctor.

Henry's expression was clouded. A thin chill hung on the edge of his words. "I've never asked anything of you except that you maintain the image that's expected of a Halston." He turned away from her and directed his remarks to the far wall. "I never demanded you sleep with me, even though it is my right as your husband." He turned to face her, his gray eyes ablaze.

She remained silent, her lips thinned in anger, nostrils flaring. He was right, he never made demands on her. Had she been too hard on their relationship? Expected too much? Henry was Henry. She should be satisfied he loved her.

She bit her lip and looked away. The day had taken its toll. Her head was pounding. She was in no mood for his sharp tongue and was quick to apologize, blaming her behavior on the day's happenings. Then she turned, walked out, and rushed upstairs to the solace of her room.

# CHAPTER 9

Before this month's scheduled luncheon Lily had to talk to Jim. Hopefully he'd be able to answer the question that still haunted her. Why did her father kill himself?

Jim's tone seemed odd as she walked in. "I was just thinking about you," he glanced at the calendar on his desk. "It's that time again," he raised his brows and twisted his nose, "lunch with mother." He paused, "you look tired, is anything wrong?"

"Something happened the other day, I have to talk to you about it." She took a deep breath, sat back on the old couch, and started relaying the details of the young girls suicide and the memories it triggered.

"After seeing the bullet hole in Dad's head I don't remember anything else. I need to know what happened. What made him do such a terrible thing? He knew suicide was wrong. What could have been so bad? Why were Mom and him arguing that night? Do you think I did something wrong?"

He shook his head, pushed his glasses up on the bridge of his nose, and cleared his throat. "I'm glad you finally remembered that night. I've always wondered why you never talked about it." He took her hand in his. "You were only five, I was eleven. How could we be responsible for his actions?" Jim walked to the mahogany buffet and grabbed two glasses, along with a decanter of Rose'.

Lily shook her head, "none for me."

"Well I'm thirsty." His hand started to tremble as he poured the wine. Some spilled some on the rug. He dropped to his knees, pulled a handkerchief out of his pocket, and frantically rubbed at the burgundy spots. "Mrs. Dilansky will be upset if I don't get this up."

Lily watched him struggle with the stain. At that moment she became aware of Jim's burden, his dependence on alcohol. It was evident that he craved the bottle more than she had been willing to admit.

"I'm sorry I interrupted, please continue," he said.

"I remember the relatives whispering about Dad, saying that he had been drinking heavily, and he was depressed."

Lily walked around the couch and examined their parents' wedding picture. She stared at her father's image and straightened the frame. "From what I remember, it was always about money."

"Mom was always on him to get a part-time job. He kept telling her he worked hard at the factory and was too tired to work more hours. That's one of the reasons Mom went to work, she was tired of struggling from paycheck to paycheck."

Jim took another sip of wine. "Mom was always conscious of what people thought about her and her family, so she made sure we were always well dressed. I remember when she made me wear a pair of wool knickers to school, I was nine. I hated them, they made me itch all over. But you, you loved getting dressed up. You'd stand in front of the mirror for hours, primping over a new dress. You use to pick up your skirt and check your petticoat, you had to be sure there was lace and ribbons on it."

"But what does that have to do with Dad's suicide?"

"I remember the relative's talking about his drinking problem and his love affair with the ponies."

Lily rushed to Jim's side. "What! He bet on the horses? How come I didn't know about it?"

"You were only five, what did you expect?" He paused, than started talking again. "Getting back to that night...from what Uncle Harry told me, Dad had more then usual to drink that night. He came home late and Mom was waiting up for him and his paycheck. The pantry was almost empty, there were only a few groceries left in the house, and she was planning to shop that evening. When he finally made it home, he handed her ten dollars. It was all he had left of his pay. He'd gambled his entire week's wages on the horses, and lost. Mom hit the roof and that's what you heard that night." Jim took another sip of wine as if the liquid could dull his memory of that fateful night.

"I remember her yelling and shouting for him to 'get out'. She accused him of being a failure as a husband and provider. Then it got quiet...and you know the rest."

Lily cringed. My god, she thought, I didn't know him at all. My memories are nothing but fantasies, nothing to do with reality.

Jim refilled his glass and walked to the couch. "Now do you see how silly you were to think you caused his death. He had a lot of problems, Lily. Believe me, I'm not sitting in judgment; I loved him despite his weaknesses. But he couldn't forgive himself. When he realized what he'd done, he took the coward's way out."

She responded sharply, "don't call him a coward! You have no right to say that."

"It's true Lily, face it. Anyone who takes his or her own life sins against God and nature."

"If she'd only been a little nicer to him."

Jim furrowed his brows. "Get real, you can't blame this on Mom. Do you know what it must have been like for her, living with an alcoholic? She gave us a preview at lunch last month, remember? He must have put her through hell."

"You know they've found that alcoholism is an inherited disease. There's a gene that's passed down from generation to generation."

Jim gulped the last of his wine and pushed his glasses back on the bride of his nose, totally oblivious to her statement. "All right, out with it. Say what's on your mind." He straightened his posture, folded his hands, and waited for her to sermonize about his drinking.

She leaned across the sofa. "Look at you, it's not even noon and you've already had two glasses of wine, and I suppose you'll have two or three martinis at lunch. You never drank martinis before. Two glasses of wine use to be your limit."

Jim looked away as if to ignore her.

"You use to talk to me, but in the last few months, you haven't said much. I miss our closeness. I miss my brother."

Jim smiled and hugged her. "This reminds me of when we were little, you'd come to me after you'd fallen, and I'd soothe away your pain by holding you in my arms. I must admit I've missed this, Lily."

He sounded tired and his arms felt weak around her. She sniffled and moved away. "Please," she begged, "I want to help."

"I have a lot of questions about my beliefs, about the Church, about life, and most of all, about God."

"Your faith was always strong, now your telling me you have questions. If you're not sure, then who can I count on? You're unwavering faith has always been my rock."

"No Lily, you're wrong. Your faith in God has been your rock, not my faith. You've always believed in the teachings of the Catholic Church. What I'm going through doesn't have anything to do with the Church. Growth is painful and right now it hurts like hell."

Jim turned away and stood up. "I'm fighting a battle with the devil himself and I'm not sure whose going to win."

Lily's thin fingers tensed in her lap. She didn't know what to say or how to comfort him. If she only knew more about the Church, than she could quote scripture and possibly comfort him.

"I wish I knew what to say."

Tenderness warmed his gray eyes and for a moment she caught a glimpse of the brother she knew and loved. "I'm glad you're my sister and I'm lucky to have you on my side. Now what do you say we meet Mom?"

* * *

When the doorbell rang she glanced at her watch, smiled, and hop scotched over copies of old newspaper articles spread across the living room floor. It was the first of the month and she knew her mom would need some TLC after lunch with grandma.

"Hi Honey," I heard our song all the way downstairs. As the words of 'There's a Place For Us' wafted across the room, Lily stepped between copies of old newspaper articles that were spread across her daughter's living room floor.

"Grandma got to you again, huh? If you're going to have lunch with her every month you've got to learn to ignore her. She's a lonely old woman with nothing to do but complain. It's an attention getter, can't you see that?"

"Well I hope to God you shoot me if I ever get like that. I wouldn't want to make you miserable like she does me."

"I won't have to shoot you, Dad and I will have you locked in a padded cell." Jody laughed and cautioned her mother to step carefully across the paper-covered floor.

"What the heck is going on here, it looks like a tornado hit. Doing research?"

"I wanted to find out more about the Professor's family and what happened to them. He never says much about it. I made copies of all the San Francisco papers I found at the downtown library."

A muscle quivered in Lily's jaw. "What are you talking about? What do you mean his family?"

"Didn't you know?" Jody eyes were as round as the CD's on her player. "They were killed in an automobile accident. A head on collision."

Lily stood blank and visibly shaken.

"Judging by your expression you didn't know either."

She winced, covered her mouth with her hand, then fell back onto the couch. She leaned over and picked up copies of the articles that described the accident, along with a picture of his wife and daughter. Lily stared at the beautiful young girl and tried to see Edmund in the girls face. She took note of the shape of her nose, the way her lip turned up when she smiled, just like Edmund's.

She breezed through the other articles. My god she thought, what a way to lose loved ones. Her head was spinning and she bit her lip until it throbbed. Why didn't he say anything?

Jody sat down beside her. "I felt so sorry for him when I was at his house. It's a beautiful old home but it needs a woman's touch. He seems so lost without his family." Jody walked into the kitchen and poured a glass of iced tea.

As Lily stood the papers slipped from her lap. Stunned by her daughter's statement, she swooped into the kitchen after her. "When did you go to his house?"

"Before you say anything, yes, I think it was a good idea. He and I hit if off immediately. He's my friend and he needs company."

Lily's stomach felt as though she were on a fast descending elevator to hell. She was trembling and her knees started to give way as she leaned against the wall.

"I helped him unpack, and while we were putting together his stereo he showed me a picture of his wife and daughter. She was Vietnamese, and beautiful. I can't imagine what it must feel like to have your family wiped out in one felt swoop. He told me that if the authorities found the person that did it, he didn't want to know because he'd kill him. I'm surprised he didn't say anything to you or Dad."

"I haven't had a chance to talk to him. The one time I did see him, Uncle Jim and he were going to lunch." In an effort to hold back her shock, Lily sucked in her breath. She couldn't let her daughter see the extent of her turmoil. Jody continued to rattle on about Edmund's house and how the two of them unpacked his things. Her thoughts stayed on Edmund, his wife, his daughter, the accident...she could only nod and smile.

Suddenly the walls of the tiny apartment started to close in on her. She couldn't let Jody see her like this, there'd be too many questions which she couldn't answer. "Honey, I'm sorry but I have to leave, I just remembered something. Let's get together tomorrow and you can tell me all about the unpacking. Okay?"

Before Jody could answer, Lily grabbed her purse, rushed out the door and down the stairs. Jody at Edmund's house! Alone! She shuddered at the thought and wrapped her white coat around her in an effort to ward off the cold, along with her fears. How could this happen? Why didn't he tell her that his wife was dead? Did he know about Jody? She leaned over the steering wheel and hoped the queasiness would leave. Her throat was starting to close. "I hate you, Edmund Vilante," she shouted.

She pushed her shoulders against the back of the seat and resolved that Jody would never find out the truth. "So help me God." Then she raced out of the parking lot and drove south on the Outer Drive. She glanced at her watch, it was after five. She thought about going home but dismissed that idea and continued to drive. She turned west, off the Outer Drive, and headed toward the loop, driving up and down the one-way streets. Suddenly a Cathedral loomed in front of her. She parked the car, walked up the front steps, pulled open the massive wooden doors, and stepped inside.

As she walked down the long, center aisle, she became aware of the high archways that appeared to be reaching skyward. The oversized stained-glass windows were brilliant blues, greens and reds, all depicting religious figures, and were brightened as the late afternoon sun filtered through and cast an eerie hue on the interior of the church.

She stopped two rows from the altar, knelt down, made the sign of the cross, and stepped into the pew. Her eyes were glued to the larger-than-life hand-carved figure of Jesus on the cross, which hung high above the altar. He looked so real. As she began to bask in His presence, she felt like she was wrapped in a fluffy blanket, safe from all that consumed her, secure enough to let her feelings flow.

"You've really dealt me a loaded hand. You didn't even give me time to recover from one dilemma and you send me more. I know I deserve it, it's part of my punishment, but now I need your help," Lily shifted in the bench, "I've really screwed up this time."

She reached into her purse, grabbed a handkerchief, and blew her nose. "As you know, Edmund's back in town, and it scares me. I never wanted him to find out about Jody, but now he's her teacher, and she's even been to his house...alone! I hope he doesn't notice any resemblance, or worse yet, see her as an interesting woman. And to really complicate things, Jody informed me that his wife and daughter are dead."

Lily rattled on, "I want to comfort him, but I don't dare. I think I still love him, but I'm not sure." She looked around to make sure no one was sitting near her. "I thought Edmund loved me. I don't understand God, why didn't he come back to me? Why did he have to marry that Vietnamese woman?"

In the front of the altar the votive candles flickered and cast shadowy images on the walls. "For years I've deceived Edmund and Henry. Forgive me for that. Then there's Jody, I've been deceiving her as well. Haven't I?"

She knelt down again and buried her face in her hands, as an even more terrifying realization washed over her. "You can't possibly want me to tell Edmund about his daughter?" She paused as if expecting an answer. Her pulse started to race along with a sharp pain huddling around her heart. "I can't do that, no matter what. I'm sorry but this is one thing I won't do."

She raised her head and looked pensively into the darkened altar area. Ignoring the mocking voice inside her head, she moved to the very front of the church. Iron stands held rows of red glass votive cups filled with flickering candles, a silent testament to the faith of those who lit them. She lit two, knelt down, closed her eyes, and whispered a prayer for Edmund's wife and daughter. Then she made the sign of the cross, turned, and walked out.

# CHAPTER 10

Lily wanted Henry's fiftieth birthday party to be perfect and suited to his impeccable taste. The caterers arrived and immediately took over the kitchen despite Emma's disdainful eye. They ignored her stares and busied themselves by preparing Henry's favorite foods. Wearing black and white starched uniforms, the servers set the tables and arranged chairs for additional seating. Vases of white and yellow Fuji mums were scattered throughout the downstairs. Bouquets of black and silver helium-filled balloons hugged the empty corners. The trio was busy setting up, they were on at seven. Bottles of fine wine and champagne were iced. The silver was polished, linen tablecloths pressed, extra servants hired, and within a few hours, two vested young men would be standing at the curb, ready to park the many Mercedes, BMW's, and the occasional Rolls.

Satisfied that everything was on schedule, Lily walked into the kitchen hoping to assure Emma that everything would be fine. Emma was in charge of the temporary help but didn't trust them to take care of things the way she did. Lily knew that her faithful housekeeper was still haunted by the memory of that Thanksgiving dinner ten years ago, and till this day, didn't trust herself or others, in her kitchen.

With twenty guests seated around the dining table, applauding Emma's culinary efforts, she proudly carried the bronzed bird on a silver tray. Suddenly she lost her footing and tripped. The cooked bird rolled off the tray and onto the carpet. She dropped to her knees and started to cry. Then quickly composed herself and began to gather all the trimmings in sight, hoping to restore the tray to its original culinary beauty.

Henry jumped up, grabbed the turkey, put it back on the tray, than helped Emma to her feet. He put his arms around the sobbing cook and assured her that everything would be fine. It was the only time that Henry insisted that Emma join them for a holiday dinner. Ever since that incident large parties made Emma nervous.

As Lily left the kitchen she ran into Henry who had just returned from a Saturday visit to the office. "It looks wonderful, Lily." He picked up a black and white napkin from the portable bar and grinned. "Everything has a reminder of my age, including the cocktail napkins. As usual, you've thought of everything. I think this will be one of your best parties yet."

Pleased by his compliments, Lily smiled.

"Remember the party you had for Jim when he came home from Nam. A scavenger hunt...I can still see our guests with lists in their hands. They ran, walked, and drove the entire perimeter of Wilmette in search of those stupid items."

She giggled at the memory. "I made a big mistake with one of the items. Why I ever put a tulip bulb on that list I'll never know. Word spread like wildfire when the crowd discovered I had planted tulip bulbs in the back yard. The following day I had to replant dozens of uprooted bulbs. My poor back."

"I can still see everyone carrying in bags of junk. That party made the front page of the Wilmette paper." They started up the stairs, "oh, by the way I invited another guest."

"What's one more, we have plenty of food. Who did we forget?"

"No one," he grinned, "I thought I'd ask Edmund. I hope you don't mind? I was to meet him for lunch last week but got involved and never called. I felt bad, so when I called to apologize, I invited him. I thought it'd be a good time for him to see his old friends. Don't you?"

His question mocked the panic swelling in her throat. Edmund coming here? She clutched the banister to keep her legs from buckling. "When were you planning to tell me?" she heard a voice unlike her own, "when he walked in the front door?"

"What's the difference? It's my birthday. I thought I could invite whoever I wanted."

Lily weighed her words carefully. "You know how I feel about him. He didn't bother with us all these years and now wants back in our lives?"

Henry retained his affability but a distinct hardening in his eyes was apparent. "He's our friend and now he's Jody's teacher. I think you should get over this thing you have about him. For God's sake bury the hatchet."

She felt herself shrinking from his cold watchful eye. She had to stay cool. "Maybe your right," she uttered, "I'll probably be to busy to talk to him."

At the top of the stairs Henry turned, "Oh by the way I have a surprise for you."

Filled with thoughts of seeing Edmund again, she suddenly became aware of the strange expression on her husbands face. His eyes danced in an eerie manner while his thin lips curled in a smug smile.

"Did you say something?"

He repeated, "I said, I'll have a surprise for you this evening, one I think you'll like."

Lily shook her head and hurried to her sanctuary, the room where she gave herself permission to unwind. "Now what? He's coming to the house and there's not a damn thing I can do about it. How the hell do I get out of this?" She'd seen him at Jim's. They'd spoken. What was the big deal?

A plan began to emerge. First she'd offer her condolences about his wife and daughter. Despite his treatment of her, he deserved better. He had a good heart, that's why she'd loved him. She shook her head. A lot had happened to all of them. Her past consisted of a one-way street, paved with her love for him. Should she call and tell him not to come? He'd respect her wishes. Or would he? He could be stubborn when he wanted.

Once she asked him to wear a suit to a party at her house because she wanted to impress her mom. He refused. He said he didn't have to impress anyone, and that included her mother. That day he showed up with an open shirt, showing off his chest and a gold medallion dangling from his neck. A quiver floated through her as pictures floated around her head.

When Lily's Victorian tub was filled with billowy bubbles, she started to step in and caught her nakedness reflected in the mirror. The vision revealed bulges of cellulite bulges on her outer thighs. She peeked over her shoulder and tried to see how badly rippled her rear end was, and gasped at the changes in her body. She ran her hands down her legs, at least they were still firm and shapely. She cupped her hands under her breasts, pleased with their firmness. Thank goodness for small favors.

She slipped into the hot bath and relished the moment. She began to relax and splashed water over herself then let it trickle down her shoulders and chest. She eased under the bubbles until they covered her body and rested her head against the pink pillow that hung from the back of the tub. A fragrance of coconuts titillated her nostrils and brought nostalgic remembrances of her vacation in Hawaii. The romantic setting; moonlight on the water; tiki torches to light the paths around the hotel, and the overpowering fragrance of flowers still captured her.

As she began to soap the upper part of her body, her hands slid across her smooth creamy skin. Her thoughts started to wander and she found herself enmeshed in a sexual fantasy. Her nipples grew hard. She smiled to herself, her sexuality was alive and well. Almost fifty and feeling horny, she laughed.

She stepped out of the tub, wrapped herself in a terry robe, sat down at her dressing table, and vowed not to allow herself the luxury of erotic thoughts about him ever again. Within a few hours he'd be here. Maybe he won't come? Maybe he wouldn't accept Henry's invitation and all the worry would be for nothing. But in case he did, she'd have a house full of guests to keep her busy and a safe distance from him.

There was a light rap on the bedroom door and before she could answer Jody bounced into the room. She leaned over for a kiss from her daughter.

"Hi, Mom."

"What are doing here so early?"

"I thought I'd come over and give you a hand if you needed it." The young girl's face lit up. "From what I saw downstairs, everything looks great. You used my idea about bouquets of balloons."

Lily frowned as her eyes scanned Jody. "Don't tell me you're planning to attend your dad's party in those jeans?"

Jody raised her brows and let out a sigh. "Of course not, I brought my black dinner dress."

"I'm sorry, I should trust your judgment. Forgive me?"

"Of course. What's wrong? You seem preoccupied. On edge?" Jody sat on her mother's bed and rearranged the lace throw pillows.

"I just want everything to be perfect."

"You've done a great job with this room," Jody said as she looked around, "I just love it. What made you go Victorian?"

Lily stretched out on her chaise and watched her daughter. "I love that era. It was one of the most romantic times in history."

"What good is this romantic ambiance if you and dad have separate rooms, unless you two are into bed hopping for a turn on?" She chuckled.

"Jody!"

"Did I say a bad word? You have a romantic bedroom including this gorgeous canopy bed, too bad you don't make use of it."

"You're father's invited your professor to the party."

Jody jumped off the bed. "You're kidding? I did too, but I didn't think he'd come. He definitely needs to get out and be with people. He stays in that house too much. I'm glad Dad invited him."

Lily paused, "do you think he'll show up?"

"If he's not here by eight I'll go get him. He needs friends, especially since the accident. We can't turn our backs on him."

"Nobody's turning their backs on him," she wrinkled her nose. "He's seen Uncle Jim and he's seen your father. I talked with him the other day. What else are we suppose to do?" She glared at her daughter. "Why all this concern about your professor, aren't you over-stepping your boundaries as a student?"

Jody's answer was sharp. "I hope you're not insinuating what I think you are. For the record Mother, Edmund and I are just friends. He thinks of me as a daughter, and treats me like one. And I think of him as my teacher and family friend. I hope this is the only time I'll have to explain our relationship."

"Well look at yourself, you're a beautiful young woman, what man wouldn't want you, including your professor."

"Geez, he's a widower, Mom. His wife and daughter were just killed. He's not thinking about women. He's trying to get his life back on track." Her eyes held a pleading look. "Can't you and Dad help?"

Lily walked around the bed and pretended to straighten the lace spread.

"Mom why don't you tell me what's really going on. What's got you so upset?"

Lily walked to the window in hopes of avoiding her daughters piercing gaze. "What makes you think anything's wrong?"

"Well you ran out of my apartment the other day as soon as I told you about Edmund's family. Something's up, I'm not stupid. You and I haven't really talked the past couple of years. Ever since I moved out of the house you seem to have shut me out. You don't share things with me like you use to when I lived at home. Are you punishing me for moving on my own?"

Lily's mind raced, but the right words wouldn't come. She put her hands on Jody's shoulders. "You're my daughter and I love you more than anything else in this world. Don't ever forget that. I would give my life for you, if I could." She turned Jody's head so their eyes would meet. "So don't ever think I'm punishing you for wanting to be on your own. I envy your independent spirit. Sometimes I feel guilty that I don't help more with your problems. By the way, how are you feeling? What ever happened with the eye doctor?"

Jody fell back on the bed.

"Well? Have the headaches stopped, or what?"

"No, I still get them, but I take four aspirins and it goes away. If they get worse I'm going to see a different doctor. If you want, you can come, okay?"

"I'd like that. Thanks for asking." Lily laid down next to her daughter. Perhaps Jody did need her after all.

"By the way Mom, I'm on to you."

Startled by her daughter's remark, Lily's heart skipped a beat. She turned to face Jody.

"You never answered my question. You evaded it by asking me about myself, a maneuver just like an attorney. It looks like Dad's habits are beginning to rub off on you." Jody chuckled. "I want to know what's really wrong. You seem so preoccupied."

Lily rolled over on her back and looked up at the ceiling. "There's been so much happening I can't get it all straight in my head. You know me, I like my thoughts organized, but right now they're doing their own thing. I feel out of control. Maybe I'm getting Alzheimers or something?"

"Don't be silly. Sometimes it helps to talk about it. Try me."

Torn by conflicting emotions Lily hesitated, than began. "A couple of weeks ago I lost one of my callers on the hotline, a young girl, just a few years younger than you, and it hit me hard. Then I did a stupid thing and went to where she lived, and I arrived just in time to see them carrying out her body."

Jody was somber as she listened to her mother.

When Lily revealed the memories about her own father, Jody sat up with a start. "What? Grandpa committed suicide? Shot himself? God, what a way to go. Why didn't you ever tell me? It must have been awful. I, um, don't know what to say. No wonder you seem so distant these last weeks. I'm glad Dorey gave you time off. You need it."

She breathed a sigh of relief as Jody veered off on another tangent. "C'mon let's get dressed," she playfully smacked Jody on her rear, "it's after six and I'm going to need time to fix this old face. Your room's ready, so you can shower and dress there whenever you like."

After Jody skipped out of the room, Lily studied her face in the mirror. She trailed her thin fingers along her nose, ending at the indentation that lead to the corner of her lip. She pulled the skin back along her jawbone, amazed by the difference it made in her profile when it was taut. Time had definitely taken its toll. Her fingers moved to smooth the lines around her eyes. Fifty. She covered her face. Where had the years gone? Why can't I remember all of it, she thought. Suddenly a feeling of loss swept over her, loss for the days gone by, and what might have been. Where do I go from here?

Bitter memories still weighed her down. I don't know how much longer I've got on this earth God, her thoughts rambled, but you and I have got to figure out what to do about me. I want to be free from this burden. I want to enjoy the time I have left, however long that is. I'm tired of hiding my feelings, I just want to be me. She implored the face staring back at her from the mirror. Just point me in the right direction, I promise I'll do the rest.

# CHAPTER 11

Lily descended the sweeping staircase and quickly scanned the crowd, looking for a glimpse from the past. Her black crepe evening gown clung to her figure and exhibited a set of full hips that tapered into a set of long, shapely legs. Just above the separation in her breasts a two-carat solitaire hung from her neck. She was regal in her gait and fully aware of the appreciative glances from the faces below.

Jody chose a long navy sheath, crowned with a single strand of pearls around her neck, and was alluring as she chatted with the guests among which were Dorey and her husband. Suzanne, a volunteer from the hotline, roamed the downstairs rooms, admiring and enjoying being a part of the luxurious lifestyle, even if it was for only an evening. The astonished look on her face when she saw the variety of antiques brought a smile to Lily's face.

Kyle Dorsett, one of Henry's partners along with his wife Joan, stood in the far corner talking to Mother and Dad Halston. Henry's father, with his standard black tux, and unlike his usual serious demeanor, worked the room as if he were running for office. He smiled and joked with the many guests. He stopped by his son, slapped him on the back, and whispered in his ear. An unlit cigar dangled between his fingers, he didn't dare light it in his wife's presence.

Jeanette Halston, the Matriarch of the Halston clan, was a picture of elegance in her brown satin cocktail dress and sported a costly diamond and ruby necklace, a gift from her husband on their thirtieth anniversary. As it lay above her breasts, it sparkled in the light. Worn only on special occasions, her sons fiftieth was reason enough to have it removed from the safe and exhibited to the guests. The soft lights brought a shimmer to her hair and complimented her peach complexion. Her royal-like bearing and soft-spoken ways sparked envy in many women half her age.

Poised at the bottom of the steps, Lily watched Henry cross the room to join his mother, who beamed with pride when her only son kissed her on the cheek. He grabbed two glasses of champagne from one of the servers then rejoined his father. Lily couldn't be sure but it appeared as if the men were toasting something, then she quickly dismissed the errant thought.

Jim and Nora stood off by themselves as if waiting to be approached. Nora, as always, was dressed as if she stepped off the cover of Modern Maturity, wearing a white long-sleeve silk blouse with a black cocktail skirt tied with a gold lame' belt. Her black sequined cocktail hat and small black veil hid her ever-appraising eyes. The one thing Lily couldn't take away from her was her impeccable sense of fashion.

Jim grabbed two glasses of champagne from a passing server and handed one to his mother. Lily couldn't help but notice how tired and old beyond his years, he looked. The white collar around his neck added brightness to his otherwise dull pallor, but traces of gray sallow tones, in his hollow cheeks, were still evident.

Lily greeted the Courtney's, the Drakes, the Anderson's, and other country-club friends as they made their entrances in elegant designer gowns, as if dressed for a white house function or the academy awards. Lily watched her mother slowly edge over to the opulent group where she was chatting. Lily introduced her, then excused herself and stopped to chat with the Haroldson's, Steinberg's and Watson's. Lily loved their tales of early Wilmette.

Pat came out of the kitchen, followed by three black and white uniformed servers. She was stunning in her low-cut, red sequined Halston. Her jutting breasts and narrow waist enticed men and drew envy from many women. A diamond encrusted "P" lay flat above her cleavage.

Lily continued to survey the room. He hadn't arrived yet. Relieved yet disappointed, she let out a sigh. When the band started to play, she grabbed Pat and steered her toward the library.

"By the way, you look exceptionally good," Pat primped Lily's hair. "Did you get a facial at Andrea's today?"

"I didn't have time." She pulled Pat into the room and closed the door. "Henry invited Edmund to the party."

"Will you relax. Here, sit down." Admiration glowed in Pat's eyes. "If you want him to eat his heart out when he sees you, you've done it girl. I wish I could see the look on his face when he sees you in this outfit."

"Be serious." As Lily sat in the winged chair she began to fondle the sequins on the hemline of her dress. "Should I ignore him?"

"What do you want to do?"

"I don't know." Lily quickly stood, peeked out the door, and checked the crowd again. "I know I have to offer my condolences about his wife and daughter, that's only good manners." She began to chew on her nail as she sat down beside Pat. "Damn, I wish I had a cigarette."

"So far your plan is sound. Why not play it by ear? First see what he's got to say. You don't have to plan every word, go with the flow, things have a way of working out."

"Sure, it's easy for you to say," she frowned, "with Henry looking over my shoulder and Jody watching every move I make."

"You've played this fucking game for twenty five-years, what's one more night. Maybe he won't even show."

"He'll be here."

Pat stuck out her bottom lip and blew air off her face. "Aren't you hot?"

"I'm warm, but it's probably my nerves. I can't think straight when I'm uptight. I've got to relax."

"That's the idea," Pat echoed, as a twinkle appeared in her eye, "and if that doesn't work take a Prozac."

Suddenly the library door opened and Jody appeared with Edmund in tow. "Mom, look who's here, Professor Vilante."

Lily's eyes opened wide and a flash of heat rushed to her face. To remain calm proved to be an effort but she managed to hide her apprehensions and extended her hand. "How are you Edmund? I'm glad you could join us. Welcome to our home." Lily was aware that Pat was staring at Edmund and she quickly withdrew her hand. "This is my best friend, Pat Cunningham. We've known each other over twenty years."

Edmund took her hand. "I'm glad you and Lily are friends. I'm sure you're the perfect complement to her, and yet in your own right a woman of magnetic beauty."

His smile dazzled Pat.

He turned to Lily, his eyes mirrored his appreciation of her loveliness. "You're more beautiful than ever. I feel like I'm at one of your sorority dances. Remember?"

A sensual glimmer passed between them. The time it took to get ready was well worth it, she thought.

"Yeah, but I wasn't born yet, so this isn't Mom's sorority dance, it's Dad's birthday," Jody chimed in.

"You're right," Edmund smiled, "and I can't imagine this world without a beautiful young lady like you—"

"I want to show you something," Jody led him to the far bookshelf. She pulled out a book and pointed to the signature, it was signed by John F. Kennedy.

"He's a hunk," Pat leaned over and whispered. Get a load of that gorgeous tan and that thick head of hair. I can feel that great chest against my breasts. I can see why you're still in love with him."

Lily pushed her elbow into Pat's side. "Shh," she put her index finger to her lips, "he'll hear you. Is that all you can think about is a man's looks?"

"Of course not, I'm also concerned with his bank account. If this Edmund of yours has money, he's too good to be true."

Lily giggled. "Listen you two," Lily got Jody's attention then grabbed Pat by the elbow, "Pat and I are going to join the rest of the guests. Jody, why don't you show Edmund the rest of the house?" She didn't wait for an answer and pulled Pat out of the library.

"When are you going to talk to him, the longer you wait the harder it's going to be? Although I think you're going to have a hard time getting him away from Jody."

"That's fine with me, she'll keep him busy. It'll give me more time." Lily caught a glimpse of Jody and Edmund as they strolled into the living room. He nodded and smiled at her guests as he walked around the room of well-dressed people.

Her attention back on her guests, Lily watched Jim exchange another empty glass for a full one.

"I saw Edmund, I'm glad he's here," Jim smiled, "we had a great time a few weeks ago. We talked about Nam and our college days, but I need to talk to him again." Jim's balance started to teeter and he caught himself by taking a step back to correct his equilibrium. Then he tried to pretend it never happened.

She didn't care what happened to Edmund in Vietnam. He found that woman there. "Where's Mom," she asked, "she was here a few minutes ago?"

"When Edmund came into the room she quickly excused herself," he shrugged, "maybe she's in the ladies room," he chuckled and sipped his drink, "it's not my turn to watch her Lily, and believe me, she does need watching."

"Be nice," she scolded, "after all she is our mother."

He held up his hand. "She reminds me of it often enough."

He laughed, but for the hard, passionless look in his eyes, it might've been funny.

"Brother dear, you'd better behave or God will get you." They laughed and he took a lusty gulp. "He already has. There's not much more he can do to me." He winked and walked away. Then he held up his empty glass, signaling the waiters to bring him another.

As the evening progressed the music grew louder. Groups fanned out and became part of other groups as couples crowded the dance floor. Lily caught occasional glimpses of her mother scooting from group to group. Odd, she thought, is my mother trying to avoid me? What's she up to?

The music stopped and a sudden drum roll interrupted the festivities. Henry and his father stepped onto the platform. Mr. Halston grabbed the microphone and instructed the servers to fill everyone's glass. Henry motioned Lily to his side. As she walked across the room she suddenly remembered that he had said something about a surprise. Was this it?

Her eyes moved about the room and stopped at the back of the room where Edmund was standing with Jim. How handsome he looks in his tuxedo, she thought, and remembered the formal dance they attended in college. He turned and caught her staring at him. He smiled. She quickly looked away and turned to her father-in-law who was toasting his son's fiftieth birthday. He thanked Lily for a lovely evening and the guests responded with applause.

"Now to serious business," he continued, "we, a group from downtown, have talked with the Republican Committee. And it is their choice, that my son, Henry Wadsworth Halston, run for the seat on the Circuit Court."

Lily's lashes flew up. When did they hatch these plans? When the applause subsided, and the guests had finished with their congratulations, she approached him. Her voice, courteous though patronizing, was demanding. "When were you going to tell me? Did you expect me to see it on television? I am your wife, you know. It would have been nice to discuss this with me."

"You know it's what I've always wanted. And this is just the first step." He smiled and nodded at the crowd while continuing to try and appease her. "Father thought it would be a good idea to surprise you. Now don't get into one of your moods." He frowned, then was quick to smile when he looked around at the crowd.

"It's over and done with, can't you be happy about it." He grabbed two glasses of champagne from a waiter and handed her one. He raised it in a mock toast, "we're in this together Lily and don't you forget it!" His tone was threatening as he clicked his glass against hers. "I'm going to need your help, so let's drink to that."

Aware that her guests were watching, she raised the glass to her lips and pretended to take a sip, then barely hugged him. "Congratulations dear, if that's what makes you happy," and mustered as much warmth as she could, "then I want it too." Pleased at her control, she realized with his running for public office he'd be away from home even more. Thank god for small favors. I'll play his game, she thought, and grabbed the microphone. She gave Henry a side-long glance, turned, and raised her glass, "to the next Circuit Judge of Cook County." The mockery of her toast mirrored in her eyes. She knew it. So did he, but the show must go on. She smiled and finished her little display of support then turned to leave. Suddenly she felt an uncomfortable energy about her, she knew someone was staring at her.

She turned. Their eyes met. Mesmerized by his stare she found it difficult to move. He started across the room towards her and she took a deep breath and stepped back. As he drew near her lips started to tremble but no sound emerged. She turned to walk away and he caught her by the elbow. With a firm grasp, as if corralling an escaping animal, he escorted her out of the room and toward the library.

"We have to talk. You've been avoiding me all night. Why?"

"I, I haven't been avoiding you, I have guests to attend to."

He continued toward the library.

"Jody told me about your wife and daughter. I'm truly sorry. I don't know what I'd do if I had to go through something like that."

He looked at her as the library door closed behind them. "It's surprising where a person finds strength. After the accident I'd wake up in the morning and didn't think I'd be able to make it out of bed. Then I'd feel a surge of energy, or whatever you want to call it, and I'd be up and about, ready to start the day."

"I said a prayer and lit some candles for your family. That was the least I could do." She was starring into the eyes of an old friend and kept any reaction to his tender look in check. Her anger was slipping away. Stay on guard she told herself.

"Lily have you heard a word I've said?"

"Of course, why wouldn't I? You always had a writers way of explaining things."

"You're lying!" He stared at her, stern in his observance. "Your left eyelid twitches when you lie," he smiled, "it always did when we were kids, and it still does." He chuckled when Lily's hand moved toward her eye.

"Remember I know what you were thinking even before you do." His brow furrowed as he steadied his gaze, he was still unable to penetrate the invisible wall between them.

"You really look great," she managed cheerfully, "it looks like California agreed with you. Did you do a lot of traveling?"

"Yes, and I regret those years on the road. I was gone almost three quarters of the year, selfish in my intent to find adventure. I never took into account the people I left behind." He searched her eyes.

"Well we all do a lot of things that we're sorry for. I wonder," she added, "if we had the chance to do some of the things over again, would we?"

"I've pondered those same questions. I wonder what would have happened if I refused to get my brother out of Mexico. Because right after I brought him back to the states he was off to Europe, and in a few months he was in another jam."

She shrugged and tossed her head. "I never expected life to turn out the way it has. I imagined a different life and now it looks like I'm going to be involved in politics."

Edmund stood and grabbed her hand. "I really need to talk to you, but this isn't the place. Meet me next week. Please, it's important."

Before she could answer Jody burst into the room, panting and out of breath. "Mom, come quick! Uncle Jim's fallen down the back steps."

Lily and Edmund brushed past her, through the kitchen, and out the back door. Jim was sprawled out on the ground, moaning something about the last step. Edmund knelt beside him and started to move Jim's legs and arms, assuring himself that nothing was broken.

Jim kept insisting he was fine and clung to Edmund as he helped him up. His glassy eyes and strong smell of alcohol spoke the truth. He didn't trip. He fell.

"He's drunk," Lily said.

"I'll take him home. He needs a cold shower, strong coffee, and a big shoulder. Get back to your guests," Edmund commanded, "let your mom know he's all right and tell her I'll stay with him tonight." Edmund wrapped Jim's arm around his neck and dragged him out of the back yard and into his car. Lily watched the tail lights of the Explorer until they disappeared into the darkness and prayed that Edmund would be able to penetrate the gates to her brothers purgatory.

Then she thought about her husband. What would Henry say about Jim's drunken behavior? If Jim had only taken off his collar...

Despite her makeup, Nora appeared pale as she rushed to her daughter's side. "Lily, what happened to Jim? Jody said he fell down the stairs. Was he hurt?"

"He had too much to drink and slipped on the porch steps. Edmund took him home and is going to stay with him."

Nora sighed, wiped the beads of perspiration from her forehead, and took a sip of wine. "I'm glad Edmund's gone," the old woman said, "I still don't like him."

"By the way, where have you been hiding all night? This is the first time I've seen you."

"I haven't been hiding, I've been socializing with your guests. I even talked with those people that work down at that hospital with you. I'm shocked you invited them into your home." Nora turned and thrust her chin towards Dorey and her husband. "Besides you've been too busy to notice what I've been doing. This is the first time you've talked to me all evening."

"Mother I have other guests beside you. By the way what did you think of Henry's surprise announcement?"

"Imagine that, a Circuit Court Judge for a son-in-law." A definite haughtiness hung in her reply. "I always knew he was the right one for you, instead of that no good 'Dago'."

Lily lifted her chin, swallowed hard, and met her mother's gaze.

"Mother's know what's right for their children, despite what they themselves think.

Lily was about to explode when Pat walked into the kitchen, grabbed her arm and started to lead her to the door. "C'mon your guests are asking for you, something about having a fund raiser at the club. Excuse us, Nora." Pat whisked Lily out of the kitchen and back into the company of her guests. None of them knew of Jim's mishap, so she didn't have to make up a story to cover up the truth.

"All right, where is he?" Pat asked.

"Where's who?"

"Don't play games with me," she said in a matter of fact manner. "You know who I mean, that gorgeous hunk of male specimen. Did he leave?"

"Yes, he's gone."

"Weeellll." Her eyes twinkled with mischief. "How was it?"

Lily smirked. "We talked for a few minutes and I offered my condolences. Then I saw the gentleness in his eyes and years of anger melted away. I hold no animosity towards him."

Pat smiled as they sat in front of the roaring fire and watched as Halston senior stirred the logs.

Lily leaned over and whispered, "I don't know what I felt. He started talking about the past and the things he'd done and about all the time he'd spent on the road. Imagine being gone nine months a year. I can't imagine that kind of marriage. One thing I'd never noticed before was his limp. That surprised me, I wonder what happened? I'll ask Jim, maybe he knows?"

"Why didn't you ask him?"

"I didn't have a chance. But he wants me to meet him next week."

"You said yes, didn't you?"

"Before I had a chance to say anything Jody rushed into the room screaming that Jim had fallen."

Pat hit the arm of the couch with her fist. "Damn, he would have to fall just when things were getting good." She paused. "Henry sure pulled a hell of a surprise tonight. I knew by the look on your face you were just as surprised as the rest of us. Once he gets this judgeship he'll be set for life."

"You're a pistol," Lily threw her head back and laughed, "when God made you he didn't bother to use the mold that the rest of us are formed from."

Pat laughed and motioned Lily to follow her into the living room where the party was still going strong. Shoes of varied colors lay around the edge of the dance floor as her barefoot friends danced to the rock and roll strains of 'New York, New York'.

Jody grabbed her mother's hand and pulled her onto the dance floor. Mother and daughter stepped lively to the music and after a few minutes Lily kicked off her shoes as Jody spun her around. Ah, such youth and spirit, she thought. They laughed and applauded when the song ended. Lily was out of breath and collapsed into the nearest chair.

"Not bad for an old lady," she panted and put both hands on her chest as she tried to catch her breath. Jody was out of breath as well and joined her. "You look tired. Why don't you spend the night?"

Without hesitation, Jody nodded.

"Great. Tomorrow morning we can go to mass and afterward we'll have breakfast, or maybe brunch."

"Whoa! Slow down. I said I'd spend the night and you've already drawn up an itinerary. I don't mind the brunch idea, but let's skip church."

"Why? What happened? You always used to go to church with us."

"Nothing happened! It's, well, it's like this. One day I walked out of church and knew I'd never be back. I feel that a church, or temple, or any organized religion, should give you a feeling, something, maybe a warm fuzzy protective thing. I feel nothing when I'm in church; I get nothing from mass; nothing from communion. I'm more peaceful when I meditate, a peace that I've never experienced in church. There have been times I'm so filled after meditating, it's, it's indescribable."

Lily leaned over and hugged her. "I'll tell you what, you sleep in tomorrow and I'll go to church. Then when I get home we can go to brunch. Okay?"

"I'd like that Mom, and now if you'll excuse me," she exhaled as if relieved, "that last dance did me in. I think I'll go to my room." She kissed her mother and father good night and went upstairs.

Lily and Henry stood at the door saying good-bye to their happy guests. "I forgot to tell you," Henry said, "tomorrow I'm meeting with father and some of his cronies at the office, you know, the big money men. I've got to get all the financial backing I can, and as soon as possible. I know you can find something to do."

Now it starts, she thought. Lily climbed the stairs to her room and couldn't help but wonder what life had in store for her next.

*Marilyn Stuart*

## CHAPTER 12

The clock on the dashboard signaled eleven as Edmund drove into Saint James's parking lot. Jim was sound asleep in the passenger seat. He awakened him and helped him out of the car and into the rectory. After coaxing three cups of black coffee and half a turkey sandwich into the inebriated priest, Edmund finally spoke.

"That sure hit the spot, I was hungrier than I thought." Edmund wiped his mouth then lit his pipe. He slipped off his jacket, loosened his tie, leaned back, and stretched his feet under the kitchen table. "Now tell me what this evening was about," his eyes were steadfast in their intent, "and I don't mean Henry's announcement. What's going on my friend? You know you won't find the answers in a bottle."

Jim pushed up his silver-rimmed glasses, walked into the living room, and came back with a bottle of Rose'. "I need some wine," his hands shook, "then I'll be able to talk about it."

Edmund jumped up and grabbed the bottle out of his hand. "No you don't. There's a problem here and I want to help, but not with this between us." He went to the sink, turned the bottle upside down, and poured the wine down the drain. "Now damn it, talk to me." He put his arm around the frail priest's shoulder and helped him back to his chair. "We went through so much shit in Nam, there's nothing you could tell me that I wouldn't understand."

Jim sat down and took of his glasses. His bloodshot eyes appeared heavy as he started to speak. "Let me ask you something, and you have to promise to tell me the truth," he spoke in a reedy voice.

Edmund agreed.

"Do you ever have dreams or visions about Nam?"

Edmund tilted his brow and looked at him with uncertainty.

"I don't mean the country. I'm talking about the fighting, the killing, bombs exploding, the burning, and the bodies. I've never been through anything so...dehumanizing. I can't put it out of my head." Jim's voice trailed off as he stared into the distance. "It's as if it happened yesterday. The memories are my constant companions, especially the one where I lost this," he grabbed what was left of his earlobe, "will the horrid pictures ever leave me?"

Edmund's voice hardened. "I had a hard time understanding that bru-ha-ha you were caught in, I heard it was horrible. In fact, Historians are calling it one of the worst battles of Nam. A lot of my buddies died in that clearing."

Jim nodded and gritted his teeth. "Do you remember the code word 'Broken Arrow'?" The tone of Jim's voice turned to ice. "It was hammered into us that when any unit was in trouble, everyone, every unit, had to come to its aid." His eyes filled with tears and despair trailed in his voice. "Why didn't they come Edmund," his face grew hard, "how could they let the slaughter happen?"

"I heard stories," Edmund said, "tell me about it."

Jim hesitated, took a deep breath, and began. "Three platoons were pinned down in the La Drong Valley. We couldn't move to safety, we were surround. Our radio operators were shouting 'Broken Arrow' till they were hoarse. But headquarters never heard us, or they chose not to. They didn't realize we were trapped, because our planes continued to drop Napalm. With the fires, smoke, and bombs all around us, we couldn't see the snipers in the trees. But we damn well knew they were there. They had our clearing surrounded." Jim took another deep breath. "Our planes made a final pass, the heaviest bombardment of 'cans' I've ever experienced. Flames were shooting up around us. I remember shielding my face from the intense heat. It was like I had always imagined hell to be. Then a wall of flames was upon us and forced us to make a mad dash across the clearing, and as we did we were picked off like sitting ducks.

"I was running with the rest of them when I heard a blood curdling yell and turned to see a sight I'll never forget. A buddy next to me was engulfed in flames, a human torch, on fire from head to toe. The Napalm had stuck to him. I grabbed him by the boots and started to pull him back into the dense underbrush where we'd have some protection. But before I had a chance to move him he stopped yelling. I tried to remove his hot blackened boots and when I did his feet came off in my gloved hands. I stood there, staring at the blackened stumps, and started to puke. When I finally stood up, there was a sea of fire around me. I was caught in a ring of raging flames. The stench of burning flesh and agonizing screams pierced my soul."

Jim started to tremble. "I heard my platoon commander yelling, 'Kill the bastards before they kill you.' I ran. Men were falling like flies around me and I couldn't do a damn thing. The snipers never let up. Then I saw something I don't think I'll ever forget." He covered his eyes.

"As our GIs ran past their wounded buddies they shot them. Americans killing Americans. I couldn't believe it. Some might have been dead, but I know for sure, some weren't."

Jim took another deep breath. "Bullets were whizzing past me as the snipers tried to finish off the crawling wounded as they slid on their bellies across the clearing. I was never so scared in my life. Some started to run and scattered in different directions, like ants running for cover. I ran like hell, back into the jungle, opting to take my chances with the VC."

Jim sighed, "men were shouting, 'jump em, shoot em, bayonet the sons of bitches' and I did. I was insane with fear and kept stabbing at anything that moved or came close. I don't know how many of them I killed," his eyes bulged, "I was like a wild man. I can still see him...a VC running towards me. I swung the butt of my gun against his slimy face and split his head wide open. As I watched his brains ooze out, another Cong came at me. I parried and side stepped, then lunged forward with my bayonet and caught him in the neck. When I yanked my bayonet to the side, it cut his throat and left his head hanging back off his shoulders, as he fell."

Edmund remained silent. Compassion tore at him as every ounce of his being ached to comfort his friend, but he also knew that talking about it was better.

"God, I was tired. I couldn't run anymore. I dropped in my tracks. Beside me lay a dead GI. I pulled his body on top of me and stayed there, afraid to move a muscle, not daring to breathe. In the distance I could still hear the agonizing screams."

He looked at Edmund and pleaded for understanding. His jaw was slack, his ragged breath coming in gasps. "I was their spiritual leader, for God's sake, and there I was playing dead, hiding under a dead comrade, afraid for my worthless life. I kept my eyes shut, for how long I don't know, all I could see was a black hole and it was sucking me in, deeper and deeper into the vortex. I fought not to be swallowed up in it, but everything got blacker and blacker. I nearly lost it that day, God only knows how and why I survived. Those men died a painful death, their bodies all torn and bloated. I should have died with them, they were in my spiritual care, and I failed them."

He took another deep breath. "I must have passed out because when I came to I could hear, in the distance, twigs crackling and voices whispering. They seemed to be getting closer. Then I heard it. English. I called out 'broken arrow' and a GI rushed to my side. Then I smelled shit and looked down. It was all over me, I knew it was my own waste and so did he. The only thing he said was 'you know Padre, we're not fighting this war for the U.S. That's bullshit. We're fighting this battle to save our ass.' You know Edmund, he was right. There were eighty-four of us that started out that day, and only twenty-two made it. Why God chose me to survive I'll never know."

Jim put his head on the table and started to sob. Edmund rushed to his side. How to comfort this shell of a man? He tried to console him by rubbing Jim's shoulders as he continued to sob. Edmund's heart ached for his friend.

When the sobbing subsided, Edmund filled their cups with hot coffee. The look on Jim's face was one of mute wretchedness. His eyes were closed and his mouth grimaced as if in pain. Edmund watched his anguish peak, then shatter like a windowpane as a raw, primitive grief, seemed to overwhelm him. Jim dropped to his knees and grabbed the edge of the table. He rested his forehead on his hand.

"My God, why hast thou forsaken me?" He made the sign of the cross then pulled himself up. He grabbed a handkerchief from his pocket, wiped his eyes, and blew his nose. The slender frame heaved like someone who had just finished a hard, cross-country run. The boil of guilt had been lanced. Maybe now, it would have a chance to heal.

The two men were silent as they drank their coffee. Jim grabbed Edmund's forearm. "Thanks buddy," the strangled whisper was hoarse, "I don't know what I'd have done if you weren't here."

"You would've had the courage to go it alone. God would've seen you through."

"I don't know about that," he shook his head, "I'm not sure about anything at this point." He buried his face in his hands. "The God I believed in would never have let this happen. How could I add to the carnage? I killed everything that came into sight, and when I ran out of ammo, I grabbed the rifles from the dead bodies. Believe me, prayer was the last thing on my mind. All I knew was that I wanted to live."

Edmund went to Jim and rubbed his shoulders again. "What happened to you happened to a lot of us. Shit, I did everything I could to come back alive, and in one piece. What makes you think you were any different?"

"God handed down commandments, one of which said 'Thou shall not kill', and if that's true, then I've sinned the most grievous of sins. If it's not, then what I've believed in all these years isn't real and not worth the faith I've placed in it. What's left then? That's the real question. I feel godless...lost in an inner space with no ties or strength of faith to keep me from floating away."

"I know, that's how I felt when I got the news about my family. It's a terrible place to be in, it's like you don't know who you are. You're numb, devoid of any feeling."

"Yeah," Jim's face brightened, "that's it. It's like being in a fog, and the only time it clears is when I'm drinking. That's—"

"Go on," Edmund said.

"I've never felt more like a failure then when I came home. The fervor and love for the priesthood was gone."

He stared off into space. "I'm not sure what to do about it."

"How about going to AA? They do marvelous things. I'll be glad to go with you, if you want."

Jim looked at Edmund. "I'm not sure. I've thought about it, but if I did, I'd have to go as a layman, not as a priest. And to be quite honest, I don't know if I'm ready."

Edmund took their cups to the sink.

"Leave it," Jim said, "the housekeeper will take care of it in the morning." He put his glasses back on and looked at his watch. "It's almost five, we've been up all night. But I can tell you one thing," his smile waned, "my heart is light, at least temporarily, and I can think again, thanks to you. You saved my life. God bless you."

Edmund walked to the door, "try and get some sleep, you have to say mass in a few hours."

Outside the rectory Edmund watched the eastern horizon begin to glow. The dawn had slipped through the crack of a new day. A cold wind brushed across his back and forced him to turn up his collar as he walked to his Explorer.

* * *

With Thanksgiving just a few days away, Lily couldn't put Edmund's plea out of her mind. He said he had to see her and explain things. When Henry left for the office, Lily sat gazing out the breakfast room window, counting the bare branches on the trees in the back yard. Should she see him? Should she ignore him? Like a volleyball being tossed back and forth over a net, her thoughts moved between the holidays and Edmund. Whenever he came to mind she would start to think about unimportant holiday trivia. Thanksgiving was the official start of the Christmas season. Time to decorate the house; shop; plan parties, the time of year she loved best.

"Are you all right Miss Lily?" Emma asked.

"Yes, thank you. I was just thinking about the coming holidays and all the things I have to do."

"Umnn," she refilled Lily's cup, "are you going to shop for the shelter again?"

"Definitely, it's what gives meaning to the holidays. I'd like you to go with me again."

"I wouldn't miss it," Emma's face glowed, "I love seeing them faces when we drive up with all that food."

Back in her room, Lily flipped through her appointment book. Thanksgiving was next Thursday. This was the last day for classes at the University. The school was neutral ground, she thought, possibly the best place to talk. Should she call? No! Surprise him. Show up when he's finished with class.

She pulled a pink wool suit from the closet and threw it on the bed. From her jewelry box she grabbed a pair of earrings and noticed the edge of the velvet liner was beginning to curl. Wedged underneath was a silver charm, a replica of an engagement ring mounted on a charm, a gift given to her almost thirty years ago. By him. She turned it over and read: 'UNTIL'.

Lily smiled. On graduation day, when they were alone on the back porch of the apartment, he had surprised her with it. She remembered how nervous he was when he pulled the small box out of his pocket. He opened it and handed it to her. She turned the charm over and read it. She threw her arms around him and whispered, 'Until'.

Persuasion had always been his style and she loved giving in to his every whim. His ideas were different than any of the other boys, including Henry. What happened to that college girl? To her ideals? Butterflies flitted in her stomach as she slipped the charm inside her suit pocket and finished dressing for her meeting with Edmund.

*Marilyn Stuart*

# CHAPTER 13

The silent halls of Loyola echoed her every step as she wandered through the long dark caverns in search of room 206. At one point she thought about leaving and slipped her hand into her pocket. There was the silver charm. Maybe they could be friends. Jody and Edmund had already met and he hadn't voiced any suspicions. Maybe her secret was safe.

"Mom!" Jody came dashing down the hall. "What are you doing here? You're the last person I expected to see in school."

Lily stammered. "Well I, I want, I thought I'd see Edmund. I haven't had a chance to talk to him, and besides I have a favor to ask. I need his help with Uncle Jim."

"What's wrong with him?"

"If you haven't noticed he's been drinking quite a bit lately, and I thought if Edmund could talk to him, maybe he could find out what's bothering him."

"Makes sense. Men don't talk to women." Jody continued down the hall. "Boy the Professor will be surprised to see you. I think he's free now." Jody opened the class door and bounced in.

Startled by the unexpected interruption Edmund looked up, his raised brows and furrowed forehead spoke to his surprise.

"Hi, Professor, look who I found roaming the halls."

He started to shuffle the scattered papers into a pile.

"I'm sorry to bother you Edmund," Lily said, "I can come back later if you're busy."

His troubled eyes opened and gave way to a sparkle. "On the contrary, I want to talk to you." He ushered his two visitors toward the front row of desks.

She felt his admiring look, than watched his expression when he looked at Jody.

"And what brings you to school today, young lady? I thought we said our good-byes?"

Jody sat with her feet propped up on the seat next to her. "We did, but I had to get a form stamped at the office so I could get reimbursed for my classes. You know this higher education doesn't come cheap."

"Well I'm glad to see you both—"

"Listen guys," Jody interrupted, "I've got a super idea. Since it's lunch time, let's go somewhere and grab a bite to eat?" She looked from one to the other. "Come on, it's better than sitting here in class."

"She's right," he winked at Lily and his mouth curled into a smile. "Great idea," he chucked Jody under the chin, "this is no place to visit with friends."

They agreed to meet at the pizza place a short distance from campus. Lily knew she and Edmund wouldn't be able to talk, but despite the butterflies in her stomach, she managed to remain calm.

Jody ushered Lily into a booth and slid in beside her, with Edmund seated across from them. After they ordered, Edmund leaned back and smiled, his voice was low and smooth. "You said you needed to talk to me about Jim." His eyes sent a different message and Lily knew it was for her. "Is he all right?"

"Well..." she started to toy with the silverware and succeeded in avoiding his gaze, "that's what I wanted to find out from you. I haven't seen or heard from him since the party. What happened when you took him home?"

"In a nutshell? He's tormented by his stint in Vietnam, and because of it, he's having a hard time handling the gruesome memories. He's a gentle man, filled with love and compassion, and fate thrust him into circumstances that the toughest of us would've found hard to handle."

"Is that why he's drinking?"

"I think so, but I don't know for sure. I asked him to think about joining AA. He's against it—"

"Uncle Jim an alcoholic!" Jody's eyes widened. "He's a priest! He should have things like that under control," she shook her head, "I'm more convinced then ever that the church is failing its priests, I still say they should let the priests get married."

"Jody, that's not the point, I don't see how being married would help your uncle." Lily looked at her daughter. Why did she insist on blaming the church for everything. "Like Edmund said, his problem is dealing with what happened in Vietnam." Lily turned to Edmund. "Can you tell me more without betraying any confidence?"

"Only that he's in a lot of pain, and filled with guilt." He nodded. "He thinks he can handle it, but I don't think he's strong enough. Fighting ghosts is rough. I know. All I can do is let him know I'm there for him. I made some suggestions, but the rest is up to him."

Suddenly the glass of iced tea slipped from Jody's hand sending the cubes, along with the cold liquid, across the table and onto the booth and floor. Jody doubled over and grabbed her head. Her hands were shaking as she fumbled through her purse. She finally found a bottle of pills and started popping them into her mouth.

Lily and Edmund grabbed the napkins and started to sponge up the wet mess. Their eyes met, and mirrored disbelief, as Jody scooted out of the booth.

"Where are you going? Are you all right?"

"Yes, I'll be okay in a few minutes. I have to wipe these spots."

"Edmund, I'm concerned about her. I don't know what to do. The headaches seem to be getting worse and she refuses to go to a doctor. I can't drag her there. Maybe," she pleaded, "if you talk to her. She respects your opinion."

He reached across the table and grabbed Lily's hand. He curled his fingers over hers. "I'll try Lily. She's complained to me, in class, about headaches." He heard Jody's footsteps and quickly pulled his hand away. "Shh, here she comes."

"I'm really worried about you. You said that if your headaches didn't get better you'd make an appointment at the doctor, remember?"

"You should listen to your mother Jody, it's probably nothing but tension caused by that fast life style of yours."

Jody cocked an eyebrow and forced a smile.

"But on the other hand," he continued, "if it's strain or tension they might be able to prescribe something to relax you."

Jody laughed. "I don't need a damn tranquilizer, if I were any more relaxed I'd fall asleep sitting up."

"I caught you doing it in class."

Jody eyes flashed. "You're a trouble maker, Professor. Thanks a lot. Now you've got Mom all worried." Her eyes sparkled again. "See the headache's gone, I told you it wouldn't take long."

Lily looked at Jody then shifted her stare to Edmund.

"Mom, why don't we invite the Professor for Thanksgiving," she grabbed Edmund's hand, "daddy would like that and so would I. Besides," she said, "it will give him another chance to talk to Uncle Jim."

"I can't accept a Thanksgiving invitation, it's a family holiday. Besides if I know your mother, she's already invited a crowd."

Lily assured him that there was always room for one more at any holiday celebration, and besides Henry would be delighted to see him again. Edmund graciously accepted.

"Listen you two, I have to go to work. Mom, I promise I'll make an appointment with the doctor, these damn headaches are beginning to bug me," Jody smirked at her mother, "I guess you win." She waved to them and headed out the door.

"Thanks Edmund, I'm really worried about her."

"Don't worry, she'll be all right, you heard her say she's going to make an appointment with a doctor." He moved his plate to the back of the booth. "Now that we're alone would you like to tell me why you really came to see me? I know it wasn't about Jim, you could have called about that."

"If you remember," she began, "you're the one that wanted to talk to me, so I thought I'd catch you at school. What was so important?"

He sat back, lit his pipe and took a few puffs. He starred at Lily in an attempt to size up the situation.

She'd never known him to be evasive, yet here he was carefully weighing his thoughts. "You're not making this easy for either of us."

"Why should I? You're the one that didn't wait." His ebony eyes sparked with anger. "You ran off and married Henry the minute my back was turned. Talk about an enigma. Why didn't you wait for me? You knew how I felt about you. I guess I was wrong about us."

Her heart pounded in her ears. "What? You're accusing me of not waiting?" She slapped the table. "I don't believe this."

She took a sip of tea and replied through tight lips. "I spent weeks on the phone calling Mexico City; talking to your mom; I even called the Mexican Consulate to see if they could locate you. And you ask me why I didn't wait? You dropped off the face of the earth. For all I knew," her lips trembled, "you could have been killed or taken prisoner by the those bandits your brother was running with."

He sat up and put down his pipe.

She cocked her head in defiance and tossed her red hair across her shoulders.

Her fixed stare bore through him. He couldn't believe what he was hearing. He lifted his chin and with a bold gesture met her glare.

"I did everything but take out a full-page ad and offer a reward for information concerning your whereabouts. You're the one that was playing 'Don Quixote' in the mountains of Mexico. You were the one that never called. You never even dropped me a card to say you were okay. How dare you accuse me of not waiting?" The heat of her anger rushed to her cheeks.

Pale and shaken, he sat perfectly still as if frozen in time. Finally his mouth popped open. He reached across the table for her hand.

She quickly withdrew it. "Don't touch me. Don't ever touch me again. If you only knew the sleepless nights I spent worrying about you, wondering if you were ever coming back. I spent hours crying, wondering, hoping, I was desperate to find you." She took deep breaths in hopes of remaining calm.

"After your long silence I went to Henry's school for a week-end and that's when he asked me to marry him. Why shouldn't I have said yes. You were the one that ran away. Thank God he was there, at least he wanted me." Blinded by her tears, she reached into her purse for a tissue.

He never took his eyes off her. He was baffled by what he'd just heard. An array of jumbled thoughts ran through his head. His tortured eyes held a glint of disbelief, but when he finally spoke, his voice was strong and insistent.

"Lily, listen to me. I did call. God knows I called, four or five times, maybe more. I always got your mother. She told me you weren't home. I told her I was stuck in Mexico and didn't know when I'd be able to get back. She assured me she'd relay the message. I also told her that I'd write with a further explanation."

She gasped. "Liar! How dare you accuse my mother." The very idea that he would blame her mother was too much to handle.

He couldn't believe what he was hearing.

"Why, why would she do that?" Lily said.

He raised his brows and opened his mouth to defend himself, but no words crossed his lips.

"You want me to believe that garbage? Well I don't. My mother wouldn't do such a thing. Why don't you accept responsibility for your actions."

"Did she give you the letters I wrote to you? There must have been at least five, maybe six?"

Excuses, all excuses. Blaming her mother was something she didn't expect.

"Judging by the surprised look on your face, you don't believe I wrote, do you? Why is it you choose to believe your mother instead of me?"

"You come back into my life after a twenty-five year absence and expect me to believe you over her, and besides, my mother wouldn't do such a thing. She couldn't. For God's sake, she's my mother, why would she want to hurt me that way."

There was a pensive shimmer in the shadow of his eyes as his face began to cloud over with uneasiness. "This answers a lot of questions. And for your information, when I finally got out of prison I called again. Your mom told me you had married Henry. How could you, after what happened between us? I thought you cared?" He took a deep breath.

"I swore I would never let anyone get that close to me again. It hurt too damn much to be that vulnerable." His eyes were icy and unresponsive. "I figured I misread your intentions. That's why I never got in touch when I got back to the states. I kept thinking that you didn't want anything to do with me. I don't think you realize the terrible consequences your mother caused with her meddling. It's hard to believe that one human being could affect so many lives. If I'd only known what she was up to I'd have gone around her, contacted your brother, or even one of our friends, anyone to get a message to you. I had no idea..."

Lily started to sob. Her voice was shaky. "Stop it," she yelled, "stop the lies. When are you going to tell the truth?" She hit the table with her fist. "You had no right. No right."

Edmund reached for her. "C'mon let's get out of here. Let's go some place where we can be alone."

"No! I'm not going anywhere with you. Not until you're ready to tell me the truth."

He thought a moment. "Wait here. I've got something to show you. It's in the car. I think you're ready to see it."

Lily stared at the twisted napkin in her hands. Within moments he was back. He sat down across from her and held what appeared to be a book.

"This will be in the stores within the next month," he handed her a book, "I want you to read this Lily. It begins when I left Chicago to find my brother. It'll explain a lot of details of what happened. You'll also be able to read the letters I wrote to you. Read the book, then make up your mind whom to believe. That's the least you can do," he hesitated, "do it for us Lily."

She looked at the slick cover. The bold lettering "UNTIL" jumped off the black-and-white cover. She reached into her pocket and toyed with the charm. Lies. All lies.

"I hope this isn't about us. My family can never know."

"I wouldn't do that to you. Personally, I wouldn't care if the whole damn world knew how I felt about you. Don't worry, I've changed the dates, names, and places to conceal the facts. Remember I had a wife and daughter when I wrote it, and I wouldn't have hurt them for the world. It's written so that no knows it's about us, not even Henry, so relax."

Lily turned the book over. The large picture on the back was complimentary to him. "When women get a look at your photograph they'll buy the book even if it's written in Greek."

"That's exactly what my publisher said, that's why they made sure I posed with an open-necked shirt and exposed my chest to all of America. But if that's what it takes to sell the damn thing, who cares," he added in a lowered, huskier tone, "it'll mean more to me what you think about it. Now more than ever."

"I don't know when I'll have time to read it. I'm busy preparing for Thanksgiving."

Edmund shrugged. "Whatever. I can't make you read it. Since you don't believe me about what happened I don't think it would be right for me to accept your holiday invitation. Give Jody and Henry my regrets. You can tell them that I had a meeting in New York with my publisher, and if I'm questioned I'll back you up." His glare penetrated her soul and she started to fidget.

"I've got to go. I have a lot to do." She picked up the book and slid out of the bench. She hurried to her car, opened the door, and slid across the leather seat. She glanced in her rear-view mirror, he was standing there, watching her edge the Mercedes into traffic. A sudden sadness crept over her as she drove away.

# CHAPTER 14

Lily finished the last chapter and stared at his picture. She ran her fingers over the glossy print then clutched it to her breast. She felt warm and fuzzy all over. It was a beautiful story and she loved it.

She glanced at the clock on her nightstand, it was six in the morning and her eyes, heavy from lack of sleep. Her eyes closed as she lay back in the chaise. Was he telling the truth? She wanted to believe him. Why bother to make up such a lie? What did he have to gain?

The first three chapters described, in detail, how he smuggled the letters out of jail, and how it cost him his weekly allowance of American cigarettes from the Red Cross. His letters were a desperate cry of a caged man, waiting to hear words of hope and encouragement from his love.

And as he waited for a reply, each letter grew more desperate, filled with many questions and misgivings. Did she still feel the same about him? Why her long silence? In some of the letters he wrote of his deepening love and asked her to be his wife. Then without a word for six months, his final letter, an ultimatum. If he didn't hear from her by the time he was released he would assume he misread her intentions and never bother her again.

When he and his brother were finally released, he called his mother immediately and she informed him of

Lily's marriage. Edmund's description of his sense of betrayal tugged at her heart. Haunted by the memory of her love, and convinced his love had been desecrated, he enlisted in the army.

A knock at the door dispelled her reverie and she quickly slipped the book under the pillow. "Come in." She sat up when Henry entered the room.

"I was worried about you. Are you feeling okay? Emma said she brought you a tray last night." He glanced around the room, "what have you been doing all this time? Your eyes are bloodshot, have you been up all night, reading?"

"I started to read," she rubbed her eyes, "and must have fallen asleep on the chaise. I just woke up."

"I won't be joining you for breakfast, I've got an early meeting at the Rotary. I'll see you tonight, have a good day." He closed the door behind him.

She reached under the pillow, grabbed the book, and gazed at his picture. Did her mother destroy the letters? She never did like Edmund. Perhaps...Lily still found it difficult to believe that such treachery could come from her own mother?

In the depth of her heart she knew. Oh God! He was telling the truth. Her mother's meddling had changed the course of her life and so many others along with it. Lily grabbed at her chest and felt a sharp pain enter her heart, as though someone had thrust a knife into it. Her destiny had been tampered with, and she felt violated to the depth of her soul.

How could she, was her only thought? There must be a logical explanation. Yes! That's it! She didn't do it on purpose, she probably forgot about the calls, than when I announced I was going to marry Henry, she didn't want to upset me by giving me his letters.

Lily believed Edmund, and at the same time understood her mother's actions without ever having to take sides. She could live with both explanations. But doubt began to creep into her thoughts, she had to know the truth. If anyone would tell her the truth, her mother would.

* * *

She rang the front doorbell. No answer. She rang it again. He didn't answer. She peered through the stained glass window. Disappointed, Lily got back into her car and started to back out of his driveway when the black Explorer pulled in behind her.

Edmund jumped out and ran toward her car. "This is a pleasant surprise. And to think I almost missed you." He stared at her. "I was afraid I wouldn't see you again."

She tried to contain her eagerness and strained to make herself heard above a whisper. The cold night air spilled a white mist from her mouth when she spoke. "I'm here," she paused and looked up at him, "to apologize for calling you a liar."

He leaned down and grabbed the handle of the door. "Come on in, it's too damn cold out here, it'll give me an excuse to see if the fireplace works." He grinned and opened the door.

"You mean you haven't made a fire in it yet? We've had some pretty cold nights."

"It's a lot of trouble to make one, and then sit and watch it by yourself."

He piled logs in the fireplace, than lit the crushed papers at the bottom of the grate. Within minutes a roaring fire filled the old brick fireplace. He made hot chocolate and carried the cups into the living room.

A playful look came into his eyes and the rich timbre of his voice matched his brawny look. "You're the first guest I've had in my home, other than Jody of course. I'm glad you're the first grownup."

The warmth in his eyes caught her off guard as she fought the cobwebs of a sleepless night. The butterflies were back in her stomach and she could feel the hair on the back of her neck as it began to quiver. Her heart beat faster. Embarrassed that he might discover what she was feeling, she lowered her head.

"I'm here to apologize. I called you a liar without giving you a chance to explain. But after I read your book I understood. But I'm still struggling to justify my mothers actions."

His full brows shot up, then drew together, as he waved the pipe smoke away in an attempt to concentrate on Lily.

"When I finished reading your explanation, I knew you were telling the truth. But I also know my mother must have had a good reason not to tell me that you had written. I'm giving her the benefit of the doubt."

"That's between you and her. Right now I want to talk to you about those years. Those lost years of our lives. You know what happened to me, but I know very little about you." He sipped his hot chocolate and watched as she stared into the fire.

She turned to him. His eyes were magnetic and her whole being was filled with a schoolgirl excitement. Her pulse was erratic. "You're staring at me, what's the matter? I haven't changed that much, have I?"

"You're more beautiful than ever, and you can still cast a spell over me."

"Still the silver-tongued orator. You could talk the devil out of his pitchfork."

He laughed. "I'm glad to see that you haven't lost your sense of humor."

Lily picked up a photo of Edmund's family. "I assume," she held the picture toward him, "this is your wife and daughter. They're beautiful. I know you must miss them. You wrote in the book how she took care of you and risked her life when she hid you. I'm thankful she nursed you back to health after your run in with the VC."

His eyes were wistful. "There were no antibiotics or medicine available so Mai Lyn used the jungle as her drug store. She was in danger every time she went into the wild to search for special medicinal plants. She wrapped my legs in the leaves and made sure every stab wound was covered. I don't know what else she did, I was out of it most of the time, delirious for over two weeks. When I came to she was sitting next to me, wiping perspiration from my forehead and smiling. She spoke in Vietnamese, of course I couldn't understand a word she said. But over the months we learned to communicate by gestures, hand signals, whatever..."

He glanced back at the photo. "Like I wrote in the book, I got her pregnant. I didn't plan on it, I just wasn't thinking. After being in such a hellish place all I remember is that I needed to be held by another human being. Call it selfish if you want." The reflected flames, from the fireplace, danced in his eyes as he blinked repeatedly at the memories.

She waited for him to continue.

He leaned forward and rested his forearms on his knees, then clasped his hands and scrunched up his face. "I had no idea if and when I'd be out of that hell hole. Her warmth and caring were the only things I had to hang on to, and for that I'll always be grateful." He lit his pipe again, threw his arm on the back of the chair, and turned to face her.

"After she had Christine, the GI's finally took back the village, by then I was well enough to join them. Saigon was ours. I wanted to take her to the hospital but she wouldn't hear of it, she was frightened of the big city. Later I found out what she endured when I left the village.

'Boi Doy' is the English translation for 'Child of the Dust'. That's the name those goddamn Vietnamese gave my daughter. She was a mixed breed, considered ugly, and shunned by the people, marked for life because I was her father." He moved closer.

"Can you imagine those people calling someone so beautiful, ugly. That's when I decided to bring them to America. Their life would have been hell if I left them behind. Fate dealt the cards, I had to play the hand."

Lily stared at the dying fire and watched the yellow and orange flames as they flickered their last dance of heat. Her solemn thoughts echoed her words. "You and I had different paths to follow. It seems as though there was a conspiracy to keep us apart. Do you suppose it was because we had sinned?"

"What kind of thinking is that?" His eyes mirrored her anger. "Since when is making love a sin? God is without judgment. It's people who put tags on everything, declare it good or bad, then spend the rest of their lives living out of that judgment." He moved closer and reached for her hand. "What happened to us was the result of the choices we made, not because a celestial big brother was controlling our destiny."

At that moment she knew the love they shared was real. He put his pipe down and stared into her eyes. He stood and pulled her up from the couch. An animal fire glowed in his eyes as he drew her close.

A sexual energy passed between them like lightening bolts shooting through her body. Her whole being was filled with wanting. She was alive and on fire with desire.

His large hands embraced her face and incited a wave of passion. "No," she muttered and backed out of his grasp. "We can't. No matter what I may feel, I'm still married. I can't be in a situation like this. If I let you kiss me we know where it will lead. I won't let it happen."

"I don't know any such thing. There have been too many wasted years." He placed his hands behind her elbows to keep her from flight. "We deserve some happiness. When two people love one another like we do, they belong together." He pulled her closer and slid his hand to her shoulders. "You're all I've ever wanted. All I've ever dreamt about."

Cheeks flushed, her breath caught in her throat. How dare he take her for granted! "Who said anything about love. I never said I loved you. Where do you get off thinking you know how I feel?" She grabbed her coat off the couch and hurried into the hall.

"Lily!"

She stopped at the front door.

"Tell me you don't love me. Turn around and look at me. Tell me I'm wrong."

She stiffened. If she didn't walk out now she'd never leave his side, and she couldn't allow that to happen. But it was what she had to do. It was what was expected. Despite her soul crying out to stay, she bit her lip and walked out the door. Blinded by tears she rushed to her car, all the while she fought the impulse to look back.

"Lily, come back! I love you." Trapped in the driveway by the Explorer, she made a sharp turn and drove over the front lawn. As she drove past the porch he called to her one more time.

"Lileeeey."

* * *

As promised, Edmund never came to Thanksgiving dinner, with Jody quite verbal in her disappointment. She believed the story her mother told; he was out of town, simplifying matters and justifying his absence. Lily postponed talking to her mother about Edmund's letters and calls, after all it was Thanksgiving, and she didn't want to cause any family friction. For the time being Lily's excuse for her mother's actions was enough to justify her silence.

Pat lingered after the elaborate dinner and finally cornered Lily in the butler's pantry. "Well? Did you talk to him?"

"Yes I did and I think we've come to an understanding."

"What the fuck does that mean? Are you two going to get together or not? And don't play coy with me Lily Halston. Your pants are probably wet as we speak."

"Pat, really. Have you no respect?"

"For who? For what? Look what the hell respect has gotten you; a hunk of loneliness that could sink a ship, along with hot pants for another man. Not that I blame you. But I must tell you, there's something about that man that bothers me. I don't know Lily, he's just too perfect. Everyone has a past, especially men."

Lily scrunched up her nose. "Now don't look for trouble where there is none. Leave well enough alone."

"All right, if you insist. I won't bring it up again." They returned to the table for a piece of Emma's pumpkin pie. After dessert Henry excused himself and retired to the study.

Pat scurried to Lily's side, "now let's finish what we were talking about."

Lily smiled. "Yes! Yes, to all the questions you're going to ask."

Pat's eyes popped open and in a loud whisper she exclaimed, "you and Edmund made love?"

"Shh!" Lily held a finger to her lips. "Do you want the whole damn house to hear you? No, we didn't. We just talked. C'mon upstairs I've got something to show you."

Pat sat on the edge of the bed while Lily fumbled through her dresser drawer and pulled out the book. "This is an advanced copy of Edmund's book, it'll be in the stores soon. It answered all my questions. According to this," she slapped the book, "he wrote me six letters and in two of them asked me to marry him. Can you imagine that? He loved me enough to want to marry me."

"You never got any those letters?" Pat was perplexed.

"Nor the phone calls. My mother forgot to tell me about his calls. And when the letters came I was married to Henry so she didn't want to upset me."

"What?" Pat's fury choked at her. Anger lit her eyes and she became indignant. "Damn that bitch. She never told you?" Pat quickly covered her mouth with her hand. "I'm sorry. I know she's your mother, but it makes me angry to think that she could have done something like that."

"She didn't do it on purpose."

"I wouldn't put anything past that—"

"The most important thing is that he thought I didn't want him. He joined the army when he found out I had married Henry. That's why there's been no communication all these years."

"Well now that you know how he felt are you going to tell him about Jo—"

"Don't you dare mention that in this house or I'll never speak to you again! Is that understood?"

"I'm sorry," she said nodding, "it's just that I'm so excited for you. You're going to see him again, aren't you?"

"I don't think so. The last time we were together he dared me to look him in the eye and deny my love for him, and I couldn't."

"You're fifty, right? More than half your life is over, maybe three quarters. I came to that realization last year and it knocked my socks right off, and scared the hell out of me. How much time do you think we've got left?"

Lily kicked off her shoes and rubbed her toes into the plush white carpeting. "What the heck does that have to do with anything?"

"Everything. If you were in your twenties you'd have your whole life ahead of you, but not at fifty. Do you want to be Henry's stepping stone for the rest of your life? Think about it, and think hard." Pat grabbed a silk pillow off the bed and began folding and unfolding the gathered material. "What about your dreams, Lily? Prince charming, the white horse, happily ever after?"

Lily tried to ignore the mocking voice inside her head and finally stood up. She put her hands on her hips. "You know you're a trouble maker. I thought I'd solved things and now you have to remind me that I'm going to die someday." She fell back on the bed with her hands beneath her head and stared at the ceiling. "You do have a unique way of looking at things."

Pat sat down beside her. "Forget the morbid aspect for a moment. You told me you don't sleep with Henry anymore, and haven't for years. What the hell are you doing to relieve sexual tension? A vibrator?"

Lily's mouth dropped open as she looked away. "I, I," she stammered.

Pat laughed. "You're turning ten shades of pink. If you're too uncomfortable talking about it we don't have to, but it's a natural part of life. The big "O" eases tensions and relaxes whatever needs relaxing."

Lily roared with laughter.

"See it's not so bad. You just have to come to terms with it. No pun intended. But if you're going to continue to see Edmund, and not sleep with him, I'll buy you one. There's no way in hell that your body will be able to handle the passion without getting some kind of relief."

Lily shook her head. "I don't know about you. Is anything sacred to you?"

Pat hesitated, than blinked. "Now that you ask, I really don't think so. I believe in being honest and living life as it comes. I like to enjoy myself and if that's wrong and immoral," she shrugged, "so be it."

"You sound just like Edmund."

"You know what they say, 'If you don't use it you'll lose it'."

Lily giggled, then grabbed Pat's arm.

"Tell me what's it like to have an affair. Weren't you scared of being caught? Didn't you feel any guilt?"

"For the record, when I was married I never slept around, I didn't have to. All my needs were taken care of at home, but I wasn't married to a Henry. I would have divorced him years ago. Now that you have someone in your life that loves you, and that you love as well, why not? Guilt? After all he is the fath—" Pat caught herself in time and quickly changed the subject.

"Look, stop trying to justify why you shouldn't. Why not look at reasons why you should have an affair. Did you know that climaxing on a regular basis is good for your complexion." Their laughter rippled through the room.

"Besides, it'll give you an excuse to get some new lingerie. You never have an affair wearing old underwear. It always has to be new; you go on a diet and exercise regularly, you want to be able to keep up with him. In case you forgot, it's not easy keeping your legs raised or wrapped around them. If you get a cramp in your leg it can be very embarrassing. And make sure you have a pedicure every week, a lot of men love to suck on toes. Maybe that's his thing."

"You're unreal. Why don't you write a book about the dos and don'ts of having an affair. For someone who's never had one, you sure know an awful lot."

"I said I never had one when I was married. In between marriages is another story. I occasionally dated married man, and that constitutes an affair. So I do put myself up as an expert."

Lily laughed and admitted to envying her friend's uninhibited sexual attitudes and behavior. "Now will you go home?" She pushed Pat toward the door. "I've got a lot to think about."

"Just remember, if you need a vibrator I'll buy you one."

Lily laughed and threw a pillow at Pat as she ducked out the door. When the door closed Lily picked up the pillow and smiled. She walked over to the phone and looked up the number for Andrea's. Tomorrow she'd make an appointment for a manicure and pedicure.

# CHAPTER 15

Thanksgiving recess was over and Loyola was back in session. With midterms looming, students arrived early, trying to catch up on their studies. Seated at his desk, Edmund prepared his notes, and wondered if Jody would be in class today? She'd missed the last two. It was so unlike her. Concerned, he called after Tuesday's class. She told him she wasn't feeling good, but assured him she would be in class today, and begged him not to tell her mother. He was hesitant but promised to keep her confidence. Had he done the right thing? Maybe he should have alerted Lily.

He stepped up to the podium and was ready to begin class when the door flew open and Jody rushed in, flushed, and out of breath. She apologized for being late and rushed to her seat. He smiled and started his lecture. He turned to the blackboard and started to write names and dates, and as he did he heard a commotion. He reeled around and saw Jody standing at her desk, holding her head between her hands, and crying out in anguish. Suddenly she dropped to the floor.

"My pills! Someone get my pills."

He ran to her side and began rummaging through her purse. One of the students ran for water.

"It's all right, just lie still. Everything will be fine." He shouted for someone to get a cold towel and lifted Jody's head to rest on his arm. He put two pills on her tongue and held the glass to her lips. She took short sips. He quickly folded his jacket and made a pillow for her head. As he put the cold cloth on her forehead he kept assuring her she'd be okay.

Within moments her color returned. She sat up and looked around. Her eyes were glazed over as she peered at the empty classroom.

"Here, let me help you into a chair."

She let go of him and covered her face with her hands. "I'm so embarrassed. That was one of the worst, it was so sudden and intense. It felt like someone was stabbing me in the back of my head. That's all I remember. What happened?"

"You collapsed. Thank goodness you had your medication with you. No more putting off going to the doctor young lady, I'm taking you to the Emergency Room. Now! This is nothing to fool around with. What if you'd been driving or worse yet, what if you were on your bike? You could've been killed, and I refuse to be a party to that." He held up his hand, "not one word out of you, is that understood? We're going to the hospital, now. If they tell me everything's all right I'll take you home."

* * *

While Jody was being examined, Edmund called Lily. Jody would be angry for betraying her confidence, but Lily had to know about the attack. He waited at the entrance to the Emergency Room until he saw the silver Mercedes tear into the hospital parking lot. Lily ran to the door.

She was out of breath, "what happened? Is she all right?" He put his arm around her shoulder as they walked back to the area where Jody was being examined.

"Calm down, everything's fine. She had one of her headaches in class and collapsed from the pain. Once I gave her the pain pills she was okay. I convinced her to come to the hospital just as a precaution. She's going to be mad as hell that I called you. I don't know why she doesn't want you to know that she's sick."

Lily walked into the curtained petition.

Jody glared at Edmund. "Mom, what are you doing here?"

"I called her," he said, "you can be mad at me, but I felt she should know. What if the tests show that they have to cut your head off to stop the headaches, your mother should know about it?"

"Ha, ha. Very funny." She rubbed the back of her head. "I suppose your right. I'm glad your here, Mom," she squeezed Lily's hand, "but I'm fine." Jody sat on the edge of the gurney, swung her feet, and waited for the doctor to sign her out.

"You came for nothing."

"It wasn't for nothing. Anything that affects you, concerns me. How many times do I have to tell you that I worry about you. I love you." Lily stroked her daughter's hair.

That could easily be Christine sitting there, Edmund thought as he stepped out of the room and looked around for a place to sit. He wanted to be sure to tell Lily about the classes Jody had missed, this was serious enough not to honor his word.

He slipped outside to grab a puff, and at the same time he hoped there'd be an opportunity to talk to Lily. He puffed on his pipe and turned at the sound of the glass doors as they slid open. Fear mirrored in Lily's eyes. Her thin hands shook.

"They want to take more X-rays of her head. The doctor called a Neurologist and he ordered an MRI and additional blood work. They said she could go home, but she has an appointment with a specialist after Christmas. What do you think is wrong?"

Edmund watched Lily pace back and forth across the hospital driveway.

"I feel so helpless."

She still squints when she was worried, he thought. "I'm sure she's all right," Edmund tried to reassure her, "at least she can't put off seeing a doctor any longer. I'm glad this happened, she can't deny the headaches any longer."

"I'm glad you called. She hasn't been herself lately, she's always so tired. Her excuse is that she's not getting enough sleep because her cat keeps her awake, or her new roommate's playing the television too loud." Lily sucked in her cheeks and rolled her eyes.

"I know she doesn't want to worry me, but there comes a point when it's time to worry."

"Lily I have to ask you something about Jody."

She stopped, her green eyes were filled with apprehension. "Come sit down."

Uncertainty crossed her face.

"Relax, it's nothing serious. There are a few things I need to know. When the doctors are finished you'll have to drive Jody home. I have one more class, but after that I'm free. Come to the house, I'll throw something together for dinner and we can talk."

She stiffened.

"What do you say?"

She bit her lip, looked away, and tried to keep her response casual. "All right. I have to see Henry first, and tell him about Jody. How about I stop by around six?"

They walked back into the ER. Jody was dressed and standing at the nurse's station. She tried to disguise her annoyance with a half smile, but her impatience was evident.

"Where were you two? I was ready to call a cab?"

"We were talking. Well, what did the doctor say?"

"My blood pressure's low but other than that they won't have any test results for another week. I have to see Dr. Knuefelt for the results. I've got an appointment after the holidays."

Edmund's smile broadened. "Good. Your mother's going to drive you back to your car. I've got to run, I've got a class."

Jody hugged Edmund. "Thanks." She stood on tiptoes and kissed his cheek. "I'm glad you were there."

"I'm used to young ladies fainting in my class and I've learned to handle these kind of situations," he laughed as he waved good-bye. Outside he watched Lily drive out of the parking lot with Jody by her side. God let everything be all right, he prayed. But the look on Jody's face, as she lie doubled over in pain, haunted him. His gut told him something was terribly wrong. He tried to dismiss it by thinking that she probably was doing too much, and it finally caught up with her. The doctor will probably tell her to relax and ease up on her hectic schedule.

Tonight's dinner was priority now. She was still his friend's wife, and despite the fact that he loved her, there was nothing he could do about it. His heart told him she still cared; his head told him different.

* * *

Lily opened the massive walnut doors and walked into the courtroom where Henry was defending a client on

Federal charges. The small room held only five rows of wooden benches on either side of the narrow aisle. A wooden rail separated the spectators from the attorneys.

"I object your Honor! The question is inappropriate and has no bearing on the matter."

The Judge, Morris Hamilton, reminded her of Paul Sorvino and was a golfing buddy of Henry's. He'd been to the house, for dinner, many times, and was active in the Republican Party.

Amid the few observers, she quietly slid into the last bench. Henry bent over to confer with his client and waited for the judge to rule on his objection. Judge Hamilton sustained the objection and Henry sat down. Henry was right again, even the Judge agreed.

Lily leaned on the bench in front of her and listened to the proceedings. Her thoughts reached back in time...

Henry Wadsworth Halston, one of those young men you passed on the street without a second glance, a bland face with straight brown hair, blue eyes, and glasses. One could picture him in a white lab coat behind the counter of a drugstore pharmacy. He was five ten and of medium build. His clothes, although the best quality and cut, were conservative.

His only goal in life was to get a law degree, as his father, and grandfather before him. His birthright forged the destiny of his future. In the upper ten percentile of his class, he loved the learning process and absorbed knowledge readily. He prided himself on being an avid reader, readily quoting facts, figures, and trivia. A photographic memory enabled him to quote intricate and remote data and made his peers shake their heads in amazement. A stickler for details, he aced his tests. Because of his high goals he studied twice as hard as his classmates.

Her mind was back in court as she listened to the testimony. From what she could garner Henry's client was accused of defrauding the government, not paying payroll taxes for part-time employees. The boring testimony droned on and she glanced at the large clock on the wall. Five minutes to four. Court would be adjourned in a few minutes. Henry conferred with his client again and then addressed the Judge.

Her husband was an honest and forthright man, a quality that had been instilled in him from the time he took his first steps. He had a hard time relating to the loose interpretations of the law that many attorneys espoused. As an officer of the court he believed the law to be black or white. No shades of gray; no latitude for individual interpretation. Guilty or not guilty. Simple. Extenuating circumstances be damned.

Lily smiled when she pictured him as a Judge, sitting behind the bench in his black robes. He'd be good, she thought. Henry firmly believed that by standing back, away from feelings, an attorney could reach logical conclusions.

When he gave speeches at the local colleges, he always engaged in off-campus debates with young attorneys who challenged his oversimplified interpretations. But he knew case law by heart, and spouted references like a child reciting ABC's. Many nights, while dining at the country club, Lily sat and listened to he and his father discuss Supreme Court decisions.

Startled when the Judges gavel sounded, signaling the end of court, Lily stood and walked to the where Henry was sitting, leaned over, and tapped him on the shoulder.

"What are you doing here? Is anything wrong? You've never come to court. Has something happened to Mom?"

"No," she whispered, "I need to talk to you about something. It concerns Jody. I know you have another one of your speeches this evening so," she shrugged, "I thought I'd catch you before you went back to the office."

He gathered his papers and stacked them in a neat pile in his attaché' case. He excused himself, shook hands with his client, and followed Lily to the rear of the courtroom where they sat down.

"Well what's so important?"

"I've just come from the hospital."

His eyes narrowed.

"Jody collapsed in school." She heard his quick intake of breath as he sat straight up.

"What! Why didn't you call? Is she all right? Where is she now?"

"She's fine now. She's home, resting."

"What happened?"

Lily relayed the events, as much as she knew. Finally, she had his attention.

"Well," the impatience in his voice was evident, "what did the doctors say?"

"I didn't get a chance to talk to the specialist. The ER doctor called the Neurosurgeon. He's the one that ordered X-rays, an MRI, and additional blood work. She has an appointment after the holidays."

"What's the doctor's name? I'll have him checked out, I don't want some quack taking care of her."

"Well the fact that he didn't prescribe two aspirins and send her home, tells me something. He's concerned enough to want to see her again."

"I still want to check him out, it doesn't hurt. She'll be all right, you know young people these days, the hectic lifestyle they lead brings on problems. Jody is going to find out that she's got to take better care of herself."

"I hope you're right, but whenever there's something going on in the brain—"

"Stop it! You'll make yourself crazy over nothing. You know how you react. Remember when Jody was four and her first merry-go-round ride? You were so worried that you had to accompany her. She was fine but you were the one that got sick and lost your lunch."

"I shouldn't have eaten those hot dogs before going on that rides."

He nodded as his lips drew to a half smile. "Remember when she had her tonsils out, you'd have thought she was having major surgery—"

"It was major! Anytime you're under an anesthetic it's serious. As far as I'm concerned, that's the most dangerous part of any operation. My baby was under the knife. What the hell did you expect me to do, go home and wait, like you did?"

His brows drew together in a frown. "That's not fair. She's my daughter too. I was trying a case that day and I couldn't get another postponement. I had to be there."

Her face quivered as her voice grew louder. "You could've asked your dad to take the case, at least while she was still under. No," she shook her head, a sneer curled her lips, "you chose to be in court. I waited alone for the doctors to tell me it was over. Whenever anything happens you're never around. Then you dismiss my feelings like they don't count for anything."

Her temples were pounding, and the pain was blurring her vision. "I get tired of being taken for granted. You treat me as though I never have an original idea or thought. It's always your way. You never consider my feelings and I'm getting tired of it."

"There you go again," he slapped his briefcase, "making something out of nothing. Why does everything have to be a big deal to you?" He stood and leaned against the back of the bench. I can't talk to you anymore. I don't know what's bothering you lately. Is it because I'm running for this Circuit Court seat?" The gray eyes peered and probed for answers.

"It's just that," she stammered, "it's, I, hell, never mind." She looked away then jumped to her feet. In order to keep her temper in check she turned and ran out of the courtroom. Damn him. How could he say I was overreacting, insinuating that I didn't know what I was talking about, and peering at me through those glasses as if I were the one with a problem. Never us, never him, always me.

* * *

"Not bad," she laughed, "you surprise me. When did you learn to cook? Your Marinara sauce is excellent, you'll have to give me the recipe."

His eyes grew openly amused. "Who'd have thought we'd be swapping recipes."

"Life is funny. If someone had told me six months ago that I'd be having dinner at Edmund Valente's house I'd have bet the farm they were wrong."

His tanned face became somber. He put down his fork and leaned across the table. "I know we got into this discussion last week," he offered, "but we didn't finish it. I don't want to upset you again. Maybe a truce is in order?"

"Maybe you're right? I agree to a truce." They shook hands across the table. "I read your book. It's wonderful! You have a unique way with words." His gaze made her feel uncomfortable. She glanced away and quickly changed the subject.

"You know this could be a beautiful room if you'd finish decorating it—"

"Lily, I'm not interested in decorating the damn room—"

"I know, it's just that I sometimes find certain subjects hard to talk about, and reliving the past is one of them."

"But we have to," he covered her hand with his, "we have to straighten things out."

"You're right." The excitement she felt at his touch, forced her to withdraw her hand. "This is as good a time as any." She took a deep breath, pushed away her half-empty plate, clasped her hands, and leaned her elbows on the table. "Let's start with your book. I loved it." Her voice was warm and contained. "I believe you sent those letters and made the calls."

"Well that's a start. It's important that you believe I didn't run out on you. But what I still don't understand, and need to know, is why you didn't wait." The expression in his currant-black eyes pleaded for the truth.

She leaned her face against her hands and held in her heart the words she wanted to scream. 'Because I was pregnant.' She wanted to tell him about her broken heart when she couldn't find him, and how she tricked Henry into making love. Her pretense, all these years, that Jody was Henry's daughter.

Like a leaf caught in a whirlpool, she felt like she was being swallowed into a pit. "If I'd known you were being held in Mexico, against your will, I never would've married Henry. You have to believe me."

He smiled and reached for her hand. This time she didn't withdraw it.

"If you remember, Henry was off at summer school, and Jim was away on a retreat, when you and I said our good-byes." Heat filled her cheeks as she recalled their last night together. "I was sure I'd hear from you within a week or two. Then as the weeks passed without any word I felt abandoned. So I took it upon myself to try and find you. Those were the darkest days I've ever known." Rigid, she held her tears in check. She smothered a sob, pushed away from the table, and darted into the living room.

Edmund scrambled after her. "I never realized you felt that way about me. You never said anything." He turned her around to face him. "Why didn't you tell me? I would have moved heaven and earth to get back to you. I never would have let you marry Henry."

Lily moved to the iced window. Swirls of frozen moisture had formed intricate patterns on the glass. She shivered and rubbed her arms, then turned to face him. "When I didn't hear from you I figured you'd forgotten about us, and had no intention of ever seeing me again." She looked away, "I thought your trip to Mexico was just a farce, an excuse to leave."

Edmund shook his head and stepped closer.

"Please don't come any closer," she held up both hands, "let me finish."

He stopped and sunk down on the arm of the leather chair. His eyes held a bewildered plea.

"I was ridden with guilt, and worried that nobody would marry me because I wasn't a virgin, so when Henry invited me up to school for the weekend, I accepted. That night we went to a party and I tried drinking away my sorrows. The next thing I knew we were in bed. And as luck would have it, I got pregnant. We were married the following month."

Lily rubbed her stocking feet across the carpet pile. She could feel his eyes penetrating her very soul and she grew nervous. Sheer fright swept through her. Would he believe her? She had to do something to change the subject. "Let's clear the table, I hope you've got dessert. I still have a sweet tooth. We can talk while we're cleaning up."

Within a few minutes the dishwasher was loaded and the aroma of fresh coffee brewing, filled the kitchen. Lily smiled when Edmund took a white bakery box from the refrigerator.

"I didn't forget about your desert fetish. Look, Napoleons and Cannolis, how's that for extra pounds?"

She grabbed the coffee pot and poured, while Edmund sorted out the dessert. She handed him a dish and he grabbed her hand.

"I'm sorry."

She stiffened. The compassion in his eyes, along with the warmth from his hand, was undeniable. Her heart fluttered like a bird with clipped wings. She lied to him about Jody and a wave of apprehension swept through her. She couldn't look him in the eyes, and turned away. "There's nothing to apologize for. That was a life-time ago."

"Maybe we can start fresh, at least that's what I'm hoping. I know you're involved in Henry's campaign—"

"No I'm not! That's his thing. He never consulted me or asked my opinion, so he can damn well do it alone. My only contribution is an occasional dinner or cocktail party."

"What does he say about that?"

"Well there's not much he can say."

He grabbed her hand again, "Lily you read the book, so you know about my marriage. You must know that I never loved Mai Lyn. I treated her well, always with the utmost respect. But my heart was filled with love for you. No matter how many assignments I undertook, the memory of you never left me."

Edmund continued to explain his relationship with Mai Lyn. Tenderness filled his eyes whenever he spoke about his daughter. But when his eyes met hers, his hand tightened around hers as if confirming her presence. Suddenly he brought her into the circle of his arms. His large hand cupped her face and held it close. She twisted in his arms and put her hands against his broad chest in hopes of moving away. She arched her back and fought to get free. His other hand clasped her waist and pulled her against him. He caressed her face, and slowly trailed his fingers down her cheek, and rested around her neck. He pulled her face to his. Then his lips brushed across hers like a warm evening breeze. His kiss, slow and thoughtful, gentle and patient, awaited a response.

Her heart was pounding and drowned out the protests in her head.

He brushed her lips with his, then released her. "You've told me what I wanted to know."

"I haven't told you anything," she sniped and fussed with her hair.

"You can't deny that you're still in love with me, as I am with you. Time hasn't erased the way we feel about one another. You make me feel like a schoolboy who's been kissed for the first time. I know you feel the same way. I felt your heart beating wildly against my chest. Don't deny it. Remember, you don't like lies. Well, neither do I."

She slowly backed away and ran her fingertips across her lips. He took two steps towards her and his lips recaptured hers, only this time, demanding more. She gave freely to her awakened passion, and kissed him with a hunger that swept away her outward calm.

He raised his mouth from hers and looked into her eyes. "Lily—"

The doorbell startled them. Edmund pulled away and moved toward the door. She wrapped her arms around herself trying to retain the feeling of his strong arms about her. Her lips were tingling with his warmth when she heard him call.

"Lily!" his scream shattered her composure, "come quick." She ran to the front hall in time to see her brother collapse in Edmund's arms.

# CHAPTER 16

Lily dropped to her knees and leaned over her brother. "Oh, my God," she gasped, "is he breathing? His face!" His body was limp.

When Edmund tried to move him, his head fell back onto his arm. "He's breathing, but he seems to be hurt bad." Edmund leaned over, than pulled back sharply.

Lily shook her brother. "Jim!" she yelled, and when he didn't answer, she panicked. "He's not responding! Do something."

"Call 911," Edmund shouted, "tell them to send an ambulance."

She ran to the phone, and when she heard Jim moan, she hung up and rushed back to her brother's side.

"He's coming around."

He slurred his words as he pleaded, "don't call ambulance. No accident. Was beeeat up. I'm not hurt. Don't fuss." He struggled to sit up, but slumped back down.

"The bathroom," Edmund shouted, "get towels and a bowl of hot water, peroxide's under the cabinet." A cursory exam revealed no bones were broken. "Maybe we can take care of him."

Edmund removed Jim's bent wire-rimmed glasses, than brushed strands of hair from his friend's face. The deep gash above Jim's eye was seeping blood and left a trail across his face and down into his ear.

Lily brought a large bowl of warm water and towels. She wet a cloth and started to dab the blood from her brother's face. "How could someone do this to him? Don't they know he's a priest?"

"We don't know what happened."

"I'll clean him up while you put on a pot of coffee. He's going to need it." She gently wiped away the blood and dirt. There was a nasty cut by his mouth, the edge of his brow had a deep laceration, and his nose was dripping blood and mucous.

"How could this happen? He never used to drink. Did he tell you anything about what's been bothering him?"

"We talked a little. I'm no psychiatrist, but it'd be safe to say he needs help. I've talked to him again about going to AA and he skirts the issue, but tomorrow I'm going to force him to make a commitment. Maybe this beating is what he needed to wake him up. Do you know if the Diocese offers counseling for its priests?"

"I'm sure as hell going to find out." She suddenly realized the implications of her brothers' careless actions. "He drove in this condition? He could have killed someone, or worst yet, killed himself."

Edmund picked up the frail priest and carried him to the couch. They removed his torn, bloody clothes. Lily grabbed bedding from the guest-room, propped his head up with a pillow, than covered him with a blanket. As she slipped off her brother's slacks, his wallet dropped to the floor. She picked it up. Empty. He was robbed. As she looked through the wallet she felt something behind the credit cards. She pulled out a creased piece of paper. As she unfolded it, a silver cross fell to the floor.

"What's this?" She picked it up, "it looks like a Greek Orthodox cross."

"Damn!" Edmund's eyes were wide as saucers, "it's the Silver Cross. One of our country's highest honors it bestowes on war heroes. I wonder how he got it?"

"Look!" She unfolded the paper. "This article is from the STARS and STRIPES, dated August 10, 1963." She read the yellowed article, gasped, than sank into the chair. "It's his, my brother received the Silver Cross for bravery in the battle of Pun—Ja—Le. I can't even pronounce it. It says he killed ten Viet Cong in a last ditch effort to save his buddies who were ambushed in a village near the Laotian border."

Her chest heaved. "Why didn't he say anything about this? Why did he keep it a secret?"

"Very few servicemen receive the Silver Cross, and those that do, their families are present at the ceremony. Why wouldn't he share this?"

"Jim and I were always close, I never dreamed he'd keep this to himself. Why wouldn't he confide in me?"

"We're not going to find out much tonight," Edmund bent over the unconscious body, "he's out like a light."

She turned and touched Edmund's arm. "Thank you."

"Thanks aren't necessary. It's a good thing he found his way here. His timing was perfect." He winked at her.

"What do you mean?" Lily blushed at the twinkle in his eyes. "You're right," she said with a laugh, "divine intervention."

Then his eyes turned somber, his demeanor serious. "We're not finished Lily," he said, as he helped her into her coat. "It's just beginning."

She leaned over and pecked him on the cheek. He grabbed for her but she spun out of his reach. "See you tomorrow morning. I'll supply the croissants and bagels, make sure you have plenty of coffee." She glanced back at the sad figure sprawled on the couch.

"He doesn't know it," she jutted her chin toward the couch, "but tomorrow he's going to confession."

After a restless night Lily woke early and dressed quietly, making sure she was out of the house before Henry came down to breakfast. By seven fifteen she was in her car and speeding away, avoiding questions that would most certainly be a part of the early meal.

Edmund opened the door in his robe. "You're early. I didn't expect to see you for at least another hour." His mussed hair and dark shadow of stubble made him look sexy.

"How is he?" she whispered, "is he awake yet? Does he have a hangover?"

"Come see for yourself," he laughed. "Hey Buddy, your favorite sister's here, and she brought breakfast."

Jim stood by the table and put his arms around her. "I'm sorry I scared you last night," he spread his arms wide, "that wasn't my intention."

"You looked awful. How many guys jumped you?" She leaned over him and tried to get a look at the gash above his eye. "I hope that cut closes without stitches."

"What's another scar? I got myself in a real mess last night. I was drunk, and was walking around a neighborhood where I didn't belong."

Edmund piped in, "that's one hell of a shiner to explain to your parishioners. Better yet, why don't you try explaining it to us."

Jim stared at the floor for a moment, then looked at them. "You deserve an explanation for all I've put you through."

She reached across the table.

He smiled, his voice resigned, as if he knew he had to tell them the truth. "I was having a really bad day, everything seemed to be going wrong. As usual Mom called, only this time she had a lot of questions about Edmund."

Lily looked at Edmund. "What do you figure that's all about?"

Edmund raised his brows and shrugged.

"After that phone encounter the Ladies Rosary Society stopped by to plan the parish Christmas festivities." He picked up his cup with both hands and sipped the hot brew. "Of course not one of them could agree on anything, especially where the Nativity scene should be. An hour wasted," he said with a huff, "just discussing should the statues go outside the church or inside, by the altar." His hands shook as he took another sip of coffee.

Lily split a croissant and scooped strawberry jelly into it, than pushed the plate in front of him. "You can eat and talk at the same time."

He took a bite, spilled jelly on his finger, and proceeded to lick it off. "Then I had an appointment to counsel a young couple." He wiped his mouth, crumpled the napkin, than tossed it on the table. "Can you imagine, me giving advice? I can't even get my own act together, much less give counsel to the poor souls of my parish. What a laugh. Then to top off the morning the Bishop called and asked me to say afternoon mass on Christmas Day, at the downtown Cathedral."

"Why would that upset you, I'd think it would be an honor."

"I told him I couldn't, I had parish activities scheduled, and he'd have to get someone else."

"Why?"

"Say mass in front of God knows how many people when I'm not even sure God is hearing my prayers." His face turned red and his eyes bulged. "Those people deserve a priest who is dedicated; one with a blind unwavering faith. That's something I don't have anymore." He held onto his mug with both hands to stop the shaking, than blew on the steaming liquid.

"If anyone's dedicated his life to God, it's you. You sleep, eat, and talk God. You've always had enough faith for all of us. Remember when Jody was five and fell down the stairs? You were the one that sat at her bedside all night, praying. You were the one that comforted me by letting me know that God would reward my faith. And you were right. She surprised the doctors with her quick recovery."

"That was a long time ago. What I believed in is no longer true. I'm all mixed up. It's like being in limbo, and that's a damning place to be."

The desperation in his voice brought her to his side. She cupped his face with her hands and stared into his tormented eyes. "You've always been there for me," she smoothed his hair and stroked his cheek, "now it's my turn. Please let me help."

He removed her hands and held them in his. "You can't, Sis. This is my battle. It's between me and God."

"That may be so, but I'm a good listener, and so is Edmund. We're not going to let you go through this alone. We love you."

He looked at them. "Maybe talking through some of this," he hesitated, "might put things in perspective." He took a deep breath and his story about Vietnam spilled out. The longer he spoke, the more his words grew thin and hollow. He talked of a deep emptiness when he found himself in the situation, to kill or be killed. All he wanted to do was save souls. He cried when he talked about his fear of dying, and the haunting nightmare of dead Viet Cong, some no older then ten or twelve.

"In the dream they're laughing as they walk toward me—"

"It's not unusual for combat veterans to dream about war, Edmund said, "I've talked to some guys who see the VC in their dreams, just like you. But when it invades their waking hours, they seek help. They know they can't lick the problem alone."

"I know, that's why I'm considering AA."

Edmund cast a narrow glinting glance at his friend. "Serious?"

Jim was quick to add, "but before I do, I'm going to have to make some major changes in my life."

"That's a cop out and you know it. You don't have to make changes in your life to go to a meeting. Just go. Don't put this off any longer Buddy. You know how you arrived here last night. Forget the beating and robbery, I'm talking about your drunken stupor."

Edmund's fist hit the table and caused Lily to jump. Then he started shouting. "Damn it, I lost my daughter and wife to a drunken driver. How can you get behind the wheel knowing you could kill someone, let alone yourself. I've had enough heartache to last a lifetime. I don't have enough in me to mourn the loss of a friend."

"You're right, it's sinful of me not to consider the consequences of getting behind the wheel when I've been drinking. I've seen enough killing to last ten lifetimes." He looked at his sister then turned to Edmund. "I'm scared. Real scared. But I'm too embarrassed to go." He stared at the floor. "Will you go with me? I, um can't—"

"No, you don't have to wear your collar, and I'd be honored to go with you. When you're ready you'll put that collar back on and be proud to wear it."

# CHAPTER 17

Lily kept busy by preparing for her favorite time of year. She made lists, planned menus, and spent hours shopping the crowded stores. Despite numerous trips downtown, and the freezing weather, she finished her shopping ahead of schedule. Three days to spare. Through all the hustle and hurry she worried about Jody and phoned daily, for assurances, that the headaches were still manageable. She called Jim as well, and encouraged him to continue his fight against alcohol.

Despite the whirlwind days, thoughts of Edmund kept intruding; their passionate kiss; their past love affair; her hurried marriage to Henry; thoughts of adultery. Guilt about her longings churned in her belly and she began to feel unclean.

Married women don't think about being with another man. It's wrong, she thought. But despite her self-recriminations, she continued to fantasize about lying next to him and feeling his touch, even imagining his lips on hers. She thought about what it would be like if he took her forcefully, than she would pretend to fight him off.

Then she'd pray for relief from her obsessive thoughts. But the longing only increased. He called her daily and told her of Jim's progress. His deep voice stirred her, and the conversation always ended with him begging her to meet him.

After weeks of saying no, she began to weaken. He finally convinced her to meet him for dinner. Neither of them would ever have piece of mind until they talked through their feelings. He assured her that he'd find a place far enough away from Winnetka, a restaurant where they wouldn't be recognized.

In complete opposition to her logic, a sense of longing drove her to say yes. He was a disturbing influence in her life. She was constantly plagued her with feelings of guilt, but her heart finally ruled, and she agreed to meet him.

She took out three outfits and laid them on the bed, then dismissed all as inappropriate. Nothing fit, and she cursed her overindulgence of sweets and wine, than vowed to start a diet after the holidays.

She pushed hangers of clothes from one side of the closet to the other, than laughed at her silliness. She had dozens of outfits, each would be perfect. Finally she decided to wear her white long-sleeved wool dress. It fit like a glove.

As she grabbed his book, she flipped to a dog-eared page, the letter that talked about his loving her. She scanned the page and found the passage, 'I have never loved anyone as I love you. I never will. You quench my thirst for life. You are my completeness. Once in a lifetime is one blessed to find someone as lovely as you.' The words jumped out at her, and brought jolts of electricity that skittered on her flesh. There was a knock on the door and she quickly slammed the book shut, then slipped it back into the drawer.

Pat barged into the room. "Hi stranger, haven't seen you in a while, what've you been up to?" She walked over and picked up an outfit from the bed. "From the look of things you're either giving half your wardrobe to Goodwill or you've got a heavy date," she smiled smugly, "and I'll bet it's the latter."

"You're funny, very funny." Lily frowned. "Why don't you announce it in the local paper."

"No one can hear me. Emma's downstairs and Henry's not home, so relax and tell me what you're up to."

Lily giggled as she hung up her clothes.

Pat stalked her and wiggled her index finger at her. "You're having an affair." She started to clap. "You finally gave in. Congratulations, it's about time."

"Whoa! I'm not having an affair, I'm only having dinner. It's not like a real date. I only agreed so he'd stop pestering me. He insists we have unfinished business."

"I agree. You won't be happy until you get this settled. You either want him or you don't. It's that simple."

"It's not simple. You forget I'm married, and it's wrong to be seeing another man, or even wanting to be with him."

"Sooo...you're having sexual fantasies about him. It's about time you got honest."

"I have no intention of having an affair." Lily moved to the window. "I'm not divorcing Henry. And," she hesitated, "I have no desire to be with him."

"Time will tell, in fact I'd be willing to bet the farm that before the holidays are over you'll be in his bed with your hot little ass scorching his sheets."

"How much do you want to bet?"

Pat tossed her head and eyed Lily as she slipped out of her dressing gown.

"I'll bet you a brand new one-hundred-dollar bill that you'll make love to him before Christmas."

"It's a bet, and you're going to lose. It'll be a pleasure to take your money." They shook on it.

"You're on. Remember you have to let me know..." the silence between them was long as they walked into the dressing room. Finally Pat broke out laughing. "I don't have to worry about you telling me, I'll be able to see it on your face. I just hope you'll be able to conceal it from Henry. You know that old saying about the smile on a dying man's face being hard to wipe off. That'll be you. But knowing Henry, I'm sure he wouldn't notice if your teeth fell out."

"You're not being fair, he's not that bad. He's been a good provider and, and I sort of—"

"What! You sort of what? Like him?" She laughed. "C'mon grow up. You either love him enough to stay with him, or you love Edmund enough to leave. That's the bottom line. And no matter how many different ways you find to deny it, that's what you're facing. The sooner you can sort out your feelings the happier everyone will be."

Lily watched her friends' image in the mirror as she pretended to fuss with her make-up. "Why don't you go home?"

"Are you chasing me out?"

"You got that right. I have to get ready and you're making me nervous."

"On one condition."

"I can just imagine. What is it?"

"I'll leave if you promise to tell me all the details in the morning. Deal?"

Lily turned and smiled. "Deal. Now get out of here."

Pat leaned over and kissed her on the cheek. "Have fun." She held up her fist with the thumb up. "I'll be thinking about you."

Lily took her powder puff that was filled with body talc, and tapped Pat on the nose. Pat kept sneezing as she left the room.

When Lily finished touching up her makeup she smiled at the image in the mirror. She liked what she saw and quickly finished dressing. Anticipating dinner with him made her insides feel like Jell-O. Excited, but nervous, she shut the lights off and headed downstairs to her car.

* * *

He only knew one thing, he wanted her. Sitting across the table from her was a dream come true. It was finally clear to him why he returned to Chicago. One reason only. To find her. He watched her sip the champagne cocktail and wrinkle her tiny nose as the bubbles burst when they touched her lips.

The restaurant was dimly lit, except for the white candles on the tables. White-flocked trees surrounded the bandstand and large wreaths with twinkling lights were mounted on the edge of the raised stage.

He stared at her and time was suspended, he wished...he didn't know what to wish...only that she'd be his. He searched her eyes for answers, then set his glass down and reached across the table. He took it in his and was struck with the changes the years had made to her face. Time had rendered her more beautiful than he'd remembered, and the intimate lighting highlighted shadows on her smooth creamy complexion, and inflamed his ache for the wasted years. The choices they'd made left no memories, no unforgettable moments to warm his heart on cold lonely nights.

He loved her, of that he was more certain than ever. He wanted to share the rest of his life with her, and was ready to make a commitment. This time he was sure. But would she have him? He breathed a deep sigh. The truth was easier then he had expected. It was different this time. He was hers', heart and soul, and the dimension of that love wouldn't allow him to ever love another. He'd tried, many times, with many women, and it never worked. Time and experience had healed his wandering heart but it hadn't erased the memories of her. He knew he would never be free of her.

He watched her sip the apricot-colored liquid, than twirl the stemmed glass in half circles, taking childish delight in the sloshing amber champagne. Entranced by her full red lips, he couldn't help but stare when they moved to speak. It was as if she were inviting him to kiss her. Her green eyes, her copper hair, and the unusual arch to her brow, fascinated him.

His eyes lingered on her round breasts. They were full, and strained against the white wool, outlining her obviously hardened nipples. Her body had matured since last he held her and enjoyed her nakedness. He'd watched her grow up and blossom into a beautiful young lady. But the woman she'd become, he knew nothing about.

He puffed on his pipe and wondered how to make up the lost time. For most of his adult life he had chased around the world, afraid to face love, afraid to make a commitment. He couldn't handle the thought of rejection. Even as a young boy, he found his mother's inability to tell him how much he was loved, was disconcerting. He longed to hear the words from her lips, but they never came. Since then he'd heard them from many a woman but it wasn't the same, they were always hollow and empty. The fear accompanied him, the fear of being abandoned.

"Edmund, have you heard a single word that I'm said?" She looked into his eyes.

"Of course. I can repeat every word, if you wish." He watched as a flash of humor crossed her face.

"This place is beautiful, and it's decorations," she flushed in embarrassment, "you know me and Christmas."

"Is it still your favorite time of year?"

"I'm surprised you remember! What else do you recall?"

He stood up and guided her to the dance floor. He swung her into his arms as they laughed at their missed steps.

"You know, we've never danced together. This is a first for us."

"I know." They took a few more steps.

"You're easy to follow."

He pushed her hair away from her ear and teased her with his warm breath. His gaze met hers and like a magnet generating an unbreakable force, he swept her around the dance floor.

She pulled away.

"What's going on Lily? Relax."

"Nothings going on." She moved away. "I can't catch my breath. Remember I haven't been dancing for quite some time."

His eyes probed hers for answers. "Are you sure that's all?"

"Of course. What else?"

He smiled, took her into his arms again and continued to dance, but held her at a distance. "Well I was hoping it was my nearness that left you breathless."

She smirked and smacked his shoulder. "Don't flatter yourself, it's just my age. I am going to be fifty." She giggled and walked off the dance floor. She stopped by the elegant twenty-foot Christmas tree that stood in the corner of the dining room. The entire tree sparkled with silver and crystal. At the very top of the tree was perched a white and silver angel with mechanical moving wings.

He raised their clasped hands to his lips, kissed her hand, than smiled and kissed each of her fingertips as they walked around the large evergreen, admiring the unique crystal pieces. "I'm so glad I've got you to share this with. It would be meaningless without you."

As they walked back to their table, he slipped his arm around her shoulder, giving her the feeling of a safe harbor. He hoped this moment would never end. What more could he ask for? He had explored the sights, sounds, and smells of her, and delighted in the renewal of feelings along with the excitement of discovery. They joked, laughed, and freely shared many serious moments as she unknowingly exposed the totality of who she had become. He wanted her and bulged with desire.

## CHAPTER 18

With Christmas a few days away, Lily found herself embroiled in a mountain of last minute details, the least of which was her charity food drive. Lily and Emma left the house early and drove to the truck rental office, where she had made arrangements to pick up a fourteen-footer. Her first attempt at driving a truck, three years ago, was a nerve-racking disaster. But today, without the least bit of hesitation, she climbed up into the cab and drove to the rear of the local supermarket, where the employees started to load fifty cases of canned goods that she had purchased the week before.

This was the fun part of her charity work. She sat high behind the wheel of the rented truck in jeans, no makeup, and music blasting away. She and Emma bumped along the expressway, heading to the homeless shelter on Madison Avenue.

Mike Zimmerman, the bearded director of the shelter, in his plaid shirt and corduroy pants, welcomed her with open arms and waved the volunteers to unload the truck. "It's people like you that make our holidays," his gravely voice rasped. He looked like a mountain man, "I know that when our food reserves run low I can always count on you. I'm grateful that you're helping these people get back on their feet."

Lily stood at the back of the truck and checked the cases as they were carried into the shelter's kitchen. "One of these days you have to come down and see the faces of the people. That's where it's at Lily, in their faces. Hope beams in their eyes when they know they haven't been forgotten."

"I did Mike. Remember, that's how I got hooked. The hospital needed volunteers to bring donations of cakes and bread the day before Thanksgiving, and I happened to be one of them. When I saw the families you fed, I knew I couldn't ignore this place. Ever since then. I've been one of your staunchest supporters."

"Well I don't know what we'd do without the food you and your husband donate. I'm grateful."

"I enjoy it. It's the only time I get to drive a truck and I love it. It gives me a feeling of power being behind that wheel. In the cab I sit up high and it's like you can see everything that's coming towards you, and I like that."

She laughed as Emma struggled to get back into the cab. Lily moved behind her and pushed on Emma's well-rounded backside, while the big woman pulled tried to herself up. For a moment, neither of the women could move, they were frozen in place, laughing hysterically, until Emma had tears dripping down her face. Finally one last push, one last tug, and she was finally in the cab. Emma sighed as Lily climbed into the driver's seat. "Don't hesitate to call if you need anything Mike," she called out, as she pulled the truck into traffic. On her drive home her thoughts were on Edmund, last week at the restaurant—

Over and over again she tried to remember every word he'd said, but it kept fading from memory. Nothing about her seemed to be functioning, not her legs, her mind, or heart. Edmund Valente was back in Chicago and she was with him in her thoughts. This was all she'd ever wanted, and to think that she'd spent years trying to get him out of her heart and mind. Damn him for coming back. Damn him for staying away. Was it all going to start again?

She felt the strength of his hands as he lead her lithe body across the dance floor, just like a river follows the curved stretches of banks. He pulled her tight against him and she felt the hardness of his chest against her breasts.

She felt the flutters in her stomach and tried to concentrate on driving. But she couldn't let the memory go. She was torn by conflicting emotions. Her proud bearing became stiff and stilted behind the wheel. She wanted him.

He had called this past week and she cut him short. Saying no to him was getting more and more difficult. She knew if they were alone, ever again, her desires would erupt and they'd make love. She had to avoid any compromising situation. Where he was concerned she was weak, and her only saving grace was separation.

He was joining them for Christmas dinner so she needed to shop for a gift, something special. A gold pipe lighter was appropriate, but as much as she would like to have it engraved, she didn't dare.

She realized she'd have little time to talk with him on Christmas. She'd be sure to arrange the seating for the holiday dinner and have him at the opposite end of he table, next to Pat. She'd occupy his time and keep him distracted, keep those dark eyes from watching her every move.

After she returned the truck and dropped Emma at the house, she quickly changed to go shopping. She visited a few specialty shops on Michigan Avenue, and as she walked past a bookstore his image caught her attention. In a window display his face smiled out at her from a multitude of slick book jackets that had been carefully stacked to create a display. A sign announced that he was a local writer, and a professor at Loyola, and would be conducting a special book signing on Wednesday, December 23rd.

She smiled as a feeling of happiness surged. Now the whole world will know their love story. But the irony brought her back to earth, no one in her family would know that the story was about her and Edmund.

"How do you like it?"

She was startled by the husky voice behind her and jumped back. "Oh," she gasped and turned, "you scared me half to death." She pressed her hands to her chest in hopes of slowing her racing heart. "What are you doing downtown?"

"Would you believe I'm admiring the display. Even though I've seen my name in print many times, it's something else when you see this kind of advertising. The publishers think the book is going to take off like wildfire, another BRIDGES of MADISON COUNTY. They're using the Chicago bookstores as a test to see if their expectations are on target." He peered through the plate glass at the brisk business inside. He pointed with his chin to the activity. "Yesterday they said sales were good and a lot of people were returning so I could autograph their copy."

"Congratulations. I think it's wonderful. I'd love to shout to the world that the story's about you and me, but I don't dare. I just have to stand here with a smug look on my face and a feeling of pride in my heart."

She pulled her coat tight around her body to stave off the cold winds that blew off Lake Michigan. They whipped around the corner unmercifully, causing her to catch her breath.

"As the inspiration for the greatest love story ever," he grabbed her arm and led her toward a coffee shop, "I'll buy you a cup of hot chocolate before you catch pneumonia."

In the busy restaurant they sipped the hot liquid as their conversation touched on Jim; the holidays; and Jody's health. Lily expressed her concern about having to wait till after Christmas for the appointment with the Neurologist.

"If it was serious the doctor would have called." He leaned forward.

She moved back quickly and leaned into the red upholstered chair, than slid her hand up and down over the hand-carved arm. Her shoes were off, and she moved her foot over the carpeting in search of one.

"What's wrong? Why are you backing away?"

"I've been doing a lot of thinking," she avoided his eyes and spoke to the cup in her hand, "there's a lot of things happening in my life. Henry wants that Judgeship, then there's Jim and his problem, and God only knows what the doctor is going to say about Jody. I can't deny that I'm worried about her." She paused and sipped her chocolate. "I just don't have time to deal with us." Even as she spoke the words rang hollow, and she knew it.

He put his pipe in the ashtray, and leaned forward with his hands splayed on the table as if about to stand. Concern flashed across his eyes as he whispered, "you sound as if you've written us off." His brow wrinkled as he focused his stare into her eyes. "I'm not going to let that happen. Never again. I lost you once, that was enough."

"Edmund, please, listen to me. I didn't plan to say anything before the holidays but since we're here maybe its time I did. This is probably for the best; for both of us. You have to stop calling me." She went over her thoughts.

"I can't meet you for dinner, or lunch, or breakfast, ever again. Since you've been back I haven't had a moment's peace. You're always in my thoughts, awake, and asleep. I long for the peace I had before you moved back. I try to stay busy, but it doesn't help. I find myself wanting to be with you, but we both know that's impossible. If I don't see you..." she shrugged and took a sip of hot chocolate, than clung to the cup as if it were a life preserver. She looked away from his glare.

His voice was thick and unsteady. "Look at me Lily," he slapped the table, "damn it! Look at me."

Her eyes darted around the room to see if anyone was looking, then slowly met his gaze.

"I love you Lily. I've never loved anyone but you. You're so deeply burned into my heart there's no room for anyone else." He hesitated, than recovered. "Don't do this to us. I beg you, don't do this to our future."

Her eyes misted and her lips drew into a thin line. They began to tremble as if to speak, but remained shut. After an endless moment she forced herself to speak with quiet, but firm resolve.

"There are other people to consider. Most of all, there's Jody. How would she react if she found out about us?"

"I know Jody," he pleaded, "give her a little credit. I think she'd be happy for you—"

"Then there's Henry and his Judgeship, it's something he's always wanted, and now it's within his grasp. There can't be any scandal surrounding him."

"We'll wait till after the election. Once he's elected you can get a quiet divorce—"

"You know I can't get a divorce, the church doesn't permit it. If I do, I give up my religion, the sacraments, and—"

His eyes widened in alarm. "Lily, your brother is a pastor, I'm sure he could get you a special dispensation."

He grabbed his handkerchief and wiped the single tear that rolled down her cheek. Than his voice broke. "I know you love me. I know it. Please, I beg you, we can work this out, we'll just have to be patient. There's an answer to everything and it's just alluding us at this moment."

"You're pressuring me Edmund." She pulled back and as she did, a heaviness fell across her chest, like an old scar that ached on a rainy day.

As he stared at her his face began to sag. The animation was gone, but he continued to probe. "Lily, what if, after the holidays, we don't see one another or talk to each other for a few months? My publisher wants me to go on tour. He's lined up some radio talk shows and autograph parties. All I have to do is find a substitute to take my classes and I'm gone. This way the family, especially Jody, won't be suspicious."

She offered no resistance to his idea. It had a calming effect on her frazzled nerves. This would give her time. Time to think and hopefully come to some different conclusions. A couple of months would be good, enough time to get her bearings back. Time to strengthen her resolve, and the possibility for a chance at happiness with Henry. Even though she loved Edmund she would use this time to fortify herself against any further advances. She had no intention of letting herself fall under his spell again. Romantic notions were a distraction she couldn't afford. She drew a deep breath.

"I think that's a good idea. A lot of things can happen in that time, and God only knows what's in store for us."

## CHAPTER 19

Numb from the speed that carved the events of the past few days, Lily found herself navigating through an emotional mine field, each step a potential casualty. Her anguish overcame her reason as she paced the hall at Highland Park Hospital. Henry was engrossed in a brief, Nora, dressed in black, looked as if she were going to a funeral, and was skimming through a fashion magazine. Jim waited in the hospital chapel for any news, and Pat joined Lily in pacing the hall outside the surgical waiting room.

Lily's throat was raw and dry. Why is it taking so long? They said it would only be a few hours."

"There's any number of reasons why doctors aren't accurate about the time. If they took Jody at nine, it doesn't mean they started operating at nine. When I had my gall bladder removed, I was scheduled for ten, but they actually started an hour later. Sometimes the operating rooms back up, and patients have to wait."

Pat put her arm around Lily, and squeezed. "If something were wrong you'd know, they'd come out and tell you. I realize you're not going to relax while she's still in surgery, but keep in mind, you're going have to stay calm for her sake. When Jody comes out of surgery she'll need to see your smiling face.

Tears teetered on her eyelids. "You're right, it's just the shock of it all." Her voice was weepy, as if on the verge of crying. "Jody and I were in the doctor's office just a few days ago, and within four days we've seen three different specialists, and they all concur. I still can't believe it. Jody with a brain tumor? Not my baby. She looks so healthy."

Pat remained silent as Lily continued to talk.

"It's all a big mistake. When they operate they'll find out they're wrong. There's no tumor."

Tears continued to choke at Lily as Pat tried to get her to accept the possibility that what the doctors were saying maybe, just maybe, was true. She put her hand on Lily's shoulder.

Lily swallowed hard and tried to hold back the tears.

"Please," Pat whispered, "don't put your head in the sand. Face the truth, if not for yourself then for Jody's sake. You told me they all read the MRI's, and agreed on the prognosis. You saw the shaded area on the films."

"But they can make mistakes. I've heard of cases where X-rays have been switched, and the diagnosis made on the wrong person."

"You're right, but not by three different doctors. Remember, Jody was rushed to the emergency room with a violent headache? You're the one that told me she's been losing weight and complaining about being tired. Those are some of the symptoms."

Lily's lower lip trembled as she looked at her watch again. Every nerve in her body was poised, ready to explode. If only he were here. She was quick to stop her thoughts about him. He's not important right now, Jody's the one in trouble.

"How can Jody have a malignant brain tumor that I can't even pronounce? She's so young, she's done nothing to deserve this. Why would God make her suffer like this? It's not fair." Her throat felt as though it were closing. She couldn't concentrate. She was living her worst nightmare. Her mouth felt like old paper, dry and dusty. "Assure me I'm not dreaming. Convince me this isn't real."

Pat bit her lip and struggled to control her tears. "When you see Jody being wheeled out of the operating room you'll know it's real. Just remember what the doctors told you, be prepared. Part of her head will be shaved and the rest, bandaged. Try to keep in mind what the nurses explained about the tubes in her nose and mouth, as well as all the machines she'll be hooked up to. You have to be strong for her. If you break down, she's going to think the worst. You don't want to do that to her, do you?"

Lily sniffled than blew her nose. "You're right, I have to pull myself together. Let's go." Without a word between them she grabbed Pat's arm, dragged her into the elevator, and rode down to the lobby. When the doors opened she pulled Pat across the lobby, out the front door, and across the street to the drug store. Lily stopped at the counter, bought a pack of cigarettes, walked outside, and lit up. She inhaled deep and started to cough.

"It's been awhile since you gave those up, you'd better take it easy with the first few."

"You mean you're not going to chide me for smoking?"

"Hell no, not at a time like this. If it were me I'd have a flask in my purse. Whatever gets you through this Lily, do it. When this is over you can always quit again. If the nicotine calms you down, go for it."

Lily continued to pull on the long thin cigarette, hoping for the numbing relief the nicotine would provide. She continued to smoke as they walked back across the street, then a few quick puffs before putting it out and going back inside the hospital.

As she approached the waiting room Dr. Berner, still in his green scrubs, approached her. He wasn't smiling. She shuddered and felt Pat grab for her hand. Henry stepped behind her and put his hands on her shoulders.

The surgeon explained that he only removed part of the tumor, the portion that was causing the headaches. The remainder of the tumor was in an area of the brain that was inoperable. The hairs on the nape of Lily's neck tingled. Her stomach lurched as if on a fast descending elevator.

He explained that Jody would be in ICU for at least twenty-four hours, and referenced a meeting he would schedule with them, in his hospital office, as soon as Jody was stronger. At that time a course of treatment would be decided upon, with careful consideration given to all options.

The blood drained from Lily's face. Her knees began to shake, and her legs went limp. "You left cancer in my baby's head? How could you?" Her skin was clammy, her temples were throbbing like a jackhammer. Lily turned when she heard Nora gasp.

"She's going to be all right? Isn't she?" Lily took a deep breath. "Is she going to die?" She stared into the surgeon's ice blue eyes. To lend her body support, Henry pulled her against him.

The doctor's hands were in his pockets, his shoulders hunched forward, his voice, void of emotion. He sighed. "Only God has those answers. That's why I want to meet with the entire family. We have to treat this as a family illness."

She leered at him, anxious to understand the meaning behind his words. Swallowing the sobs that rose in her throat, she looked up. "What are the chances that the tumor will begin to grow again?"

Doctor Berner took Lily by the arm and escorted her and Henry into the doctor's lounge. "It will grow again, but there's a procedure that we follow in cases like this. A conference is set with a group of specialists. They'll be an Oncologist, a Diagnostic Radiologist, a Pathologist, and the Radiation Therapist. Of course I'll be there as well, along with the both of you, and Jody. It's through conferences like these that we decide the course of treatment best suited to the patient. We'll have to wait until Jody is a little stronger." He quickly excused himself and acknowledged he'd be in touch.

An unaccustomed pain shot below her breast. Lily turned when Henry shuddered and drew a deep breath like he'd been struck in the face. Her own breath came in shallow gasps. She felt his arms around her as she continued to cry.

A hint of a tear crept into Henry's eyes, but he could only stare. She'd never seen him upset about anything, but she knew this had taken him by surprise. He finally cleared his throat, and found the words to take control of the situation. "Why don't you and Pat meet me in the hospital cafeteria. I'm going to send your mother home, there's nothing more she can do here. I'll look for Jim and let him know what's happening."

Lily met Pat in the hall. "Come outside with me, I need a cigarette." Lily took a few deep breaths, wiped her face with Henry's handkerchief, and continued to smoke. After taking a few deep drags she started to cough than glanced at Pat. "The doctor never answered my question about Jody, he never did say if she's going to make it."

"How can anyone say when we're going to die. Doctors have been wrong, more than they've been right. I don't think they say too much nowadays."

"Don't kid yourself, they sure as hell do. Only they use big words, like prognosis, inoperable, and medical terms that I can't even spell."

"You told me he'd have all the experts in for a meeting. In the meantime why don't you write down all your questions, then ask the experts when they're all together." Lily quickly lit another cigarette and wandered aimlessly around the parking lot, constantly checking her watch. She felt so helpless and wanted to scream. Then for the hundredth time she whispered a silent prayer to St. Jude. Now all she could do was wait. But for what? To see if her baby was going to die? Somewhere deep with her being her soul began to weep, it knew the truth.

After a few minutes she looked at her watch again, Henry and Jim would be waiting. She stepped on the cigarette and hurried back into the hospital. "Where's Jim?" Lily looked around the cafeteria. "I thought you were going to get him?"

"I looked all over the hospital, went back to the chapel, but he's no where to be found. Maybe he had to go back to the parish, a previous appointment or something. I'll call him later and inform him of the diagnosis. I sent your mother home. I told her we'd call tonight. Please Lily, don't forget to phone, she's very upset about this."

"I'll call her," Pat said.

Lily nodded and sat back in the metal cafeteria chair. The sound of clanging trays, joking staff, and talking visitors infuriated her. She turned and glared at them. How dare they joke at a time like this? My daughter has cancer. How can the nurses enjoy their lunch.

Lily weighed the structure of events, then winced and started to grind her teeth. Hoping for some reassurances, she started to question Henry. "Do you think she's going to be all right?" Her hands were clenched. "You're the one that deals in facts. Tell me! Do you honestly think Jody is going to be all right?"

"I can't tell you that, I'm not a doctor. I don't deal with the unknown like the medical community does. But one thing I do know, whatever happens, we can handle it." He covered her hand with his.

She jerked it away. The sharp anger in her voice bordered on hysteria. "I don't want to handle it, Henry. Do you hear me. I don't want to handle it." She folded her arms and her body became ramrod stiff. "I want my daughter to be well, to be free of cancer. I want her to live." She started sobbing again. "I want to hold her in my arms just like I use to when she was little. I want to take away her pain, and assure her that everything will be all right." She glared at him.

"What do you want from me? I'm hurting just as much as you. You aren't the only parent, I raised her too. Why are you angry with me? I'm not the enemy, the cancer is what's destroying her brain."

Lily's eyes flashed. "With all the modern-day shit that we invent, why the hell can't doctors find a cure for brain tumors. All the money that people give for research, and for what?" Her nostrils flared, and she felt weak and vulnerable, in the face of that dreaded word. She licked her lower lip, and managed to quell her anger. She looked around, finally aware that people were staring.

Embarrassed, she took a few bites out of her sandwich, and kept checking the large clock on the cafeteria wall. Only thirty minutes had gone by. It was torture having to wait to see her daughter. "Damn it, why is it taking so long for her to come out of recovery?"

"Lily, don't swear, it doesn't help anything."

She glared at him. "It helps me and I'm going to say shit, damn, and hell whenever I feel like, whether you like it or not. Shit, shit, shit."

Pat's eyes flew open. Henry stood and walked out of the cafeteria.

Lily turned to Pat. "What was that look for? What did I say?"

"I don't know if you're aware, but you just as much as told your husband you were going to do what you wanted, weather he liked it or not."

Lily smiled. For the first time in their marriage she'd told Henry no. "And you know what, it felt good. Let him go off and pout, I don't give a shit. I've got Jody to worry about, and I don't have the time or the inclination to cater to his selfish whims." She threw down her napkin on the half eaten sandwich. "C'mon let's go, I want to wait for Jody in her room."

The smell of disinfectants reminded her of the days when her mother washed the bathrooms with Lysol. The stark white walls, the array of monitors, and the number of patients shocked Lily's senses when she walked into the IC unit. As much as the doctors had warned her, and as many details as Pat recounted, it wasn't enough to prepare her for what she saw.

The massive white bandages on her daughter's head struck her immediately. She grabbed the doorframe to keep her legs from buckling. All the wires, leading from Jody's chest to monitors behind the bed, overwhelmed her. Bags of Glucose and blood, hung from a stainless-steel tripod, and dripped their life force into her daughter's arms and hand. A tube protruded from Jody's mouth and another from her nose. Her blue-veined eyelids were deathly still, her breathing erratic.

As she approached Jody's bed a shrill sound pierced the silence. Something had triggered an alarm. Lily jumped, her heart stuck in her throat. Nurses pushed by her to Jody's side. Lily froze as she watched the team frantically work on Jody. Then they stepped back. A wire on the heart monitor had come loose. False alarm. Lily's legs turned to Jell-O as she struggled to remain standing. She swallowed hard and moved to Jody's side. Cloaked in helplessness, tears began to roll down her cheeks as she stood by her daughter's bed.

She slowly reached for Jody's hand, careful to avoid the IV. Henry came in, pulled a chair near the bed, and motioned Lily to sit down. Seated next to her daughter, she started to smooth the few strands of damp hair off Jody's forehead. She studied her daughter, a portion of the tumor was still in her head, she thought. The doctor's said it would grow again, like some monster eating up her brain. How can something so ugly be inside someone so beautiful?

Lily looked at Henry when Jody moaned, than jumped to her feet and bent over her. "Jody, it's Mom. I'm here, Honey."

Jody's eyes opened slowly, a weak smile formed on her face. Tears glistened on Lily's pale face when Jody squeezed her hand. She leaned over and kissed her on the cheek then watched as Jody fell back into unconsciousness.

She looked at her daughter's hand. Even asleep, Jody clung to her, like a person awash in the sea clings to a life preserver. Lily leaned over the bed and whispered to her sleeping child. "Don't worry Baby, I'll be here when you wake up. Sleep in peace, God knows you need it."

Pat tiptoed to Lily's side. "I'm going to leave now. I'll be back tonight. If there's anything you need, call."

"Thanks for being here." She hugged her friend.

Jody stirred and slowly opened her eyes. She tried to move her lips.

"Don't try and talk, you have a tube in your throat. The nurse said they'll remove it shortly, so just close your eyes and go back to sleep."

Jody drifted off again. The next hours passed quickly and brought a constant parade of nurses checking Jody's vital signs. Through it all, Lily never let go of her daughter's hand. She was convinced Jody could feel her presence and she wanted her to know that she was at her side.

As Lily sat at her daughter's bedside her thoughts carried her back to the time when she first felt the light tickles in her stomach as Jody announced her presence inside her womb. The sheer delight, of carrying Edmund's child, overwhelmed her. Then as the months passed, the nudges became kicks, until finally her baby was ready to enter the world, screaming at the doctors for disturbing her comfortable surroundings. Henry was at her side, but that didn't prevent the tears she shed because of Edmunds absence at his daughters birth. Henry assumed the tears were those of joy, and acknowledged his happiness at having a daughter.

As she emerged out of her memories, reality hit. Oh my god! Edmund. He doesn't know about Jody! This is his child laying here, his flesh and blood, with a brain tumor. What to do? A sense of panic welled up inside her. He had to know.

His publisher would know his schedule. She'd call Edmund, wherever he was, and tell him about Jody. She knew he'd come for both their sakes. And God know she needed his assurances and comfort to get through whatever lie ahead. But she couldn't let him know that Jody was his daughter.

Lily spent an agonizingly sleepless night in the armchair, never moving from Jody's side, and thankful the tube in her throat had been removed. When morning came, two nurses removed the tube from her nose. The only tubes left were the IV and the morphine machine.

What a god sent idea, that pain machine. No nurse to call, no shot to kill the pain, only a button to push when the pain became unbearable.

Jody smiled as her mother gently washed her face. Her voice was scratchy. "That feels good Mom, so soothing," she glanced at the blankets in the chair, "looks like you spent the night here. You didn't have to, but I'm glad you did. I felt better knowing you were here. I wasn't afraid to go to sleep because I knew you wouldn't let anything happen to me."

"That's what mothers are for." She turned Jody's face toward her. "I'm here to look after my baby, and I'm glad to see you haven't outgrown your need for me."

"I don't think I ever will, Mom. I love you."

"Your father was here most of the day, so was Grandma, Uncle Jim, and Pat, the whole gang was rooting for you."

Jody's voice sounded fragile, "Mom I know the doctor talked to you. What did he say? No bullshit, because if you don't tell me, I'll find out when he comes in to see me."

Lily sat down on the edge of the bed, careful not to disturb the Heparin Lock in her daughter's hand. "He told us that as soon as you're feeling better, probably within the next few days, he's going to schedule a conference with a group of specialists, including your Dad and I. That's when they'll outline a course of treatment."

Jody stared at her mother. "But what did he say about this head of mine?" She ran her fingers across the bandages on the left side of her head.

Lily took a deep breath as helplessness and dread swept over her as she attempted to repeat the doctor's words.

Agony spread across her daughter's face as her brows furrowed deep within her forehead. Her mouth went slack and her eyes widened. Then she started to tremble. "You mean they didn't get it all?" Her voice choked when she started to scream. "Do you know what that means?"

"It doesn't mean a damn thing. You'll probably have to get some treatments to get this thing shrunk, or eliminated, or whatever they do with tumors." Lily bit her cheek and a funny taste permeated her mouth. As she moved her tongue around her mouth she realized, that in her effort to stop her tears, she'd bitten down so hard that her cheek had started to bleed. She swallowed the bitter taste of her bloody saliva and prayed for strength.

Fear swirled wildly in Jody's eyes. "Mom, I'm not a child. I know that cancerous tumors continue to grow. Once they open you up and the air gets to them, the growth is accelerated." Jody shuddered.

Lily reached out and held her in her arms. "Listen to me, and listen good. This isn't the only hospital, and these aren't the only doctors. There are a lot of options available to us." Lily watched Jody struggle with the enormity of the implication and silently willed her own body to relax.

Suddenly Jody shrieked, "Mom, I'm scared. I don't want to die. Help me, please."

Lily drew her daughter into her arms. Her breathing became shallow and quick as she rocked her back and forth. They were reaching beyond their own understanding for something, anything, some force that would bind them together. Forever. "I love you and I will be here with you, no matter what. I'll do everything within my power to get you well."

Jody lay back on her pillow.

"Let's wait to see what the doctors have to say. Then we'll know for sure what we're facing. Okay?"

Jody nodded, then turned solemn and silent.

Lily knew her well enough to know Jody wasn't taking her word for anything. She knew panic was rioting within her. And her daughters silent stare was distant and unblinking as if in a trance. Lily pulled her chair closer to the bed and sat quietly at her side, allowing her daughter the solitude of her thoughts. Jody needed time. Maybe God would have mercy on this child and give her the strength she would need to handle this life-altering situation.

A team of doctors walked into the room and Lily left her daughters side to wait in the hall. She heard loud talking, then mumbling at the nurse's station. It was evident they were changing shifts and it was the first time she became aware of time. It was after three, and she hadn't slept or eaten since yesterday noon. Pangs of hunger turned into loud growls in her empty stomach.

The doctors' left, and Lily hurried back in. The nurse was washing Jody so Lily slipped into the bathroom and looked into the mirror. She was pale, and there were dark circles under her eyes. Yesterday's makeup was gone, except for some smeared mascara, creating even darker shadows. She washed her face, brushed her hair, put on some fresh lipstick, and walked back to Jody's bedside.

Jody sounded tired. "I'm glad somebody looks better than I do. You looked like you had been through the wars, but now you're gorgeous." Lily's stomach started to growl again, and Jody encouraged her to get something to eat.

Lily agreed. She smoothed Jody's blankets and fluffed her pillows. She kissed her daughter, then dashed outside to grab a quick smoke. When the nicotine high had cleared her head, she went back into the hospital cafeteria, where she sat and nibbled on a sandwich. She was tired but fought her body's craving for sleep, hoping that a second cup of caffeine would give her a needed lift. A hand touched her shoulder and jolted her from her thoughts.

"I didn't mean to startle you," Pat apologized, "I just came from Jody's room. She said I'd find you here."

"Thank God, I need someone to talk to. How was Jody when you left?"

"Her eyes were red and puffy, like she'd been crying, but other then that, she seemed fine. I brought her flowers and we talked for awhile, then she said she wanted to rest, so I came down to find you."

"I had to tell her that the tumor was still in her head." Lily shuddered. "She cried like a baby when I told her and begged me to help. I've never felt so helpless in all my life. I'd give my life for her, switch places in a heartbeat. I'll never forget the look on her face when she found out they left some of the tumor in her brain. When I think about it now, I shudder."

"She needs time to digest what's happening, and so do you. None of us were prepared for this. We all need time to adjust. Have you told Edmund yet?"

"I can't! He's out of town on a book tour. I don't know where to reach him."

"Not to worry. When I go home I'll call the publisher and see if they can track him down."

"He's crazy about Jody, and he'd be angry if I didn't try to reach him. If you could do that it would help a lot. I don't think I'm in any state to try and find him." A sadistic laugh overcame her.

"You know what this reminds me of? Twenty-five years ago, frantically trying to locate him to tell him I was pregnant, and here I am again, trying to find him." Her laugh was almost sadistic. "Nothing changes, does it?"

"You can't blame him for not being here. Remember you told him you didn't want to see him. He had no choice but to go on tour. What did you expect him to do?"

"I don't know, this is 'Deja voux'. And I don't like it."

"I'll bet when I find him, and tell him what's happening, he'll be on the first plane home. I know it."

"You're probably right." Lily stood up and grabbed her purse. "Let's go, I want to see Jody. Then I've got to go home and get some sleep before I fall on my face. Henry will be here soon so I won't have to worry about leaving Jody alone."

"Lily, she's not alone. This is one of the best hospitals in the area, and her room is shouting distance from the nurse's station. If she needs anything, they're right there."

"You're right, I have to let go. I have to trust that God will take care of her, but it's so hard."

# CHAPTER 20

The days passed in a blur. Every waking hour was spent at her daughter's bedside. Henry cancelled his speaking engagements so he could spend time with Jody. Lily kept trying to reach Jim, but to no avail, and was concerned about his silence, but she had to focus on Jody, after all, Jim was a big boy, and could take care of himself. Jody was the one who needed her now.

Finally the day of the consultation with the medical experts arrived. Surely they'd have some good news, there'd been a mistake, no malignant brain tumor. Oh what a joy at the thought, but just in case, she had a laundry list of questions she needed answers to.

Henry and Lily wheeled Jody into the conference room. Three doctors, seated at a long conference table, in the middle of the room, were scanning charts, and acknowledged their arrival with a nod. Lily scanned the room for Dr. Berner, but he hadn't arrived yet. Two young women in white lab coats walked in with additional charts, and sat across from the other doctors. One physician clipped six head x-rays to the lighted wall panels. As they were being seated Dr. Berner and a nurse walked into the conference room.

He mouthed polite salutations to the Halstons and went directly to the wall of X-rays. He pointed out to the meeting participants, along with the Halstons, the inoperable areas of the brain, and explained the dangers, and why it was inaccessible to a surgeon's knife. He moved to a plastic mock up of the brain and started disassembling the myriad of parts, pointing to the parts of the brain that were affected by the tumor. When he finished, he introduced the other participants seated around the table, then sat down.

Lily, Jody, and Henry were silent as they listened to the expert medical staff discuss the different ways to attack the cancer, talking as if they weren't even there. Each suggested different approaches, but the bottom line didn't change. Her condition was terminal.

The team of specialists never blinked an eye as they conversed about the prognosis, options, and treatments: radialtherapy; chemotherapy; pressure on nerve tracts; various drugs; finally zeroing-in on how best to slow the growth. They suggested Jody volunteer for clinical trials. No guarantee's, but something might come of the new medications, all of which were still in experimental stages.

The doctor's words echoed in Lily's head: physical and mental deterioration, deafness, blindness along with personality changes were all discussed and agreed on as inevitable, when the tumor began to grow again. Convulsions and paralysis were possible side effects she might have to contend with. In the final analysis, with all the years of expertise in the room, no one knew the exact course this tumor would take.

The doctors were a fine tuned act, and made sure they said the right words, at exactly the right time. Each specialist spoke when Dr. Berner signaled, and not before. They artfully dodged the one question that Jody posed.

"How long?"

They looked at each other, none of them dared to venture a guess. Dr. Berner cleared his throat, then spoke in a slow precise manner. "Six months, twelve at best," to the best of his professional judgment she'd have four to six months of almost perfect health. Then as the tumor grew larger, the headaches would return. Eventually she would lose control of her limbs, and be bed-ridden.

The meeting was adjourned as quickly as it was called to order, leaving the Halston's stunned and speechless and attempting to deal with the news. Jody spun her wheelchair around to face her parents. Her hands skimmed the wheels and grabbed them hard as she could until her knuckles turned white. Her chin sunk to her chest and she started to whimper like a baby. She raised her head and looked at her mother through tear stained eyes.

"Why, Mom? Why me? I don't want to die, I'm too young. They didn't give me much time. Six months?" She swallowed hard. "It's too short." She clasped her hands in her lap and lowered her head again. "I'm scared!" She looked to her mother, then to her father with the frightened look of a young child trying to understand what was happening to her.

"Mom! Dad! Please do something," she sobbed, "help me. I don't know what to do?"

Lily knelt down and embraced her daughter. "Sshhh..." she stroked her hair then kissed her on the forehead, "it'll be alright." Lily glanced up at the ceiling and squeezed her eyes shut in hopes of stopping the tears from running down her cheeks. The pain in her heart felt like a knife had been thrust into it. "We'll figure out something. I don't know what, but we will." She put her hands on Jody's cheeks and wiped away the tears.

Henry put his hand on his daughter's shoulder. Jody grabbed at him as if she was drowning, and he was her life preserver. He cleared his throat.

"First of all, we need time to digest what we've been told. I'm going to the office and get on the phone to the country's top neurosurgeons, and the Ketering Cancer Institute as well. I'll find out all I can about the new drugs, as you know, I do have a few connections in the medical field." He started pacing as if giving an opening statement to a jury.

"I'm not taking anyone's word about anything. If we have to, we'll travel around the world until we find someone who can help."

Jody looked up, grabbed her robe, and wiped her tears with it. "First off, young lady," Henry cleared his throat again, "we have to get you home. You'll stay with us, your room is ready."

"I've had a day or two to think about the 'what ifs' and I've made some decisions. Dr. Berner said he'd release me tomorrow. I'll go home with you, but when I finish with the chemo and radiation, I'm going back to my apartment—"

"I won't hear of it. You can't stay alone. You're—"

"I'm what Mother? Say it," Jody glared, "don't beat around the bush. I don't have the gift of time." She wheeled herself to the door and spun around. "Didn't you hear what they said? I'm going to die. I want to spend what little time I have left, living. When my body no longer responds like it should, I promise I'll come home, that's when I'll need you to take care of me."

Jody started to cry again. Lily swallowed hard. She had used up all the words she knew to comfort her daughter. What could a mother say to a daughter who has just been told she has less than a year to live. For once, Lily couldn't make it better. All she could do was pray. Pray for a miracle. Surely God would hear her pleas. After all, he was a good and just God. She paused in her rampant thoughts.

Then why did He let her little girl get this terrible cancer? Why not someone else's daughter? Why not one of those girls on drugs? Why not one of the prostitutes that walk the streets? No one would miss them. Why Jody?

Henry took the lead and pushed the wheelchair back to Jody's room. No one spoke. When they finally reached her room, Lily helped Jody into bed and started to pull up a chair.

"Mom, don't be hurt, but I want to be alone. I've got a lot of thinking to do. I have to set some priorities. I know you have a lot to deal with as well. Please go home before I break down again. I really need to be alone."

Reluctant to adhere to the request, Lily and Henry finally left their daughter alone. Once outside the hospital, Lily forgot that Henry was beside her and lit a cigarette.

"What are you doing?" his brows furrowed in surprise, "I thought you gave those up years ago."

"So!" She took a deep drag and let the smoke out her nose. "I need them now."

She turned, continued to puff on her cigarette, and headed toward her car. When she reached the Mercedes, she leaned against the side and continued to smoke as he drove away. Suddenly she heard the screech of brakes and jumped out of the way, as a car pulled alongside her. Edmund!

Tears brimmed in her eyes when she saw the anguish on his face. He jumped out of the car, threw his arms around her, and drew her close. She shivered in the warmth of his arms and pressed her cheek to his chest. She felt the beat of his heart as it pounded wildly against her cheek. She pressed closer.

"I'm glad you're here, this has been a terrible nightmare. You can't imagine what's been happening."

He stroked her hair and whispered words of comfort. "Shh, Pat told me everything," he moved his hands across her arms, "you're shivering! Let's get out of here. Follow me." He helped her into her car, leaned across the steering wheel, and brushed his lips across hers.

"We can talk at the house. You're no longer alone, I'm here to stay, no matter what."

Emotionally and physically exhausted, she sank into the couch and watched him build a fire, stoking it till the orange and yellow flames leaped high into the blackened chimney. He set mugs of steaming hot chocolate and cookies on the coffee table in front of her. She kicked off her shoes, curled her legs under her, and grasped the hot mug in her cold hands. As the blood started to flow through her fingers she sipped the hot liquid.

"Is it all right to leave your book tour? I wasn't sure if I should call you?"

His voice was thick and unsteady. "Honey, for God's sake, I had to come. These past few months I've gotten to know Jody and I love her as if she were my own. She's one of my favorite people." He took out his pipe and lit it. "It's been less then a year since I lost Christine, and I can still remember that feeling of devastation. I had to be here for you, to share this sorrowful moment."

"Edmund, why is this happening?" she sighed, her eyes leaden in their sockets.

"I drove myself nuts trying to find answers to questions like that when my wife and daughter were killed. All I've discovered is that God doesn't answer 'why' questions. And He's not about to. He expects us to have enough faith to trust Him. Our sorrow forces us to reach deep within ourselves to achieve some peace."

She put her drink on the table, covered her face with her hands, and tried to quell the onslaught of tears. Edmund pulled her to him and held her tenderly in his arms. His steady gaze swept her along a river of emotions as she struggled against the need to be closer to him. The compassion in his eyes touched her soul. His warm lips brushed hers like a feather, gentle yet exciting. In his eagerness to comfort her, his hungry lips covered hers. Then he kissed her eyelids and tilted her head as his hot lips slithered down to the pulsing hollow at the base of her throat, forcing a moan to escape her lips. His mouth covered hers again and left her on fire.

Lost in the sanctuary of his arms, all thoughts of Jody were suspended in her building passion, as the feeling of impending loss was overcome in her love for him. Beside the shadows of the dancing flames, he eased her to the floor.

Eager to respond to the urgency of his exploratory kisses, her body ached for the long denied touch of her beloved. She was swept away by the touch of his lips on her ivory flesh as he began to explore her body. His lips moved down her neck and shoulders, and she melted in his arms, like butter in the noonday sun. His naked body melded with hers and in that moment they were suspended in time.

Like a blind man exploring new terrain, he touched every part of her body. She was eager to follow the uninhibited dictates of her body. "You knew I'd come back to share your heart break."

She nodded, slid her arms around his neck, and pulled his head down so their lips could meet again. With his steamy flesh next to hers, she raked her nails down his back, grabbed his buttocks, and pulled him on top of her.

"Yeesss," he whispered as he entered her warmth.

She wrapped her legs around him in a fleshy vise and began to move beneath him. Her willing body cried out for his love and he responded by wrapping his arms around her body and gazing down at her. Her hips thrust upward and met his downward plunge as her body swallowed him even deeper.

As quickly as their passion had overtaken them, it subsided. She was finally empty of physical desire and lay basking in the glow of spiritual unity, filled with love for the man who lay on top of her. She clung to him and started to breathe fast and hard as his passion began to rise again.

In the shadow of death they experienced the great miracle of love. Did the Angel of Death have to be present in order to bring the Angel of Love out of hiding? To know the depths of despair and the heights of ecstasy within hours of each other was unbelievable.

Still reeling from their passion, she fought to stabilize her emotions; her marriage on one side; Jody and Edmund on the other. As they lay on the living room floor, their moist flesh touched as she turned to watch the rise and fall of his chest in peaceful slumber. She clutched the blanket against her naked body and fell into a blissful sleep. After a short time she opened her eyes and started to trace her fingers across his chest. She burrowed closer to his warmth, and pondered what his first words would be. Would he tell her he loved her or speak of the pleasures she brought him? Would he speak of the love they shared, and the beauty of her body?

His eyes still closed, he began to nuzzle against her.

"I wasn't sleeping." He opened his eyes and turned to face her. His hand cupped her breast. "I'm almost afraid to open my eyes, afraid that it's all a dream." He lifted up on his elbow and rested his head in his hand.

"Lily," he pushed her damp hair away from her eyes, "I didn't plan this. My heart was aching and I took you in my arms in hopes of comforting you. I love you, and I needed to show that love, especially when you were hurting."

"I wanted you Edmund. Every part of me cried out for you. I needed to feel alive. These past few days I've been in another dimension, almost dead. At times I'm here, and then it seems like I'm gone. It's hard to explain, but thanks to you, I can feel again, and I hurt. I hurt for me, I hurt for Jody, and I hurt for you." She shivered and pressed closer to him.

"I don't know how to stop this terrible ache."

Edmund clasped her hand and began to kiss her fingertips. "Take my love and use it as a healing force. Let me be your strength, it will help you through this. Please, let me be a part of that sorrow."

She stared at him. "How do I share my pain with you? Too many years have passed between us. I've forgotten how to share anything."

"It wasn't like that a moment ago," he touched her, "you willingly shared yourself with me. Now share your feelings. It's easy, just let them out."

She didn't want to talk about her feelings. All she wanted was to bask in the afterglow of his love, but he wanted to know what she was thinking and feeling. He was asking to look into her very soul.

"Tell me what's really going on up there." He leaned over and kissed her head. "Let me inside so I can really get to know you. Don't hide from me. I want to know every part of you, every thought, every emotion."

She rolled over and turned away.

He moved closer and held her hands.

"Why are you pushing me for answers," she whined, "what do you want from me?"

"I want to know you, really know you. How you sleep, what you look like in the morning, what you're thinking."

"Please Edmund, give me some space. I'm not used to sharing any part of myself. There are things about me that have to remain secret. If not, we'll both be sorry we went down this path."

He pulled her to a sitting position and brushed the hair from her eyes. "I can't let it go. I feel there's still a wall between us, and I have to find out what it is." He looked away, than turned back. "Is it Henry?"

Lily shook her head.

"Then it has to be Jody." He squinted, tilted his head, and stared into her eyes. "What aren't you telling me about her? Is there something more that the doctors told you? Is it something about you? Tell me. Whatever it is, I can help." Far back in his eyes there was a hint of dismay. Desperation chilled his face and was indicative of an imagination running rampant.

Lily thought a moment, then spoke. "Jody is your daughter." The dreaded words were finally out.

Edmund's mouth moved, like a fish out of water and gasping for air.

"What? What did you say?" He shot up. "What are you talking about?" His eyes darkened as the truth of Lily's words seeped into his soul.

How could she have said the forbidden words? Why did she utter the truth? Shocked and speechless, she fought her way back to the moment, only to realize he was waiting, waiting for her to clarify her words.

She was horrified at her unsolicited confession. Her eyes filled with tears as she nodded confirmation.

Edmunds eyes glazed over and remained riveted on Lily as he began to back away. He slipped into his pants and began to pace in front of the fireplace.

Her heart was pounding as she put her clasped hands over her mouth as if to stop any further utterances from slipping out. The fire flickered, and cast ominous shadows across his face that mirrored a gamut of emotions. He continued to pace without even so much as a glance toward Lily.

"Talk to me, say something, anything."

Then as abruptly as he'd gotten up, he sat down in front of her. She felt herself shrinking from the coldness coming from his eyes. "You're telling me that Jody's my daughter? How could that be?" He shook his head like a man dazed from sleep. "You just told me that you slept with Henry, and you had to get married because he got you pregnant."

"I told you only part of the truth. When you and I made love, that one time, I got pregnant. Why do you think I was so desperate to find you?" She shivered and wrapped her arms around herself. "I did everything humanly possible, God knows I tried. I was pregnant," her voice dropped to a whisper, "and you were nowhere to be found. I even thought about having an abortion." She shook her head at the shocked look on his face. "That's right. But I couldn't do it. I'd already sinned, and to kill our baby, this life I was carrying inside of me, would be more offensive to God then what we'd done. I couldn't live with that. I even prayed that God would take me then I wouldn't have to make any decisions."

She brushed the blanket across her face in an effort to dry her tears. "The only plan I came up with was to find Henry and trick him into going to bed with me. Three weeks later I told him I was pregnant. And the rest, you know."

His expression grew still. His eyes, hooded like those of a hawk, grew dangerously dark. Lily shivered. All he could do was gape in stunned silence. He couldn't hide his feelings, he was never good at that, and continued to stare at her. His lower lip started to curl with disgust. His face grew hard.

She looked into his eyes, that only moments before had expressed tenderness. Now there was anger spewing from them. He leaped up and walked around the couch. He fell back onto the settee and pierced the silence with an agonizing cry. Then he hunched over and wept out loud.

Suddenly she felt her nakedness, and quickly covered her body with her coat, then dashed to the couch to comfort him. She wrapped her arms around him and cradled his sobbing body. Slumped over, his head on her chest, he clung to her like a drowning man. She started to massage his shoulders, then held him close and allowed his grief to run its course.

The sobbing finally subsided. His muffled words drifted into the room. "This can't be happening. It just can't be. God wouldn't be so cruel as to take another daughter from me." He clutched her tighter. "That would be the cruelest of things to happen to any human being. I don't deserve it, I've always tried to do the best that I knew how. I never purposely hurt anyone." A moment of silence passed between them.

"Maybe this is the way He's making me pay for running away from responsibility." Without warning he sat upright, his eyes rolled with wild furor. He grabbed Lily's arms in a vise-like grip, and started to shake her. "You had no intention of ever telling me she was my daughter," he hissed, "did you?" His face was inches from hers. "Answer me, damn it." He shook her again. "Did you?" He finally let go and moved away.

"Were you going to let her die without ever telling me she was mine? How could you rob me of the joy of knowing and loving her as a father." He pulled her so their faces were inches apart. "You weren't going to tell me, were you?" He pushed her away.

Lily started to shout, "I didn't know what I was going to do. I hadn't heard from you in twenty-five years and all of a sudden you walk back into my life. Did you expect everything to be the way it was before you left? Well life doesn't work that way. It moves on. I had a daughter to consider." She ran to the couch and knelt in front of him. She put her hands on his knees.

"Understand," she pleaded, "she was uppermost in my mind. Do you blame me for not wanting to disturb her world."

"What are you going to do about...?"

Her words faltered and died on her lips. Her heart felt the grip of his steady, cold, gaze. The tension between them increased with frightening intensity. He was changing before her eyes, a volcano on the verge of erupting.

He gripped her wrists, moved her hands from his knees, and stood up. He put on his shirt, and his hands started to tremble as he fussed with the buttons. "How many times are you going to lie to me? What else haven't you told me?" His cold words were like a slap in the face.

Silent in the face of his accusations, she could only stare at him. Then, as though someone lit a fuse within her, she exploded. "How dare you!" Her face turned red, and she started to tremble. "How dare you use that tone with me. Yes, I lied, I lied in order to survive. I lied to give our daughter a name and a decent life. I knew Henry could give her the things you couldn't. He was responsible, and provided a stable and secure environment for her to grow in."

"How the hell do you know what she needed? You could have at least tried to get in touch with me?" His words were like a stiletto that pierced her heart.

She snarled and crossed her arms. "Really? Where Edmund? Let's see. Mexico, Vietnam, or Timbuktu? Who the hell knew where you were?" She moved closer, and stood with her hand on her hips. "Before you throw your righteous indignation in my face you bastard, remember you had every opportunity to call me. You knew Henry's last name. You knew how to get in touch with Jim, after all you ran into him in Vietnam. Damn it, don't you dare accuse me of anything. I did what I had to in order to protect our child."

He held his hand out as if patting the air. "I'm leaving before we say things to one another that we'll regret," his voice was cold and distant as he finished dressing, "I have to be alone. I've got a lot of shit to sort through. When I get back, don't be here. If you only knew," he said in a choked voice, "what holding you in my arms meant to me." He looked away as he searched for the right words.

"I thought I knew you, I thought I loved you. But that's all been blown to hell. I have to step back and see where I stand in all this." He hesitated, then in an acid voice he yelled, "go home Lily. Go home to Henry where you belong. You could never feel safe and secure with me. Isn't that right?"

"Edmund! You can't leave. Not now. I love you." Her arms were outstretched.

With had one hand on the doorknob he turned and smiled. "Boy you can turn it on and off like a light switch. Now you've decided that you love me. To quote you, 'what about Henry and Jody?' What about them Lily?"

"This is about us. You and me," she screamed, "leave them out of this." Tears coursed down her face.

He shook his head, "don't you understand? What you fail to realize is that they're already in it. They're a part of our life, and I'll be damned if I know what to do about it. I've got to get the hell out of here." He pulled the door open and rushed out.

The cold air rushed into the room and Lily started to shiver. What if he decides to tell Jody? Would he do that? She had to stop him. She couldn't let him tell her, not now that she was fighting for her life. She took a deep breath and forced herself to calm down. Edmund wouldn't do that. He wouldn't do anything to hurt Jody. Now that he knew she was his daughter, he'd do all within his power to keep her alive. He loved her.

She returned home to a darkened house and was glad Henry had retired early. She went directly to her room and tried to analyze all that had happened. Later that night, in the privacy of her own bedroom, she wrote:

*My Dearest Edmund,*

*I'm sorry I never told you that Jody was your daughter, I regret that more then you'll ever know. If only there had been some word from you, some gesture that you still cared. But in all honesty, I don't know if I would have left Henry.*

*I'm ashamed to admit it but I do like the comfortable life that he's provided for Jody and me. Through the years, every thing has been fine till you showed up and disturbed my very soul. I knew I loved you, and if I were really honest with myself, I'd have to tell you that I've never stopped loving you. Not for one minute did the flame of love ever die. I may have buried it but, it was still there.*

*I've done some things in my life that I'm not particularly proud of and not telling you about Jody was one of them. Now that she's sick, I don't know how to remedy that. I can only hope that your love for me will overcome any other feelings you might have about me. And hopefully, in time, you will understand why I kept it from you.*

*My time with Jody is precious and I must savor every moment we have together. I have to keep her well and happy until...God knows the answer to that one. Speaking of God, I only hope he can forgive me for betraying my husband as I lay with you tonight. Henry deserves better.*

*Maybe time will give us the answers we seek. I love you my darling, and that love was rekindled this evening. I shall never love another as I love you...*

# CHAPTER 21

A week had passed with no word from Edmund or Jim. Her brother hadn't been to the hospital to see Jody and Lily was concerned. It wasn't like Jim to shirk his priestly duties, but because of his drinking problem, she worried more than ever. What could be so important as to keep him from seeing his niece? Whenever Jody needed spiritual help, Jim's reassurance that God hadn't forgotten, pulled her through some rough times.

Lily was relieved when he answered the door. "I was worried about you." She gave him an extra squeeze. "Why haven't you seen Jody? What happened to you at the hospital?"

He walked back from the kitchen with two steaming cups of coffee. A far off pain seemed to glow in his eyes.

"What's wrong?" she asked.

He pushed his wire-rimmed glasses up the bridge of his nose several times.

"You've used every imaginable excuse why you haven't seen Jody, and I don't believe any of them. You can't lie, least of all to me. Tell me what's wrong, maybe I can help."

"You've got enough on your plate without worrying about me." His voice was flat, and his eyes avoided contact. "I'll be all right. I'm coming to some conclusions about my life," he gave a pathetic shrug, "although I still have a long way to go."

Lily got the point. It was evident he wasn't ready to share his problem. "I want you to hear my confession. I need to be free of this guilt I'm carrying."

His curt words tumbled out. "We're not in church, wait till Saturday."

"You've never refused to hear my confession. Why now?"

The tremor in his voice frightened her. "I can't hear your confession. I can't hear anyone's confession. I can't administer absolution. My soul is damned."

"What are you talking about?"

"Don't you understand?" His voice raised an octave, then slowly mellowed. "Things are different now."

She laughed nervously. "What are you talking about?"

"You won't leave me alone until I tell you, will you? Just like Mom, always poking and prodding." He chewed his bottom lip, a habit from childhood, a dead giveaway that he was struggling with himself. "All right," he smiled tersely and looked away, "I'm leaving the order. I can no longer be a priest. I've failed God, and my fellow man."

The shock was as great as if someone had doused her with a pail of cold water. "You don't mean it?"

He sipped his coffee, and watched her move about the room. "You've told me many times that we all go through troubled waters at one time or another. Just because you're a priest doesn't make you immune to depression."

"You don't know what you're talking about." He took off his glasses and rubbed his tired eyes. "When I went to the hospital chapel to pray for Jody, I couldn't. I could not utter one word of prayer for my niece. Instead I found myself cursing, I repeat, cursing the very God I professed to love."

He hesitated as if searching for the right words. "I'm suppose to pray for others, but I can't. I'm the shepherd, ordained to lead the flock." He smacked his fist in his hand. "I've been damned, punished for my sins." He sunk to the edge of the couch.

Lily sat next to him. "Jim, please don't talk like this. Don't you believe in God anymore?"

"I don't know." His tone was flat and cold. "I don't know what I believe. AA is helping me confront my drinking but it didn't prepare me to face the reason why. As the truth of why I drink begins to surface I'm having a hard time facing it, much less dealing with it."

"What's so terrible that you don't want to feel it? Why do you think you've failed God?" She hesitated, then continued. "You've been devoted to God all your life, you've always loved Him. Ever since I was a little girl you talked about being a priest. You told me that the day you were ordained your heart was so full you thought it would burst. Remember?"

"Yes, but that was before Vietnam." His face hardened. "Everything's changed. Jody's illness is the icing on the burnt cake. I can't take any more."

"Does it have anything to do with that medal you received?" Astonishment touched his face and his thin lips drew tight across his face. She knew she hit a raw spot.

His face blanched. "How did you find out?"

"That night at Edmund's, your wallet fell out of your pocket. I opened it to see if you'd been robbed, and that's which I noticed the old newspaper article. Edmund and I read it. Why didn't you tell us? We're your family and we have a right to know about your bravery."

He walked to the cabinet, turned, and snarled at her. "Just because you're my sister doesn't give you the right to snoop. If I wanted you to know I would have told you years ago." His voice trembled. "I didn't, did I?"

Lily jumped when his fist hit the table.

"Why didn't I?" he shouted, "because it's my cross." He threw his head back, laughed, and took off his glasses. "They gave me that cross and I've been carrying it on my shoulders ever since. Ironic, isn't it?" He walked around the easy chair and rubbed the fabric with his thin fingers.

Lily's stomach felt queasy, and she offered a silent prayer for strength. "Jim, talk to me. Please. You're scaring me when you talk about leaving the Church. I've always relied on your faith, but now, the way you're talking...help me to understand."

"How can I when I can't even comprehend what's going on. Do you know what it's like to be empty inside? I feel like a hollow shell." He stared past her. "In the chapel that day, I knelt down to pray, prayers I've recited all my life, prayers that always brought me peace."

Her head was spinning. She couldn't believe what she was hearing.

"I tried to pray, but the words wouldn't come. Fearful that I was loosing my mind I tried to recite a different prayer. The same thing happened, a silent emptiness. I began to read the prayer of supplication from my missal...nothing. Empty words echoed in my head."

He took a deep breath and continued. "I finally put the missal down and tried to meditate, hoping the flow of spirit would return so I could pray for Jody's recovery. The longer I sat there the deeper I sank into an empty pit. Everything I knew and cherished had slipped away. God, the Church, prayers I'd recited all my life, all gone. I tried to hang onto something. Anything. But whatever I reached for disintegrated. It was like standing on a sandbar that was dissolving beneath my feet, and I didn't know how to get off. So I just sat there, numb, and divested of my identity."

His voice quivered. "I was never so scared in all my life. I didn't know what to do." He licked his lips, like a man dying of thirst. "I wanted to hit the nearest bar but I couldn't move."

"Maybe," she offered, "you've been too busy trying to run this parish, taking care of everyone except yourself."

"Maybe?" He stared at her and gripped the back of the chair. "All I know is that it's gone. Whatever you call it, it's gone. There's nothing left of the calling. That's why," he said in a choked voice, "I have to leave the priesthood. I always felt that I had a solid foundation of faith, an invisible rock, and that no matter what happened I could always fall back on it. But if I continue, I'll collapse in on myself."

"Instead of leaving," she bargained, "why don't you take a leave of absence?"

"If I thought it would help I would, but there's more to this. Much more."

"Have you told Mom about your decision? This'll kill her. You've been her pride and joy, her son the priest."

"I'll tell her, but not just yet. I want to have everything in place before I break the news. Please, don't say anything. I promise I'll tell her myself."

Lily agreed to keep his secret and he sighed with relief. His mouth was pale as well as his cheeks and his head shook with regret. Finally, he put his frail shoulders back and sat up straight. A slight smile came to his face as if he'd rid himself of a heavy burden.

"Jim you've got to see Jody, she's wondering why you haven't been to see her."

"I know. Thanks, Sis."

"For what?"

He chuckled. "For hearing my confession. Now that you know, I can finally face Jody. I don't know if I'll be able to provide any support, but at least I'll be there with her."

"Did it ever occur to you that it just might be enough? As long as she knows you care. I suppose Mom's filled you in about the diagnosis."

He put his arm around her, "this is a terrible thing to happen to such a young and vibrant girl who's just beginning her life. Why couldn't it have been me? My life is over, I wouldn't be missed."

"Stop talking like that. You're just feeling sorry for yourself. Start feeling sorry for Jody." Lily felt her anger building, and fought to hold it in check. "And if you can't do that then feel sorry for me, I'm losing a daughter, my only child."

"I'm sorry, I can't seem to say or do the right thing. Truly, my heart aches for Jody, but it aches more for you, and those of us that will be left behind. If it's any comfort, I still believe in an 'After Life'. I'm convinced that when our soul leaves the body it enters another dimension where we continue to live on. But where God fits into this equation I don't know. That doesn't help right now but it's all I have to give. I'm emotionally bankrupt and have nothing to draw on. Forgive me for failing you." Tears filled his eyes.

"If I can't count on you, who have I got?"

"You have yourself. I'm not your strength, I never was. You have more strength than you realize. Trust yourself to know how to handle this."

"I don't want to be strong, I want her to live. I want everything to be the way it was. Why is everything falling apart?"

"You're a fighter. You've always been an inspiration to me."

Her mouth dropped open.

"I've watched you surmount problems that I wouldn't dream of tackling."

"Me! An inspiration? To you? I've never done anything to inspire anybody."

"You're wrong Lily. Think back. Every emergency in your life you were alone, and you did what you had to. You got Jody to the hospital when she shattered her kneecap. The same when Mom fell. You didn't call any of us." He shook his head. "You dragged her across the lawn and into your car. And it's a good thing you did, she'd thrown a clot and if it weren't for your quick thinking she'd have died."

"That was nothing. It was something I had to do."

"See, that's what I mean. You don't even think twice. You just do it. It's evident to everyone except you. Once you realize who you really are, your strengths, your goodness, your generosity, your life will change. I know it."

"What do you mean it'll change my life?"

"Lily, this isn't the time. Let's leave that discussion for another day." He looked at his watch. "Don't you have to get to the hospital?"

Lily jumped up. "I told Jody I'd be there first thing this morning. She's being discharged tomorrow and they have to teach me about her care."

"Tell her I'll be by to see her this afternoon," he said, and walked her to the door, "take care."

* * *

Lily was stunned when she walked into the hospital room. Jody was wild-eyed and started to shriek. "It's about time you got here. I've been calling the house all morning. Where have you been?"

Unnerved by her daughters' behavior, Lily threw her coat on the chair. "I'm sorry Honey, I went to see Uncle Jim. I wanted to see if he was all right."

Jody glared at her. "Uncle Jim is a big boy, he can take care of himself. I need you now."

Jody never talked to her this way. Why was she so angry?

"What is it Honey, what's bothering you?"

"What a stupid question." Her face twisted in anger, and her eyes bugged open. "I'm dying, or haven't you heard."

Her anger slapped at Lily with a brute-like force. "Stop it," she yelled, "right now! You're not going to die. There are lots of people who have cancer, and beat it. So can we."

"Are you on another planet?" Jody started to laugh hysterically. "It's incurable. I have six months. I won't be around at Christmas. I'll be dead." Jody's shouts filled the room. "Do you hear me? I'll be dead before the holidays."

Lily shook her daughter. "Stop it!" she yelled and sank onto the bed. She pulled Jody close and felt the tremors in her body as she continued to sob. She rocked her back and forth all the while fighting the screams that were lodged in her own throat.

"We're going to beat this. These aren't the only doctors." She forced Jody to sit up and look at her. "Don't you believe in miracles? I do."

The sobbing girl collapsed in her arms. "Oh, Mom."

Lily held her and bit down on her lip to prevent the tears that were sitting in wait. "Shh," she whispered, "it's all right. We'll find a way. I don't know how, but I'll do everything in my power to help you." Lily handed her a tissue and waited until she blew her nose. She wiped the tears on her cheek and sat up.

"Look at me."

Jody eyes were downcast.

"Look at me I said, and listen. Really listen."

Jody looked up.

"Do you believe I have your best interests at heart?"

Jody nodded.

"Do you believe that we can lick this thing?"

"I'm not sure. I'm not sure about anything anymore, but I'm willing to try. I have to get strong and I can't do it by myself. I need you, Mom. If the treatment doesn't kill the cancer you have to promise me that you'll quit saying I'm going to be okay. Deal?" She stuck out her hand for a handshake.

"I want you to make an appointment for me at the beauty shop. I want to get my hair cut, the nurses butchered it when they shaved part of my head." She held up the short strands of hair. "I might as well have it cut real short."

Lily ran her hands over her daughter's head. "I can remember curling your hair when you were a little girl, such beautiful long hair. I just hate to see you cut it."

"I have to, I have to beat the cancer to it. If I cut it I won't be as devastated when it starts to fall out. In my own way it'll be a victory of sorts."

"What else are you planning?"

Jody said she would stay with them while going through Chemo and after a month or so, move back to her own apartment.

Lily agreed.

"I haven't seen the Professor in over a week is he mad at me?"

Lily swallowed hard.

"I've read that some people, when they find out you have cancer, are afraid. Like it's contagious or something." She looked at Lily. "But I can't imagine that about him."

Lily shook her head. "He flew in from his book tour as soon as he found out."

"He dropped this off for me a couple of days ago but I haven't seen him since." Jody reached over to her stand and pulled out his book.

"He signed my copy, look what he wrote."

> *To a wonderful young lady, the apple of her teacher's eye.*
>
> *You couldn't be any closer to me than my own daughter and I love you as if you were.*

Lily gasped. She quickly excused herself and raced into the bathroom. She gripped the edge of the sink and forced herself to breath slowly. He didn't tell Jody she was his, but he came damn close. She splashed cold water on her face and repaired her makeup.

"Mom, have you read his book? It's beautiful. He must have really loved that woman. After reading this," she held up the book, "I wanted to rush out and find a boyfriend and fall in love. She sure was lucky."

Lily swallowed hard. "What do you mean? His book is fiction."

"The first thing the Professor taught us was that all fiction is based on fact. On life. And a writer can put any spin on it that he wants. He also taught us that in order to write about the depth of human emotion, and to convey it to the readers, we have to experience it ourselves. Pull from within, from the depth of our souls."

"To me it's just another book, only this time I know the author."

"Sheez! How unromantic, Mom. Quit being so somber; let loose; live a little..." Jody's voice trailed off, as her words echoed in the sterile hospital room.

On Lily's way home from the hospital the tall spires of St. Norbert's beckoned to her. The empty church was dim, and streams of sunlight filtered through the stained-glass windows and cast large eerie shadows across the aisles and pews. She slipped into a bench, knelt down, and started her prayer.

"I told Edmund about Jody and he's very angry. He hasn't called or made any attempt to see me. I hope I did right by telling him?"

Lily took a deep breath and sighed. "Maybe I've lost him but if that's the case I want you to know that I love him and always will, but now I need to talk to you about Jody. The doctors have told us that she has six to eight months to live and I can't believe that. This is not your will, it can't be. How can you allow something so devastating to happen to someone so innocent? I want you to know I'm going to fight you every step of the way. You're not going to take her from me, not as long as I have a breath left in me."

She looked up at the stained glass window of Jesus surrounded by children. The sunlight had highlighted the blue and green pieces of glass, as well as the golden halo that circled his head. "I know you care. Despite the fact that I haven't always done right by you or always obeyed your commandments, I'm asking you to spare my little girl. Give me her pain, take my life instead—"

The hollow echo of footsteps down the aisle startled her. She turned and gasped. "What are you doing here? You're the last person I expected to see in church."

Edmund slid next to her. His voice was resigned. "Maybe it's the best place to talk. I was on my way home from the hospital when I saw your car parked in front of the church. It's not hard to miss that silver Mercedes with the white kitten peering out the back window."

Lily smiled as streams of golden light washed over his face. He was a handsome man, but today his dark eyes lacked luster and appeared troubled.

"Lily, I've come to some decisions. This past week's been hell for me. I couldn't talk to you until I figured things out and I'm finally at a place where I'm comfortable with the decisions I've made. Now I need to tell you. After all, they are about us, and Jody."

Her joy turned to fear. His voice lacked emotion and it chilled her. The muscles in her stomach were clenched tight and she found herself torn between hope and fear. He reached for her hand.

"I love you Lily and I'm not going to let you go. God only knows how much time we have left, and I want to spend what's left of our lives with you. I've wasted too many years searching for something, only to discover you're all I've ever wanted. Your love is the only thing that can satisfy this longing inside of me."

Lily opened her mouth to speak but he stopped her by putting his finger over her lips.

"Let me finish, then you can talk."

She pressed back against the hard church bench and tried to subdue her soaring heart.

"I want you to ask Henry for a divorce."

She shook her head.

"I want you to marry me." He held her by the shoulders. "I know he's running for office, and I'm willing to wait till it's over, but not a minute longer. If you want me to talk to Henry with you, I'm ready."

She leaned over and kissed him. "I love you more then you can ever know. If you only knew how long I've waited to hear those words. That means you've forgiven me for not telling you about Jody?"

"Of course I've forgiven you. I was never angry at you. It was just the shock of discovering that I have another daughter and then," he rubbed his forehead, "to realize that she's dying. I'm still trying to deal with the loss of Christine. And now," he shook his head and wiped away a tear, "now I have to face the same thing with Jody."

He hesitated. "That's why I've made up my mind that Jody has to be told. She needs to know that I'm her father. God has given me a second chance and I'm going to spend whatever time there is left, with her. I don't want it to be as her professor, I want to spend it with her as her father."

Lily gasped and pulled her hand from his. "You what?"

"You heard me, I want her to know about me. She has a right to know, and I'll tell her if you don't."

"I can't believe what I'm hearing. You say you love me and in the next breath you want to destroy my life. How can you?"

He leaned forward and grabbed her arms. "We have to set things right. Don't you see Lily, we can't start our life together on lies. It's the only way."

"No, I don't see it that way. Jody is sick and you want me to tell her that the father she's know all her life isn't her dad, but oh yes, your professor is your real father. If the cancer doesn't kill her the shock of this revelation will." She shook her head hard. "No Edmund, I'm sorry I can't do what you're asking. My daughter's life, her well being, is more important to me, especially now—"

"More important then her knowing the truth? You're willing to let her go to her grave believing that Henry is her father—"

Lily swung around and felt the hot sting on her hand as it landed on his cheek. He grabbed her wrist.

"Feel better? You can run all you want from the truth but our daughter is going to die." His voice held a hard edge. "I've checked with doctors about this type of brain tumor, and they've confirmed Dr. Berner's prognosis. She doesn't have that much time. You have to face the truth. The time for running is over. Slapping me may make you feel better but it isn't going to change anything."

She beat on his chest with both fists. "No! You're lying. She's not going to die. They've made a mistake. They're wrong. I know it."

He wrapped his arms around and pulled her close. She crumbled into his chest. She gasped for breath and looked up at him, her eyes were filled with tears.

He moved the damp curls from her face. "Remember," he said, "I'm her father, and I've only got a few months to get to know her, you've had her all her life. Please don't deprive Jody and me of the joy of knowing one another. Don't you realize how much we're alike?" His eyes possessed a sheen of purpose.

"Did she tell you about the time I rode on the back of her motorcycle while we raced through town? She nearly succeeded in scaring the hell out of me. Tell me that she's done that with Henry. Go ahead Lily, tell me that she's had fun with him"

She searched for answers but her heart knew he was right.

"I'm bringing Jody home tomorrow. She'll be with me a couple of weeks, then she wants to move back to her apartment. Somewhere in that time frame I'll talk to

Henry about a divorce. I'll let him know that I'll stay until after the election. That's all he's interested in anyway. My main concern is what he'll say when I tell him about Jody. What if he doesn't believe me and insists that Jody take a blood test? Then we'll have to tell her."

"First things first. When do you plan to confront Henry?"

"Probably in the next day or two. I doubt if he'll say anything to her right away. He wants to sit on the bench and if for no other reason, he'll maintain his silence. You know him and his proprieties. He wouldn't want anything to ruin his good name."

Her tension was easing. "Will you promise not to say anything to Jody until we can tell her together?"

Edmund nodded. "But don't take too long. Suddenly time has become a precious commodity, and we have to make the most of what we have left."

# CHAPTER 22

Jody was coming home today. Emma and Lily had worked in Jody's room for days, trying to think of everything she might need to make her stay comfortable. They bought a white wicker breakfast tray and glued yellow silk flowers around the sides. Lily purchased extra bed pillows along with a cobalt blue moiré hassock so Jody could rest her feet on whenever she'd sit in the chair. Lily was anxious to see her daughter's reaction when she saw the four-foot teddy bear she bought at Marshall Fields. Emma had bandaged part of its head in white gauze to replicate Jody's bandages.

When Jody entered her room she squealed with delight at the bandaged bear sitting on her bed. She hugged her mother and Emma. "I love it Mom, he's adorable. He's going to be good company these next weeks."

Emma's heart was warmed by Jody's reaction. "Let me help you, little one. I'll unpack your things."

Jody walked over to her closet and laughed. "I'm only staying a couple of weeks," she said as she moved dozens of hangers around. "Did you bring my entire wardrobe?"

"Of course not, I just brought casual clothes for you to lounge around in."

"I told you, I didn't want you to fuss. I know you haven't paid attention to what I've said, but can you at least keep it down to a minimum? If you and Emma are constantly flitting around, you'll make me nervous."

"I'll try," she said, "but you know me. In the meantime I thought we'd have dinner in your room this evening, just the two of us. Your Dad has one of those political dinners this evening. He told me to give you his love, and he'd see you later."

"Well, it's good to see you're in capable hands young lady," Nora said as she swept into the room. She was openly amused by their surprise at her unexpected arrival. "I know your mother will cater to your every whim, she likes to do that you know." Nora hugged Lily while Jody watched her mother and grandmother. Lily winked at Jody.

"Mother, what a nice surprise. Is that another new hat?"

"Well if you'd come to see me more often, I might have the opportunity to show them to you."

"Don't start," Lily warned, then changed the subject. "Have you heard from Jim?"

"No!" Nora was clearly annoyed. "That's why I'm here. I need to talk to you."

Jody teased her. "And here I thought you came to see me Grandma, I'm disappointed." Jody's face sagged as she quivered her lips in mock sadness.

Nora shot her a distasteful look. "No you're not, but it does sound nice," Nora smiled. Jody excused herself and walked into the bathroom. Lily sat on the edge of the bed and watched her mother as she paced back and forth. Lily kicked off her shoes and started to rub her feet over the carpeting.

"Have you heard from your brother?"

"Yes, about a week ago, he was on his way to the hospital. He said something about giving you a call, and the three of us getting together for lunch."

Nora smiled, delighted at the idea. "Other than our regular Saturday?"

"Of course, what's so surprising about that?"

"Nothing, I just can't remember when we had an impromptu get together other than the holidays or our monthly meetings. It'll give me an excuse to buy a new outfit."

"Don't try to lay a guilt trip on me," Lily shot back. "You know I've got a full agenda. My life keeps me running in different directions, and now with Jody sick, I'll be lucky to find time to talk on the phone. You have to be a little understanding, especially at a time like this."

"I'll bet you've had time to see Edmund."

"Of course, I saw him at the hospital, and I ran into him at church. Why?"

Lily heard the shower running and knew Jody couldn't hear them.

Nora peered at Lily. "I never would have thought of him as a church going person. I wonder when he got religion? Was it in that Mexican jail?"

Surprised by the comment, Lily spun around to face her mother. "How did you know Edmund was in jail? No one knew that." Before the flustered woman could answer Lily took her by the hand and guided her into the hall where they couldn't be over heard. "Now," the steel in her voice seemed to unsettle Nora, "go on, tell me if you can, about this Mexican jail."

Nora stammered, "I read it in his book."

"No Mother," Lily put her hands on her hips, "try again. It isn't in the book. The only people that knew about his stint in jail were Jody and I, and she didn't have a chance to tell you. Now, do you want to explain how you knew?"

Nora walked to the end of the hall, stared into the gold leafed mirror, and pretended to adjust her hat. Lily continued to pressure her for an answer.

"Well, I'm waiting. Tell me."

Nora remained defiant despite the force of her daughters questioning. She took a deep breath and finally responded. "Remember when you couldn't find Edmund, well he called a few times. He even had his friend call. He wrote some letters and sent a telegram. I burned them all," she blurted out. "I didn't want you to make the same mistake I did. Marrying someone who couldn't take care of you. Your father was born poor and died poor." The distaste for her husband was apparent, and dripped from her lips. "I wanted a better life for you."

Lily was blank and shaken. "How could you?" she chastised. "How dare you interfere with my life?" Lily was livid. "I wasn't a child. I was a grown woman, able to make my own decisions–" Lily's voice broke in mid-sentence.

Nora started putting on her coat.

Lily grabbed the coat from her and clutched it to her breast. "No you don't, you're not leaving here until you tell me. Why did you do this? I'm your daughter. You're supposed to love me?" She hesitated. "That's not love, that's..."

Nora stared at her daughter for a moment. "I'm your mother, and mothers know what's best for their children."

"What a crock. If you knew what was best for me then you'd have known it was Edmund I loved, not Henry."

"You're not faultless in all this young lady," Nora sneered. "Why didn't you bother to wait for him, huh? You were pretty quick to marry Henry. Was it because," she paused as if savoring the moment, "you wanted Jody to have the Halston name?"

Frozen in a stunned tableau, the two women stared at each other. Nora snapped her mouth shut as Lily gasped, stunned by the blunt disclosure. Disbelief, then anger flowed in Lily's eyes. "You knew? All this time you knew, and you let me carry this burden all by myself. I would have given anything to have a mother to confide in—"

"Of course I knew. There's no such thing as a seven-month pregnancy, especially when the baby weighs almost seven pounds. I'm not stupid Lily. Maybe Henry believed you, but not me."

"Why...why didn't you ever say anything?"

"What was there to say? You made the right decision by marrying Henry. Look's like you did all right." Nora pointed around the house.

"Don't you understand, I loved Edmund?"

"Phew," she spat, "love can't pay the bills."

Too stunned to cry, Lily could only glare at her mother. Then her mood veered sharply to anger. Her nostrils flared. "You say you love me, and you claim to have loved daddy, but you don't even know the meaning of the word. All you care about is your own selfish interests. Don't you ever mention Edmund or my father to me again, if you do..." Lily stopped short of physically shaking her mother and realized the extent of her rage. She grabbed her hands and held them in front of her as she fought the gut wrenching anger raging within.

"What were you thinking when you decided to play God with my life?"

"I told you, I wanted you to have the best, and as it turns out you got it. What's wrong with that? A mother always wants what's best for her daughter. Henry was better for you then Edmund. That's why I did what I did.

And if it hadn't been for you and Edmund's sin, Jody wouldn't be dying now."

"What the hell are you talking about?"

"God is punishing you for your sins by taking Jody away from you. And you don't have to swear."

Lily gasped; her fury was beginning to choke her. She stuttered then started to shout. "You hypocrite. How dare you tell me that God is punishing Jody for my sins? Is that what the church teaches you? If that's what God is all about, I'll have none of it. You're a sick old woman, and right now I'm ashamed to call you my mother. The name used to mean something special, but not anymore. I've been longing for a mother who was sympathetic and cared about me. Someone who'd be my confidant. But you're none of those. All these years you've been sitting back and waiting for God to have his revenge."

Lily tried to control her heartache. "How could you say you loved me, while all the while waiting for the hand of God to fall on me?" Tears started to fall from Lily's eyes as she glared at a woman she thought she knew. She shook her head; unable to comprehend that someone, in this day and age, could believe that God was responsible for Jody's malignant brain tumor. Lily bit her lip; her hands were still shaking from the confrontation.

"I want you to leave," she shouted, and threw her black coat at her mother. "It makes me sick to think that you blame me and Edmund for Jody's illness. I can't even look at you without feeling disgust and pity. I feel sorry for you. You're a lonely old woman, and you'll stay that way till the day you die. And the irony is that you'll probably outlive us all. But you know what, maybe its poetic justice. You'll have to live the rest of your life alone, without a person to care about you. Then you can see what your stocks and money will do for you. Now get out."

Lily opened the door, and stood to one side as the old woman walked out. Nora rushed down the cement stairs and never looked back. Lily was still fuming when she slammed the door and marched into her room. An intense sensation in the pit of her stomach made her gag. She gulped and forced the nausea to subside as a feeling of desolation swept over her. She leaned against the closed door and buried her face in her hands. What have I done, she thought? I've never spoken to her, or anyone, in that tone, or said such awful things. She tried to excuse her own actions, but try as she might, couldn't absolve her mother. She had no right, she thought, to do what she did to Edmund and me. Then to tell me that it's my fault Jody's sick. She shuddered and drew in a sharp breath.

"No more!" Her mind was made up. "I'm not going to let you get to me. No more, Mom." She slapped her hand against the door. "This is the last time you'll interfere in my life."

A knock on the bedroom door startled her. She quickly wiped her tears and Jody walked in. "What's wrong? I heard loud voices." The young girl shook her head. "Did you have a fight with Grandma?"

"Well I wouldn't exactly call it a fight. It was more like a difference of opinion."

"Well whatever it was, I heard you all the way in my room. I hope you didn't let her get to you. You know she loves to push your buttons. She knows how to get a rise out of you."

"Well I'm not going to give her the opportunity to do it again. I doubt if I'll be seeing her for a while. I'm going to be too busy taking care of my little girl." She forced a smile and put her arm around her as they walked back into Jody's room. "You're the most important person in my life and I want you to be as comfortable as possible while you're here."

"Mom," Jody cocked an eye, "Grandma is so obvious. I don't know why you can't see it. She could easily be a case study for my psyche class. She's deathly afraid of being alone in her old age. And for some reason she thinks that her money's going to take care of her, but you and I know it won't. It's people that take care of people. You know she's afraid of being put into one of those homes."

Jody laughed. "I wouldn't be a bit surprised to find out that she's planning to have you take care of her in her old age. But for now all she really wants is attention from you and Uncle Jim."

"She's not easy to be around," Lily sighed. "I've tried for years to get close to her, but she's put up a wall, and I can't get through. She's always on the attack."

Jody smiled. "Natch! That's her protection. Like they taught us in school, if she doesn't let you in, then she won't miss you if you withdraw. Have you ever noticed she doesn't let anyone see her cry? But I'll bet you that she spends many lonely nights in her Condo...crying."

"I doubt it. She's a tough old bird."

"Remember," she pointed her finger, "if she's a tough old bird, theeennn...so are you." She wiggled her finger in a circular motion, and jabbed Lily in the chest. "It's in the genes."

Lily grabbed Jody by the waist and started to tickle her. "Are you insinuating that your mother is old? Huh! Huh!

Jody started laughing and tried to get away. "Stop it," she laughed. "You know I'm ticklish." she screeched as her mother increased the attack. "Stop it, you're not playing fair, I'll wet my pants." Lily and Jody stood up and panted as they tried to catch their breath. "In all seriousness, you're tougher than you think." You're strong," her warmth touched Lily. "I've always hoped to be like you when I grew up—" She smiled and kissed her mother on the cheek. "I'm glad to be home Mom. Really. I'm glad you're here for me to lean on. I know I can count on you." Her eyes began to fill with tears. "Teach me how to be strong?"

Lily surged with self-confidence and threw her shoulders back. They walked into Jody's room with their arms around each other.

* * *

Lily was happy that Jody was home. Now she could keep a watchful eye on her. The down side was their semi-weekly visits to the hospital. Jody's reaction to the chemotherapy was horrible. Within hours after treatment she became nauseated, and at times, it lasted for days. As soon as she felt better, it was time to go for another treatment. It was a no win situation, and she wasn't holding up as well as they'd hoped.

Jody's jovial personality was gone. Still at odds with her fate, she sought to find definition and purpose for her life, the why and wherefore of her short existence. The high point of her day seemed to be when Henry came home. Her first question was if he'd found a new doctor, one that didn't concur with Dr. Berner and his associates. Jody was still hoping for a miracle, after all the doctors said that hope kept many a patient alive for years beyond their forecasted time.

Lily kept herself busy by searching out every alternative medicine and treatment for her daughter. They attended laugh therapy sessions. They read all the books available on nutrition and had Emma prepare special meals. They read brochures about herbal therapy, and even considered flying to Mexico to see an ancient Indian healer. Lily was determined to have Jody utilize everything that was available, but questioned the Mexican connection. After further inquiry, she nixed the healer and centered her attention on what was available in the Chicago area.

Jody started meditating, something she'd practiced on and off for the past five years. For at least an hour a day, she sought the solace of a stilled mind. She read that there had been cancer remissions when the patient pictured the cancer cells being eaten by her healthy cells. She started the regimen by picturing her blood cells, dressed as soldiers, and marching around her brain, destroying the tumor piece-by-piece until it was so small she couldn't see it any more.

When she found time, she read literature authored by researchers regarding cancerous brain tumors, and their rate of growth. She was also interested in the side effects of the tumor. To face death was one thing, but the devastation that it could cause her body scared her more than dying. She talked to Lily about what could happen, but Lily dismissed it and assured her that everything would be all right.

Jody found those reassurances empty, and hard to deal with. She'd prided herself on dealing with facts, and her mother's refusal to face them worried her. Jody gave Lily all the reading materials, and begged her to study them.

Jody was still learning to deal with her sudden bouts of anger whenever she thought about her future. Never to know the feeling of walking down the aisle as a bride kindled the anger. When she thought about the love that was in her heart, and the fact that she would be denied the chance to give it to a man or a child of her hers, the child she'd never carry in her body, the bitterness grew. There were nights she lay in the darkness and cursed God, the God she once professed to love. She railed against the universe for being born, and wished her time on earth was over...now.

Her face was sallow and drawn, and the area under her eyes grew darker from the effects of the Chemo. Despite the recent haircut, her thinning hair was evident. The dresser drawers were filled with colorful scarves from well-wishers. On days she wasn't scheduled for chemo she read, and tried to absorb all the knowledge the world had to offer. She was determined to learn all she could in the next six months.

The fact that there were no more headaches was a blessing. The new nightmare was the nausea and weakness. She dropped eighteen pounds in three weeks, and Lily worried about keeping food in her daughter. No matter what she put on Jody's plate, it ended up being upchucked into the toilet. Tea and crackers seemed to be the only things she tolerated, and Lily knew she couldn't survive on that. The doctor kept prescribing different medications for her upset stomach, but nothing seemed to help. She watched her daughter deteriorating before her eyes.

Jody was in a constant state of anger, not that Lily blamed her. She too found herself angry at the world, and God. Lily found herself reading the obituaries, and noted the ages of the people who'd died. Much to her surprise thirty percent were under thirty-five, something she didn't expect. The statistics stared her in the face. I always assumed she'd bury me, she thought. Nature didn't intend for parents to bury children. But if the doctors were right, she'd have to bury her only daughter, and she couldn't face it, and constantly fought the morbid thoughts.

Since Jody's illness, Henry and Lily spent even less time together. Their conversations were limited to Jody's situation, and Lily's involvement with doctors and treatments. Henry put his political agenda on hold, and spent evenings with his daughter, or researching articles about new cancer studies. When he found one that sounded promising, he'd talk to Jody about entering one of the programs. She wouldn't hear of it, and refused to put herself through some experimental program, like some guinea pig. That wasn't for her.

Lily and Edmund managed to steal an occasional moment away from the daily ordeal. He was anxious to talk to Jody but agreed to wait until she went back to her apartment. That's when Lily would ask Henry for a divorce. It would be a lot easier without Jody there. Lily didn't know what to expect from Henry and a shouting match was the last thing she wanted. Lily's anger lay just below the surface of her calm demeanor, and she knew that if Henry started pushing her buttons she'd let him have it.

Lily told Edmund about her run in with her mother and Jim's plans to leave the priesthood. With all that was going on in her life she definitely wasn't in any frame of mind to take any guff from Henry. She knew that asking for a divorce would be rough, but telling him that he wasn't Jody's father was another matter entirely. She searched her heart but couldn't anticipate his reaction.

First of all, would he believe her, and if he did, would he step aside and allow Edmund to be a father to Jody? What a laugh, she thought. Here I am, married to a man for twenty-five years and I haven't the slightest clue as to what he'll say or do. She had to be ready for the consequences of her decision.

Pat had been in Florida for the last ten days and was expected back today. Even though she called daily to check on Jody, there was much Lily had to tell her. So much had happened since she left, and Lily needed her confidant. She had to tell her about Edmund and her plans to ask for a divorce. If anyone would be honest, Pat would. Lily was counting on her for so many things, including feedback about the different doctors and treatments.

As soon as she arrived home Pat hurried across the lawn into Lily's house. "Look at that tan," Lily exclaimed. "Did you spend every waking hour on the beach?"

"Of course," Pat preened. "At the prices I was paying, I wanted to get as much sun as I could. I think I'm tanned down to my bones. I could pass for black if my lips were bigger."

"Two weeks in the sun didn't effect your mouth. Too bad that didn't get burned, you might have a gentler tongue." Lily laughed and hugged her friend then ushered her into the library and closed the double doors behind them.

"What's up? Why the secrecy? Is Emma here?"

"Yes, and I don't want anyone to hear us. Are you ready for the big news?"

"Of course," she looked at Lily. "You didn't! You finally told your mother to go to hell?"

Lily nodded. "That's only part of it. Come sit down." She looked at her friend then cleared her throat. "I'm, going to ask Henry for a divorce." She exhaled a whooshing breath and waited for Pat's reaction.

Pat was stunned; her wide-eyed expression displayed utter disbelief. "You've got to be kidding! Judging by that damn smile, I guess you're not. What the hell happened? What made you finally decided to make the break?" Before Lily could answer Pat continued to question her. "It's Edmund...isn't it?"

Lily jumped up from her chair and hugged Pat. "He's asked me to marry him and..."

Pat leaned forward, "And, and what? Damn you, tell me."

Lily's eyes crinkled, she loved the look on her friends face, "I said yes." The two friends embraced. "I told him about Jody." Lily felt Pat stiffen, then heard a gasp seep from her lips.

Pat pushed away from Lily. "You did what?" She sat down. "How could you do something like that?" Then she whispered, "how did he take it?"

Lily proceeded to tell Pat about the past two weeks. "I go away for two weeks and you're whole life changes. It's like you're a different person."

"Everything started happening so fast, starting with Jody, then Edmund, and finally my mother. I don't think I could have planned it better. Edmund made me realize the fragile quality of life. None of us know how long we have left. In fact I don't know if I'll see my next birthday."

Pat chimed in. "Don't get morbid on me."

"I'm not. It's just that when Jim told me about leaving the priesthood, he confessed his admiration for my strengths. Then Jody said she wanted to be strong like me. I couldn't believe they were talking about me. Can you imagine? After thinking about it for a while, I started feeling stronger. And it's beginning to feel natural."

"Well it's about time. I've been telling you that for years. You're not the mealy mouthed, frightened little girl you pretend to be. You really are a strong, independent and caring woman, able to make it in today's world. You don't need anyone or anything. You're just like me."

Lily walked to the window, pulled open the drapes, and let in the morning sun. "Well you were right, until your last point. I need Edmund," she said emphatically.

"Listen, don't fall into that trap. You can stand on your own two feet," she pointed her index finger at Lily, "but you choose to stand next to Edmund. Can you distinguish the difference? It takes you from a needy position to one of sharing and power. Understand?"

Lily nodded and walked back to the chair. "It makes sense." She artfully switched subjects. "You'd have been proud of me when I asked my mother to leave the house."

Pat's mouth popped open. "You what?"

"You heard me," she said. "I asked her to leave. Edmund was right but I refused to believe him. She knew where he was the whole time. She decided she didn't want me to marry him, so she burnt the letters, and never told me about them, or where he was. Would you believe she knew I was pregnant with Edmund's baby?"

"That doesn't surprise me. Mothers usually know those things. Remember she's seen your body change through the years, and I'm sure she saw the changes while you were pregnant. But why didn't she ever confront you?"

"I don't know," Lily was puzzled. "That's her thing. But what really did it for me was when she said it was God's punishment that Jody had cancer. That's when I lost it. For the first time ever, I swear I could have slapped her. Imagine hearing my own mother tell me that it's my fault that my daughter's going to die."

"I know you didn't buy into that. It's that old time religion talking. That was the only way the church had of controlling people. They put the fear of God into them and it governed their lives. Many still believe it today. Your mother is a perfect example. That my friend is one of the reasons I left the church. I couldn't handle the bullshit any more." She tilted her head, and squinted her eyes. "What's this about Jim leaving?"

Lily threw her hands up in frustration. "I don't have all the details because he refuses to talk about it. It has something to do with Vietnam, and what happened there. Edmund seems to understand Jim's dilemma. The church teaches that killing is a mortal sin. And there he was, forced to kill to save his own life. I don't think he's ever gotten over it, and drinks to forget. AA doesn't seem to be doing any good. Can you imagine my mother when he tells her about his plans to leave the church? She's going to die. He's her pride and joy, her son the priest."

Pat was unmoved. "I'm sure God himself will hear her cries. I wonder whom she'll blame for her sons problems? Maybe she'll finally take a look at her life and see what she's done to the both of you. Maybe she'll find the right place to lay blame."

Pat got up and walked toward the door. She motioned Lily with her head.

"She's really not that bad. Jody pointed out that she's probably very lonely. You know Pat, I wish with all my heart that she and I were close. I've always felt there was something missing in my life and I finally figured it out. I wanted a close relationship with my mother, but she wouldn't let me. She didn't let any of us close to her. I don't know if it was due to my father's suicide or if she was like that all her life. Now," she shrugged, "I have nothing but pity for her. I wish I could feel love, but I can't."

"Don't start blaming yourself for not feeling good about your mother. If you do, she's succeeded in laying a guilt trip on you, and I'm sure you don't want to carry that baggage. You've got enough right now."

They strolled into the kitchen. "Look at this." Lily opened the refrigerator and pulled out a platter of turkey sandwiches. "It's like Emma can read my mind." She set the dish down and grabbed a bottle of wine. "How's about a glass with lunch?"

Pat parried in surprise. "You, drinking at lunch." She feigned mock surprise, and raised her hands in the air. Then she placed them on her cheeks and started to shake her head. "Something has shook you to you're very core," she said, and used an exaggerated southern accent. When she stopped clowning her voice was sharp. "I like the fallout. By the way where's Jody?"

"She insisted on going home to her apartment to get her stereo. I hope this means she plans to give up her apartment and stay here."

"Now don't go getting your hopes up. You know what Jody said, and I can't say as though I blame her. She's trying to maintain some semblance of life, as she knew it, for as long as possible. You have to allow her this time."

The joy left Lily's face as the realization of Jody's future intruded. She tried to quell her spirit, troubled as it was, by listening to Pat talk about her Florida vacation. After many nights of soul searching, her head still swirled with doubts as to the reality of Jody's condition.

What happened to the levelheaded woman she knew herself to be? Here she was, ready to change her whole life. Ready to abandon everything she believed in, everything she'd been taught. And for what? What was this illusive thing called love? I'm even sounding like a song. What's going on? Then she heard Pat's voice.

"You know Lily, I hate to say this—"

"When has that ever stopped you?"

"Be serious. Talking about religion, and God, and all that stuff, a thought struck me." She laid her hand on Lily's arm and looked into her eyes. "Just pretend for a moment. What if God sent you Edmund at this horrible time in your life?" Pat held up a hand to quiet Lily's protest. "What if Edmund is back in your life to help you though this, and at the same time to let him have a little time with his daughter?"

Lily stared at her in awe. It made sense. Maybe there was an overall plan involved in their lives, and she pondered the possibility. Maybe they were nothing more than pieces of a chess game, being moved from point to point by the hand of destiny.

"For a loud mouth blond, you sure as hell make sense at times. I can buy into that. The church always said that God never gives you more than you can handle, and I don't know if I could go through this without Edmund at my side. You know I've been pretty mad at him, maybe I should talk to him this evening, and ask for forgiveness."

"Who Edmund?"

"No," she rolled her eyes, "God. I'm talking about God. I've spent the last few weeks cussing Him out, and telling Him what I thought about life, how it sucks and all that."

"You mean to tell me," Pat said mockingly, "you're not afraid of Him?"

"Why should I be? What have I got to lose at this point? He's taking the most important thing I have on this earth."

"Did it ever occur to you that Jody is not yours? She belongs to the universe, and is only on loan to you. As an instrument of Spirit, you gave her entrance into this world, and raised her the best you knew how. If the universe decides to call her back, you have nothing to say about it."

Lily looked at Pat and saw tears fill her friend's eyes. She reached over. "What's wrong?"

"It's something I've never told anyone. Something I've lived with, all these years. Maybe it's time I tell you." She hesitated, and then took a deep breath along with a sip of wine. She put her glass down and started.

"When I was married the first time, I focused on finding someone with a lot of money, and Mike had plenty, or so I thought. After we were married, I found out he didn't have as many assets as he claimed. In fact, the few assets he did have were cashed in and invested into the stock market. Every cent we had went into the market. We were house rich but poor as church mice. And as luck would have it, he made wrong choices, and the paper was worth more then the stocks."

Lily listened.

"I found out I was pregnant, and till this day I don't know how it happened. But I couldn't let the pregnancy interfere with my plans to divorce him. I knew that if Mike found out I was pregnant, he wouldn't let me go. You know, all that macho bullshit. So I made a choice that day, and I've regretted it the rest of my life. No doctors would perform an abortion so I talked to one of my friends. She told me about a woman who did it at her house for two hundred and fifty dollars. I had no choice but to call."

Pat took another sip of wine. "Well to make a long story short, she botched the job, I hemorrhaged, and was rushed to the hospital. They performed an emergency hysterectomy. Evidently she'd punctured the uterine wall, and I nearly bled to death. Talk about punishment, I've been carrying around all kinds of shit for that murderous act. And when I think about Jody, I sometimes feel that I gypped the universe out of one of it's children, and it's paid me back by not letting me have any more."

"Pat I never thought...I just figured you didn't want any kids."

"Oh, I keep kidding myself, but I'd love to have a daughter like Jody."

Lily felt her stomach tense. The anguish on Pat's face was overwhelming. Her heart ached for her friend. Just imagine, she thought, after all these years, you still don't know what secrets people carry in their hearts. And here I am condemning myself for loving Edmund. She shook her head.

"Pat, I'm sorry. Truly sorry. I didn't know. The more I think about it, it explains why you've always showered so much attention on Jody. I've been happy to share her with you." Lily leaned over and hugged Pat. "I love you, my friend. We'll get through this, I know we will, so help us God."

# CHAPTER 23

Jody's stay at her mother's house turned out to be much longer then planned, and it thrilled Lily to have the time with her daughter. She hoped Jody would change her mind about moving back into her apartment, and move back home, permanently.

One afternoon Lily walked into Jody's room and was surprised to find her packing.

"Before you say anything," Jody said, and kept packing, "give me a chance to explain. I've been doing a lot of thinking, and I can't shake this feeling that time is hovering, like the heavy burden it is. I have so much to do, and I don't know how much time I've left to do it in. That's why I've got to leave."

"But you can't go to an empty apartment. Who's going to fix your meals; remind you about your medicine; drive you to the hospital? You know how sick you get after your treatments."

"I've thought about that, Mom." There was a quiet determination in the young girls' voice. Her green eyes fixed on her mother, "and you're right. That's why I've decided to go to one of those cancer treatment centers, that's if you and Dad will help with the cost because my insurance will only cover part of it."

"Of course we'll help. What kind of place is it, a hospital like your father was talking about, where they experiment with new cancer drugs?"

"No, it's nothing like that. You know me and pain, I couldn't handle that. This is a residential hospital with a home-like atmosphere, and every patient there has cancer. I'll be sharing a bungalow with another woman who's fighting for her life, just like I am. The staff prepares your meals, provides medication, and administers the Chemo and radiation. My doctor's orders are followed to the tee but what's more important, right now, is the support."

"What support? I don't understand? We've been supporting you though this."

"I'm not talking about that kind of support, what I'm missing is the therapy groups, women who discuss their fears; their hopes; their dreams. They talk about dying. Women who are going to survive, and women who are going to die. All of us together, fighting this cancer scourge."

Lily's heart squeezed with fear. "Where is this place? Around here?"

Jody shook her head. "No it's in Zion, Illinois. That's why I have to live there."

Lily flopped into a chair. "So far away," she said, "why there? I can't let you go, I want you near me."

"You don't understand," Jody said as her eyes took on a hard edge, "I'm not asking for permission, I'm telling you. I've already made the arrangements, they're expecting me later today."

"You're leaving today? I, I can't believe you're doing this. Why?"

"It has nothing to do with the care you've been giving me. I couldn't ask for a better nurse, friend, and mother. But anytime I look into your eyes I see pity. And I want to see life. I see fear in your eyes, and I feel it in your touch. I can't be around that, at least not now, not while I still have a chance to beat this thing." Her eyes started to mist.

"Don't misunderstand, Mom, it's only natural you should feel the way you do. But I have to be around people that have the same disease; that are feeling the same things I am, and experiencing the same highs and lows. Please understand, I have to do this."

"Can I come and see you?"

"No," she said gently, "not until I get the lay of the land. But I promise I'll talk to you everyday, that is if it doesn't interfere with what I have to do for me."

"Well then I'll drive you there, it'll give me a chance to see where you'll be living."

"No," she said, and continued packing. "I've made other arrangements. Edmund is going to drive me. Please don't be angry with him, I was the one that asked. I didn't know how you'd take the idea of me going away."

"He never mentioned anything to me."

"I just made up my mind yesterday. I knew that if you drove me we'd cry all the way, and right now I can't afford those negative emotions. I have to use all my energy to fight this thing, and I am going to fight it Mom! I've read about remissions, and they claim the whole self has to be involved in the healing process. I need to utilize every ounce of energy I have left in me to get rid of this thing that's growing in my head."

Lily mulled over her daughter's words. And the more she thought about it, they made sense. She should be in a place with other women who had cancer. Maybe being with others like herself would give her the strength she needed. Hopefully God would let a remission occur.

Lily hugged her frail daughter. "I wish I could provide the support you need. I love you Honey, and whatever you decide is all right with me. Please call, and let me know how you're doing, I even want to know about the bad days. Promise?"

"I promise. I love you, and thanks for picking up the tab. It's my last shot at life, and I have to take it, no matter what."

Lily caught her breath, and bit her tongue as she reached for Jody's hand, but despite her effort to contain her heartache, tears forced their way out.

"Mom, stop it. Now is not the time for tears, there'll be plenty of time later. And if I do my work, maybe they'll be tears of joy. At this point God only knows."

Lily's house was quiet once again and echoed the emptiness in her heart. The stereo was silent; no more echoes of a young girls giggles; and she was back to dining alone. Every time she walked by Jody's room she peeked in, reassuring herself that her daughter would be back. She'd only been gone a few hours, but it seemed like forever.

When Edmund returned he called Lily. He told her about the hospital and his positive impressions of the doctors and staff, as well as Jody's upbeat attitude.

Convinced that her daughter was in good hands, Lily questioned Edmund about Jim.

"He's still attending AA, at least that's what he said. And he's thinking about getting a sponsor. But I still can't get him to tell me what's really at the bottom of all the drinking. He won't take that last step and confide in me."

"I hope he can turn things around." Lily kept waiting for Jim to call and wondered if he was still planning to leave the church. Perhaps he'd changed his mind? Maybe no news was good news. If not, when was he planning to tell Mother? Lily dreaded the day; she knew the scene would be absolutely horrendous.

That evening Henry came home all excited about a call he'd made to his fraternity buddy, a Neurosurgeon, who promised to get in touch with specialists in England. He'd heard they were doing experimental work with Taxatir, a drug produced from the needles of a European tree and the clinical studies were being conducted at the MD Anderson Cancer center in Texas. He also discovered, from one of his clients, about alternative medicines that were being tested, and the research that was being conducted with plants in the Rain Forests of the Amazon. But all were far from complete. It would take time, a luxury Jody didn't have.

Lily wanted to confess her fears about Jody but didn't dare. He never showed an ounce of fear, and often looked down on those who did. So that evening, during dinner, she put on her best smile, and thought about how he'd react when she told him that Jody was not his? Edmund was pressuring her. Would the truth bring about a change in Henry's attitude towards Jody? Would he expect Lily to leave the house when she told him about Edmund? No, he wouldn't do that, after all he knew Jody would be home in a month, and she'd need her.

Feeling nervous, she started to clear her throat when Emma finished serving coffee. "Henry, I have to talk to you," she swallowed hard, and tried to get the lump out of her throat.

"What is it? C'mon out with it," he looked at his watch, "I've got a speech to write."

Despite the twinge in her stomach, she took a deep breath, sighed, and finally said the dreaded words. "I want a divorce."

He laid down his spoon, leaned back in his chair, and starred at her. His eyes were cold and proud.

"I'm afraid that's impossible."

"Why? We've been pretending to be happily married for years, it's about time we put an end to this charade."

"You may think it's the right time, but I don't. You see my darling wife, I've worked too hard, for too long, to get to this point in my life. And I'm not going to let a divorce stain my good name. So the answer must be an unequivocal no." He wiped his mouth, than threw the napkin on the table.

She gasped, than snapped her mouth shut. After seconds of deafening silence she found her voice again. "Why would divorce put a stain on your name? Half the people we know are divorced."

"You're quite right, but they aren't running for the Circuit Court."

Relieved, she stood up. "Well if that's the only reason, I'm willing to wait until the election is over, even until you're sworn in."

"Why are you standing, for God's sake? Sit down, we have to finish this discussion."

Annoyed that he was right again, she sat down.

"Look at you, you're annoyed with me. Why? You're the one that wants your freedom. And if you're willing to wait until after the election, I have no objection. I'll give you a quiet divorce," he leaned toward her; his eyes were like icy pools and caused her to shudder. "And I do mean quiet. No newspapers; no local TV news; nothing. Understand? I want this kept under wraps as long as possible."

Lily shook her head. "I'd never do anything to embarrass your good name. God forbid that should happen. But answer me one thing, is that all you care about? Don't you want to know why?"

Suddenly he stood up, pushed the chair from behind him, and turned to catch it before it fell to the floor. His voice thundered through the dining room. "Do you think I'm blind? Or stupid? I know you've been seeing Edmund. That's why you want a divorce. You've never stopped loving him, all these years he's been between us."

"That's a lie. I buried him over twenty years ago, and never gave him another thought until last July when you showed me that newspaper article. And if you'll think back, I didn't want to see him; you were the one that invited him here. You're the one that kept insisting I have dinner with the two of you. I didn't want this to happen, but it did. And now with Jody so sick, I had to tell you."

"I'm surprised it took you so long. I've given the two of you every opportunity to be together."

Her eyes shot up in dismay. Why do you think I kept accepting all those dinner invitations?"

"Don't feed me that bullshit that you stayed away nights so I could see Edmund. You went to every one of those dinners because you want that judgeship more than anything else in this world. You'd sell your soul to the devil if he could get you that seat. You would have attended those meetings whether Edmund was in our lives or not. Who the hell do you think you're kidding?"

"I'm warning you. Take heed. If there's even a hint of scandal," she saw his hand begin to tremble when he pointed at her, "you two will be sorry. I don't care if you sneak around like some common whore, I just don't want the rumor mill running rampant."

She glared at him. She couldn't believe what she was hearing. Her husband was approving of her affair. Did he loath her that much? Did all these years mean so little to him?

Henry walked back into the dining room and threw some papers across the table. "I want you to take a look at these."

She picked up the discolored legal papers, which had yellowed with age, and slowly read the date, nineteen seventy-five. Her name as the plaintiff, in a divorce suit, jumped out at her. She was too startled to offer any words. Shock touched her pale face, and she sat there, blank and shaken.

After she regained her composure she started to read them again, and now her blood began to boil, and her stomach muscles tightened in anger. She felt the heat of rage radiating from her cheeks.

"All these years you've wanted a divorce? Why didn't you file for it?"

"I didn't want to be the bad guy. You see," he smiled smugly, "if I filed, public sympathy would be in your court. But if you filed, all the voters would be on my side."

"You bastard. You know what you can do with these papers?" Enraged by his self-serving logic, she started tearing at the aged documents until they were in hundreds of tiny pieces. She leaned across the table, and threw them in his face. His complacent expression never changed. His cold stare continued as bits of paper floated through the air, landing on his head, his lap, his nose, and the table. He never moved a muscle.

Rancor sharpened her voice. "All these years I thought we had a marriage, but I can see that I was wrong. And I kept blaming myself for our inability to talk, when all along you'd cut yourself off from me. For some reason you built a wall and there was no letting me in. I've been such a fool."

"Don't lie to an attorney, I've seen better than you. I know better, Lily. You never loved me. You've always wanted him. I was just a handy convenience for you. You only loved the money I supplied so generously."

Stung by his remarks she finally shot back, "and you loved the idea of having a gracious hostess for all your dinner parties, and client gatherings. It was a trade off."

He peered at her. "I thought that when I moved out of the bedroom you'd dissolve this marriage, but you hung on and kept spending the money as if it were going out of style. You used me Lily, and I can't forget that."

She tried to catch her breath, to hold her rage in check, and keep the festering wound from exploding. "Yes, I used you, I had to. I wanted Jody to have a good name, and upbringing, and I knew that was one thing you could provide." She decided to let him have it. "Why do you think I married you? It was for your name only. I wanted my daughter to have the Halston name. For your information I was pregnant when we got married, but not by you! Jody's not your daughter!" She paused. "I guess we're even now."

As he looked at her, a satanic smile crossed his thin lips. She was breathing fast and heavy, and grabbed the edge of the table as she waited for him to explode at the bombshell she'd dropped.

"I was wondering when you were going to get around to telling me. You must have really considered me a fool. I bought your story about the pregnancy at first, even the fact that Jody was two months premature. But for the last twenty years I've known Jody wasn't mine."

She turned to face him directly. "You're lying. You're just saying that to get back at me."

"No, I'm not." He studied the tabletop, then looked up at her. "Remember when I became a partner in Father's firm? Each of us had to have partnership insurance for a million dollars. Before I could get the insurance coverage I had to have a thorough physical, and that's when I found out I was sterile. From what the doctor could determine, it happened when I had the mumps. I was ten."

Her body stiffened, her facial muscles grew taut. His words appeared to bounce off her. Then without warning she started to laugh, and continued laughing, hysterically, giving him the impression that she was out of control.

He began to fidget in his chair, his look of triumph turned to fear. His smile slipped, and his brows displayed furrows of concern.

Still laughing wildly, she rose. "You know the irony of this whole damn thing? I thought I was fooling everyone, when in reality I wasn't fooling anyone, except myself. My mother knew, you knew, and the only one that doesn't know is Jody." She leaned across the table. "We can't tell her the truth, at least not now. She has to get strong and fight this cancer. We can't tell her anything."

"Well," he said wryly, "for once I agree with you. Jody can't know a thing, it would destroy her."

"Why didn't you tell me you knew? That explains the wall between us. Aren't you going to ask me who the father is?"

"She's Edmund's daughter. It was obvious; you were in love with him. So when you wanted to make love, that weekend in college, I took advantage of the situation. I hoped you'd forget him, but I soon discovered I couldn't begin to compete. Little did I know you were carrying his child when I held you in my arms." His eyes darted around the room. "But you know what Lily, I think I still would have married you. You stuck by your part of the contract. I never had to worry about you doing anything to ruin the Halston name, and I was right. Your catholic upbringing, along with your social skills, proved to be an asset."

Her jaw dropped as a myriad of feelings washed over her. She felt violated, and raped of her self-respect. She had been used like a piece of merchandise. He wasn't, at all, what she thought. He was cold, calculating, a user, and a master of deceit. She opened her mouth to speak, then changed her mind, and started to walk out of the room.

The sound of his voice stopped her in the doorway. "Remember, we have a deal. Not a word to Jody, and no meeting in public."

She turned, looked at him, and walked out.

* * *

She pulled in behind the black Explorer and ran to the front door where Edmund was waiting with open arms. Instantly warmed by his embrace, she felt his strength seep into her when she pressed her body against his. She started talking as fast as she could, trying to relay everything that happened between her and Henry.

"The important thing is that he knows. No more lies; no more sneaking around; it's all out in the open. All that matters now is our love, and Jody's welfare. The worst is over Lily, now we can concentrate on getting our daughter through these next few months."

Lily leaned against Edmund's shoulder as they sat on the couch talking about Jody. Together they'd figure out a way to beat this. "By the way, tell me more about the hospital where Jody's staying."

"They gave me the cooks tour, along with a great orientation. They thought Jody was my daughter," he looked at Lily and smiled, "I'm still not used to the idea."

He continued relaying his observations. "They have all kinds of cancer patients, newly diagnosed, as well as patients in advanced stages. It's a state of the art medical-care facility. Their nutrition, and psychosocial support programs are like none I've ever seen. They're breaking new ground every day, regarding their mind-body connection program which is built on the foundation of Psychoneuroimmunology."

"Huh?"

"That's exactly what I said when I heard the word. From what they told me, this program provides patients, and their family members, with individual, and family counseling sessions; support groups; instructions on relaxation, and stress reduction. They have an extensive medical staff. It really sounded great. In fact I meant to tell you, when I got back I checked their license, and accreditation. From what I found out our daughter is in a highly accredited, blue-ribbon facility."

"Does Jody have any input into what's happening?"

"That's why she wanted to go there. The treatments are tailored to the particular type of tumor, and its behavior patterns. As a group, they search out viable options that are most effective, along with available treatments, or a combination of old, and new. Along with everything else, they provide pastoral care."

"Well if it's all you say it is, I'm glad Jody's there, but I still wish I had her with me. I miss her—." Lily's composure slipped and she leaned against Edmund.

"I know," he patted her, "but if Jody is fighting we have to fight too. We can't give in to negative thoughts. Whenever you start to feel afraid, picture her healthy, running, dancing, or whatever you can see in your mind's eye. It helps dispel the fearful thoughts. I did it a couple of times last week, and it helped."

They discussed what would happen when Jody came home, and how they'd tell her about Edmund, and agreed it should be together. But it all depended on Jody's condition; her health would dictate their timetable.

## CHAPTER 24

As the black Explorer traveled north towards the Wisconsin border Lily was deep in thought as she watched the bare brown landscape whiz by. The silence between them was deafening. She wondered if he was experiencing the same uncertainty that was raging through her. Why did Jody want to see them? Was she all right? Jody wanted Henry there but suggested that if he couldn't make it, maybe Edmund could.

"What are you nodding about?" Lily asked.

"Oh," he shrugged, "I was just thinking. You and I, here together, it feels right. After all these years I finally feel I'm in my right place, and with the right person. I feel—"

"Connected?"

"Yea, that's the word, connected. It's like I'm part of you, and we're part of something. Even when you leave me I continue to feel your presence." He pressed his clenched fist to his chest.

"I used to hate the dry barren landscape of winter but today I don't see it dry and barren, I see the rightness of it. Does that sound silly?" Lily asked.

He glanced at her, than fixed his eyes back on the road. "That's the way I've always felt when I'm with you, the rightness of us. I'll never know why I didn't call when I got back from Mexico. The only excuse I can come up with is that I didn't want to see the woman who didn't wait for me. You know men and our egos; we let them get in the way of our own happiness. And this time it robbed me of my life."

When they walked inside the main building of the cancer center, Lily and Edmund were greeted warmly, and ushered into a cozy living room environment. Soon Dr. Joyce Framingham, staff physician, who specialized in family counseling, joined them. Her coal black eyes were magnetic, and filled with warmth and understanding.

The doctor smiled, and invited them to be seated. She pulled up a chair and faced them. "The day your daughter called you she was quite ill, and dealing with a bout of depression. I suggested she call you. From what I understand you two are quite close."

"We are, and it's still hard for me to believe she's in this place. I fluctuate between the reality of it all, and the pangs of denial. I'm having a hard time accepting what's happening to her, and at the same time I'm angry that it had to be her. Then I get mad at myself for being angry, because if I'm angry then it means I'm admitting she has cancer. Does that make any sense?"

"What you're experiencing is normal. Family, as well as patients, experience similar emotions," the doctor brushed a loose strand of hair behind her ear, "maybe not in the same degree, but I can assure you they experience the seesaws of an emotional ride to hell, and back. Jody's been stuck in denial. She thought she had accepted the cancer, but somewhere deep inside, where it really counts, she continued to deny it. With the help of her support group she realized she couldn't keep denying something so evident. Once she was able to accept her fate the anger hit big time, and she fluctuated between anger and depression for days. She couldn't find her way back."

Lily detected concern in the woman's voice.

"I thought that seeing you, might help her through this stage."

"I'm glad you called Doctor, but I don't think I've accepted it either." Lily turned to Edmund and he grabbed her hand.

The doctor nodded. "Many times we find that loved ones help them come to grips with their cancer. Jody has a devastating intrusion in her body, and she's reacting accordingly. You see Mrs. Halston, it's just as important for Jody's prognosis that you deal with this problem as well. You have to realize that your daughter is seriously ill, and we still don't know how well she'll do in treatment."

Lily turned to Edmund.

"None of us know how long we have on this earth, and that includes our cancer patients. We constantly remind them that the most important time there is...is now. And that's all there is. They can't waste time looking back, and they can't involve themselves in an uncertain future. But if they live in the present moment, their lives will be full, far beyond their wildest dreams. I know, I'm a cancer survivor," she smiled at their astonished look.

"I've been where most of these women are, and I've learned that though I've survived the five-year marker, I could get hit by a car tomorrow, and be gone in a heartbeat."

"I agree, but when it happens to someone so young—"

"Life doesn't come with guarantees, Mrs. Halston. Research shows there's a noticeable difference in patients that accept time as an ally and concentrate on living, versus dwelling on the illness."

Lily moved to the edge of her seat. "I want to help Jody as much as possible. What can I do?"

"First, and most important, you have to face your own fears. Your daughter has a cancerous brain tumor. Once you accept that fact you'll emerge with more self-respect, more self-love, and more courage. If you continue in denial you're wasting valuable time, time that you will never have again. And as you must know by now, time is a very precious commodity."

She poured them a cup of coffee. "The most important thing you can do for your daughter is to stop denying that she has cancer. Once you do this, prepare yourself for an onslaught of anger which you're sure to experience. And I guarantee you will. And it's normal to be mad at the world at this stage of your acceptance."

"I've noticed that I've been losing my temper over things that normally wouldn't bother me," Lily said.

Edmund chimed in. "Has Jody accepted the idea that she has cancer?"

"She's working on it. I believe she's gotten past the denial, but there are times I still detect some anger, and wonder if she's really let it all out."

"How do we help her? Do we talk about it? Do we ask her how she's feeling?"

"I understand your concern, Mr. Valenti. Act as normal as possible, and talk about the things you always talk about. Make plans for the future, but not too far down the road."

Lily gasped.

"Yes, Mrs. Halston," she took Lily's hand, "talk about what you're going to do when she leaves here. Ask her how she's going to feel when she's finished with the Chemo. Find out what she wants to do when she goes home. Don't worry; she'll know her limitations. The worst thing you can do is let her see fear in your eyes. That fear reflects back to her, and we don't want that."

Lily's head was swimming. She didn't want to accept the fact that Jody had cancer; didn't want to say the words; didn't want to be here. She turned to Edmund as he questioned when Jody could come home, and about her continuing treatments at the local hospital. He also asked about Jody's return to school.

She nodded in the affirmative. "Remember the patient knows what she can and can't do. By the time Jody leaves here she'll be emotionally, and spiritually strong enough to deal with whatever life holds for her. Come on, I'm sure she's anxious to see you both."

She showed them the way to Jody's cottage, and warned them about her physical appearance, reminding them that radiation and Chemo weren't chemicals that were easy on the body, and every person had a different reaction.

When Jody stood up to greet her mother, Lily felt the nauseating sinking of despair. Emotional explosions began to fill her soul. She was stunned and sickened at the sight of her daughter's emaciated body, and a bitter cold began to settle in the caves of her broken heart. Edmund grabbed her hand and squeezed it as they walked towards Jody. He smiled and put his arms around his daughter, and it gave Lily a moment to catch her breath.

Jody's thick blond hair was gone with only patches and clumps on an almost baldhead. The surgical scar was visible, still red and swollen. Jody, always petite, looked even smaller and emaciated. Her youthful glowing complexion was gone, replaced by a gray and sallow complexion that augmented her high cheekbones, and made them appear to protrude beyond her narrowed face. Her large luminous green eyes were dull and lifeless. The shapely lips, once rosy with color, were cracked and pale. Her haunting expression was that of a Holocaust victim.

Lily's body constricted from the shock. Despite her own emotions, she threw her arms around her daughter and sobbed. Jody cried as well, and time stood still for both mother and daughter. No longer could they deny what was happening, in one another's arms they each found their moment of truth, and it hurt like hell.

Edmund grabbed a box of tissues from the table and handed it to them. Jody was the first to speak, "I'm glad you're here," she mouthed 'you too', to Edmund. "Dad couldn't make it? Is he in court?"

"Yes," Lily replied, and avoided her daughter's eyes; "he said he'll be here on the week-end, if it's all right with you?"

Jody shook her head, "c'mon," she tugged on her mother, "I want you to help me put on a scarf. I feel naked walking around here with this cue ball for a head."

Lily swallowed her horror and put on a smile.

"They say your hair will grow back when the treatments are finished. How many more do you have?"

"I'm not sure," she said, and wrinkled her face, "it can't be soon enough. Would you send one of my wigs with Dad?"

Lily nodded and helped her daughter tie a yellow scarf around her head.

"What's hard to handle is the nausea, sometimes the medication doesn't help, and I keep throwing up. I probably scared you to death when you saw me. I'm really not in as bad a shape as I look, I just happen to be one of the unlucky ones that doesn't tolerate medication well. You know how I've always felt about taking pills of any kind. Even aspirins."

"They seem very nice here," Lily assured her, "in fact we spent some time with Doctor Farmingham. I hope I can remember everything she told us."

"It's really not as complicated as it sounds." An air of authority permeated Jody's voice. "There are certain disciplines that I have to master, so by the time I leave here I'll be a pro. C'mon we've got time before lunch so let's talk about something else."

"Of course, that's why we're here."

Lily wandered around the small cottage, and it allowed her time to regain her composure. The living room was simply arranged with a turquoise patterned couch pushed against the far wall. A solitary window provided a view of the grounds, as well as needed sunlight, into the drab room. The kitchen was tiny but utile with a small glass-topped table and four white wrought-iron chairs, over which hung a three-bulb chandelier.

Jody had her own room, thank good for that, Lily thought.

"Where's your roommate?" Lily asked as she walked out of Jody's bedroom. "Will we get to meet her?"

"They took her to Chicago for consultation with another Oncologist. She's forty years old, and has breast cancer. She's been in remission twice, but this time she's fighting the clock, and doesn't know if she can beat it."

"Well," Edmund said, "that means we have you to ourselves. Now do you want to tell us how you're really feeling?" Edmund grabbed Jody's hand and patted it.

"I'm doing as well as can be expected. I'm not scheduled for any treatments today so it's bound to be a good day. I'm learning that a small thing, like no nausea, is what makes this day great. There's so much I took for granted. But now I consider it a blessing to have lunch, and enjoy the feeling of a full stomach."

Jody's child-like smile touched Lily's heart, and a flash of hope skipped through her. She quickly tried to dispel it, as the doctor advised and reminded herself that her daughter had an inoperable malignant tumor. She had to realize that Jody—she stopped her thoughts just short of saying the word.

She grabbed Jody's hand as the three walked to the main dining room. Lily listened as Edmund and Jody discussed her writing, along with plans for her motorcycle, weather she should sell it or keep it. Jody shared her plans about a trip to San Francisco, and her timetable regarding her move back to her apartment.

When Edmund put his arm around his daughter, the love in his eyes was undeniable. Jody bubbled over with excitement when he challenged her. He bet her that he could walk faster backward, than she could forward. Of course he lost, but well worth it to see Jody laugh, especially when he veered off the sidewalk, tripped on a rock, tumbled sideways, and rolled down the incline.

Their day passed quicker then any of them wanted. It was time for Jody to meet with her support group. It was important that she attend these sessions, so their good-byes were short. Lily hated good-byes, the word always felt sad, and somehow final.

Edmund and Lily drove out the gate in silence, comforted only by each other's presence. "I'm glad we had a chance to talk with the doctor," Edmund began, "what she told us is important. I can understand how it will help Jody."

"Seeing Jody today made me realize how sick she really is. I feel like I could kill someone right about now. I'm doing everything in my power to stop from kicking out this damn windshield. It's a good thing I'm not driving or I'd run this damn car into a building."

Over and over Lily kicked at the dashboard. Her anger nearly choked her. "Damn it I've never felt this way before. I've always had a handle on my emotions."

"But you've never been through anything like this," he said, "I've lost one daughter, and I know about anger. And now I'm about to lose another. Only this time it's different. With Christine it was sudden. One moment she was there," he flicked his lighter and puffed on the pipe, "the next she was gone." He blew out the flame, "I think the shock," he nodded absently, "Yes! The shock is what I had to deal with. Now I'm learning to take one day at a time, and not spend time looking for miracles. While we're busy chasing a mirage, we're missing the biggest miracle of all, the life that we have to enjoy. I want to experience every bit of pleasure in the time I have left with my daughter. I've made up my mind to live these next months as we've never lived them before. When Jody comes home, the three of us are going to be inseparable."

"That means she'll have to be told about us as well, and about who you really are—"

"That's what it means, Lily. She's bright and intuitive, and if I start spending all this time with her she's going to wonder why. She might question Henry."

"You're right. It's just that it's going to be so hard. I don't know how she's going to react. How do I prepare her?" A horrific thought occurred to her. "What if she never wants to see me again?" Torment was eating at her from the inside.

Edmund patted her hand. "Now how can you even imagine that? Just listen to yourself. Do you feel so insecure in her love that you'd think your daughter wouldn't want to see you again? C'mon, get real. Sure she's going to react. Anyone would. There are a lot of questions you'll have to answer, and be ready for her anger at not telling her sooner, but I can help there. Remember, I'm going to be at your side when we talk to her. Your days of being alone are over."

* * *

Each day brought new questions; new unexplained feelings; new frustrations. One night Lily woke seething with rage. The suffocating sensation tightened her throat. She realized she was mad at Jody; angry with her daughter for putting her through this; angry that she was depriving her of years they could have together. Then shame marched through her emotions and filled her full, now she had to face all these feelings. Good thing Doctor Framingham warned her. Finally Lily had given herself permission to rant and rave.

She found it inconceivable to imagine an actual ending to her own life, let alone Jody's. She'd always associated the ending of her life to a malicious intervention from the outside; by someone else; an accident. Even dying of old age was difficult to imagine. She just never considered her finiteness. So who could she punish for what was happening to Jody? Who could she hate? Only one person was responsible for her daughters terminal illness; the same source that could remove it.

With a definite plan in mind, Lily made a pilgrimage to church, only this time with renewed hope. Because she'd accepted His will, she was convinced He'd hear her prayers, and cure Jody. She was ready to make a deal, anything that would save her daughter.

She slid quietly into the pew, careful not to disturb the few women who were kneeling in silent prayer. She thought hard about her proposal. Either way she'd be the looser, and she knew it. Her heart was heavy, but she had no choice as she fought to control the spasmodic trembling within her.

"Dear God, hear my prayer. I've tried to be a good servant, and follow your word. You brought Edmund back into my life, and for that I'll be eternally grateful.

You know how much we love each other. The secrets I carry, deep within the recesses of my heart, are known only to you. You understand my love for Edmund, and you know the love I have for my daughter. But this day I make you this solemn vow. If you'll let Jody live, I'll never see Edmund again. I promise on my life to stay married to Henry, and be a good wife; go to church every day; take communion, and be eternally grateful that you spared her.

I beg you to answer my prayer." She took a deep breath. "I love Jody so much; I can't imagine life without her. I want to keep her close to me a little longer. Please don't take her from me." She slumped over. Her head rested on her clasped hands and she sobbed. The spasms in her stomach intensified as she continued to watch and listen for some word, some sign, some feeling, anything to hang on to. She welcomed any ray of hope, any answer from God. Any sign.

Finally a tingling numbness moved through her entire body as she sat motionless and silent. No sign. No acknowledgment. Only a feeling of emptiness. She became more uncomfortable, by the minute, as her dismay grew. Tired of feeling hopeless and engulfed in bitterness, she wiped the tears with the back of her hand, and walked out of church, numbed by the experience. She realized her present composure was a fragile shell around her.

She looked at her watch. Damn, why did she have to meet with her Mom and Jim? But she had promised her brother she'd be there when he told their mother he was leaving the priesthood. It might be just the jolt she needed to teach her a lesson. And being there to see her reaction would be great. Talk about payback. After all the shit she pulled.

Suddenly Lily found herself looking forward to the occasion; perhaps her mother would finally come to realize what the real world was about. And maybe, just maybe, she'd get rid of those silly ideas about God and punishment.

Earlier, Jim and Lily had discussed the possible reactions their mother would experience, and how they would handle it. They were ready. Jim chose his living quarters to tell his mother about his decision. It was the housekeeper's day off; the three of them would be alone.

The cold winds of March whipped off Lake Michigan and left a chill that penetrated her bones. Lily braced against the cold and ran into the rectory. After the usual greetings the three family members sat down around Jim's dining room table. Nora, in her typical style, was going on about trivial subjects when she turned to Jim.

"What's the occasion? Lunch at the rectory? What's going on?" Her mouth spread into a thin-lipped smile as a muscle flicked in her jaw. She stared at her children. "You two have been awfully quiet. Normally one of you finds a reason to disagree with me."

"Mom," Jim began, "remember the last time we had lunch and you accused me of having a drinking problem? You told me I was becoming an alcoholic. Well you were right, I'm not becoming one, I am one."

Nora's smile quickly faded. The loud clank of her fork, as it dropped to the dish, startled Lily. Nora's lower lip quivered. Her face took on the likeness of a marble effigy of contempt.

"I've been going to AA meetings. In fact, I go every day. The worst part is, I'm still drinking. I know I've got a lot of problems to handle, and that's why I wanted to talk to you."

Nora's eyes iced over. "If you're going to AA, how come you're still drinking? I thought they're supposed to help? Maybe you need to go to a different group? Maybe you need to see someone else?"

Jim propped his glasses back on the bridge of his nose. "It's not like that, Mother. Before they can help me, I have to help myself. That's where the problem lies, with me—"

"Don't say that, there's nothing wrong with you. You've been a perfect son. You're a perfect priest. God chose you. You're blessed with a Holy calling."

Lily noted how well Jim was doing. He didn't need her help. At least not yet. He walked to the cabinet and brought back three glasses, along with a decanter of wine, and immediately filled all three.

"I don't want any wine, and I don't want you to have any either."

"It's not what you want that counts any more, it's what I need that matters." His hand trembled as he took a sip. "And right about now I need a glass of wine."

Lily took a sip and put her glass down. "Mother," she began, "let him finish telling you about his decision. Why don't you have some wine? It won't hurt you."

Nora peered at both Lily and Jim. "All right, but what are you two up to? Are you trying to get your hands on my stocks?"

"Sheez," Lily blurted, "for once in your life quit thinking about yourself. There are people here who need to say something. Why don't you give Jim a chance to explain things to you?"

Jim looked at Lily through the bottom of his empty wine glass. "Mother, I've got a lot of problems that I have to deal with, that's why I'm leaving—"

"Leaving! You can't leave this parish, you can't." Nora threw her napkin on the table. "He said no! The bishop promised. I have it in writing." She realized the words had slipped out, and quickly snapped her mouth shut. But it was too late.

Jim's voice resonated. "What are you talking about? The bishop promised? Promised what?"

The silence was deafening as they waited for Nora to answer. Suddenly Jim hit the table with his fist. "Answer me damn it. What did the bishop promise?"

Nora started to sob, and looked at Jim. "Years ago when you came out of the seminary, I had just received the insurance check from your stepfather's death. So I prayed to God, and asked him what I should do with it." She sniffed and blew her nose. "Then one day the answer came." she smiled, "I went to the bishop and told him that if he assigned you to St. Jerome's I'd give fifty thousand dollars to the Bishops Relief Fund."

Jim lunged forward and knocked the chair down as he stood and started around the table to his mother's side. "What!" he screamed. He quickly deflated his anger, and smiled through his tightly clenched teeth. "And, he took it?"

Nora nodded.

"Why? Why did you have to pay off the church to keep me close? You profess to love God, and have faith in his will. Then why in the hell didn't you have enough faith, and trust that he'd send me where I was needed."

Nora started to cry again. "I didn't want to be alone. Lily was married, she had Henry and Jody." She dropped her eyes and twisted a handkerchief in her hands. "I had no one, so I needed you near me. You were all I had left."

Lily was speechless. The bishop taking a bribe? She pictured the scene and smiled.

"Tell me how you managed to keep me here all these years. Tell me!" he shouted, "if you don't," he shook with rage, "I'll shake it out of you."

He started towards her. Lily jumped in front of him. "Don't worry I'm not going to lay a hand on her, as much as I'd like to." He looked down at the sobbing woman and demanded the truth. "Tell me."

Nora began to tremble then started to stutter. "Every year, I, I write a check for ten thousand dollars to the church, and they keep you at St. Josephs."

Jim shook his head as he picked up his chair. He sat silent, disgusted by all he'd heard. He poured himself another glass of wine and drank it in one gulp. A deafening silence hung over the room. Minutes passed. Then Jim turned towards his ashen gray mother. Her hands were still trembling. Suddenly Nora's arms dropped to her side.

"No one has the right to interfere in my life. That includes you, Mother. May God forgive you for what you've done. In your desperation to keep me close you've created a chasm between us that may never be bridged. Like I started to say," his soft voice lacked emotion, "I'm leaving the priesthood. I've talked with the bishop, and as soon as they find a replacement, I'm gone. This is probably my last month as a priest. I will never hold the Eucharist again. I will never say mass again."

Nora stopped crying. She starred at her son, her eyes wide with shock. She stuttered, than started to gasp for air. "I, I, I." She grabbed her throat with her left hand, as if fighting for breath. Her hand waved wildly out of control then dropped to her side. The woman sat motionless, only a soft hissing sound escaped her lips. Then her mouth went slack.

"Mother," Lily shrieked, and yelled, "I'll call 911." Jim remained on his knees in front of his stricken mother, rubbed her hands, and tried to get her to talk. There was no response. The blank stare, the slack lips and drool told it all. Nora had retreated to a safe place where she no longer had to deal with disappointment.

Lily waited for the ambulance and ran to the window every time she thought she heard a siren. Despite Jim's cajoling, there was no response from his mother. Finally the ambulance was at the rectory. Lily stayed by her mother's side till they arrived at the hospital. When she stepped out of the ambulance she expected to see Jim following behind, but he wasn't there. Lily shook her head, and rushed into the Emergency Room. Her mother needed her now. Jim would have to wait.

# CHAPTER 25

It was a cool, but sunny spring day with lilacs budding throughout the city, casting a lavender hue over the stone buildings and concrete walks. Heads of tulips pushed through the dark brown earth with their promise of a living display of color.

On one of her regular visits to see her mother, Lily decided to take the long route to Skokie, and enjoy the spring floral concert. The Forsythia's were in abundance every-where she looked, their blaze of flaxen yellow flowers graced homes, fields, and strip malls. Jonquils were bursting with yellow pride, and challenging the tulip blossoms. All nature was ready to start life anew.

As she drove along the winding roads she rolled down her window to breath in the aroma of new life. Spring was finally here. It'd been a long winter, and she wanted to put it behind her, but couldn't. She was still angry, and hurt by her mother's manipulative actions in her life, Edmund's, and now Jim's.

As she drove the main road, the tops of the buildings of the nursing home came into view high above the treetops. The winding drive curved among stately oaks and maples, finally leading to the H shaped buildings, with steeped roofs topped with red-clay shingles.

Nora's small, but austere, room held a single bed with two tables gracing either side. As she had for the past months, Nora was sitting in her leather chair. Her pink robe covered a pale pink nightgown. The scuffs, that Lily had bought, protected her limp, spider-veined, feet.

Lily brushed through her mother's hair. She touched Nora's cheeks with a little color and dabbed cologne behind her ears, all the while talking to her as if she could understand. Test results showed Nora to be in the best of physical health. Her heart was strong, no evidence of aging like arthritis, osteoporosis, or arteriolosclerosis. There was no physical reason why she should be in this catatonic state, and the doctors didn't know how long she'd remain non-communicative. The psychiatrist felt it was an escape mechanism, and they didn't know what would bring her back. The longer she stayed withdrawn, he cautioned, the harder it would be to bring her back. They encouraged Jim and Lily to continue daily visits, and to attempt to interact as though nothing were wrong, but at this time they didn't hold out much hope.

Despite years of aggravation with her mothers' behavior, Lily didn't want her last years to end this way and felt more helpless with every visit. Jim lied to his mother, and told her he'd changed his mind, and was staying on at the church. No response. Not even a twitch. Finally after another long day at the hospital, Lily, exhausted and sad, dragged herself home. She was surprised to find Henry at home, it was much too early.

"How's your Mom? I presume you've been to see her."

"No change."

He followed her into the living room.

"She just sits there and stares into space. The doctors don't know if she'll ever come back." The leather made a whooshing sound as she sank down on the couch. "I just wish there was something more that I could do to help her." She kicked off her shoes, curled her legs under her, and rested her head on her hand.

He sat down beside her, and attempted to comfort her with his reassuring words. "She's getting the best of care. That's the most you can hope for."

She studied his face, and nodded. "I know, it's just that I have such mixed emotions where she's concerned. I hate her for interfering in my life, and despise the way she's treated me. Yet I feel badly for her. You know Henry, there's no one that comes to see her, except Jim and me. She has no friends."

"Well the way she treated people," he sat back and sneered, "did you expect anything different?"

"I see the life she's created, and I feel sorry for her. She was so afraid of being alone, and now," she paused, "she's totally alone in her mind, a place where nobody can harm her. I want to cry but I don't have any tears left."

Henry coughed and turned on the television. "My campaign manager told me to watch the evening news, Townsend is announcing his candidacy for the same Circuit Court seat I've got my eye on. I want to hear what the thrust of his campaign will be."

Mark Townsend, a dark haired man in his late forties, spoke. "I am formally announcing my candidacy for the Judicial Circuit Court seat #8. When elected I pledge to aggressively fight to make the judicial changes you demand. I will stop letting prisoners off with light sentences, and I will enforce the three strikes you're out law. But before I start giving speeches, and tell you why I deserve your vote, I have a confession."

He towered over the thin brunette woman standing by his side. He put his arm around her shoulder, and gave her a charismatic smile, then turned to the camera. "I have been married to my lovely wife Sandra for twenty-five years. We've been one another's rock, and I didn't realize what she meant to me. I was unfaithful in the early years of our marriage." He swung her into the circle of his arms. His eyes reflected his sorrow.

"Sadly, it's true. It happened almost twenty years ago, and I've been sorry about it ever since. We decided to bring it into the open, and beat the tabloids or opponents to the punch. I want all my cards on the table and prove to you that, painful as it is, you have my word that there will be nothing that I'll hide from you when I'm elected." Townsend's campaign headquarters exploded in a thunderous round of applause.

Henry smiled, and hit the remote. He sat and tapped his fingers on his knees. Finally he stood up and a smug look crossed his face. "After that confession I'm assured of that judicial seat. In fact, it's in the bag. He just handed it to me on a silver platter."

Lily cocked an eyebrow.

"I'm going to tout my perfect record, both personal, and professional, every chance I get. My father always told me to keep my nose clean, I'm glad I took his advice. Just remember what I said," he cautioned, "I expect you to play the role of devoted wife till this thing is over. Then you can do whatever you like. You owe me." His lips were pulled thin, and his eyes challenged her to disagree.

She was trapped. Edmund wanted Jody told that she was his daughter. Henry warned her not to disturb the status quo. But Edmund insisted on spending more time with his daughter. And she too was hopeful they could spend the time together as a real family, but now...

If the three of them were constantly seen together, rumors would start, and the election would be in jeopardy. She couldn't do that to Henry. She'd promised. "I gave you my word," she said, "and I intend to keep it. You just make sure you treat Jody like she's your daughter."

"You forget Lily, I've known I wasn't her father since she was two. Do you think that I can stop loving her or caring for her just because you and Edmund have finally decided to claim her as yours? She'll always be my daughter, no matter what you and Edmund do. I'm sure Jody will feel the same."

He started to walk out of the room, than turned. "Oh, by the way, they're holding a big banquet at the Shriners' this Saturday, I expect you to be there." With that he turned and left the room.

Lily stuck out her tongue, wrinkled her nose, then started to stomp her feet. "Ooohhh, I hate it when he talks down to me. I hate it when he gives me orders." He'd always given the orders but for the first time she realized how much she disliked it. A gamut of perplexing emotions ran through her. She sat back and thought about what she was feeling, and it was humiliation and anger. Her eyes conveyed the fury within her. But she couldn't blame him. All these years she gave away her power, and allowed him to treat her this way.

The more she thought about it the angrier she got. She hit the arm of the chair with her fist, and moved to the mahogany desk where she opened the top drawer. She dug underneath a stack of papers, and pulled out a pack of cigarettes she'd hidden weeks before. She took one out, lit it, and puffed away, as if trying to fill the room with smoke. A spiteful and defiant smile molded her face as she walked out of the den, blowing smoke all the way up the stairs to her room.

* * *

Lily could barely contain herself as the words played over and over again in her head. 'Come and get me, I'm ready to come home.' Jody had finished her treatments. Two months away from her daughter seemed like an eternity, and Lily's spirits were soaring.

When Lily arrived at the hospital Jody was dressed, and waiting. She smiled and grabbed at her blond wig, "well how do you like it?"

"It looks great. You look so much better then the last time I saw you," Lily squeezed Jody, "you even feel like you've got some meat on those bones."

"When they finally stopped the Chemo I was able to keep food down. Then I couldn't stop eating."

How healthy she looked! "I guess all that worrying was for nothing. You look as though you could run the hundred-yard dash. You've even got some color back in your cheeks."

Jody leaned over the couch. "Mom I want to talk to you before we leave."

"My, my, we sound serious," Lily joked.

"I am. You have to understand where I was before I came here and where I'm at now," she held up her hand, "and please don't interrupt. You know you have a way of doing that." Her face screwed up.

"You're right Honey, I'm sorry. I'll do my best."

"I, I'm facing some pretty heavy stuff in the months ahead. Before I came here I was hoping for a miracle. I thought I'd have a remission and the tumor would go away just like in the movies. Mom, we have to face the facts, that's not going to happen." Jody became teary-eyed and reached for her mother's hand. "I know that now. And I want to help you realize it too."

Something was different about her daughter, and the strangeness of Jody's words smashed at her. As she stood she jerked her hand away, and clasped it to her breast. She turned away and hastily wiped a tear. "I won't listen to you talk like this. I didn't come here to talk about dying. I still have hope."

"Damn it! You promised to let me finish. You think this is easy for me? Respect me enough to hear me out. Please don't make it any harder than it is."

Lily apologized and sat down.

"Before I came here I couldn't accept the idea that I was going to die. I was too young. I kept hoping that it was all a mistake; maybe they were wrong, maybe the

Chemo would take care of everything. Well that's not going to happen."

Jody took a deep breath, smiled, and continued. "When I finally stopped denying the facts, I became enraged. Why did it have to be me? 'Why God,' was my constant prayer, please let it be someone else. There's so much I want to do. There are so many things I want to accomplish, places to see, and people to meet. And the more I thought about it, the angrier I got. It was as if this was happening to someone else, and I wanted that other Jody to come back, the one that had all the plans, and dreams for the future." Jody paused. "Are you listening? It's important that you really hear what I'm saying."

"I'm listening."

"The treatments have not, I repeat, have not shrunk the tumor. There is no remission Mother. No remission."

Lily bit at her lower lip and choked back her inclination to deny Jody's words.

"It's all right. Really. I've faced it. And I'm here for you," she stooped down and placed her hands on her stricken mother's knees. "We can face it together. I've gone through the depression, now it's your turn." Jody stood and faced the window.

"It's not going to be easy. I cried for a week straight, and felt sorry for myself about everything. It was a real pity party." Jody smiled. "The support group was great, I couldn't have made it through this without them. Meditation helped a lot. I worked on making peace with my body, and with God, and in so doing came to terms with what was happening: anger; rage; sorrow; and disappointment. You know Mom, all those things come from fear. Fear of dying. Until I faced that fear I couldn't make any headway. And face it I did."

Jody's eyes mirrored peace. "It was the hardest thing I ever had to do. There were many days I wanted to pick up that phone and call just to hear your voice. I wanted you to hold me, and tell me everything would be all right, to fix the hurt, just like you did when I was a little girl. Remember," she said smiling, "when I nearly cut my fingers off in the lawnmower, you held me all night and rocked me to sleep." Jody wrapped her arms around her middle. "I wanted to feel that security again. But from what I learned in therapy, this was something I had to work through, alone. No one could do it for me. No one could take the steps for me."

Lily's emotion-filled voice cracked. "Jody, I'd have come. You know that."

"I know but that wouldn't have helped me get to where I'm at today." She put her hand on her mothers shoulder. "After I faced the fears, I had no fight left. I remembered yelling, 'I give up God. What do you want from me? I've done everything humanly possible.' I can't be sure what happened after that." Jody's voice was steeped with excitement. Her face became flushed.

"Well, tell me. Calm down, and tell me."

Jody took a deep breath. "Some time had passed, and I was still crying. As a tremendous feeling of emptiness engulfed me I raised my eyes skyward. The deep feeling of loss came from the deepest part of my soul.

I was staring at the sky when a billowing cloud drifted across the heavens toward me. Suddenly it took a sharply defined path and started toward earth. At that moment my heart exploded with a joy I've never known. Instantly I became the joy itself, and I expanded to where I knew no boundaries, and I was part of everything. I experienced an ecstasy of knowing, a total understanding of life. Of God. As if everything that was unknowable, suddenly became known. I dropped to my knees, I was on holy ground, I was "IT", and as "IT", I had transcended time, place, and flesh. Then as fast as it came it was gone."

Lily felt a cold chill slither across her skin. The hair on her arms and neck stood up.

"When it was over I was filled with an indescribable, pleasurable pain. Pleasure with the ecstasy of the moment, and pain that it had left me. My body felt like a marshmallow, light and fluffy. I tried to understand what had happened, and as much as I understood everything during that moment, when it was over, I knew nothing. I can only remember some vast and infinite jubilation, something so great that the desolation I'd felt prior to this experience, remained only an illusion. It was then that I realized the cancer had lost. My spirit had won. The cancer could no longer control my life."

Lily reached for her daughter and hugged her. They cried in one another's arms. "I've heard about this happening to people," Lily said. "Some call it Rapture, others say it's a Beatific Vision. Whatever, you are truly blessed."

"I called Uncle Jim to tell him, and he came to see me that same day. He looks terrible, Mom. I feel so sorry for him. He told me what happened to Grandma."

"Did Jim tell you what he thought about the vision?"

"As I was telling him he started to cry. I didn't know what to do. He just sat there and sobbed. Then he hugged me and said I was blessed. He said there weren't many people who experienced what I did or at least not many who talked about it. He said that he experienced something similar when he was lying on the floor during his ordination, only his wasn't as illuminating. He said I was given a gift from God, and that he envied me my innocence. He said I was chosen and asked me to pray for him. I don't understand." She looked out across the room.

"Can you imagine, Uncle Jim asking me to pray for him? And I did, that same evening. When I get home he and I are going to have another talk. Maybe," she shrugged, "we can help each other."

"Quit going off on a tangent, finish telling me what happened."

"When I got up from my knees I was filled with a tremendous peace. No," Jody shook her head, "I was Peace. Something I'd never felt before. No thoughts were running around in my head, only a strange silence, and I felt stronger than I had in a long time. Can you believe it, I was happy? For an instant it felt like this past year was only a nightmare. Then I touched my head and felt the incision. No dream, everything was real. But why did I feel so good? Nothing had changed."

Jody paused a moment. "But it had! I felt different on the inside. I felt love! Joy! Beauty! I haven't felt those things since they told me the news. In fact I don't think I could have cried if they told me my best friend had died. Later that day, I found myself humming."

Jody looked at her mother and smiled. "But I also know that I'm going to die. This I know for sure. But it no longer scares me. It's not the end of the world, only the end of my world as I know it."

A soft glow settled on her. "There's another place I'm going to, and I don't know if it's what you call heaven. I don't know about any of that, I just know that it's not the end of me."

"I'm really trying to understand," Lily said, "I'm trying to be strong when you talk about dying."

Jody handed her mother a tissue. "Be happy for me, Mom. I'm finally at peace about all this. The reason I'm telling you this is because I want you to be at peace as well. I want you to help me enjoy the time I have left. I want to live every moment as though it will never end. I don't want the rest of my life to be about dying, I want it to be about living. Right now I want to taste good food, see strange lands, and go shopping with you. I want to enjoy the days I have left but I can't if every-time I look into your eyes I see sorrow and fear."

"You're asking me to forget that you're going to die?" Lily bit her lip. She had to sheath her inner feelings.

"Mom," she screwed up her face, "we all have to die. The difference is that I know when. You don't. In that sense I'm lucky. I have time to prepare for my transition. I want you to find your peace with what's happening. Can you do that?"

"I'll try Honey," she nodded, "I really will." She became increasingly uneasy under her daughters scrutiny.

Jody stood behind the couch and started to massage her mother's neck. "I know you will."

During the daylight hours Lily remained strong as she had promised. It was at night, in the solitude of her room, that the tears fell, the place where she buried her face in the pillow to muffle her cries. She couldn't let Jody know she was pretending.

Jody loved Emma's cooking and proceeded to eat everything in sight, much to Lily and Emma's delight, and fulfilled their mission to fatten her up. Laughter rang in the Halston house again. Henry was out of town so Edmund visited Jody every morning before class. They discussed Jody's return to class; they kicked around the idea of a trip to San Francisco, a place she'd always wanted to see; and talked about seeing her byline in the Tribune. They even considered cruising the Greek Isles.

A definite time schedule had developed. Everything they planned had to be accomplished in the next three or four months, hopefully six. Lily's heart leaped with joy at seeing the past reunited with the present. A father and his daughter, sharing life, a dichotomy to be sure. She could only imagine what it must've been like with

Christine, and how empty his life was without her. Soon he'd experience another loss, another daughter. Her heart was torn, and she wept inwardly. He didn't deserve this, no one did.

The following Wednesday Edmund and Lily helped Jody move back into her apartment. When Emma and Lily finished shopping, cooking, and baking, Jody's cabinets were full. Her freezer was brimming with prepared meals: casseroles; roasts; complete dinners that she could slip into the microwave, giving her home-cooked meals whenever she liked.

Pat visited Jody every afternoon, and brought bouquets of fresh flowers from her back yard. Yesterday, a huge bouquet of lilacs, today, yellow tulips in a crystal vase. The day before, every known fashion magazine, fourteen in all. Then they'd sit on the couch scanning the fashion pages for the latest trends, and eye-catching accessories.

When Lily watched Pat with Jody, laughing and carrying on, she thought about what a wonderful mother Pat would've made.

* * *

Edmund and Lily finally found time to enjoy each other. With her days divided between checking on Jody, and running to see her mother, Lily was exhausted. Edmund's suggestion to drive to Wisconsin sounded great, and being alone for a whole day would be heavenly. Despite her heavy heart she promised herself to enjoy their time together.

A few miles down the road they turned off the main highway and drove down a shale pathway. The rough road bounced them about, until finally the glistening vision of a lake loomed on the horizon.

"Hot dog, I was wondering if I could find this place again. It was over twenty-five years ago that I was here. A bunch of us guys camped out for the week-end, this was one of the most secluded spots I'd ever seen."

He helped Lily out of the car, grabbed the picnic basket and handed her a blanket. They strolled down a path that eventually lead to a beach. Lily felt the pine needles, soft and slippery, beneath her feet. Not a cloud in the sky, and the forecast of a seventy-degrees was perfect for a spring picnic.

Rays from the mid-day sun filtered through the green, statuesque pines and created shadowy designs on the ground. Lily kicked a pinecone out of her path, and noticed a chattering squirrel sitting at the base of a tree. Edmund grabbed a slice of bread and threw it as the squirrel stood on its hind legs and stared at the two intruders.

The woods were saturated with the musty fragrance of nature. Lily inhaled the cool air, and watched Edmund spread the blanket at the base of the single pine tree that stood on the shoreline of the lake. He removed his vest, and leaned against the tree trunk. He gazed out at the water as the noon light played tenderly upon it. Located on either side of the bleached white sandy beach, stood tall reeds and grass shoots that twisted and bent at the whim of the breeze.

"This is beautiful," she said, "I'm glad you remembered this place."

He pulled her down beside him. "I wanted us to be alone. I didn't feel like being cooped up in a restaurant or hotel room."

"I haven't been on a picnic..." she paused and rolled her eyes back trying to remember, "at least twenty years."

He opened the basket and pulled out a bottle of Zinfandel and a silver corkscrew.

"You've thought of everything." She smiled and handed him the glasses, "even stemmed glasses."

Edmund held up his glass and invited Lily to join him. "A toast, my darling. A toast to us, and our life together."

In the middle of the lake a silvery blue fish leaped, suspended momentarily in mid-air as it gulped at the bugs, and then returned to it's life giving liquid, sending ripples in all directions.

"Too bad I don't have a camera," he said, "what a wonderful picture that fish would've made."

Lily smiled, broke off a piece of Italian bread, and started to nibble on it. She looked at Edmund, and was surprised by the intensity in his eyes. A smile moved across her face, and her heart leaped when his grip tightened. A physical need kindled inside her but she quickly dismissed it with a laugh.

"What's so funny?"

"I was just thinking–" she didn't dare tell him, "just thinking," she looked away, "about the first time we made love. Remember how nervous and scared I was. I wanted you to make love to me, but I was so dumb. I didn't have the slightest idea what that entailed."

Edmund swept her into his arms and pressed his lips to hers. She succumbed to the sweetness, and warmth of his lips, and responded equally. Like a turbulent surf, a heavy pounding swelled in her breasts, and issued a primitive need that washed over her.

With a hunger too long suppressed, she wrapped her arms around him, and pressed against him. He untangled her arms from his neck, and held her away. He trailed the back of his hand across her cheek. His fingertips played lightly over her lips, like a blind man committing their form to memory.

Ignited with desire, he pulled her close. Her mouth, warm and pliable, parted easily to the teasing penetration of an exploring tongue.

He was breathing hard, but managed to push her away. "We'd better stop now or I'll ravage you."

"I know," she smiled.

He grinned and laid her back in his arms. He stared into her eyes. "I love you my Darling. My world is complete when we're together." He brushed her loose strands of hair to the side. "I can't wait until Jody knows about us. I dream about her calling me Dad, Father, or whatever."

His eyes sparkled when he spoke about his daughter, but guilt continued to slap at her. She hadn't told him about Henry's objection to Jody being told anything right now.

"Where were you Lily? I lost you for a moment. You're going to have to learn to shut your head off."

"I'm sorry Edmund it's just that—"

"I know. I'm satisfied just being with you." He leaned over her and kissed her eyes, nose, and chin. "We don't have to make love, as much as I'd like to," he quickly added, "you have to be mentally free, and I don't feel you are."

"You're right." She looked up at the blue sky, her brow wrinkled. "I wonder if I'll ever be free again." She exhaled a deep sigh, and looked at him. "With my mother in a home, and Jim with his drinking, did you know he's leaving the priesthood?"

"He's what?" Edmund sat up. "When did he tell you that? I spoke to him a couple of weeks ago and he didn't say a word."

"I'm sorry, I thought I told you. That's what threw my mother into a catatonic state. She couldn't handle the shock of her son walking away from the church."

"We have to talk to him, and tell him about us, and Jody. Maybe once he sees he's not the only one with problems...are you game?"

"Of course. I care what happens to him. Anything that I can do to help."

"That's all we can do is try. Maybe we can convince him to open up."

Lily leaned across the blanket. "I love you Mr. Valenti."

Edmund smiled, his white teeth contrasted with his rugged complexion. "I know." He pecked her lips with his. "And I love you, Lily Halston. Together we can handle anything."

## Chapter 26

Days turned into weeks, and weeks bordered on months. Lily watched her daughter grow stronger, making it even more difficult to accept Jody's prognosis: she looked so well, so alive. But Jody never let her forget her prognosis. Whenever Lily talked about remission, she'd remind her that the tumor was still growing inside her head.

"It seems as though I've tapped into a reservoir of creativity that goes beyond my deepest expectations. Even the professor has commented on the depth and strength of my writing."

"I've read some things you've written recently. They're marvelous. If you can tap into that reservoir to create, it should be able to heal you as well. Have you given up?"

A suspicious line appeared at the corner of Jody's mouth as she sat on the floor by her mother's feet. "I haven't given up," she clutched her blouse near her heart, "my life is a gift, every day is a gift. Let me spend it as I please? Why can't you understand that?"

"No, damn it, and you have no right to expect that of me. I'll fight for your life to the very end." Her face softened as she stroked Jody's cheek. "I can't do anything else," she whispered, "can you understand that?" A tumble of confused thoughts and feelings assailed her.

Jody went to her CD player and put on their favorite song, 'There's a Place For Us'.

"What are you doing? Why are you playing that song? Are you trying to taunt me?" Lily's eyes started to mist. Her emotions seemed out of control.

"No, Mother, I love you. I want you to accept the inevitable. I have. What aren't you at peace about? Maybe I can help." Jody hesitated. "What I've learned from all this is that peace doesn't come when the soul has unfinished business. Search your heart and see what you've left undone. Then maybe peace will fill your heart, they way it has mine."

Lily shook her head. "I don't know what you're talking about. You're not making any sense."

"When I took care of my emotional baggage, and came to grips with what was happening to my body, a deep sense of peace and harmony set in. A feeling of having done what I came here to do, a sense of accomplishment; a feeling that it was all right to leave."

Lily stared at her daughter. "I envy your courage. I can feel the peace around you," she looked down at her hands, "but I'm not there yet."

"Get to the bottom of things that you need to face. Despite the pain, look at them, and you'll be on your way."

"I don't know what I have to face? I don't even know what you're talking about." She searched anxiously for the meaning behind her daughter's words.

Jody looked at her with a discerning eye. "C'mon Mom be honest. You and the prof...Edmund"

"What are you talking about?" A thought tore at her insides. Did she know?

"You know very well what I'm talking about. You're an entirely different person when you're with him. Remember when we went to Brookfield Zoo, you were actually humming. I've never heard you do that. You were happy being with him, and that's okay. I can understand about you, and Daddy. He's a stuffed shirt, and you've acquiesced to his style of living, but it's not you. I know you haven't slept together for years." Jody hesitated. "Now tell me you don't know what you have to face."

Lily stared at her. She started to squirm and stalled for time to gather her thoughts. But hearing the words aloud, and from her daughter somehow made it easier.

"I love Edmund, Honey. I've loved him ever since we were kids. I suppose I can tell you now, he's asked me to marry him."

Jody hugged her. "Oh, Mom, I'm so happy for you. You two belong together, I can see it, and I can feel it. Have you told Dad yet?" Lily nodded.

"What did he say?"

"I told him a month ago. He wasn't surprised or so he said. We had words, but that passed. As usual he wasn't the least bit disturbed, or at least he didn't show it. He said it was a long time in coming."

"I'm happy for you and Edmund, but I'm sad for Dad." She moved her head from side to side. "His whole life has been the law. I wonder what he's going to do without you?"

"You're kidding, aren't you?" She looked at her daughter in interested amazement. "Judging by your expression, I guess you're not. Don't worry he'll do just fine without me. When I'm home he's always buried in a brief or looking up some case law."

Jody wrinkled her eyebrows. "I've seen him pace the floors when you were working late at the hospital. When he'd hear you drive in, he'd rush back to his chair, pick up a book, and pretend to read. He didn't want you to know he was worried."

"Well. Maybe he did it, once. He's never really been that concerned about me."

"Oh, c'mon," she eyed her mother, "I know, I lived there too. I watched him pace the floor when you were out. And that week when you and Pat went to the mountains; he was like a lost puppy. He walked around with a long face, and kept asking me if you had called. When I told him to call, he wouldn't hear of it. He said he didn't want to disturb you."

Surprised by the information, Lily tried to picture Henry missing her. "If that's true, why didn't he ever tell me?"

"He's not like that. He has a hard time showing affection, for anyone. You know something? He's never told me he loved me or even put his arms around me, not even with this cancer stuff. Strange," her voice softened, "I know he loves me. I can tell by the way he looks at me. I feel his concern. He's got so much locked up inside him. If he could only let it out he'd be a different person."

Lily marveled at the wisdom spewing from her daughters' lips. "When did you get so smart?"

"Remember when I told you about reaching into the deep recesses of yourself," her eyebrows shot up, "that's where the answers are. Maybe not the ones you want to hear, but you get answers. All you have to do is get rid of the concepts about anyone or anything, and the truth surfaces. It's that simple"

Lily laughed. "My daughter the philosopher."

"When are you and Edmund getting married? Soon, I hope? You know I have a right to be there."

Lily took a quick sharp breath. Her heart started to pound like a trip hammer. "What do you mean you have the right to be there?" She held her breath.

Jody smiled. "Well you're my mother aren't you? And he's my Professor. Somehow I feel responsible for bringing you two together. If I hadn't signed up for his class we might not be here talking about him."

Lily exhaled. "You're right Honey, but your dad wants me to wait until after the election. He feels it could hurt his chances for the Judgeship. I agreed."

"You can't," Jody cried out, "I don't have that much time." Tears filled her disappointed eyes. "I want to see you and Edmund married. I have to see you married to the man—"

"Don't cry, Sweetheart. We'll figure something out. Everything always works out for the best. This will too," she dabbed at the tear-streaked face with a tissue, relieved that Jody didn't know her true parentage and thrilled that she wanted to attend their wedding. If only she could make it till Christmas.

What was it the doctor told them to watch for? The first sign would be headaches. Then her vision would start to blur, and it would be more painful for her to lie down then to sit up. Several months later she'd lose her motor skills. Lily gasped. "What's wrong? You look pale. Do you feel all right?"

Lily forced a smile. "Of course, I was just thinking about marrying Edmund, and I started to get nervous and excited. He has that effect on me. By the way, when are you two leaving for San Francisco?"

Jody's voice was filled with excitement. "Edmund made reservations for next week. I'm so excited; I've never been to California, or San Francisco. I can hardly wait. I wish you were coming with us. I know you can't, it wouldn't look right."

Lily harbored the same thought. But in deference to Henry she chose to stay behind, and give Edmund and his daughter this time. Alone. A time that was long overdue, no matter how impermanent.

"I'm glad you understand," she smiled, "this will be a good time for Edmund to show you his old stomping grounds. I think you're good for him, Honey. I'm sure the two of you will have a lot of fun. And no riding those crazy motorcycles out there, you know how I worry."

"I'm not afraid of anything anymore. What's there to be afraid of? Dying? I'm going to do that anyway, and soon." She laughed.

"You have a sick sense of humor, young lady. Just make sure you call me when you get there. Don't forget to take your medicine and don't give me that patronizing look, I can still take you across my knee."

"You're a great mom even though you're kind of old fashioned."

Lily tapped her daughter across the rear, then walked out of the apartment happier then she'd been in a long time. Wisdom comes from many sources, she thought, even one's own children.

* * *

Edmund opened the front door. Joy bubbled in his laugh, and shone in his eyes. He kissed Lily, and ushered her into the house. "This is a nice surprise, to what do I owe this pleasure?"

Barely able to contain her excitement, Lily grabbed Edmund's hand and screamed, "she knows! Jody knows!"

He fell back in his chair. "How did she find out?" His brows rose as he sat up straight. Then he wrinkled his face. "How did she take it? How did she find out I'm her father?"

"Oh! No, I'm sorry. I didn't mean that. What I meant was I told her about you and me. Well, actually, she told me that we were in love. I just confirmed her suspicions. I told her that you asked me to marry you."

He managed a reluctant smile. "How did she take it?"

"She was thrilled. She's felt for a long time that we belonged together."

His broad smile returned. "A girl after my own heart." Lily groaned and sat back in the chair. "It broke my heart when she said she wanted to be at our wedding." She sat up, than leaned forward. "I don't know," she said, and shook her head in sadness, "if she can make it that long. She's in great shape now but according to the doctors she can start–" she faltered, than rolled her eyes upward, "all of a sudden she could be bed ridden. I didn't know what to tell her, so I explained about waiting until after the election. But all she wants is to be at our wedding. What are we going to do?"

"Well," he clamped his jaw tight, and stared, "we know what the signs are, and she's had none of them so far. In fact, the other day she complained about gaining weight. So, I'd say she's holding her own. I wouldn't be taking her to San Francisco if I thought she couldn't make it."

He filled his pipe then lit it. After letting out a puff of smoke he tapped the bowl of his pipe in the ashtray. "Give me some time to think about this. Maybe we can have a mock ceremony, you know, a pretend service, this way she could–" he shook his head from side to side. "That wouldn't be fair. She's been deceived long enough. No more lies. What's the chances," his eyes narrowed to slits, "that Henry would change his mind about a divorce before the election?"

"Are you kidding? He's told me, over and over, that this has been his life's goal. He's not about to do anything to spoil his chances, Jody or no Jody. I have to respect his wishes; after all he gave our daughter a home and a good life. I owe him that much. When I leave, he'll have nothing but the law. We'll have each other."

Edmund reamed out his pipe, refilled it and puffed on the stem as he lit it. He cleared his throat, and spoke with hesitation. "I don't know Honey, I don't have any answers right now. We've got some time to think about this, I'm sure there's a solution. I've always believed there's an answer to every problem." He raised his brows, and continued to puff on his pipe.

"You make it sound so simple."

"It is. Just knowing there's an answer is what helps me let go. And when I do, the answer comes. Strange isn't it. One thing I've discovered, everything in life is simple. We're the ones that fuck it up. Nature displays its individuality within the framework of its own simplicity. Everything fits together baby, just like you and me."

For the first time since his return to Chicago there were no shadows. Like the brilliant sun, her heart radiated joy and sang with delight. His mood, euphoric and gentle, made her feel like a cork bobbing on the surface of placid water. She grabbed his hand and expressed her contentment with his presence, grateful that she had been blessed with his love.

* * *

Jim stumbled into the rest home, staggered down the hall, and bounced off the walls as he weaved toward his mothers' room. He took a deep breath, and paused before going in. He walked over to her dresser and picked up a photo of her, Lily, and himself, taken on the day he was ordained. He laid it down with the picture face down.

Next to it stood a twelve-inch statue of the Miraculous Infant of Prague, gowned in white, and robed in a flowing red cape. The cherub like face was framed in light brown curly hair, and on its head rested a golden crown. She'd always kept this statue on her dresser, and he was glad Lily brought it with.

Nora sat in her beige leather chair, ten feet from the television, that same blank stare frozen on her face. Jim waved his hand in front of her. No response, not even a blink. Forlorn, he plopped down on the edge of the bed. Why had he come?

His speech was thick and slurred. "I've had too much to drink." He wiped his hand across his mouth, and pointed a shaky finger at her. "I know you don't like my drinking, but you don't know what's going on." He shook his head. "Maybe it's for the best. Having the damnedest time kickin this demon." He slid out a flask from his jacket, and took a swig.

"One step forward, then back two. Then need more wine. But I made a discovery...Vodka gets me there quicker. That way I don't have to drink as much to get rid of the pain. You should've tried this Ma, it's great."

He paused, than wobbled to her side. "You knew you had an alcoholic for a son," he wiped his mouth with the back of his hand to remove the spittle that dribbled down his chin, "you knew, didn't ya? Always knew when children were in trouble. You saw me drinking a lot of times. I'm the one that didn't know I had a problem."

He dropped to his knees in front of her, grabbed her hands from her lap and started to kiss them. "I'm sorry Mom for doin this to you. I never realized my leaving the priesthood would have this effect on you. If I'd only known." Tears filled his eyes and trickled toward the corner of his mouth. He kissed her hands again and laid his head in her lap.

"I should've lied. Should've told you I was bein transferred to another parish, out of state." He rocked back and forth as the sobs wracked his body. He moaned repeatedly. "If I'd only known, if I'd only known. Please forgive me, I didn't mean to hurt you. I was only doin what I knew I must."

He raised his head and wiped the tears with the sleeve of his shirt. Then he put the flask to his lips, and took a big gulp. The burning liquor hit his stomach. He coughed, than wiped his mouth with his hand and took another swallow. He looked out the corner of his eye at his mother. He corked the flask, and struggled to find the inside breast pocket, then lost his balance, and fell. He slowly picked himself up and crawled to his mothers' chair.

"This is my confession. I wanna tell you the truth. AA says you have to ask for forgiveness. I'm doin a totally selfish thing, but I have to, so I can go on."

He made the sign of the cross, raised his eyes heavenward and began, "bless me Fath–," he stopped and dropped his eyes. The vacant orbs stared into space. "Bless me Mother for I've sinned. I confess to you that I have disobeyed the fourth commandment. I took the life of a human being. I killed not once, not twice, but many times. It happened over and over again."

His pulse was erratic and he became afraid. He gasped, and started to pant as the memory of those days filled him with terror. "I couldn't stop. Once they started comin at me I started shootin. When that didn't stop 'em, and they kept comin, I started swingin, bayonet in one hand, my knife in the other, cuttin whatever crossed my path. I saw one man's hand hurl through the air and watched another mans head hang by a thread. I even stabbed one of em so hard his blood squirted all over me. I tasted it and wanted to throw up." He shook his head to disperse the sweat that poured from his brow.

"No time, didn't have time. More comin at me." He nodded as he replayed the action in his head. "Had to keep killin. It was them or me. I didn't wanna die. I don't remember how long."

He relaxed his position. "I heard gunfire from my flank, it was our guys comin over the hill. The killin was finally over."

He sank back on the floor, his face wet with tears and sweat. He was nauseated, and tried to catch his breath. As he tried to stand he fell back. He rolled over on his stomach, and threw up on the floor.

He kept retching with his face in the vomit. He propped his forearms on the floor and pushed up into a kneeling position. Then he held on to the legs of the chair, where his mother sat, and slowly picked himself up. He weaved to the bathroom, grabbed a towel, wiped his face, staggered back into the room and attempted to wipe up his puke.

He threw the soiled towel in the shower stall and knelt against his mother's side. "I haven't told you the best part," he laughed sadistically, "the real kicker to this tale, your son the priest, the one who swore to keep God's commandments, killed a lot of men. Know what," he giggled, "I enjoyed it!"

He stood up, and continued in a raspy voice. "Enjoyed it so damn much, probably do it over gain if I could. Felt good killin em. Felt powerful like—" he stopped, and carefully considered his words.

"I felt like I was God." His eyes glowed with a savage inner fire. Then he paused and stared out the window. He began to moan and repeatedly stroked his breast. "I liked the feelin when I was killin. It was me, lowly Jim, who had the ultimate decision as to whether they lived or died." He turned back to face his stone-faced mother.

"God help me."

He staggered over to the edge of the bed, slumped down, and buried his face in his hands. "No way! No, no, no! He pounded his head with his clenched fists. "I'm a priest. Priests don't kill, they save souls. I can't stay, got to leave the priesthood. Pretending to be somethin I'm not is getting to me." He looked at his mother and hoped she'd somehow heard his confession.

"Know it all," he swung his arms wildly. "This poor excuse of a son you've raised has turned out to be a failure, a killer, a poor example of a man." He took out his handkerchief and wiped his face. "I've broken every one of God's laws. Sorry Mama," his voice cracked, "I can't be a priest any longer. I hurt you. Sorry I did this to you. Can't hide my dark side any longer. Have to face it."

He knelt down in front of her and took her blank face into his hands. He kissed both cheeks and looked into the unseeing eyes. He tilted his head to the side and spoke in a child-like voice. "Forgive me Mama, I didn't mean to hurt you. I just wanted you to be proud of me. I have to try and go on. I thought about takin easy way out, like Dad. But when it comes to takin my own life, I'm a coward. Couldn't do it, putting a gun to my head is insanity."

After a long silence he began to giggle and threw his head back and roared. Gales of laughter shattered the silence. He pushed his glasses back on the bridge of his nose, kissed his mother, and turned away. He gasped at what he saw.

The door was partially open and revealed Edmund and Lily behind it. His fists were clenched and started to tremble. He started to scream. "How long have you been standing there? How dare you." He glared at them as his lips continued to move in silent tremors. "How long?"

"Long enough," Edmund replied, "long enough my friend to find out what's going on."

"Why the hell didn't you knock?"

"We did," Lily said, "but you were talking so loud you didn't hear us, so we decided to let you get it off your chest. We came to see Mom and tell her about us, but instead we found you."

Jim staggered backward, bumped into the bed, than caught himself before he fell. Edmund rushed into the room to help steady his friend. Than Jim reached into his pocket for the flask Edmund quickly grabbed it out of his hand.

"No more, it's all over. You don't have to hide in there any longer. Everything's in the open, and now you can look at it. The worst is over."

Not trusting himself to speak, Jim loosened his grip on the flask. Edmund grabbed his hands, helped him to the bed, and urged him to sit down. Jim grabbed Edmund's shirt and pulled him close.

"Help me. Please help me! I'm lost. Please God, have mercy on me."

Lily sat by his side and put her arm around his shoulder. "I love you Jim. There's nothing that you can do or say that can ever change that. I know God feels the same. Remember we're all human. God doesn't expect perfection. If we were perfect we wouldn't be on earth. I believe we're here to learn lessons, and all we can do is our best. I don't think he expects any more of us. Do you?"

Jim stared at his sister. "I don't know about God any more. I don't know about anything."

"Stay and visit with your mom, Lily," Edmund said, "I'll take Jim home, then come back for you."

Jim hugged his sister then turned and walked out with Edmund at his side. Lily looked at the silent woman, and sighed.

"You missed it Mom. You missed seeing the best part, your son as a human being and may God bless him for it."

# CHAPTER 27

Pat walked into Nora's room with a bouquet of roses in one hand, along with a gold and white striped hatbox hanging from her wrist. In the other hand she carried a large soup tureen. "Hi Nora. I know you don't like me, but that's okay, the feeling is mutual. But I don't like to see anybody in your situation. No matter what."

Pat arranged the roses in a container and continued to talk to Nora. "I'm here for two reasons, the first is to give you this new hat. I hope you like it." Pat opened the box, arranged the large white picture hat on Nora's head and adjusted the large brimmed hat so the red rose was on the side.

"I've come to apologize for calling you all those names. Not that you didn't deserve it, but I feel bad now that you're like this. But god damn it Nora, why the fuck did you interfere in your daughter's life? She deserved better from you. You thought you knew better, but I've got news for you, you didn't. Or did you? And that brings me to the second reason I'm here."

Pat turned Nora's chair around to face her. "I know you can't hear me, but I've just got to tell someone what I've been up to. You know me I've got a big mouth and what I'm doing is almost as bad as what you did."

Pat rose and started to walk around the room. "When I met Edmund I really liked him, and believed he was perfect for Lily. But something kept eating away at me.

Something about that man, he was too perfect, if you get my drift."

Pat took a rose from the vase and put it in Nora's lap. "I don't want Lily to get hurt again, so I've done something I'm not so sure about. I've hired a private detective to check up on Edmund's past."

Pat took a deep breath and turned to see if there was any reaction from the old woman in the chair. Nothing. "Do you know something about him that you've never told anyone? I know that despite your fucking bad manners, you're no fool. What did you know about this man that made you so desperate to save Lily? If there is something, I hope I can find it. Who ever thought you and I would ever be on the same side. I feel like a god damn traitor."

Pat looked into the mirror. "I sure hope Lily won't hate me for doing this, but she's going through enough shit and I don't want this man to destroy what's left of her." Pat took the rose from Nora's lap and adjusted her hat again. "Well I feel better now that I got that off my chest. I sure hope you feel better Nora, but I can't help but wonder about the irony of you being rendered silent."

Pat smiled and walked out.

* * *

In order to fulfill Jody's wish to see her and Edmund married, Lily knew she had to talk to Henry again. She hoped to convince him that she could fly to Mexico and get a quiet divorce. No one in the state of Illinois would know anything about it.

Their meeting was short and to the point. Henry was vehement, he would not agree to a divorce until the election was over. He wanted Jody to have her wish, but he had a lot at stake and couldn't justify years of work and planning against one wedding. His only concerns were Jody's health, and his campaign.

Lily understood his point of view and didn't push him to change his decision. She didn't want to make waves.

* * *

"Well, look at you Missy," Pat said, "don't you look cool. Is that outfit new?"

Lily smiled and twirled like a fashion model at the table in the Country Club dining room. "Jody and I've been doing a lot of shopping. This one's from Fields."

Lily returned the compliment. "That red halter dress is sexy!"

Pat wrinkled her nose and adjusted her silicone breasts into the cups of the dress. "I've ordered you a drink, a Bloody Mary. By the way I went to see your mother yesterday."

"You did?" Lily frowned. "I thought you didn't like her."

"I never said I didn't like her," her tone was defensive, "I didn't like the way she treated you and the way she tried to run over everyone. Besides, it was a totally selfish visit. My garden's filled with roses and I needed a place to take them. Besides, I wanted to ease my conscience."

Lily raised her eyebrows. "About what?"

"Well," she smiled coyly, "whenever I mouth off about someone, and they get sick I feel bad, maybe even a little guilty. So," she raised her shoulders, "to ease my conscience, I do something nice. In your mom's case it was for naught." She wrinkled her nose and raised her penciled brows.

"She didn't even know I was there. She just sat there, staring off into space. A new summer hat didn't evoke the slightest reaction. Nada. I even took a tureen of my famous 'Polish Penicillin' chicken soup, 'good for the soul' and all that crap."

Lily smiled. "I don't know if I've ever told you, but I appreciate you being my friend."

"Stop, already! You're going to have me crying." Pat mimicked tears by dabbing at her eyes with the napkin. "I can't afford to have my make up smeared. You never know who I'll meet." She rolled her eyes and wiggled her raised brows.

Lily gazed out the large picture window that overlooked the eighteenth hole. A warm July sun cast its heated glow over the golfers as they sat patiently in their white canopy golf-carts, waiting to tee off.

Lily jumped. "I forgot to tell you. Remember when I saw Edmund's picture in the paper, announcing he was coming back to Chicago? Do you remember me telling you that I woke up that morning with a feeling of foreboding, and Henry pooh-poohed it?"

Pat nodded, "Vaguely."

"Well, the same thing happened yesterday. Only, this time it was worse. I woke up in a cold sweat and my stomach was tied in knots. I was trembling. I thought I'd had a nightmare. Then this terrible feeling came over me, like I was enveloped in a cloak of fear. I haven't been able to shake it. Something terrible is going to happen."

Pat slapped her hand. "Phoo. It's probably all this shit catching up with you." She sucked the last of her drink through the straw and the slurping noise broke the tension. "You haven't had time to deal with one thing then you're hit with something else."

"I don't know," Lily shifted in the chair, "this feeling has something to do with me." She shivered for a moment. "I can still feel it."

"Well," holding her empty glass aloft, Pat motioned the waiter for another round, "have another drink, and order the pasta with garlic. You know what they say about garlic," her eyes narrowed when she made a sour face, and spoke like 'Count Dracula'. "It wards off the evil spirits."

"Be serious, will you?"

"I can't. You've been through so much shit, serious is out. By the way how's Jody?"

Lily began to feel the effects of the vodka, and started to unwind. "She and Edmund left a couple of days ago for California. Jody's always wanted to see San Francisco, and since he's lived there, he was thrilled to be her guide. I'm just glad they have this time together."

"That's great, but why didn't you go?"

"How could I? If anyone found out I was with Edmund, and still married to Henry, it would be the end of the election. I couldn't do that to him. After all, I promised."

"Bullshit. Henry said he didn't care if you saw Edmund, as long as it wasn't in public? C'mon Lily you should be there with them, you know, one of those family things. Who knows if you'll get the chance to interact as a family ever again? I think you should get on the next plane and spend a day or two with them. Once you're gone what's Henry going to say. There's nothing keeping you here, unless you feel you have to take care of Emma."

"Very funny." Maybe it isn't such a bad idea, Lily thought. San Francisco was far enough away, and she could bunk with Jody, so reservations wouldn't be a problem. Maybe she could pull it off without hurting anyone. She and Henry didn't have any friends or relatives in the Bay area so she wouldn't have to worry about bumping into anyone.

Pat signaled the host for a phone. She pressed in seven digits and handed the phone to Lily. "This is my travel agent, make a reservation on the next plane to San Francisco. I'll drive you to O'Hare and pick you up when you return."

Lily's hesitation was short lived. Excited, she grabbed the phone. The seven o'clock flight to the Bay area would be fine, with a return trip scheduled in three days. Pat nodded as Lily laid down the phone.

"Now that wasn't so bad was it?"

* * *

As the taxi pulled around the hotel's circular drive the jacketed doorman opened the car door. He snapped his fingers and motioned for a bellhop. Two enormous glass doors opened and Lily found herself in the busy lobby of the St. Regis.

A familiar voice rang out. "Mom, over here." Jody rushed towards her with Edmund in toe. She threw her arms around her mother. "You must have been reading our minds. Edmund and I were just saying that we wished you were here. When we got back from Seal Point your message was waiting."

Edmund kissed Lily on the cheek, and nuzzled her ear. "I'm glad you're here too."

"I didn't want to interfere with any plans the two of you made, but Pat convinced me I should come. That's not true, she only nudged, and here I am. We only have a few days, so let's get busy."

Edmund held Lily's hand as Jody rambled on about all the things they'd seen and done. She talked about the cable cars, and described how the big orange bridge disappears when the fog rolls in from the bay. She went on and on about the bridge at night, the stars above, and the mountains as a backdrop. She talked about Fisherman's Wharf and the cruise around San Francisco Bay.

"Dinner is always at a different restaurant, and when I think I've found my favorite, he finds another, even better." She turned to Edmund; her eyes twinkled with a child-like delight.

They stopped at Jody's room. Edmund unlocked the door and pointed a finger in mock consternation. "Listen you two, I'll give you a half hour to get ready. I want to show you the city by night."

"I'm so happy, Mom," Jody began, "with Edmund as my guide I'm seeing this city from a different point of view, his. He doesn't see the old decaying buildings or the dirty streets or the weird characters. He sees the stories behind each one of those old facades. He tries to imagine who lived there fifty years ago and the problems they might have faced. He's really an interesting man. I've seen another side of him, a side I'm sure many people don't get to see. And I'm learning so much about writing, I just wish I had the time to write a nov—"

Jody stood silent at her mothers' side. "Tomorrow we're going to take a ride into the wine country. That should be fun, especially now that you're here." She squeezed her hand as a knock sounded at the door.

"Geez, that was the quickest thirty minutes ever."

Edmund strolled into the room with two splits of champagne immersed in a silver wine bucket. "I think this surprise visit deserves a toast." The corks popped, and Edmund poured. "Now what shall we drink too?" He studied them for a moment. "I know," he smiled and held up his glass, "to the two most exquisite women in the world. And," he gulped his drink than refilled their glasses, "they both happen to be mine."

Jody giggled, "I'll drink to that," and took a sip of the bubbly liquid.

Lily took her turn, and lifted her glass. "I think we should toast our guide. I know he's going to make the next few days memorable."

"Wow that's a heavy order, but I gladly accept the challenge. Now it's off to dinner at Augustinos', and I'll fill you in on this evenings itinerary." He showed them Market Street, Giadelli Square, and then on to the Embarcadero. The pier was crowded, laden with cargo. They shopped all of Chinatown and Jody fell in love with an oil portrait of an Asian girl, with large sad eyes, holding her pet cat. Edmund carried the oversized painting in and out of the small shops in China town, grumbling playfully, as he knocked into shelves.

Jody spotted a quaint storefront, off Main Street, and pulled her mother into the tiny shop. It was so small Edmund couldn't maneuver the painting among the tiny aisles, so he put it by the door and proceeded to scan the crowded shelves for interesting merchandise.

Jody drifted to the rear of the store, and began to browse through the dusty shelves filled with old merchandise. Her eyes opened wide as she reached far back on the dusty shelf. She held a miniature house in the palm of her hand. Its tiny front door swung open, and the windows moved up and down. Most amazing of all, the handmade bamboo house had a purple roof.

"I've got to have this," Jody exclaimed, "I don't know why but I feel a connection to this house, it makes me feel good."

An aging Asian peered at them through strands of beads that hung over a side door. Dressed in his native silken kimono, his Fu Manchu mustache hung to his chin. He wore a bowl shaped skull-cap on his head, and his hands were folded and encased in the opposite sleeves of his gown. As he passed them he bowed, and in short choppy steps, shuffled to the front counter.

They followed him to the front of the store, and Jody carried the purple roofed house in the palm of her hand as if it were made of fine glass. In broken English the shop owner inquired, "you know meaning of loof?" he pointed to the purple roof.

Jody shook her head no.

"This house for you?" He pointed to Jody.

"Yes, I just love it. The purple roof is such a unique idea."

"Purple loof mean, he who get house with purple loof is blessed." He pointed to Jody. "It mean you spend eternity with Budda."

Jody was speechless, and glanced at her mother and Edmund. "I knew it was for me. It feels good just to hold it."

The shopkeeper carefully wrapped the bamboo house in tissue paper and placed it in a box. He smiled at Jody and she smiled back, it was as if the two of them shared a secret.

As they left the store Lily wondered about Edmund's philosophy. 'There are no accidents'. 'No coincidences.' Here was Jody walking out of the store with a miniature house that, according to an old Chinese proverb, would guarantee her eternal life. How interesting, she thought.

After their jaunt through Chinatown, Edmund drove to Mission Dolores, Golden Gate Park, Telegraph Hill, Point Lobos and the opulent Nob Hill area. At the end of three hectic days, while driving back from the wine country, Lily slipped off her shoes, and rubbed her tired feet into the carpet of the rented Lincoln. As they neared the hotel she tried to slip her shoes back on but they wouldn't fit. Her feet had swollen so bad that she had to walk through the hotel lobby, barefoot.

She turned to Edmund and started to laugh. "No more, I give up. I've had enough. It's time for me to go home. I'm going to need a vacation from this vacation."

He winked at Jody. "Well I'm surprised you were able to keep up as good as you did. You've done well, I'm proud of you." He leaned over and kissed her, then dropped his head back, and roared with laughter.

"What's so funny?"

"You," he laughed and pointed to her feet, "if you could only see what you look like walking across the elegant lobby of the St. Regis dressed in your yellow Armani pants suit and carrying your yellow shoes in hand. Who knows, you might start a new trend. But you know what? I'd love you whether barefoot or clad in designer shoes, you're still the only woman for me."

Lily blushed. She caught Jody's reaction, and saw her smile. Edmund tucked Lily and Jody on either side of him, put his arms around their waists and pulled them close.

Jody looked at Lily, then Edmund. "I can't tell you how much this has meant to me. I hate to see it end. The only thing that helps is knowing that we can do this when we get back to Chicago."

He looked at Lily with a challenging glint in his eyes. She knew he wanted to tell Jody the truth but couldn't. She kissed him on the cheek then spun out of his reach. "Well I've got to start packing. If I miss my plane, and Pat has to sit at the airport, you'll hear her yell all the way to California."

The jumbo jet winged its way east across the states, it's powerful jet engines hummed monotonously and lulled

Lily into a light sleep, for what she thought to be minutes. Suddenly she woke with a start. Her heartbeat was rapid, and her palms were sweaty. She opened her eyes, and tried to catch her breath. That same damn feeling, she thought. She felt clammy as the foreboding feeling of impending danger enveloped her. She scanned the darkened cabin and looked at the other passengers, some of whom had propped their pillows under their heads, enabling them to doze. She forced herself to take slow deep breaths. What was she being warned about?

For the rest of the long flight home Lily tried to ignore her heart palpitations. Was it a warning that the plane might crash? Wary, she kept a watchful eye on the activities of the stewardesses, looking for any signs of distress on their faces as they moved leisurely about the cabin.

The intercom broke the silence as the voice of the pilot announced their approach to O'Hare. They would be on the ground in less then twenty minutes. The 'fasten seat belt' sign flashed, and her fear eased when she felt the thump and screech of the wheels when they touched down on the tarmac. What were her feelings trying to tell her?

* * *

A week later Jody and Edmund returned from San Francisco. Lily was at her daughters' apartment with an arm full of groceries. "Mother, I'm the only one living here. I don't have a roommate anymore. Do you think I'm feeding the whole building?"

"Of course not," she shrugged, "it's just that I don't want you to run out of food. You know Emma, she's always baking and cooking."

Jody looked at her mother and smiled. "Of course, this is all Emma's idea."

Lily stopped in the doorway to the living room. "Ugh!" The entire floor was covered with greasy motor parts. "What the heck are you doing now? What's all this?" She pointed to the debris that littered the floor.

"I decided to take apart my motorcycle. I'm cleaning it, and putting it back together. It helps me keep tabs on my coordination."

"What does that have to do with anything?"

"I figure, if I can work with all these tiny parts, and see them as well, that means I'm still holding my own. It means," she said quietly, "I haven't lost any muscle function. This exercise tests brain skills and hand dexterity. And so far all my parts are still working. Look," she pointed to the engine, "I put it back together."

Lily shook her head. "I don't know about you. Where in the world did you ever get that idea? It's wild, but it makes sense."

Jody giggled as Lily carefully stepped over the motorcycle parts while attempting to make her way into the kitchen. Dark circles had settled in the pockets under Jody's eyes. Their usually lively sparkle waned with weariness.

"You look tired. Are you feeling all right?"

Jody stretched her arms and arched her back. "I just feel a little achy." She rubbed her arms. "Relax! It's got nothing to do with the cancer, just too much sight seeing in California. We haven't been home that long. I just need to catch up on my sleep."

Relieved, Lily picked up Jody's clothes, and carried them into the bedroom. She went to the nightstand to put away Jody's scarves and noticed an open book, evidently one that Jody had been reading. Curious, she picked it up and read the title. Horrified, she dropped the clothes and ran into the kitchen.

She threw the book 'Final Exit' on the table and screamed. "How dare you! To even have this in your house."

Jody spun around, glanced at the book, then at her mother. "I was just reading it, I—"

Lily screamed with rage, moved toward her, and before she realized what she was doing, she slapped Jody across the cheek. "How dare you even consider reading this?" She grabbed Jody by the shoulders and started to shake her.

Jody gasped. "Stop it! Please Mom, you're hurting me."

Jody's cries jolted Lily back to reality. She was breathing fast and backed away. Her daughters' eyes reflected her own horror. Lily gasped, rushed to Jody, took her in her arms and wept. She smothered kisses on her reddened cheek and hoped her kisses and hugs would undo her actions. "Please forgive me. Oh Baby, I'm sorry. Forgive me?" Sobs continued to rock her insides.

"There's nothing to forgive. I'm sorry too. I didn't–"

Lily hid her face in her hands. "I, I don't know what came over me. I've heard about this book at the Crisis-line. It tells people how to, to commit suicide. Doesn't it?"

Jody nodded.

"I thought you were reading it so that you could–"

"Mom. Please. Stop crying and listen to me." She took a tissue, wiped her eyes and blew her nose. "I wasn't thinking about anything when I read it. Honest!"

Lily swallowed hard, looked at the floor, and nodded. She touched her daughters' reddened cheek then leaned over and kissed the inflamed flesh.

"I've never slapped you, but when I saw that book I got crazy. Forgive me, I beg you. I'm so sorry."

Jody patted her mothers back. "It hurts me to see you cry, Mom. There's nothing to forgive, I love you, and the fact that you're so concerned about me that you don't want me to give up."

Jody's voice deepened. "Listen to me! I'm a fighter! I'm not about to give up! Do you hear what I'm saying? I'm going to live to the very end."

A smile crossed Lily's face but her misery was like a steel weight. She bit her lip again until it throbbed. The very thought that she could slap her daughter caused her to tremble.

"Sit and calm down, I'll get us a stiff drink. How does a diet coke sound?"

Lily tried to smile but her throat ached. She picked up the book and dropped it back on the table as if it were a hot piece of coal.

Jody quickly grabbed the book and stuck it in a kitchen drawer. Her tense jaw displayed her deep frustrations as she carried the iced glasses of cola to the table and handed one to her mother.

Lily blew her nose then looked in a compact mirror, and attempted to wipe off her smeared mascara. She was ashamed for reacting in such a violent manner. She never realized how deep her feelings ran, concerning suicide. Even though she'd sinned by making love to Edmund, it was nothing as bad as suicide. Suicide was a final slap in the face against God. Suicide was damnation.

She reached for her daughter's hand, and pressed it to her lips. "I love you more than anything on earth. Just the thought of you leaving sooner then God intended upsets me. I'm sorry. I promise that it will never happen again. It's your right to read whatever you want. Though I don't like it, it's still your right."

"I know Grandpa committed suicide and I know how you tried to save that girl on the phone. I'm going to cherish every healthy moment I have left. Why would I want to cut that time short?"

They sat in silence as the wall clock ticked the seconds away. Their time together was limited, and the echo of the large timepiece brought that reality home, and caused Lily to shiver. In her head she counted the seconds slipping away, and wished she could stop it's forward march.

# CHAPTER 28

The purple-roofed house sat on Jody's nightstand, a constant reminder that time was growing short, and to live everyday to the fullest. Convinced that the planet earth was not her final resting place eased her mind and brought joy to her final days.

She needed to talk to her father regarding legal matters and made an appointment to see him. The partner's names were carved in large gold letters and framed the wall behind the receptionist's desk. The hunter green carpeting was plush and elegant. The massive walnut furniture gave her the feeling of authority, and old money. Henry's secretary, Susan Moyer, an attractive woman in her fifties, had been with her father since she was four, motioned her into his office.

Henry walked around his desk and grabbed Jody's hand. His gaze was sharp and assessed her every move. "Since you insisted this meeting be strictly business, please be seated," he indicated the armchair directly in front of the desk. He sat down, and leaned back in his leather swivel chair. "Now tell me what is this about young lady?" He smiled.

"First of all I want to be assured that even though you're my father, this meeting will remain on a professional level, okay?"

Henry nodded. "It does my heart good to see you smile again. You always did have a beautiful smile, just like your mother."

"Thanks, Daddy." Jody straightened her posture in the high-backed leather chair. "I need you to take care of a few legal things," she removed a pad from her purse, "if that's okay?"

Henry never batted an eyelash, he grabbed his black Cross pen and started to take notes on his yellow legal pad.

"I have an insurance policy for twenty-five thousand dollars. I want you to make sure that it goes to the homeless shelters I've specified on this piece of paper."

Henry stared at her, than tensed his jaw. He kept moistening his dry lips.

"Is this uncomfortable for you, if it is, one of the partners—"

"Don't be silly," he forced a smile, "I wouldn't let anyone else take care of this." He put down his pen, steepled his hands and sat back. "I'll admit I don't like thinking about this, let alone talking about it, but I know it has to be done."

His eyes were full of pain as he listened to his daughters last Will and Testament. "Make sure Edmund gets my motorcycle, I know he'll ride it. The car, my college graduation gift, shouldn't be too difficult to unload, here's the title along with the rest of the papers." She handed him an envelope. "I'll take care of the furniture before I move back home. Nostradamus is at my friends and they love him as much as I do. They want to keep him, so he's taken care of." She checked her list.

"By the way is it all right that I move back home?"

Henry stopped writing and dropped his pen. He got up and sat in the chair next to her. He pulled it close and took her hand in his. "You don't even have to ask. It's your home. You know that."

"I guess," she looked away, then back at him, "but I needed to hear it from you. You've never said anything since I've gotten sick, and I thought, I don't know, that maybe, you didn't want me around when I get really bad."

"Oh Jody," despite his discomfort he took her in his arms. He took her by the shoulders, moved her back and looked directly into her eyes. "If it were up to me I'd have never let you move out," he winked, but his mouth was grim, "we'll be there for you for however long you need us."

Her eyes blurred. "Oh Daddy I know you love me, I just wanted your reassurance."

Henry coughed, wiped his eyes, then walked back to his chair. He sat down and picked up his pen.

"I also want a Living Will signed and witnessed as soon as possible. All right?"

Henry nodded.

"And I want to donate my organs, all the ones they can use. I'd like to think that I've given something back. I won't need them anymore, and there are so many people who might have a better life because of my useable parts. Lastly," she tapped her pencil against her lips as if weighing her thoughts before speaking, "I want to be cremated. You have to make sure Mom doesn't insist on burying me in a Catholic cemetery, it's a waste of valuable space. And I don't want any viewing or any of the pizzazz that goes with it. Funerals remind me of a pagan ceremony and I don't want anybody looking at my body."

"I promise." His brow creased and he folded his hands. "You're going to have to discuss these things with your mother as well, otherwise she'll fight me on it."

"I know, but I'll wait a while. When the time gets closer I'll tell her."

Henry finished writing then looked up at Jody. He averted her eyes by pretending to check his hand-written notes. Beads of perspiration formed a shiny film on his forehead. He cleared his throat, wet his lips that were moving, but with no sound emerging from them, as if he didn't trust himself to speak. "Never in my wildest dreams could I have imagined discussing my daughter's will at this early age."

"Dad I hate to ask you this," she paused, "but can Edmund come to the house and visit me? You know, when I can't get out of bed?" She studied his face looking for any sign of distress. "I know about you and Mom. She told me she asked for a divorce. I was hoping, that despite the situation, you'd let him come to see me."

His eyes were sad as he continued to doodle on his scratch pad. "What's happened between your mother and me has nothing to do with you or your friends. Even though Edmund is the man your mother's going to marry, he's still your friend and I'll honor that. I'm not the ogre you think I am."

"Whatever gave you that idea?" She shook her head and shifted in the chair. "I never thought of you that way. But I do know you were disappointed when I was born. You wanted a son. A lawyer. His picture hanging in the gallery next to yours."

Henry's eyes opened wide, and he let loose with a deep belly laugh. "Young lady, where in the world did you ever get that idea? Honestly," he held his hand up as if being sworn to tell the whole truth, "all I cared about was that you were healthy." His face softened, "in fact I can still remember feeding time, as I watched you guzzle milk from your mother's breasts. I sat on the bed beside her with your tiny fingers curled around mine. I'd never experienced anything like that, I was speechless, and filled with awe at the miracle before me. Then your mother put you in my arms—" he turned away, then looked back.

"When I held you in my arms that first day, and felt your warmth, and smelled your talcum fragrance, I swore that I'd work hard to give you everything a child could want. I've tried to keep my promise."

"Oh Daddy," she smiled through her tears and looked back at him, "I thought you were mad at me because I didn't want to be a lawyer."

"Disappointed, yes. Angry? Never. Honey, I could never be angry with you, I love you. You're my precious daughter. No matter what."

Jody rushed to his side and threw her arms around his neck. She whispered in his ear as she hugged him. "You know, you've never told me that you loved me. Those are the words I've waited to hear."

"But I believed my actions showed you how much I loved you, even if I never said it. That's why I've worked so hard, I wanted to give you everything because I loved you."

Jody stood up and put her hands on her hips. "Sheez! We women like to hear it once in a while. Those words effect us more then you'll ever know."

He continued to fidget and cleared his throat. "It's just, I mean, I never heard those words from my parents. I didn't think it was important."

"Well, I've heard it from you today and you've made me very happy. You've given me a full life, and for that

I'll always be grateful. I'm glad you're my Dad." She stroked his cheek then started back around the desk.

Suddenly she cried out and grabbed the edge of the desk. She gasped, grabbed her head, and pointed to her purse. "My pills," she moaned, "in my purse." She held her head and started to whimper, "hurry."

Henry helped her into the chair and put two pills in her mouth. Her eyes were shut tight as if trying to shut out the torment. When the pain began to ease Jody opened her eyes. Henry was kneeling beside her, his facial muscles taut.

"When did the pains start? Your mother hasn't said anything about it."

"Getting worse," she gasped and rubbed her head, "ever since I got back from San Francisco. The pain feels like a knife is cutting into my head. I haven't said anything to Mom. Please, don't you," she clutched at his jacket sleeve, "I don't want her to worry. I've got a few more things to do before I move back home. If she knows the headaches are back she'll insist on moving me tomorrow." She shook her head and mouthed the word please.

He smoothed the hair back from her eyes and nodded. "When do you think you'll be moving back?"

"I talked to the doctor and he says I can increase the pills from two to four. When that doesn't help—" she looked away, her expression became set, "then I'll have to be ready to take the next step. We talked about morphine or something like that."

"All right. You'd better prepare your mother and if she doesn't say something to me in the next two weeks I'm going to tell her. You know she'll dog you."

The pills finally kicked in. "Well," she stood and shouldered her purse. She straightened her skirt, "I think I've got everything taken care of. Send me the bill, Counselor."

* * *

The doorbell rang and much to Edmund's surprise it was Henry. He swallowed hard and threw open the door. Henry's pale face, and set chin, suggested that he was on a mission. His medium build was tailored for a designer suit and despite the hot August day, not a drop of sweat graced his brow.

They politely shook hands with Henry's eyes subtlety darting around the sparsely furnished living room. He cleared his throat. "You're wondering why I'm here. Believe me I wouldn't be if I didn't deem it necessary. Jody just left my office. She's the reason I have to talk to you." A distinct hardening graced his eyes.

"I don't know if you're aware of it but Jody's headaches have returned. She's on double pain pills, and you know what that means. She hasn't told Lily yet. She said she needs a few more weeks of independence before moving back home."

Edmund rubbed his brow and wiped the moisture on his pant leg. He reached for his pipe and filled it with tobacco. Henry sat perfectly still, barely moving a muscle, his bearing stiff and proud.

For Henry to come here it must be serious, Edmund thought. He took his time filling his pipe and then proceeded to tap the tobacco. He knew Jody's headaches were a collateral issue and not the real reason for the visit.

Henry waited for Edmund to light his pipe then spoke with a quiet emphasis, as if in control of the entire scene. "Of course, she'll stay with Lily and me till the en—" he cleared his throat again. "She asked me if I would object to you coming to visit her at the house. I couldn't deny her that wish; after all you are her father. I checked my schedule for the next three months. I have a lot of evening meetings planned, especially as the election gets closer, so don't worry about me interfering with the three of you."

He hesitated momentarily, than pointed his finger. "But I am going to fight you both on one thing."

Edmund's heart jumped in his chest. Then with the discipline he had learned so long ago, he consciously slowed down his erratic pulse, stopped all thought, and quieted his mind.

"I know Lily told you I wouldn't give her a divorce till after the election and I'm still standing by that. But now I have to insist that you and Lily say nothing to Jody that I'm not her biological father."

Edmund tapped his pipe in the ashtray. "Who the hell do you think you are, insisting on something like that?" He slammed his pipe in the ashtray, stormed to the fireplace and leaned against it with his elbow on the mantle. He turned to face Henry, eyeball to eyeball.

"I'm her father, and if I choose to tell her the truth there's nothing, or no one, that can stop me. Lily doesn't want to upset Jody and that's the only thing that's kept me, so far, from telling her. So don't come here insisting on something you have no control over. You know this wouldn't even make it to court. The laws on my side on this one, Pal."

Edmund returned to his chair, knocked the wattle from his pipe, than pointed the stem at his friend. "I don't want to get into anything with you, we've been friends a long time and I don't want it to end like this. I was hoping we could be civil about things."

Henry was silent as if forming a legal argument for a jury. Edmund studied him and tried to anticipate, from the grim expression on his face, what was going through his mind.

Henry's cheek muscles twitched and then as he was about to speak, he looked down at his hands for a moment, then up at Edmund. "If this were about the three of us I'm sure we could come to an amiable compromise, but it's not." His eyes flashed as he held his head high. The edge in his voice was unmistakable. "Now I'm fighting to keep my daughter, or at least keep the truth from her. It's all I have left. Do you think I'm going to let you take her from me?"

"Aren't you the one that always touted the law? You said it was the only thing that you could rely on. According to the Halston hiatus, everything is always black or white." Edmund leaned forward and rested his forearms on his knees. "Well the black and white of this is I'm her father. You're not! It's a fact that can be proven by a simple blood test."

Henry glared and began to mentally stalk his opponent. As he slowly approached, he was on the lookout for the weak point in Edmund's argument. His forehead was damp. His mouth, a thin slash, was turned downward.

"I don't deny you're her father. I've lived with that fact a hell of a lot longer then you. Every day of my life I watched my daughter become just like you. There are times when she's doing something and not aware that I'm staring at her, I see your face." For a moment Edmund thought Henry was going to cry, but as always he took control of his emotions, and an invisible wall descended.

"Try as I may, I can never forget she's your daughter and sadly, I'll never have a child of my own." He took a deep breath and continued. "Despite knowing Lily had lied to me about being her father, I gave her my name, and all the things she needed and wanted, while she was growing up. You know I could have divorced her? Then she and your daughter would have been out on the street. But I didn't want that, I loved, and wanted the family I'd been given."

Henry stood, straightened his shoulders, and cleared his throat. "You owe me big time for the years I've cared for your daughter, years you were chasing around the world, searching for, who the hell knows what." He walked to the fireplace and turned to face Edmund. "I don't want her to go to the grave thinking I've lied to her all these years, or that her life's been meaningless. She deserves better. She doesn't have the time to sort through it all. She's got enough to deal with. We'll be lucky if she's with us till Christmas."

"Well I appreciate your concern, but you have to see my point as well. I want her to know I'm her father. I want to hold her in my arms and tell her she's my daughter. I want to tell her that I love her. Can you understand that?"

Henry sucked in a deep unsteady breath then exhaled. "Yes I can, especially since you've lost your other daughter. Believe it or not the only thing that concerns me is the effect it will have on Jody. We can't lose sight of that. What's important here is that she's going to need all her strength to stay alive? I don't want us to add to her pain, she'll have enough of that in the days to come."

Yes the road that lies ahead will be rough. Henry's point was well taken, Edmund thought. His jaw ached from clenching his pipe stem. He swallowed hard and tried not to reveal the depth of his anger. Life had dealt him a loaded deck. His argument was lost. He couldn't win, no matter how close to his chest he played his hand. He made an effort to remain calm as he stood toe to toe with Henry.

The two men stood in silence and appraised each other in hopes of anticipating the others next move. Then suddenly Henry turned and walked to the door. With one hand on the knob, he paused and turned. "I'll make a deal with you Edmund."

A chill pierced him as he glared at his one time friend. "Go ahead, I'm listening."

"Lily informed me that you and she want to be married as soon as possible and Jody wants to be at the wedding. Maybe you two should get married," he paused, "maybe it's time Lily learn the value of money and the rewards it can bring." He sneered as he glanced around the room.

Edmund gritted his teeth and fought to control the impulse to smash his fist into Henry's face. He was itching to smack the smirk off of it.

"I'm willing to let Lily off the hook. She can fly to Mexico and get a quickie divorce. Then if you like, the two of you can be married there, and have Jody as your witness. I won't stand in your way. I don't think it'll be too difficult to keep the marriage a secret until after the election. Then I can leak the news that I'm divorced and there will be no questions asked. By that time Jody will be too sick to know what's going on." He paused to clear his throat.

"But there's one condition. Jody can never know the truth. She can't know that I'm not her father." His cold eyes glinted with pleasure at the astonishment registered on Edmund's face. "Do we have a deal?"

Edmund lunged for him and grabbed Henry by the collar. He drew his arm back, his fist was inches from Henry's face, ready to slam into his jaw. "You son of a bitch," he shouted, "I could kill you." At hearing his violent words, he quickly let go of Henry's collar, and backed away. He took deep breaths as Henry smoothed his jacket, and straightened his glasses.

"I thought you were set on having Lily wait until after the election because you were worried about losing? She honored your request."

"That's all changed." He straightened his jacket and tugged at the lapels. "I've heard my opponents views and heard him confess to adultery. I'm not worried anymore. With a background such as his, he doesn't stand a chance. The public doesn't want adulterers in office."

Edmund shuddered at Henry's self-righteous attitude and felt the ice of hate spread through his gut. "Bastard! You're forcing me to choose between making Lily my wife now and granting my daughter her one wish, or telling Jody that she's mine and denying her the happiness of being at our wedding. The only thing she's ever asked of us."

Henry shrugged as a grim smile played at his lips. "See, nothing changes. It's still a matter of black and white. Definitive choices. We always have them. I'm giving you and Lily a choice. Now it's up to the two of you to decide. You can't have it both ways. It's either black or white. You decide."

Henry turned, started to walk out the door, then added, "Oh, one more thing, Lily's not to know about this meeting or the whole deal's off. Don't bother to see me out, I know the way."

As the door slammed shut Edmund's fist hit the wall and pieces of plaster fell to the floor. He grimaced in pain and started to rub his bleeding fist. For the first time in his life he experienced an overwhelming feeling of helplessness. "Damn!" He rushed to the phone, made a quick call to the airport, and ran out of the house.

* * *

Lily greeted her mother with a kiss on her cheek. "I brought you some of your favorite candy, peanut butter cups. You know how you love them." She pulled a chair beside Nora, whose face had grown bland with time. What was once a chin of iron determination now displayed the faint line of an aging jaw. The oval face was pale, but still rigid in her silence.

Lily brushed her mother's hair. Webs of silver strands peeked through her dark tresses. Her mother had never let a streak of gray show, but now, what was the point. "You told me you knew about Jody," she fussed with the brush and untangled some strands of hair.

"Why you never told me, I'll never know. Now," she stopped brushing for a moment and stared at the mute woman, "I'm faced with something similar, and I need to talk to you about it." She resumed brushing her hair.

"I know you can't answer, but if your heart can hear me, I need your help. You've never let anything stop you from voicing your opinion before, and I know you won't this time."

Lily finished fixing her hair and picked up a jar of hand cream from the dresser. She took her mothers frail hands, first one, then the other, and rubbed them with hand cream. "Edmund wants to tell Jody that he's her father. Oh Mama, I don't know what to do." She stopped rubbing for a moment, and looked at the blank face. "I don't think he should. Jody's got a lot to deal with, why should we add to it. He sees her all the time and that won't change, whether he tells her or not."

Lily unwrapped a piece of chocolate and slipped it into her mothers' mouth. Nora chewed the chocolate and Lily took a piece for herself. "I know he lost his daughter in a terrible accident and he's only known about Jody a short time, but now he's going to lose her too. None of that will change if he tells her. It can't bring Christine back."

Lily looked at the same empty stare and knelt down beside her. "I know you can hear me. You can't fool me. Now, back to Jody. There's a part of me that wants her to know. I promised her I'd never lie and I haven't. I just didn't tell her the entire truth, and it's bothering me. I wonder if she has the right to know who her real father is. Then I worry how it will affect her; then I wonder what it will do to Henry; then I think about Edmund, and how he'll handle it if she doesn't know the truth."

Lily rose and started to pace the tiny hospital room. She glanced back at her mother, than looked away before sitting down again. "I don't know what to do? Should I tell or not? Will it hurt her? I've prayed for an answer and all I get are more questions. Help me! Break out of that prison you're hiding in, and talk to me. It's not so bad out here. You're strong, you can face anything. That's what you taught me. Now prove it."

Knowing Nora's strong will, Lily expected her to look up, and start giving orders. But nothing happened. She shrugged and went to the dresser to unwrap another piece of chocolate. When she turned around her mother was no longer staring at the television, she'd turned her head, and was staring at Lily.

Lily rushed to her side. "You can hear me! I knew you could! You can hear me!"

Nora didn't blink an eye or move a muscle. She sat perfectly still with the same blank stare. Lily rushed out of the room, and came back with the floor nurses, trying to explain how her mother had moved her head to look at her.

The nurse sat Lily down on the side of the bed and explained that occasionally, and they don't know why, patients will sometimes respond to stimuli, such as just what happened. It means nothing. As they continued talking Nora slowly moved her head back to the television and resumed her original position. She was still hiding, comfortable, and protected in her silence.

In her heart Lily knew that her mother was trying to communicate. As always, she was trying to tell her what to do. Lily moved to her mother's side and continued to talk to her as she watched for other signs. But Nora just sat there, back in her mental labyrinth, safe in her inner world.

After minutes of quiet introspection Lily jumped up.

"I got it Mom! I got your point. I've finally sorted through it all. You're a living reminder of what can happen when you keep the truth from those you love." She stroked the arm of her mother's chair.

"Look at what happened when Jim sprung his secret on you. And look what happened to my life when you hid the truth from me about Edmund's whereabouts. I can't go on deceiving her any longer. She has a right to know. Just like I had a right to know about the calls and letters.

Jody can decide how she wants to handle it. She can ignore Edmund and consider Henry as her real father, or she can accept Edmund as her father and include Henry in her life. The only thing I risk is her anger and I'm willing to risk that in order for her to know the truth."

# CHAPTER 29

The sleek Lear jet climbed into the late afternoon skies, miles over the regional airport, with a flight plan filed for Dore County, Wisconsin. A place of solitude and beauty, a place where he could get lost, a place to get his bearings and make sure his fucking head was screwed on straight.

He could hug a tree, as his African friends taught him, or walk the forests immersed in silence, as the Navajos showed him. He could sit quietly beneath the tall bristling pine trees, and feel at one with his surroundings, as the Tibetan Monks do. Now was the time to make it all work. He had to get rid of his demons once and for all. His bearing was stiff and proud, but his spirit was in chaos. Tormented by confusing emotions he fought to make some semblance of what had just happened. He had to find peace.

In the excitement of coming back to Chicago, finding Lily, and discovering Jody, he'd gotten lost and forgotten his nemesis. Then finding out that Jody was his daughter...was he trying to replace his beloved Christine? Not fair to Jody or to Christine's memory. Each of them is an individual and can't be replaced by the other.

Who the fuck said time heals all wounds? Christine died a year ago and the wound is still open, and bleeding. So big, so frightening. Was his thinking about

Jody and wanting her to be told about her parentage, selfish or selfless? He shuddered. He had to get back in touch with his dark side, to focus on his fear of commitment, and his relentless pursuit of women. No matter what'd he'd become, he couldn't hurt Lily again, she'd suffered enough.

He lifted the nose, took the jet high above the clouds, leveled off, and headed north. To the west the sky was ablaze with remnants of the setting sun, daffodil yellow, flaxen gold, salmon pink next to terra-cotta red, all feathered by brilliant shades of orange, a sunset unsurpassed.

His facial muscles went limp as the tension began to drain from his face. His shoulders drooped when he put the plane on automatic pilot, sat back, lit his pipe and thought about his options. He'd try and get back tomorrow, hopefully with enough wisdom and strength to hear his own drummer dictating the path he was to walk.

* * *

Jody moved back home after Labor Day. Despite her assurances that she was fine, Lily knew what it meant. She hadn't talked to Edmund in a few days and was anxious to see him. She was eager to tell him about her decision to tell Jody that he was her real father. She knew he'd be pleased and had been rehearsing, in her mind, how they'd tell her. Now they only had to decide where and how to tell their daughter the truth.

Edmund called and asked her to meet him, they had to talk. He sounded different and she tried to put her finger on the difference. There was something strange in his voice, something she'd never heard before. "Are you all right?" she felt his hesitancy to answer.

"I'm fine," he assured her, "I've never felt better."

She hung up, not convinced and was even more anxious to see him. She wanted to see the look on his face when she told him that she agreed with him, they should tell Jody the truth.

Later that evening she and Edmund drove to a quaint restaurant just off South Shore Drive. Her concerns, as to his state of mind, were unwarranted; he was jovial and very much at ease.

Marco's was noted for their baked Ziti a La Romano. Wax laden Chianti bottles held a stub of a candle, and sat on red-checkered cloths. The waiter returned with the wine and spoke to Lily and Edmund in Italian as he lit the candle. Lily clicked her glass against Edmund's then sipped the sparkling red liquid.

"Umnn, this is good." She put her glass down. "Edmund, I've decided that we should tell Jody the truth."

Edmund was quiet for a moment, than started to twirl his glass by the stem. He studied the sloshing red liquid as it stained the sides of the glass. "I've given it a lot of thought as well, and I agree with your original plan. Now's not the time. It can only startle and confuse Jody."

There wasn't a strained muscle on his face as they discussed telling Jody about her heritage. His eyes sparkled and he hummed while scanning the menu. Something's different about him, she thought, something's changed. It was subtle, but intriguing. She watched, listened and tried to define the change. Maybe the fact that his book had made the bestseller list? No, that's not it. He seems to have a sense of quiet confidence about himself, a sense of reliance, trust? He's always been so decisive. Yet now he's avoiding the issue of telling Jody that he's her father. Why?

"You're skirting the idea, Edmund, why?" Was her original decision not to tell Jody the right one? She thought.

"I've given it a lot of thought and realized I was trying to replace Christine with Jody, and that was wrong. We could hurt Jody by telling her the truth, especially at this time."

Lily questioned his decision. She knew he hadn't spent enough time mourning the death of his wife and daughter. And from the psychology courses she took, she knew he was still probably recovering from the shock. But something wasn't right. Why the sudden change of heart?

Henry was in the library when Lily arrived home. Once again she broached the subject of divorce and to her surprise, he agreed. He even gave her the name of a Mexican lawyer, Juan Garcia, and assured her that this man could be counted on to follow through. When she told him she'd be married in Mexico, and that Jody would be there, he congratulated her then walked out of the room. He left Lily to wonder what did he have up his sleeve?

Surprised by Henry's change of heart, Lily began to mutter a prayer of thanks then rushed into Jody's room to tell her the good news. Then she called Edmund. When she hung up she called the attorney Henry suggested, and he recommended they start divorce proceedings immediately. While waiting for the divorce to be final, she and Jody could play tourist and investigate the city. By Labor Day she would be divorced and Edmund could fly down and meet them.

While she and Jody were airborne, Lily continued to wonder why Henry had changed his mind. That was so out of character for him. As the plane winged its way south, a tinge of fear slipped in. This was stupid. Why in the world would she feel fearful about divorcing Henry? It was what she'd wanted ever since Edmund's return. So why the sudden fear? Why now, when all her dreams were about to come true?

She knew she'd always face the unknown married to Edmund, as opposed to the dull, predictable life style she had with Henry. She willingly admitted her trepidation. A period of adjustment was certain, but she was willing to work through it, convinced that their love would survive.

She'd been very comfortable during her marriage to Henry, never wanting for material things. Now she was going to be living in an old house, in a neighborhood that was considered financially unstable, and she didn't have the slightest idea how much money Edmund had or was capable of making. What was the going rate for a new professor? About seventy thousand? Then she remembered his book, maybe fifteen or twenty thousand? She knew Edmund would never agree to join the country club. As she compared the two lifestyles her stomach suddenly felt queasy. Her decision was under attack.

Jody woke from her catnap, scavenged through her purse for pills, and swallowed two. Lily still wasn't comfortable about Jody accompanying her to Mexico, but she'd been so insistent about going, she couldn't have stopped her if she tried.

Lily closed her eyes again, and despite her financial concerns, her love for Edmund was like a soft downy blanket, warm and snugly. She'd learn to live without the things she'd been use to. Walking away from the country club activities would be easy. She'd remodel Edmund's house so that it would be pleasing to them both.

A sense of peace settled over her. She grabbed Jody's hand and squeezed it as the plane made its final approach into Mexico City.

* * *

The small white stucco bungalow was one of many bordering the main Inn. Each guesthouse had its own private pool, and when Lily and Jody saw the flowers floating on top of the blue water, they slipped out of their clothes and jumped in. Refreshed, they dressed, ordered food and drinks from room service and spent the rest of the evening discussing Lily's wedding plans.

The next morning Juan Garcia, a short slender man, who if he stood sideways would go unnoticed, met them at the main pool, legal papers had to be signed before he could file for her divorce. His dark eyes beaded as he appraised the two women. He handed them a list of the local restaurants along with a Spanish/English dictionary and cautioned them to take a cab wherever they went.

Jody mimicked his suave manner and roving eye. "He's flirting with you." Lily protested but was pleased.

The next day's festivities started with margaritas in the courtyard, where long banquet tables were laden with every imaginable Mexican dish. All during the brunch Lily kept close track of the number of times Jody reached for her pills. Despite her daughters' denial, her headaches we're getting closer and closer. Every six hours, then every four hours. Now it was only three hours since Jody took her last dose, and she was looking for the prescription bottle again.

Finally she chanced Jody's anger. "Honey, you're downing those pills like they're candy. Do you know it hasn't even been three hours, and you're taking them again? Is it getting worse?"

Jody assured her the change of climate was at fault, the heat and humidity, and added that the doctor cautioned her this might happen. Of course, Lily didn't believe her and was uneasy throughout the day.

"I wonder when Mr. Garcia will have the divorce papers? It seems like it's taking forever?"

"Chill out, Mom. You're like a young schoolgirl. It's only been four days. Remember he said it could take a week. Relax, Edmund will be here soon enough and you'll be Mrs. Edmund Vila."

"Chill out? If I were anymore chilled out I'd be an iceberg. I've been saying it over and over again, Mrs. Edmund Valenti, trying to get use to the sound." She giggled then became serious. "But I keep getting this feeling...what if something happens and we can't get married?"

"Stop already. You know Edmund loves you."

"I know. It's just that I've waited so long, I'm afraid I might not get my wish. It seems too good to be true. Experience has taught me that life can throw you a curve when you least expect it. I guess I've learned not to expect too much of anything."

She stroked her daughters' head and brought up the subject of her headaches again. "Remember Honey," she cautioned, "we don't have to stay. If the pain gets too bad, we can go home. Garcia said he could mail the divorce papers."

"Nonsense, I want to see the two of you married. I'll be all right. I promise if it gets too bad I'll let you know. Okay? Besides, it won't be much longer. I can stand anything for a short time."

Lily stared at her daughter. The blush in her cheeks was fading. The gaunt gray tone was hard to hide. The dark circles under her eyes had returned, and framed her once sparkling eyes, now dull and sad. As Jody was getting dressed, Lily could see the sharp angles and protruding bones on her daughter's frail body, and chided herself for being pre-occupied with the divorce and upcoming marriage. Jody was slowly slipping away and there wasn't a damned thing she could do.

Overwhelmed by the feeling of helplessness, she bit her lip as she watched her daughter. Let them hurry with the divorce papers, she prayed, so I can take her back to Chicago. She's so frail.

Despite her pretense that all was well, Lily considered taking Jody home. While Jody dozed at poolside, Lily walked into the lobby to check the flights back to Chicago. She started back for the pool and saw Jody, clutching her head, reaching blindly for her pills. Only two hours ago she'd taken two.

She turned back to the airline reservation desk and booked a flight that left Mexico in two hours. If they hurried they could still make it. She'd let Jody stay poolside until everything was packed. She'd have to be firm. Jody would fight her on this but with their bags packed, bills paid and reservations made, Lily would have her way.

Much to Lily's surprise when she told Jody about the change of plans, she started to cry. "I'm sorry Mom. Forgive me, I know how much you wanted this."

Lily wrapped her arms around her. "Listen young lady, your health is my number one concern. How can I even think of getting married when you're in such pain? It's just like the doctor said, isn't it?"

Jody hesitated a moment then shook her head. "I wasn't going to tell you but now that we're going home Mom, I'm scared. The last couple of nights I've had a funny tingling in my left arm and hand. I didn't want to say anything because I wanted to see the two of you married."

"Don't be foolish. I love you for caring about me, but it's more important that we get you back home. Now!" She pulled a hankie out and wiped the tears. The haunting look in Jody's eyes almost undid her composure. "Edmund and I can be married in a quiet ceremony back home. You can be there just like we planned. Just the three of us, all right?" Jody nodded and brushed her hands across her cheeks to wipe her tears.

Lily's words choked in her throat, they were as hollow as the feeling inside. She lied about being married in Chicago. She knew it could never be.

* * *

Edmund opened the front door and was surprised to see Pat standing there. She pushed open the door and marched inside. Edmund smiled. "Would you like to come in?"

"Don't you dare be glib with me. You, you, hustler."

Edmund put his head back and began to laugh out-loud. "Lily never told me you were a comedian."

She shoved a manila folder under his nose. "Well you won't think it's funny after you read this."

He sat down, pulled out his pipe, and started to read the contents. His smile waned. His eyes grew overcast. "Where the hell did you get this?"

"I hired a private detective."

He sputtered, "you what?"

"As much as I wanted it to work for you and Lily, you seemed too perfect to me. There's skeletons in everyone's closet, and as you can see, you're no exception."

"I can explain all this," he waved the papers at her.

"I sure hope so Edmund. I don't know how the hell I'm going to tell Lily about what I've done."

He got up, walked to the fireplace, tapped his pipe on the stones and proceeded to fill it with tobacco.

"Well I'm waiting. I want to hear you get out of this one, Romeo."

"Most of my adult life, starting when I fell in love with Lily, I've run from commitment. And Lily was no exception. I didn't try hard enough to find her and that was fine with me. As much as I wanted to be with her, a fucking commitment scared the hell out me."

"But what about your wife and daughter?"

"When I got Mai Lyn pregnant I knew it was my responsibility to care for her and the child. But that's totally different then commitment. To me commitment is a total giving of one's self to another human being. Physically, emotionally, and spiritually." He sat down next to Pat.

"On assignment I hungered after, and sought out different women, just as your file outlines. Being there for a short time I was able to excuse my behavior. I rationalized the many love affairs by telling myself I wouldn't be around long enough to make any commitments."

Pat listened.

"I never loved Mai Lynn the way I love Lily. I felt sorry for my wife, you know, coming to a foreign land and all. My love for Christine was another matter. In fact, I had just resigned from the magazine so I could spend more time with her when I got the news of her death. I was devastated, convinced that God was punishing me for my treatment of women. Using them and all—"

"Edmund, we're not talking a few females here. From what they were able to uncover, your partners number close to one hundred, if not more, over the past twenty years."

Edmund shook his head. "I know, that's why I got help. Counseling, for two years, and what I discovered is—"

"And what's that?"

"Well if you'll let me finish," he took a drag on his pipe, "growing up, my mother and father were the happiest people on the planet. Then one day I saw my father leaving the neighborhood saloon with a redhead on his arm. I ran home to tell my mother but when I got there, I knew I couldn't break her heart."

"Edmund, are you trying to tell me you fucked every skirt you could find because your father cheated on your mother?"

"No, that was just the beginning. Then my favorite aunt divorced her husband. Next I had an army buddy who committed suicide when he found his wife in bed with another woman. And the examples go on and on. You have it there in your report."

"It sounds like a bunch of horse-shit to me."

"I don't give a damn what it sounds like to you. It's the truth."

"And now you want to marry Lily? Why the sudden eagerness to make a commitment?"

"I told you, Christine's death had such an impact on me, I was forced to search my soul, and in the process realized my lack of responsibility to those women. I used them, plain and simple."

"You sure as hell did. And now you want to use Lily the same way."

Edmund jumped up. "Is that what you think?"

"Well after seeing this, what the hell am I suppose to think. I don't see any fucking wings growing out of your back. Maybe a tail growing from your ass?"

"You're so fucking funny. If this weren't so serious I'd laugh."

"You're right about that. This is serious. I'm the one that's caught in the fucking middle of your god damn past. I wish I hadn't snooped. Now I have to decide how, when, and if I should tell Lily."

"Pat, look at me. You said you had the feeling I was too perfect. Well since you found all this out, do you still feel the same way?"

She shook her head. "Ha!"

"Well that should tell you something."

"Shit, it tells me nothing, except that you're a god damn liar."

"I have never lied to Lily. Never."

"Okay, so you didn't tell her the whole truth. Is there a difference?"

"I suppose not, but if I told her about my past, do you think she'd have opened her heart to me. She needs me at her side, especially now. Don't spoil it Pat, I swear I've changed. There's nothing more I want then a commitment to Lily. I finally realized that's what's been missing in my life. I needed to make a commitment to another human being. I've made it to Jody, and because of that commitment, I feel like a man for the first time in my life. I've finally grown up."

He turned away, blew his nose, then turned back to face her. "Consider the repercussions of any decision you make. Many lives will be affected. But if you decide to tell her, do me one favor?"

"What's that?"

"Give me the chance to tell her first. It won't hurt as bad coming from me."

Pat stood up. "I'll make you that promise, but fuck, right about now I need a drink. I hate meddling, and this has taught me one hell of a lesson. Mind my own damn business."

# CHAPTER 30

Edmund met his two favorite people at O'Hare airport. They conveyed their mutual disappointment at having to return early but he allayed their fears with a solemn oath: Jody would be present at their wedding.

As the black Explorer pulled into the Halston driveway, Lily was surprised to see Henry's car. He was home earlier then expected. Edmund jumped out of the car, unloaded their bags, and left. As his car backed out of the driveway Henry came out on the front porch, his face pale and pinched. He carried in the bags and urged Jody to rest. He made an appointment with the doctor, and left.

As Lily walked upstairs it suddenly dawned on her, she was still Mrs. Henry Halston, not a name she planned to still have. She stopped in Jody's room, and they talked for a few minutes. Dark circles ringed her daughter's eyes and she urged her to try and get some sleep.

After Jody was tucked in bed Lily went to her room. The muscles in her neck and shoulders screamed for relief. She was exhausted and threw herself on the bed. She crumbled the spread with her clenched hands, as a solitary tear trickled down her cheek to her lip. She rubbed her face on the rose-colored coverlet. What do I do now?

Jody wanted to be at their side when they were married, and now...Lily paced her room like a caged animal. This had never really been her home; more like an institution maintained by the stockholders of a major corporate structure, the Halston Clan, insuring future generations a solid structure. Trapped, and too tired to fight her despair, she fell into a deep sleep.

A loud knock awakened her, it was Jody. "Mom, we have to leave in twenty minutes for the hospital." Lily couldn't believe she'd slept through the night. Thankfully Emma had brought her coffee to the room. The nutty smell cleared her head as she gulped the steaming brew. Why the rush? She knew what the doctor was going to say and visualized the cancer zapping every ounce of Jody's energy. Now they were forced to play the waiting game. Wait for what everyone knew was the inevitable. Everyone knew the final result, it wasn't a game, it was a sentence.

Dr. Berner examined Jody and ordered a barrage of tests. Due to the frequency that Jody was taking her medication, he increased the strength and cautioned her to rest more. And 'no driving'. He explained that as she grew weaker, she would experience difficulty getting around and he didn't want her under needless strain. He pointed out that the more energy she conserved, the longer she could maintain some quality to her life.

He wanted Jody to think about going back into the hospital when the cancer rendered her incapacitated. As before, Jody was adamant. Under no circumstances would she go back into the hospital. Never.

Doctor Berner nodded, handed Jody and Lily some brochures about Hospice and assured them that it was a viable alternative. Along with new prescriptions, Jody asked for her medical records and MRI's.

On the way home from the hospital, Jody asked Lily to drive to Evanston, she had an appointment with another doctor. Surprised by the request, Lily agreed. Jody was seeing another physician and Lily was more then pleased. Jody explained that this doctor had been referred to her by one of the patients at the cancer center.

She'd been to see this doctor twice before, and assured her that Doctor Coggins was different than any doctor she'd met. Unlike most physicians, she believed in a patient's freedom of choice, never dictating a course of treatment, only presenting available options.

She believes patients have a right to self-determination.

Jody hadn't given up, Lily thought, that's good. The idea that she was seeing another doctor meant she was still fighting. "Mom," she said, "I don't want you to let dad or Edmund know I'm seeing her. As far as the family is concerned we weren't here today. Promise?"

Lily nodded. Was Jody seeing some kind of quack? Why the mystery? Why would she want to keep this doctors' visit a secret?

By the time they reached Dr. Coggins' office, Jody was alive and animated, just like her former self. "I know you'll like her, Mom. She reveres and respects life, and believes all terminally ill people should retain their dignity and self-respect. Most of all she respects the decisions and feelings of the terminally ill."

Jody was talking in a way she hadn't heard before, and using words in different contexts, and Lily wasn't sure what it all meant. All doctors wanted the same thing for their patients.

Jody continued. "Her goal, above and beyond everything, is to preserve the personal freedom of the individual, and you know how strongly I feel about that. Everyone knows what's best for themselves."

What did Jody want from her? She mulled over her daughters words. Curiously uneasy, she tried to ignore the voice stirring in her head, when the nurse ushered them into the doctors conference room. Lily and Jody sat in front of a large glass topped walnut desk, under which were snapshots of children, presumably hers. One wall of the small room was filled with floor to ceiling shelves of medical reference books. Mounted on the wall behind the desk were framed degrees: the University of Chicago, Certification of residency at the Mayo Clinic, internship at Boston University Hospital, and an announcement of appointment to the Board of Directors of Mercy hospital in Chicago.

Thoroughly impressed, Lily's fears of an unscrupulous charlatan were finally put to rest as a woman of middle age walked into the office. She smiled and sat down at the desk. She acknowledged Jody and introduced herself to Lily. Her blonde hair was coiffured in a chignon, Princess Grace style, sparse make up, and deep-set gray eyes. She could easily be a movie star, Lily thought. Why was she a doctor when she could be in Hollywood?

"Has Jody told you why she's asked me to talk to you?"

"She said something about you being the kind of doctor that allows the patient to have choices as to their course of treatment."

"That's right Mrs. Halston, and I also give second opinions as I've done in your daughter's case. I concur with Dr. Berner as to her prognosis and treatment. But where he and I differ, as do many of my colleagues, is that I believe a terminally ill patient has the right to self determination regarding their life's termination."

Lily sat back in her leather chair.

"Your daughter has sought me out for my advice, as well as my help, and that brings us to the reason she wanted me to talk to you."

Lily began to squirm. Her stomach felt queasy as she struggled to understand this meeting.

"Dr. Berner and I agree as to the course the tumor will take. The brain is the seat of intelligence, as well as our emotions, and the idea that intelligence and consciousness are threatened, as in your daughter's case, is hard to accept. But Jody has come through this process with a good attitude. The main problem she faces now is the crowding, or 'Mass Effect' that is beginning to occur. Because the tumor is enclosed within the skull and vertebrae column, it has a limited area in which to grow. Pressure from the expanding tumor can displace adjacent structures with repercussions to numerous other organs, and body functions. Already Jody's headaches are becoming very painful, and soon she'll experience sporadic bouts of blindness. Then as the tumor presses on vital nerves she'll encounter paralysis on the left side of her body, then uncontrollable convulsions, rendering her incapacitated."

Lily dug her nails into the chair. She looked at Jody, and to her surprise, Jody appeared serene.

Jody smiled at her mother. "I know you didn't know all the details about what it will be like as I near the end, but I found this out when I was at the hospital. I'm glad they were honest with me. I had to know what to expect so I could plan accordingly."

"You know your dad and I will be there with you, we're not going to let you go through this alone. You can count on us."

"I know, that's why I want you to listen to the rest of what the doctor has to say."

The attractive woman got up, walked to the front of the desk and leaned against the edge. "Each of my terminally ill patients approaches death in their own private way, as I know you, and your family must be doing. But where I enter the picture is that some of my patients revere life, as does your daughter, and they want to retain their dignity and self-respect as they approach the end of their physical life."

She leaned closer to Lily. "She is going to need your help. This is something she can't do alone."

Pressure mounted in Lily's chest and her heartbeats were erratic as she listened to every word.

"At this point in her illness, Jody doesn't want to be hospitalized. She's made legal provisions, a Living Will, to make sure that doesn't happen. There are many of our institutions that believe life should be prolonged no matter what the prognosis, no matter the level of suffering. I believe, as many of the medical community are now espousing, that pain is a personal issue. No one can determine the level of pain any one individual can endure. Each of us experiences it at different levels, just like each of us experiences life at different levels."

Dr. Coggins took a deep breath and continued. "Your daughter has decided that when the time comes, and the pain is to intense for her to handle, and her body no longer responds to her commands, she wants to take some pills, and go to sleep—"

"What?" Lily slipped to the edge and turned to Jody. "You brought me here to listen to this, this, so called doctor tell me that you want to commit suicide."

She shot up out of her seat and began to pace. Her voice was unsteady as she leaned on the back of her chair. "Never!" She pointed a finger at the doctor. "I will never let you do this. Never help you. I'm shocked that you would even consider it." She turned to face them and threw her head back in laughter. "You want me to help? You must be nuts. Do you think there's something redeeming about taking your own life?"

Jody grabbed her mothers' hands. Lily stiffened in horror and tried to pull away.

"Mom! You have to listen," Jody implored, "you have to put your own ideas and beliefs aside. Listen to me; I'm your daughter. Do you love me?"

"Of course I do. That's a silly question to ask."

"Well then how can you even consider letting me go through what we all know is inevitable? Mother, I'm going blind. I won't be able to see you any more. Then the paralysis will set in and no one knows how bad that will be. God! I won't be your daughter." Jody's eyes glossed over, her mouth drooped, and she leaned into the chair. Her voice was hoarse with emotion.

"I'll only be a semblance of my self. The headaches will be unbearable. I've lived my life as I saw fit, short as it may be. Please let me die as I choose."

Jody led her mother back to the chair and gave her a glass of water. Lily took a sip and coughed. She gasped as panic slid through her. Her heart felt as though it were imbedded in an ice-bank. She pressed a clenched fist to her mouth.

The doctor continued. "I realize there are a lot of questions you must have and I'll try to answer as many as I can. Most people don't give this much thought till they're faced with it. Remember this is something your daughter wants. I'm here to help, if I can."

Dr. Coggins moved back behind her desk. "I also want you to be aware that in almost every hospital in the United States doctors order what we call a Morphine Drip for terminally ill patients. As their patients level of pain increases so does the morphine and within a short time they're pronounced dead. Are you aware of the significant message here? If that's not assisted suicide, I don't know what is. Only nobody talks about it. But in your daughter's case, we're doing it with pills.

When it's over, I'll come in and sign the death certificate. Of course you can't tell anyone about this because once you deal with the moral issues of your daughter's decision, you have to face the legal implications. Assisted suicide is illegal in forty-nine states, Oregon is the only state where the voters have accepted it as an alternative to suffering, and now it's being tested in the courts. And believe me Mrs. Halston, that's all this is, your daughter's alternative choice to suffering."

Lily leaped to her feet and started to shout. "I'm surprised the name on your office door doesn't read 'Doctor Death.'"

"Mother! How can you be so cruel? Remember," the hard cool tone was unmistakable, "I asked her for help. She's at high risk just talking to us about this, and she's going out on a limb for me. It's her compassion for her patients that allows her to do this. What you don't realize is that I'm going to do this, with or without your help, and there's no way you can stop me. This is my life, and my body, and I am the only one who can determine what I'm going to do with it. And there are no laws on this planet that can stop me."

Jody took a deep breath. "Mom, we put dogs to sleep that we love because we don't want them to suffer, we shoot horses when they break a leg because we don't want them to be in pain. Why do you want me to suffer? I deserve better than any animal. I deserve to die with dignity."

Jody sobbed and continued in a low, tormented voice, "Mom I've thought about this ever since I found out what I was facing: bedridden, blind, convulsions, the next thing to a vegetable. That isn't living. I don't want to be trapped in a body that will imprison my spirit. This way I'll be sure that my soul will continue on it's journey to fulfill its destiny. I have to be free and I want you to set me free. You gave me life, now I'm begging you to set me free. Help me be born into my next life. Please mother, I beg you. Allow my spirit to go on to the hereafter."

Jody blew her nose and looked at the doctor. Dr. Coggins placed an arm around Jody's shoulder. "If you choose to do this, Jody has a prescription for the pills she'll need. She has the instructions on how to use them; she can share this with you later. It will be up to her when she wants to take them. Please notify me ahead of time so I can be sure I'm in town. Then I'll wait for the second call. Remember," she cautioned, "this has to be kept secret."

Lily watched the doctor's lips move as she tried to focus on what she was hearing, but the sound of the physician's voice was muted. "I have to caution you Mrs. Halston," she moved directly in front of Lily, "you're in for a roller-coaster ride. You're going to go from the heights of optimism to the depths of despair. But Jody will need you to help her cope and through it all, you're going to think it's unnatural and unfair. You know what? It is. Just give yourself the same emotional leeway that you give her and you'll both get through this."

She moved back behind her desk. "Jody has a lot of courage for one so young. She must love you very much to ask this of you. To be so secure in your love that she wants you with her for this, her last act on earth, is a very special gift. I know the terrible turmoil you'll be facing the next few months, so please call me if you have any further questions. Hopefully I can answer them, or if I can be of any help in any other way don't hesitate. And you Jody, I need to see you in two weeks."

In the hour and a half that it took to drive back to Wilmette, a silence hung in the air. Lily pulled into the driveway, shut the ignition off, and stared out the window.

"I know this comes as a shock," Jody said, "but there's no one else. I'm not going to press you for an answer now, there's still time. I realize there's a lot for you to think about. Believe me, it's the humane way. I pray you don't wait too long to give me your answer, because, I'll—"

"You go in, I want to be myself." She felt trapped and turned to her daughter as a whoosh of air escaped her lips. "You've pulled the rug out from under me and I've got to get my bearings."

Jody nodded, leaned over and kissed her mothers cheek. Lily tried to arrange her thoughts but they continued to scramble. She floundered in an agonizing maelstrom. Her misery was so acute that she began to experience physical pain. She bit her lip until it throbbed like her pulse.

The sound of screeching brakes brought her back to the present as a large black car loomed before her at the intersection. She slammed on the brakes and barely avoided the car in front of her. Shaken, she realized she couldn't drive in this distracted state. She looked around and didn't recognize the street names. Suddenly the sun caught her attention as she made a sharp turn and headed east. Lake Michigan wasn't far.

Edmund! Oh my God! She'd completely forgotten about him. He'd never allow it. If he ever found out, it would create an iron wedge between them. He'd never forgive her. He'd leave her. Just the thought of Edmund knowing any of this terrified her.

She couldn't ask his advice; forget about Henry; she didn't dare talk to Pat; and she definitely couldn't count on Jim. For the first time in her life she was totally alone. The choice was hers, and hers alone. A choice no mother should have to make. Right, wrong, or otherwise, she had to decide. Despair pulled at her like a rip tide, sucking her down into a bottomless abyss. Whatever she decided, she'd have to live with this nightmare and suffer the consequences of her decision. She was damned! Caught in a web with no way out.

After parking the Mercedes at Montrose Ave beach, she reached into the glove compartment and groped at its contents until she'd found a crushed cigarette pack with two crumpled cigarettes. Her hand shook as she lit one.

She walked a short distance to the jagged rocks that acted as a barrier against the turbulent waters of Lake Michigan. The angry white caps smashed against the rocks with the force of hurricane winds. The cold wind whirled around her body and caused her to shiver uncontrollably. The darkened sky loomed with black swirling clouds and cast a morose hue on the earth as dark as her own.

Helping someone kill themself was illegal in the state of Illinois. A stiff jail sentence was handed down if caught. They called it accessory to murder. She couldn't even imagine the look on Henry's face if someone wanted him to do this. She giggled out of fear, than grew serious. If she were caught, he wouldn't defend her. He'd probably lead the lynch party.

How do I reconcile this? All my life I've tried to help people to live. God is the only one to make a life or death decision. How can I go against everything I believe in?

She looked skyward. She'd rot in hell through eternity for doing something like this. At the thought of a doomed future, she quickly lit her last cigarette. Anxious to escape the cold whirling winds she hurried back to the car.

"Damn!" She ground the cigarette with her toe. A single thought kept surfacing. She loved her daughter more than anything else on this earth. Jody has been the most important thing in her life, how could she even consider helping her take her life?

*Marilyn Stuart*

# CHAPTER 31

October was coming to a close, and the nights had grown colder, bringing with it a strong promise of an early winter. A month had slipped by since Jody had asked Lily to do the impossible and neither had spoken of it since. Each passing day Lily watched Jody slipping away from her. The narcotic medication merely dulled her senses and when wracked with severe pain, all Lily could do was try to comfort her. Sometimes she'd hold her in her arms and stroke her head until she fell asleep. She tried cold compresses to her forehead, which momentarily dulled the pain.

Some nights Lily would sit on the edge of Jody's bed and read to her until she fell asleep. But when the pain was at its peak, she'd crawl into bed with her and hold her in her arms until it passed.

Jody's sporadic bouts with blindness were devastating. Lily was forced to stand by and watch her daughter grope around the room, hands outstretched, stumbling over things on the floor, and bumping into furniture, always refusing her mother's help.

Jody's conditioned deteriorated at a much faster rate than she anticipated and it ripped at her heart to see her daughter so helpless. Her legs and arms were black and blue from bumping into things, and Lily wondered if she'd be able to be strong enough for her. Could she do this? Did she have the strength to see this through to the end? She didn't know.

Jody fought to maintain her independence, and read with a veracious appetite when her sight would return, endeavoring to read every book in the house. Many afternoons Lily took Jody for a drive. But today Jody looked exceptionally weary.

"Are you feeling all right? Is something wrong?"

Jody only glared, her eyes filled with reproach. "Why? What makes you think something's wrong? How could anything possibly be wrong?"

Lily remembered that Dr. Coggins mentioned something about a sudden change in personality, and not to be alarmed. Was this it? "Fresh air will do you good. You've been cooped up in this house all weekend, it's time you got out. C'mon I'll help you get dressed."

Jody shot back. "When are you going to understand that I'm the only one that knows what's good for me? Since when did you start considering my welfare as your most important concern?"

"Jody, I can't believe you're saying such a mean thing. We can go for a ride later if you like, possibly tomorrow. Maybe you should rest now. Is there anything I can get you?"

Jody's eyes were cold and unrelenting as she stared at her mother. Lily tried to read behind those glaring eyes, but failed. With no reply from Jody she turned to walk out.

"I hope moral issues aren't what's keeping you from making a decision about helping me die. I think that would be the least of your quandary."

Lily spun around. She stopped dead in her tracks, bit her tongue, turned, and walked out of the room. Hopefully this personality glitch would pass?

Later that day Jody was her old, loving self and apologized to her mother for the outburst, explaining she didn't know what had come over her.

With Jody's cries for help during the night, and her own embattled thoughts, the days found Lily in a muddled state. She was unable to concentrate and wished she could get some rest. She leaned against her bedroom door, buried her face in her hands, slid down to the floor and cried. She tried to keep up a front for her daughter and for Edmund, but it was draining every ounce of energy from her. To make matters worse, there was no one to share this hell with. She couldn't bear the thought of living without Edmund if he discovered what she was considering. She couldn't chance it. She'd waited too long for his love, and didn't want to anything to jeopardize it.

She needed to find an acceptable alternative for Jody and decided to start with Hospice. Hopefully they would provide the solution.

June Simons introduced herself. "Your doctor informed us about your daughter over three months ago. We tried to get in touch, but we never got a reply. We talked with a young lady."

Lily nodded. "That was my daughter. I don't think she wants to hear about your organization, that's why I'm here."

June pulled up a chair. "I'll tell you what I can." She leaned forward, "Hospice of Chicago is an organization privileged to provide pain and symptom control, education, guidance, understanding, friendship, caring along with love, to help overcome life's ultimate challenge."

June continued. "Based on a team concept, Hospice care focuses on alleviating the physical, emotional, and spiritual symptoms which accompany illnesses that have failed to respond to curative measures. The primary objective is to keep the patient at home in familiar surroundings. Support by the Hospice team is always available, by phone or visits, on a twenty-four hour schedule, seven days a week. Under the guidance of the primary physician, the skillful teaching of the Hospice nurses, counselors, clergy and volunteers, you're intimately involved in the care of your daughter as a part of the team."

Lily perked up. Maybe this was the answer. Could they provide the special kind of care Jody deserved? An alternative to a hospital death? A way out of Jody's request?

"We step into the case when there is less then six months."

She looked into the folder and nodded. "I see from your daughter's prognosis that we could be of some service to you now. How is she doing?"

"Not too good. My problem is to convince her about your organization. She's very independent and doesn't want to depend on anyone except family for help. Even then, she fights to hold her own."

"That's not uncommon. Patients try to hold on as much as they can for as long as they can. Then, when they see they need help, beyond that of what the immediate family can provide, they finally call us."

"You don't know my Jody. She's stubborn."

"Well, we come to your home, talk with her in private and explain our program. Maybe she'll listen to a stranger."

Lily's heart fluttered. Twenty-four-hour nursing care, pain management, psychological counseling, even a priest.

"Mrs. Halston, you have to understand, it is inconceivable for our unconscious to imagine an actual ending of our life on earth. That's why some fight it to the very end. But when there's no unfinished business, the patient experiences a sense of peace and harmony. A sense of having done what needed to be done. It's a feeling of accomplishment; a knowing that's it's all right to leave. We work to help them realize that. If a patient dies in familiar and loving surroundings, it requires fewer adjustments for them. I can understand why your daughter doesn't want to go to a hospital. It is an impersonal, mechanical, and a dehumanizing way to die. I know that when a person is severely ill, they're often treated like a person with no right to an opinion. I've had personal experience with that."

She fixed them a cup of coffee. "We believe the only way to master death is to challenge it. We do everything to keep our patients alive, comfortable, and pain free."

Lily's hopes were suddenly dashed to the ground. She remembered Jody's words about doctors handling the way she would die and she didn't want that. She wanted that ultimate decision. She wanted to be released when she decided and in the way she wanted. She didn't want to be locked in her body any longer then necessary. Lily had to try and convince Jody differently.

"I want you to be aware of something Mrs. Halston," the woman continued as if reading Lily's thoughts, "a fear of pain causes some to consider euthanasia and enlist the aid of those close to them. It is against the law in this state, and really won't help anyone. I know," the woman paused and looked knowingly at Lily, "your daughter isn't considering this or you wouldn't be here."

Lily's head started to pound like a giant sledgehammer and echoed in her temples. Did she know that Jody had asked her for help to die? She stiffened. "That is one thing I wouldn't even consider. I don't believe in suicide."

"I'm glad to hear it. Now when do you think we could come and talk to your daughter? There isn't much time left. It would be better if we got to know her now. Time helps build a bridge of trust between patient and caretaker. I feel the sooner we talk the better."

Lily stood up. "I don't know. I'll have to talk to her and get back with you. I'll call you in a day or two with her decision. I've got to make her listen, and hopefully understand."

It all sounded good, exactly what they needed. But she knew Jody wouldn't go for it. Anything that prolonged her life was against Jody's wishes. The quality, not quantity of life, was Jody's primary concern.

A bitter battle ensued, Lily's heart against her head, god against the devil, and forced her to decide what was right for Jody and what was right for her. And if she decided in favor of her daughter, how could she live with herself? It went against everything she held dear; everything she had based her life on; everything she believed in. A morose sorrow centered in her chest and made her feel like a block of lead.

Deep inside her being, despite her prayers, Lily knew Jody wouldn't be with them for the holidays. Her anguish was unbearable, and she was riddled with guilt about not being able to share this burden with the man she loved. She felt a wretchedness of mind she'd never known before. How could Jody put her in this position? Her body shivered. How could she ask her to do such a terrible thing? How could she expect her to give up all she believed in to help her end her life? She'd be free but Lily would remain with the heartache, along with the guilt of such an act. Jody was asking her to chance going to jail, and worse yet, losing Edmund.

A sudden chill hung on the edge of her thoughts. Then a deep silence invaded her. Her anger finally became a sigh of her acceptance of Jody's death. This was really going to happen. Jody was going to die. The total acceptance left her reeling and filled with a deeply rooted anger. The admission that she was angry with Jody for dying and angry with her for asking her to help, was dredged from a place beyond logic and reason. She felt bereft and desolate. As the indignation finally subsided, a strange feeling overcame her. An unexplainable clarity began to seep in. She stepped on the gas and drove to the rectory.

She'd been avoiding Jim and Edmund for the past week, fearful that they'd be able to see into her heart and know what she was contemplating. She couldn't chance it. But now she had to talk to her brother, he'd give her direction, an answer to her spiritual dilemma.

Mrs. Dirwinski directed her into the sacristy where Jim was busy clearing out his personal items. His hands trembled when he reached out to clutch her hand. He put his arms around her.

"I'm glad to see you. How's Jody?"

"She told me about your visit. Day by day I see her life slipping away. That's why I'm here, I have to talk to you."

He became rigid and forced a smile.

"What's your view on death?"

Jim dropped the books he was packing and spun around. "What kind of a question is that?"

"I need to talk to you about it. We haven't had a chance to talk for quite awhile, and right now I need some brotherly advice," their eyes locked, "I have no where else to turn."

He continued to throw his books and papers into the open boxes.

"You and Edmund have each another, you should lean on him. I can't help you." He threw the last of his mementoes into the box.

As she sank into a chair beside the shelves, he turned around to avoid eye contact. Shoulders slumped, he finally turned to her, the pain in his eyes was evident.

"Jim! You've never turned me down when I needed you. What's happened?"

"Lily I can't help you! I can't even help myself out of this darkness." He gnashed his teeth. "I'm no good to anyone, not even myself." He put his hand out and watched it quiver. His other hand snaked out to hold it steady.

"Look, I've got the shakes so bad I can't even hold my hand still. I've got to get away from here, and all this place stands for."

"You can't run away, you take your problems with you. That's a lesson I've had to learn. You've always been here for me. What am I going to do if you leave?"

"Lily you're the strongest of us all. You've survived everything and you'll muster the strength to survive Jody's death. I just wish I could say the same."

"You've been my anchor, my port in a storm. Whenever I didn't know where to turn, you were there for me."

He sat in the chair next to her. "My replacement will be here in a few days. Then I'm gone."

"Where? You can't go. I need you. Jody needs you."

"Lily, please understand, I can't be of any use to anyone until I find myself. And I can't do that here."

"Why do you have to leave? Come and stay with Henry and me, at least for a while. Until Jody—"

"I've seen enough dying to last a lifetime. I can't handle any more death, especially a vital, young person like Jody. It breaks my heart to see what the cancer is doing to her."

He brushed his hand through his thinning hair and pushed his glasses back on his nose. He seemed to come to an agreement with himself. "I'm going back to Vietnam, leaving on Saturday."

"Vietnam! Why in the hell would you want to go back there? I thought those were sad times, filled with horror and bloodshed. Why would you dredge all that shit up again?"

"I have no choice Lily. You'll never understand, and if it makes you feel any better, I don't either."

"Bullshit!" She swallowed hard, lifted her chin and met his weak gaze. "Give me some credit. Try me."

The features on his face grew hard and a muscle twitched in his jawbone. Through clenched teeth and in a barely audible voice he mumbled, "I've been trying to handle this problem by going to AA. There have been days when I've gone to meetings three times, just to stay sober. It seemed to help for a while, then the hell starts again. One of the twelve steps is forgiveness. I have to forgive all wrongful action I've taken. But you know what, I can't get past that point. I can't forgive myself for the wrong I've done. And until I'm able to do that I'll never be whole. I'll never be able to get a handle on the drinking."

"But why Vietnam?"

"That's where I lost it."

"Lost what, for God's sake?"

"My soul. God forgive me, but that's where it all started. I have to go back, and hope that God will be with me on this journey out of hell." He turned to his sister. "Pray for me Lily. Pray that I find peace, because if I don't, I'm cursed to roam this earth as if in hell. Damned forever." He sank to his knees and buried his face against her thighs.

Her heart ached for her him. She whispered, "I love you", and began to rub his back, like a mother soothing a hurt child. And all she could do was hold him close, and whisper over again, "I love you."

Jim stood, said a quick good bye and turned back to his packing. Lily moved to the doorway, her own tears still choking her. She turned for a final look at the broken man, than walked out the door. Would she ever see her beloved brother again? She swallowed the lump of despair that had swelled in her throat and pressed her face to her hands.

Wasn't a life of devotion to God enough to save him? Where was God in his hour of need? Why had he been abandoned by the God he loved, and had sacrificed his life for? Feeling bitter, Lily shook her head. If he couldn't come to grips with God, how could she expect to? She shuddered at the thought. Would God abandon her and Jody as well? She turned away from the car, and ran into the church. She slid into the back pew and knelt with her head buried in her hands. Her mind was languid and without hope. She was cold and alone.

God's abandoned us, she thought. We're on our own. What more could He do to us? He allowed Mother to be put in an institution; he's forsaken Jim in his hour of need, sending him off to Vietnam; and now he's allowing Jody to die a hideous death.

She gasped for breath as her throat tightened. What was happening? Fear cloaked and seduced her to acknowledge what she was thinking. Finally she screamed into the empty church.

"I don't believe in you. No more. You don't exist. You're dead."

She felt as though she'd been struck in the face. She shook her head, and her mouth twisted in an expression of hate. "Lies, all lies. If you were real you wouldn't let these things happen. A loving God wouldn't do that, especially to those who have been loyal servants. I believed you to be a loving, compassionate, understanding and all knowing Being. But what I've believed in all my life doesn't fit that picture any longer. I feel like I've just discovered that there's no Santa Claus."

Tentacles of anguish squeezed around her heart as she walked out of church. She couldn't pray. Her mouth felt like old paper, dry and dusty. When she reached the door, she turned, looked at the cross that hung above the altar, shook her head and walked out.

Outside, she found the cold air soothing. The stinging chill cleared her head and little by little a feeling of strength crept back into her body. And without as much as a glance back, she drove away. There was only one more thing to consider before she could give Jody an answer.

*Marilyn Stuart*

# CHAPTER 32

November's frosty winds squalled across Lake Michigan, forcing cold streams of air to swirl around the Halston house. The trees were barren and stripped of their leaves as the bending tendrils danced to the sharp winds, creating a daunting wintry chill. The days grew short and the nights were endless for the occupants inside.

The fireplace in Jody's room glowed, it's embers constantly tended by Lily or Emma. Lily seldom left her daughters side, she read to her, talked about the day, reminisced about her childhood, or just sat and tried to ease her pain and discomfort. Now Jody lived in a permanent world of gray, foggy images, devoid of color, brightened only by the sunlight.

The morning light finally intruded on the two women. Lily stretched her cramped muscles and checked to see if Jody was still asleep. She slipped out of bed and crept into her room to shower.

Refreshed, she went back to Jody's room and quietly opened the door. She gasped at what she saw and ran to her daughter's side. Jody was on the floor, her arms were flailing, her body convulsing. As instructed, Lily cradled her head in her lap, and with a teaspoon she grabbed from the bedside table, pressed her tongue down. Violent spasms jolted her daughter's body, as if it were trying to shake loose from it self. She pinned her daughter's arms between her legs and waited for the convulsion to end.

Her heart was being ripped apart as she held onto her daughter. The pain in her heart became a sick and fiery gnawing. Tears blinded her and slid down her cheeks as she held Jody close until the seizure had subsided. Lily laid her daughter flat on the floor and propped a pillow under her head. She grabbed Jody's paralyzed left arm and stroked it as if she could bring life back to the withered limb. The same with her leg, it too was paralyzed.

Jody's eyes fluttered open and she managed a smile. Then she gazed up at Lily with the blank stare of a blind person. She reached up and grabbed for her mother. "Please help me, Mom." She gasped for breath, "I don't know how much more I can take." She licked her cracked, dry lips. "I'm trying to be strong," she said as she moved her head and sank back against Lily. "There's not much left of me."

Lily pulled her to her breast and cradled her fragile, almost lifeless, body in her arms. She moved her hands over her face. "I love you my darling daughter. I can't stand to see you suffer. No more! Your suffering is over." She bit her lower lip so hard that she drew blood. The salty metallic taste in her mouth was strangely comforting. "Enough is enough! I'll help you Honey. God knows I love you too much to see you in this kind of pain. I'm sorry; I should have made up my mind sooner. I've been selfish. But now Baby, my precious gift of love, I will give you what you want. Your freedom."

The feel of Jody's protruding ribs against Lily's chest made her choke with helplessness. Her swell of pain was beyond tears and her last traces of resistance had vanished.

Tears fell from Jody's sightless eyes and her facial muscles relaxed. Her smile was angelic.

"Don't cry," Lily whispered, "it's going to be all right. I promise. Come," she helped her up and eased her toward the bed. "We have to get you back in bed."

She propped pillows under her head, filled the wash-basin with tepid water and started to wipe her gaunt, gray face. Gone was the peachy glow, along with the sparkling eyes; gone was the lively smile that always brought her joy.

"What day is it?"

"It's Monday, November 6th, the day before the election. Why?"

"Call Doctor Coggins. Make sure she's going to be in town this week. Tell her you've decided to help me. See if she has any further instructions. I don't want to botch this. That would be terrible. Tell her I'm not sure what day, but it will be sometime toward the end of the week."

"I'll call her as soon as Emma comes up with your breakfast. Promise me you'll try to eat. By the way, do I need to have the prescription for the pills?"

"I've had them for the past three months. I know the instructions by heart, but I want you to know everything as well, especially what to do afterward."

Lily was fluffing Jody's pillows when a knock came at the door. Emma walked in with a tray of juice, liquid oatmeal, and a soft scrambled egg, foods easy to swallow and digest.

While Jody attempted to eat, Lily went to her room. She sat on the edge of the bed, achy and exhausted. Like Jody, she too had lost weight and appeared haggard. Her eyes burned from a lack of sleep. She buried her face in her hands and wept.

"God forgive me for what I'm about to do. Edmund, I'm about to take the life of our daughter. I hope someday you'll be able to forgive me."

Suddenly there was a knock on the door, and Edmund walked in. How desperately she needed to cling to him. Guilt tore at the inner core of her soul. She pressed against him, and took comfort in his strong arms.

"It's all right, let it out. It's been too long. You need to unload." He rubbed her shoulders and pulled her head against his chest.

"What are you doing here? You usually don't come till the afternoon when I take my nap."

"I know," he stroked her hair and kissed her teary face. "Something told me to come now. I've just come from Jody's room. She put her arms around me and cried." His eyes glistened with tears. "So did I." He dabbed her eyes with his handkerchief, then wiped his.

"How is she, really? More important, how are you?"

"Oh Edmund, I don't know how much more my heart can take. She's suffering so. It's killing me to watch her die. She had her first severe convulsion this morning. The others were nothing compared to this one. How can we let her suffer like this?"

Their cheeks were pressed close together, allowing his tears to mix with hers. Torment still gnawed at her and her head felt as though it were in a vise. She had to push him away in order to catch her breath.

"I talked with Jody a few minutes ago," he said. "She's cheerful. If I didn't know better, I'd say she's happy. You'll see, everything will be all right, Lily. I've talked with the doctor and from all the signs; he feels that her time is short. It'll be over soon. Jody and I've been talking and I know how she feels about things. She's strong and her convictions will carry her through. Don't be less than she is. Be strong for her. Just awhile longer."

"I'm trying. It's just that sometimes I feel so, helpless. Useless—"

"Why don't you rest awhile? I'll stay with Jody the rest of the afternoon. You'll feel better once you've had a little sleep." She rested her cheek against his chest, closed her eyes, and felt as though she were fading away. No energy to fight anymore, it was all slipping away.

She lay across the bed, her face propped on an outstretched arm with her other arm covering her eyes. She heard the door close and immediately sat up. She reached for the phone and dialed Doctor Coggins.

* * *

It was late the next day, and the elections were finally over. There was a light tap on Jody's door. By the look on Henry's face, Lily immediately knew the news was true. He'd lost the election. Henry looked around the room and swallowed hard. Posters hung on the walls. 'YOUR HONOR' on one, another 'CONGRATULATIONS, and a third, 'WE LOVE YOU'.

As he approached Jody's bedside she threw a hand full of confetti at him, missing him by more than five feet. But Henry spit and sputtered, pretending that she'd gotten the confetti in his mouth and hair.

"Lily, I'd like to be alone with Jody." He smiled bitterly, "take a break and visit with Emma for a few minutes, she's still in the kitchen."

"Call me when you're finished," she leaned over and kissed Jody on the cheek. "I'll be downstairs."

"Sorry Dad, I wish you'd won. I wanted this little celebration for you anyway. I hope you don't mind? I love you. Whether you're a Judge or not, you'll always be my Dad."

Lily closed the door. She walked downstairs and thanked the powers that be for letting Henry have these last moments with his daughter.

Henry strolled into the kitchen, walked into the pantry, took out a bottle of bourbon, grabbed a shot glass and carried them to the table. He poured the whiskey into the glass and gulped it down. Then he sat down beside Lily, oblivious to the fact that he wasn't sitting in his regular place, something he'd never done. A glazed look of despair masked his face. His lips drooped, his eyes narrowed and appeared to melt his granite appearance. His expression was one of mute wretchedness as he looked at Lily and downed another shot of whiskey.

"I don't know what happened today. I can't believe it. It's over. Everything I've worked for, gone. Years of hard work wiped out in one day." His shoulders sagged as he leaned on the table. "My life is ruined."

Lily reached across the table and placed her hand over his. "Ruined? How can you say your life is ruined? You lost an election, that's all. They'll be other elections, other opportunities." Irony dripped from her mouth. "You're daughter is dying, there won't be anymore Jody's. That's more precious then you've ever realized. But all you can think about is that goddamn election. I feel sorry for you."

"I know. That's what makes this even more difficult." He reached for the bottle of whiskey and poured himself another drink. This time he filled the glass to the rim. He took a couple of swallows and put the empty glass down.

"What are you talking about?" she asked.

His tone had a degree of warmth coupled with concern. "These last weeks, seeing Jody the way she is and remembering her the way she was, hit me harder than I thought it would. You know that I was raised with the mandate from my father that a 'Halston never loses'."

"My God Henry, you're human. You're father can't expect the impossible. You ran the best campaign you could and that's what's important."

"Lily, I've lost a hell of a lot more than the election. I've lost the last twenty years of my life, years that I could've spent with my daughter." He fought the tears. "Now I won't have a chance to ever make that up." He stared at her for a moment then looked at his hands. "And, I've lost you too."

Lily swallowed hard. This seldom seen tenderness, shocked her. She studied his face. A muscle flickered at his jaw as his brows drew downward in a frozen stare. He took another swallow of bourbon.

"Henry, I loved you through these years. I wasn't in love with you, but I respected you for everything you were, and all that you are. It's not the end of the world. You can run for office again."

His tongue was thick from the alcohol. "You're wrong, it is the end of my world as I know it." He twisted his hands and continued, "I've been a focused, goal orientated, idiot that I am and never realized or appreciated what I had. I kept trying to accumulate more, and in the process I lost my daughter and the woman I loved." He hesitated, than took another swallow.

"You know what Jody told me," he looked up toward the ceiling and smiled. "She wished that she could be here to see you and Edmund married. She said she knew we didn't belong together and hoped I'd find happiness, like she had."

"How can you say you loved me? You were never affectionate; you never held me, except during sex. We never discussed our hopes, our dreams, or our life together. It was always your way: your ideas, your plans."

Henry finished the bourbon and pushed away from the table. He bit his thinning lip. His face was somber as he tried to prevent the nervous twitch that was taking hold of his cheek. Suddenly he threw his glass at the wall and it smashed into thousands of shards. When he turned, his clenched fists were pressed against his chest. Then he started shouting, "God damn it! I feel it here. I feel everything in here." He started to pound on his chest. "But I can't get it out, it sticks in my throat, and it's enough to make me puke. I feel everything." He cried openly.

"Every pain she's experiencing," he looked upward, "I feel, God forgive me, but I can't show it. I just can't." He continued to pant and wept aloud. Then his eyes grew remote as he struggled to gain a somber face.

Her tears choked her as she approached him. In an effort to comfort him she leaned over and started to put her arms around him.

He stiffened and pulled away. Composed at last, he pulled out an envelope from his breast pocket and handed it to her. "This came for you, last week. I thought I'd keep it until after the election." He went to the door, turned, and rested his hand on the doorframe, as if it would support his wobbling frame. "By the way, I'm moving out tonight. I'll be gone till it's over. You and Edmund can be married here, if you want. I won't interfere."

He walked out of the kitchen with the bottle of bourbon in his hand. Lily ripped open the envelope. Inside were her final divorce papers. Finally! She clutched them to her breast and thought for a moment. Then it hit her like a bolt out of the blue. In an outburst of rage, she hit the table.

"That son of a bitch. That bastard's had these divorce papers all this time. Why? What did he hope to accomplish? To think that Jody could've been at our wedding and seen us married, breaks my heart. Now it's too late. She won't live long enough to see us married."

Lily stared out the kitchen window into the back yard. The bright moonlight was shining on the bare branches and caused the shadows to dance and play on the back porch. She threw her shoulders back and started up the stairs. The time left with her daughter was short.

* * *

Late the following day Pat walked into the house. "Edmund called, and we talked."

"About what?"

"Nothing really. He said that you needed a few hours away from here. He's picking you up shortly and taking you to dinner. Hurry and get showered. I'll stay with Jody. How's she doing?"

Lily caught the glimmer of a diamond on Pat's left hand. She grabbed it and brought it to her face. "What's this? When did all this happen? How did you meet this one?"

"You'll never guess! I answered an ad in one of those Personal columns."

"You what?"

"You heard me." She held her hand up and giggled when the light played through the prisms of the large stone and cast a variety of colors on the wall. "I answered an ad in the paper. Would you believe, three months later he proposed. Listen, I know I talk a lot about independence, and not needing anyone, but you know me, I'd be lonely going through life alone. These last few months I've learned how precious time is and I don't want to spend another minute alone."

Lily shook her head and smiled.

"You look horrible. You're going to need a major make up job to look presentable for Edmund." Pat wrinkled her nose and walked to the stairs with Lily. "I'm glad he's taking you out of here for awhile. By the way, how's Henry handling his defeat?"

"I haven't seen him since last night. For the first time ever he showed me he had feelings. You know Pat, I really do believe he cares. But for some reason, he chooses to keep it locked up."

Lily continued. "I got my divorce papers yesterday. Officially, I'm a free woman." Pat smiled and put her arms around Lily as they walked upstairs.

Edmund waited patiently while Lily finished putting on her makeup. She tiptoed into Jody's room, kissed her on the cheek, then nodded to Pat and mouthed thank you, then waved as she tiptoed out of the room.

"Give Edmund my love, Mom. If I'm asleep when you get home, wake me. Please. I need to talk to him. It's important."

"All right Sugar, we won't be gone long."

A few blocks from the house Lily and Edmund walked into Albertos, the most public place to be seen. On Edmund's arm, she nodded at the people she recognized. After being seated at their table she moistened her dry lips and looked around.

"We don't have to stay," he said, "if you're uncomfortable."

"Hell no. It's just that it feels a little strange, I still feel married. I wonder if that feeling will ever leave?"

"Probably not. I'm not going to give you a chance to get used to being a divorcee. I plan to whisk you away to my private hideaway and marry you as soon as we can."

She smiled as he leaned over and kissed her.

"I wish I could take all this from you," his eyes were dark with concern, "better yet, I wish I could go through it for you."

"Tell me," she looked at him for a long time and searched his eyes, "I need to know. How were you able to handle the death of your daughter, especially under such horrible circumstances? It must have been painful. Forgive me Darling, but I need to know."

"I'm not going to tell you it was easy, because it wasn't. I still hurt, even now when I think about that young beautiful life snuffed out like that." He snapped his fingers. "Such a waste. I thank God she didn't suffer. When I think of what Jody's going through, I'd trade places with her in a minute, if I could. I don't know how you do it."

Lily shrugged. "I have no choice. I love her. I'd do anything to help her, anything to ease the pain."

"I know what you mean. I wish we could do something about all the people who are suffering. We do nothing except sit, watch, and pray. I can understand why Doctor Kavorkian gets so many requests. Why the state of Michigan put him in jail, I'll never know. They should give him the Medal of Honor."

Lily shuddered. Did he know what Jody and she were planning? Why did he mention Dr. Kevorkian?

"The only comfort I get when I think about Christine, and that terrible accident, is that the coroner assured me she died instantly. No pain."

His face was contorted, his brows drawn together as memories of that fateful day rekindled and replayed his familiar pain.

"I'm sorry, Honey," she stroked his hand, "I didn't mean to bring up painful memories. Hearing you talk about it has helped. A lot. Just being with you fills me with courage." She squeezed his hand and rubbed the back of it on her cheek. "I know this may sound silly," she lowered her eyes, "but, I need to know you love me."

"Lily." He grabbed her hand and squeezed tightly, then pressed her fingers to his lips, and kissed her fingers. "I love you more than you'll ever know. I love you more than life itself. I can't imagine my life without you in it."

"You say that now, but what if, in the future, something should happen. What if you find out something bad about me that would cause you to stop loving me?"

"There's nothing that you've done, or could ever do, that would change the way I feel about you. We're meant to be together. Nothing or no one can change that. I love you my dearest and always will." His eyes sparkled as he handed Lily her glass then raised his to propose a toast.

"To our wedding day. Tomorrow."

"Tomorrow?" She bolted up. "We can't do that. There isn't enough time."

He smacked the table with his palms. "Listen, it was Jody's wish to see us married, and married we'll be. I'll be damned if I'll let anything stand in the way of fulfilling our daughter's last wish. Henry's gone, right? Well...?"

"I'll get Pat to be our witness. Jody can be my maid of honor. What about a minister?"

"I've a dear friend who is a Religious Science minister. I know he'll be happy to marry us. I'll call him tonight and tell him to be at the house tomorrow at noon. How's that time with you?"

"When we went to city hall a couple of weeks ago to get our marriage license renewed, I thought you were nuts. You kept saying: never give up, just know it will happen. I didn't have faith, but you did."

"Jody asked me to bring you back to the house. She wants to talk to you. This will be perfect, we can tell her together."

"Of course I'll come. I love being with her. Anything for my little angel."

# CHAPTER 34

Lily sat up straight and swung her feet to the floor. The chaise wasn't the least bit comfortable and it caused the muscles in her back to ache. She stood up, put her hands on her lower back and started to stretch. The cramping in her legs and back, from another sleepless night in the chaise next to Jody's bed made her wince. She moved to Jody's bed, and smiled. How peaceful she looked. The clock in the hall chimed nine, Edmund would be here at noon. Still a lot to do.

She tiptoed out of the room and made her way downstairs. Emma was busy preparing breakfast when Lily told her the good news. Her musing look spoke louder than any congratulations she could offer. Immediately the Irish cook started planning the wedding lunch.

Pat called. The flowers were ordered and would be delivered by eleven. Everything was coming together. All she had to do was get dressed. Suddenly panic shot through her. "What am I going to wear? I don't have a wedding dress." She ran upstairs and started rummaging through her closet. She quickly spotted a white outfit hanging at the back of the pole. She pulled it out and laid it on the bed. Tags were still on the sleeve. Jody helped me pick this out, she remembered, it was when Henry and I were suppose to go on that Alaskan cruise, one of many planned trips that never happened. It would be perfect. Jody will know what I look like since she's already seen me in it. She carefully laid her wedding dress on the bed, than walked back into Jody's room.

"Mom, I don't want to be in bed for your wedding, I want to be dressed and sitting in a chair."

"But you're so weak. Wouldn't it be better if you stayed in bed."

Jody's jaw was set.

Despite her weakened condition, Lily thought, it might be good for her to get dressed, and sit up. Lily knew Jody wanted to be a part of the festivities and readily agreed. She told her about the minister, and how Pat was handling the flowers and decorations. The wedding lunch was Emma's project.

Emma shuffled into the room carrying a breakfast tray. Lily excused herself and used the time to get ready. Thank God, Jody would be there, her last wish would be fulfilled. Some small solace, she thought.

She took a quick shower, put on her make up, but decided to wait to get dressed, knowing she'd have to get Jody ready first. Emma was leaving Jody's room with the breakfast tray in hand. Lily stopped her and checked the tray. Emma shook her head, her brows were raised in concern. Jody had hardly touched her food.

"I tried, Miss Lily, I really tried. I even tried to spoon feed her, but she gags on it. It's too hard to swallow, she says. She says she's saving room for my special wedding lunch. She don't know it yet," she winked, "but I'm going to hold her to it. I'll be making many of her favorite things, foods she won't be able to refuse."

"Um, you smell good," Jody sniffed the air and turned to her mother, "are you ready?"

"Almost, I want to get you dressed first. Is there any particular outfit you want to wear?"

"Yes," she pointed in the direction of the closet, "it's hanging in there, all the way at the back. The ice-blue dress I bought for that cocktail party the paper gave." Jody was silent for a moment. "You know Mom, that seems so long ago, a lifetime away."

"I know!" She went to her side and brushed a strand of hair from her cheek. "What say we get started," Jody smiled.

Lily bathed her daughter's parched skin and gently brushed her hair, noting the tufts of hair that remained on the brush. She dabbed a little blush on her gray gaunt face and applied a bit of lipstick. She stood back, looked at her, and tears started to form.

"Mom! Don't you dare cry. I know you. You're probably standing there, admiring me, and all your mascara is running down your cheeks. Stop it. This is your wedding day, a time of joy. It's your time to be happy. They'll be plenty of time for tears. Save them for later."

She maneuvered Jody's legs over the edge of the bed, lifted her hands over her head and slipped the silk dress over her. How loose it fit. A once lush body had filled it perfectly. She moved the brush through Jody's hair then clipped a pair of tiny pearl earrings onto her lobes.

Just as she was finishing, Pat walked into the room, carrying three large bouquets of white flowers, and her florist in tow. He carried white satin ribbons and two large arrangements of white carnations and roses. Pat motioned the florist to bring one of the floral pieces to Jody. Her fingers moved around the edge of the flowers, then down the stems, and smiled when she inhaled the aroma of the fresh roses.

The florist started to set the arrangements around the room. Pat narrated his every move to Jody, as he draped the white satin ribbons around her bed and had them cascading from each of the four posts. He put the floral vases on a table near where Jody would be seated and one where the bride and groom would stand to say their vows.

When he finished the bedroom it resembled a small private chapel. Tall candles were lit and stood in a row, creating an aisle for Lily to walk down. Pat left no detail out as she described every movement to Jody as her favorite florist transformed the bedroom into a wedding chapel.

Lily watched her daughter's face, fascinated by what she saw. There was an unbelievable influx of energy. Jody was beaming. Pat propped extra pillows behind Jody's back and made it easy for her to rest before the ceremony. Pat ordered Lily to go to her room to get ready. Everything was set. Jody's final wish would come true.

Lily slipped into her room and put on her dress. She sat down at her dressing table and plugged in the curling iron. There was knock on the door. It was Edmund.

"Go away! Your not suppose to see the bride before the ceremony."

"Lily this is important, I have to talk to you before we say our vows."

He walked into the room, took Lily by the hand and sat her on the edge of the bed. His gaze sharpened.

"Edmund, what is it? You're scaring me."

He swallowed hard. "Lily there's something I have to tell you. I can't say our wedding vows without you knowing the whole truth about me."

She let go of his hand and his face began to cloud with uneasiness.

"Everything you read in my book is true, only I left out one major detail. I did try to get in touch with you when I was released from that Mexican jail, but when I heard you were married, a part of me was actually relieved."

She stared at him in a questioning silence.

"Yes, relieved. I didn't want to make a commitment to you, and this was the easy way out. I could always say it was you who didn't wait and thus avoid facing my responsibility in the matter."

"But that's in the past Edmund. We're starting our new life today."

"There's more, let me finish." He measured her with a cool appraising look. "As I traveled the world I used women. Many women, every gal I met became a potential bed partner. No respect for who or what they were. My only goal was to get them in my bed."

He hesitated as if thinking about his deeds. "Then when Christine was killed, I sought help. I couldn't handle the loss of my daughter, along with the guilt, at the way I treated women. I finally realized I was running from commitment and blaming everyone except myself. And God knows I've suffered." His gaze lowered, as did his voice.

When he looked up tears were rolling down his cheek. She reached for a tissue and dabbed under his eyes. She smiled as she lifted his face. "Now it's my turn. I have something to tell you."

He cleared his throat. Two deep lines of worry appeared between his eyes.

"When my mother got sick, I had to pack her things before I could sell the condo. Among her personal items I found a journal where she kept tract of her donations to the church, as well as your activities."

Edmund's mouth dropped, his jaw went slack. He was too startled to offer any objection.

"Yes. Throughout the years she paid some of your friends, at the paper and magazines, to confide in her about your many liaisons. How the hell she did it, and why, I still don't know. The only thing I can figure, is she wasn't sure that she did the right thing by not telling me about your letters and calls. So to ease her guilty conscience she needed to prove to herself, over and over again, that she was right about you."

Edmund shook his head. "You've known all this time?"

"I was shocked at first, but I loved you so much, the past didn't matter. You were with Jody and me now and that's what was important. I knew you loved me and I was right. Here you are, ready to take that big step."

He grabbed her and held her close. "Thank you for believing in me."

"Now that there are no lies between us, are you ready to become Mrs. Edmund Vilante?"

"I've been ready for twenty-five years. Now, will you leave, I have to finish dressing."

He brushed her cheek with his lips and started to whistle as he walked into the hall.

She dabbed some Chanel on her neck, behind her ears and on both wrists, then stepped back to take one last look in the full-length mirror. Satisfied she looked like a bride, she grabbed the single white orchid, and walked out.

Edmund turned when the bedroom door open. He smiled at the sight of her. "I've never seen you look so beautiful." She approached his side, joy moved across her face and shone in her eyes. She was dressed in a white gown of soft jersey, her hair was curled and swept up on her head, held only by a wide band of white satin ribbon. White sandals encased her feet.

She knew from the glitter in his eyes, the effect she was having on him. She reveled in his open admiration, and a warm tingling stirred in the pit of her stomach. A light from the window shone on his handsome face, like beams of icy radiance. Tall and distinguished in his tuxedo, his broad chest was encased in a white starched shirt.

She returned his disarming smile with a blush as she walked slowly down the make shift aisle, across the room and into his extended arms. She stopped directly in front of her daughter, who was sitting in the chair beside the minister. Emma was behind Jody and wiped her nose with a handkerchief, while holding onto Jody's shoulder. She provided Jody with needed support to sit up for the ceremony.

Lily knelt down in front of Jody and described the dress she was wearing. Jody smiled as her hands touched her mothers' hair that was gathered on top of her head.

"You feel like a roman goddess, Mom." Lily watched the vacant eyes. A tear hung on her lashes, then worked its way loose and trickled down her cheek. Edmund grabbed her hand and squeezed it. She looked up at him and nodded.

He glanced at Pat and winked. She nodded and smiled back. The couple turned to face the minister. Lily looked at Edmund, than glanced over her shoulder at her daughter. Tears were rolling down Jody's cheek. She put her bouquet in Jody's lap and turned to Edmund to speak the unrehearsed words.

"As we join hearts today I thank God for the special miracle that you are. To share our days and nights is a blessing. Our memories are my treasure. Being together is my prayer come true. The closeness and understanding we share is something I've never had with anyone but you. You're my life-long companion, my lover and best friend. I love having you in my world. I know, that no matter what comes to us, we can handle it, because we have each other."

Edmund grabbed her hand. "When I met you, I had no idea how much my life was about to change but then, how could I have known? A love like ours, rarely happens in a lifetime. You are my miracle. You are everything I've ever dreamed of, the one I thought existed only in my dreams. The happiness you bring me is the thing I'll never be able to get enough of. With you by my side, anything and everything is possible. You are and always will be, the love of my life."

The minister reached for his handkerchief and blew his nose. Pat wiped the black mascara from beneath her eyes and Emma kept sniffling as she leaned over and put a box of tissues on Jody's lap. Then the final words.

"I now pronounce you man and wife. You may kiss your bride."

Edmund took Lily in his arms. She gave herself freely to his kiss, and felt the warmth and moistness of his lips, which were more persuasive than she cared to admit. She gasped and slowly drew away. She turned to Jody and Pat.

Jody reached out to the newlyweds. "You don't know how happy the two of you have made me." She nodded and asked Pat to bring the surprise. Pat took out two envelopes from the dresser drawer and handed them to Jody. Jody stared at Edmund and Lily as if trying to break through the darkness.

"This is something for each of you." She pressed them to her breast, then handed the envelopes to each of them. "You have to promise me, both of you, no matter what, you won't open these until...until after I'm gone. Promise?"

* * *

After the wedding lunch, Pat went home to be with her fiancée, and Emma went back to the kitchen to clean up. As arranged, Edmund went home and left Lily to spend the next few precious days with Jody.

As the light of day dimmed to the stealth of approaching darkness, Lily carried an open champagne bottle, and two stemmed glasses into Jody's room. She put them on the bedside table and retrieved the two hidden bottles of pills from the bathroom. She went back downstairs, and brought up two sherbet glasses filled with butterscotch pudding, Jody's favorite.

"You know Honey, I thought we'd said everything. But somehow, I feel there's more, but the words won't come. I miss you already. My heart feels as though it's being ripped to shreds. And if there's anything left inside, it's pure sadness. It's like a part of me is dangling by a thread, soon to be severed and lost. Gone forever. They say your spirit doesn't die, it lives on, but that's a lot less than I'm ready and willing to settle for. I don't want your spirit, I want you. I thought I'd be ready, but I'm still so angry Jody—"

"You can be angry later, right now I need you, especially your courage and strength." She looked toward the window, where she thought the sound of Lily's voice was coming from and then back. "I don't know what I can say to you except thank you."

Jody took a deep breath. "I'm ready. Did you crush all the pills and put them in the pudding?"

"Yes."

"Just give me a little at a time. I'll swallow slowly, this way I won't throw them up."

Lily's hands were trembling as she slowly spoon fed her daughter, wiping away the occasional pudding that seeped out the side of her mouth. Lily pleaded, "help me Jody. I don't think I can go through with this."

"Yes you can. You must. I'm counting on you. There's no one else. I need your strength along with your eyes. Don't disappoint me. Not now, not that I'm so close."

She watched her daughter try to swallow miniscule amounts of pudding, sometimes gagging, but finally getting it down. Each swallow a struggle, but in time the dish's were empty.

"Pour each of us some champagne," she said, "the doctor said the alcohol will speed up the process. Besides, I didn't have a chance to toast the beautiful bride, my Mother."

Lily filled their glasses and made sure Jody's was only half full, than handed it to her. The sightless eyes stared at Lily. She raised the glass in a toast and smiled. "Thank you for the greatest gift of love that you could ever give me, my freedom from this wretched body. Thank you for making the choice to help me. I know you struggled with it. Before today, your gift of life was unsurpassed. But with this last unselfish gesture, I'll be able to take your gift with me wherever I go."

"When you were born they put you in my arms, and now you're leaving this earth in my arms. It can't be any other way."

Jody put the glass to her lips and sipped it slowly, then continued to sip it until the glass was empty. Lily swallowed her champagne in one gulp and hoped that it would quiet her pounding heart. She quickly poured herself another. She was numb, frozen in a dramatic void. She didn't dare think because if she did, she'd bolt from the room. Instead, she forced herself to focus on the task at hand.

She glared at the miniature house with the purple roof. "You really love that little house don't you?"

"Yes, and after I'm gone, I want you to take it with you when you leave. Let it be a reminder. Look inside the house now."

Lily picked it up and tried to look into the tiny windows.

"The house is empty, isn't it?"

"Yes. It was that way when you bought it."

"Mom," she said softly, "just remember, that house represents my body. In a few hours, I'll be gone. This body will be empty, just like that little house. And whenever you feel sad let that house remind you of the emptiness of your sorrow. I've left my earthly house, and moved into one of my Father's mansions. Now promise me you'll remember that. Will you?"

Tears flooded Lily's eyes. She swallowed hard. Nothing could stop her heart from shattering into a million pieces. She had to take a deep breath to quell the trembling in her limbs as she counted out the pills that were left and put them in the proper sequence. She crushed the lethal doses and put them on a spoon topped with a scoop of pudding. Jody took each spoon and swallowed. She gagged several times, but managed to get it down. Thirty minutes later all the pills were gone.

Lily crawled into bed beside her daughter and slipped under the covers. Propped against the pillows, she drew her daughter into her arms and held her close to her heart.

"Remember what the doctor said about my losing control of my bowels. Promise not to let them find me laying in a mess."

"I promise, Honey. I love you and I'll be here till morning, till the doctor comes. Pray with me that God will forgive us for what we've done and remember what you promised. A sign. Any sign. Let me know you're all right and that we did the right thing."

Jody nodded and closed her eyes. A strange look crept over her face. It wasn't a smile as such, but a peaceful look that a deep sleep brings.

Lily started to rock Jody like she did when she was a baby, than started to hum her favorite song. The words slipped out in a soft whisper as she sang:

"There's a place for us, a time and place for us,
hold my hand and I'll take you there,
take my hand and we're half way there,...
somewhere...someway
we'll find a new way of living..."

She couldn't remember the rest of the words so she started to hum, while continuing to rock her daughter. An hour passed, she looked down at Jody's darkened eyelids. She watched to see if there was any flickering. No noticeable reflex movements, so she concentrated on the steady up and down rhythm of Jody's stomach, the only sign she was still alive.

Lily continued to rock her daughter, careful not to disturb the almost lifeless body. Her arms were weak as she struggled to keep her daughter close to her heart. An endless stream of tears dropped on Jody's forehead. A leaden pain lay in Lily's breast.

"Don't weaken," she chided herself and bit her lower lip. "You agreed. You have to finish it, see it through. You can't let her down. Not now! No matter how it hurts, you have to be strong to the end. Hold her close to your heart, let her feel it beating until the very last moment. It will be her final memory of you, as it was her first."

Lily glanced around the room at the satin ribbons, the flowers, the chair where Jody sat and listened to her and Edmund express their love. Jody had been present for their marriage and she never knew that Edmund was her father. Lily sighed, the lump in her throat melted and her voice filled with anguish as her head fell in sorrow.

Her crying stopped and suddenly her daughter's body started to wrench. "Easy Lily," she told herself, "the doctor told you this could happen." She looked down at Jody's chalky white face and saw a greenish-yellow slime oozing out of the side of her mouth. Lily started to gag and bent forward in an effort to stop from vomiting. She looked at the ceiling and gulped air, using every ounce of strength to push back her own bile. As the feeling passed, she took tissues and wiped the corner of Jody's mouth.

Lily's temples were pounding. Her pulse was racing. It felt as though someone was pulling her heart out by its very roots. Piece by piece, it felt like her insides were collapsing. She took deep breaths in order to keep a clear mind and stay focused. She couldn't let Jody down, not now.

"Please God, let it be over soon. I don't know how long I can do this. I know you're here with me, even if I said I didn't believe in you. I know I couldn't have come this far without you. Take her. Please! She's suffered so much. She deserves better. She's my baby." She pressed Jody close to her heart and kept rocking.

"I've done all I could to help her make this journey, the rest is up to you. Guide her! Let your Divine Light illuminate her path though the tunnel and into your waiting arms where I know she'll live forever."

Jody's legs started to jerk. Her lifeless body was filled with tremors and spasms, more activity then it had know in the last month. Lily grabbed Jody, held her tight, and remembered that the doctor had described how the muscles might react. Slowly Lily began to massage Jody's leg and within a few minutes the spasms stopped. Lily sighed and leaned back against the pillows again.

She kept her focus on Jody's chest and stomach. The breathing motion had slowed down even more. Each time the lungs fell in search of a new breath, the longer it seemed to take for them to rise again. Suddenly there was a gasping sound. Life, fighting for its very existence. Again and again she heard Jody gasp in search for the vital air needed to sustain the body.

"Take her, damn it! Take her," she yelled at the top of her lungs. "She's all yours, why prolong this. She hasn't been mine this past year. You gave her to me twenty-six years ago. Well damn it, you got what you wanted. You won. Why are you taking your sweet time?"

As suddenly as the eerie sounds started, they stopped. No more rising and falling of her chest. No more horrid gasping. No more slime oozing from her mouth. No more pain. No more Jody.

Numbed from the pain in her heart, the tightness in Lily's chest slid away, like someone had pulled the cork on a drain. She saw the small house on the nightstand and a smile moved to her lips. Jody's words echoed. 'I'm no longer in that house mom. I'm in one of my Father's many mansions'. Lily stared at the lifeless body in her arms. The silence was overwhelming. And Lily screamed.

"God, my God! Help me." A chill coursed through her, and her body wretched as her sobs grew louder and louder. Her tears were no longer individual droplets but a continual stream of salty liquid. She grabbed a tissue and wiped away the mucous from her nose along with the tears.

Her sides ached as she eased the tight grip on her daughter's motionless body. Lily felt like she had been fragmented into a million pieces, like treading water and having nothing solid to stand on, nothing to hang on to. She wiggled out from beside Jody, and with every last bit of energy, laid her daughters body across the bed. As the doctor warned, during the process of dying the body sometimes excretes feces as part of it's final purging. She took off the dress and washed her daughters body. She put Jody's favorite pink nightgown on her lifeless form. The worst was over.

Lily looked at her daughter's body, smoothed her hair back from her eyes and started to talk to her. "I know you're at peace, but now I have to search for mine. When morning comes, I'm leaving this house." She fussed with the nightgown and pulled it down to cover her ankles.

"I'll carry you in my heart the way I carried you in my body. We'll be together always. No one will ever know when I'm thinking of you. Only you and I will be aware of our secret place." Lily lay on her side next to Jody's body.

"I think you've helped all of us get a little closer through your ordeal. Please Jody, remember your promise. You said that no matter what, you'd give me a sign...anything. I have to know you're all right."

She went to the window and watched the blackness of night turn an early morning gray, that period of limbo before the dawn slips in. The morning light would usher in a new day, unimpressed by the life that had just been snuffed out. Life went on, and so would she.

Lily dialed Doctor Coggins, then grabbed the purple roofed house and peered inside. It was empty. She smiled and walked downstairs. She unlocked the front door, than went back into the living room to wait for the doctor.

The front door chimed, and before she could open it, Edmund walked in.

"What are you doing here, how did you know—"

"After our wedding, Jody and I talked for a bit. I had a feeling she was saying good-bye, but when she asked me to be here at six this morning I knew that it was the last time I'd see my daughter alive. She made me promise to take you away from here and that's why I've come." He put his arms around Lily and held her tight. She looked into his eyes.

"As soon as the doctor comes, we'll go. How about some coffee?"

He nodded.

"I could use a cup too." They walked hand and hand into the kitchen, aware that this was the first day of their life together and despite the sorrow she carried, it was the first time in months her heart knew joy.

While the coffee perked, Lily and Edmund walked out onto the porch. A misty drizzle filled the air with a damp aroma and gave off a promise of spring. They sat down on the wicker love seat. Edmund pulled out the two envelopes from his jacket that Jody had given them on their wedding day.

"She asked us not to open these till she was gone. I think it's time we read what she wanted to tell us."

Lily nodded. Edmund tore open his sealed envelope and started reading aloud.

***Dear Dad,***

***No doubt you're surprised by the greeting, me calling you Dad. I've known for some time that you're my real father.***

Edmund looked at Lily, his eyes were open wide, his jaw dropped and caused his chin to rest on his chest. "Did you tell her?"

"No, I wouldn't have without you present. Finish reading her letter, maybe she'll tell you."

***In case you're wondering how I found out, it happened one afternoon when I was looking for more books to read. I found a copy of your book Until in Mom's room and in it, a note that she had written to you. I read it and I'm glad I did. When I found out you were my Dad, my heart did flips. It was one of the happiest days of my life.***

***Time after time I've turned to you for understanding, guidance, and encouragement...And time after time you've been there for me, helping, caring, sharing my joys as well as my disappointments.***

***It means so much to me to have someone like you as my father. I think of you constantly with love. I only wish we would have had more time together, but fate didn't allow it. I'm grateful for the loving and happy times we did spend together.***

***Take care of Mom, I know she's going to have a rough time of it. I love you,***

***Your daughter,***

Edmund reached for a handkerchief, wiped his eyes and blew his nose. He put his arms around Lily and hugged her. "She knew Lily. She knew I was her father. That's all I could ever ask for. She knew." He covered his face with his hands and openly wept as his shoulders rocked back and forth.

"Thank God." Lily held him close, he couldn't have had better news.

When he regained his composure he handed her an envelope. "Here, open yours."

As she did a piece of paper slipped out and onto the floor. Lily picked it up and started to read it aloud.

**MISS ME—BUT LET ME GO**

**When I come to the end of the road**
**And the sun has set for me,**
**I want no rites in a gloom filled room.**
**Why cry for a soul set free**

**Miss me a little—but not too long.**
**And not with your head bowed low.**
**Remember the love that we once shared,**
**Miss me—but let me go.**

**For this is a journey that we all must take,**
**And each must go alone.**
**It's all a part of the Master's Plan,**
**A step on the road to home.**

**When you are lonely and sick of heart,**
**Go to the friends we know,**
**And bury your sorrow doing good deeds,**
**Miss Me—but let me go.**

**Author Unknown**

Lily grabbed Edmund's arm and squeezed it. He responded by pulling her close. "You know she's right. We'll miss her terribly but we have to let her go." He wiped Lily's tears. "Now read your letter."

***Dear Mom,***

***I'll never be able to thank you for what you did for me in life. You gave me hope. You gave me understanding. You gave me strength. You gave me the important things I need to take on this new journey. Most of all, you gave me freedom, and in that freedom I found the very depth of my love for you. Allowing me to lean on you is what gave me the strength to hang on as long as I did. I'll always be grateful to you for everything...I love***

***you. You're the best. I'll be waiting for you to join me. But for now, live life to it's fullest. Live it for me as well as for you.***

***Your loving, grateful, daughter,***

The letter dropped from Lily's hands. She wept aloud and tears scaled her cheeks as she looked out into the morning sky. "Look, there's a rainbow." Her voice was fragile and shook with emotion. She shivered with fatigue as a chill danced through her limbs. They stared into the sky and watched the clouds slowly part, allowing rays of the morning sun to peek through to warm the earth.

Lily started to cry again. She knew in her heart that the colored sky was her sign. She whispered, thank you for keeping your promise, Jody. If anyone could do it I knew you would. I love you.

"That rainbow is Jody's doing, it's a sign for us. She's in her right place."

Lily nodded as tears clung to her eyelids. They walked back into the house to wait for the doctor. The aroma of freshly brewed coffee filled the kitchen. Edmund poured each of them a cup. "I'm going to fill my heart with every remembrance of her. And together we'll build our life, my Darling. Just like Jody would have wanted. In fact, last night I started a new book. I'm calling it, "Dear Jody."

Lily smiled. The peace she'd sought for so long, finally descended. God was in his heaven and all was right with the world. With Edmund at her side, life was beginning anew. It's good to be alive, she thought. Thank you God, thank you for my life, and for your gift of love.